MiSS QUiNCES

KAT FAJARDO

Color by Mariana Azzi

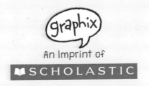

graphix

An Imprint of

SCHOLASTIC

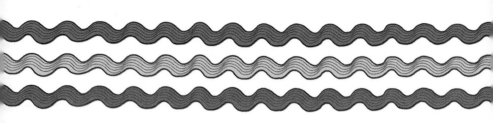

All rights reserved. Published by Graphix, an imprint of
Scholastic Inc., *Publishers since 1920.* SCHOLASTIC, GRAPHIX,
and associated logos are trademarks and/or registered
trademarks of Scholastic Inc.

Library of Congress Control Number: 2021937053

ISBN 978-1-338-53558-7 (hardcover)
ISBN 978-1-338-53559-4 (paperback)

12 11 10 9 8 7 6 5 4 3   22 23 24 25 26

Printed in Mexico   200
First edition, May 2022

Edited by Cassandra Pelham Fulton
Lettering by E. K. Weaver
Book design by Shivana Sookdeo
Creative Director: Phil Falco
Publisher: David Saylor

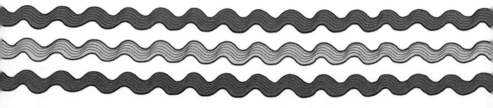

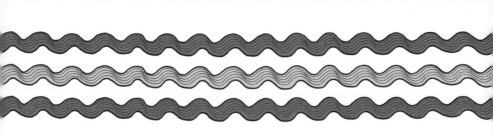

For Mami, Papi, and
Clau, and for my fans,
Pablo and Gloria

CHAPTER ONE

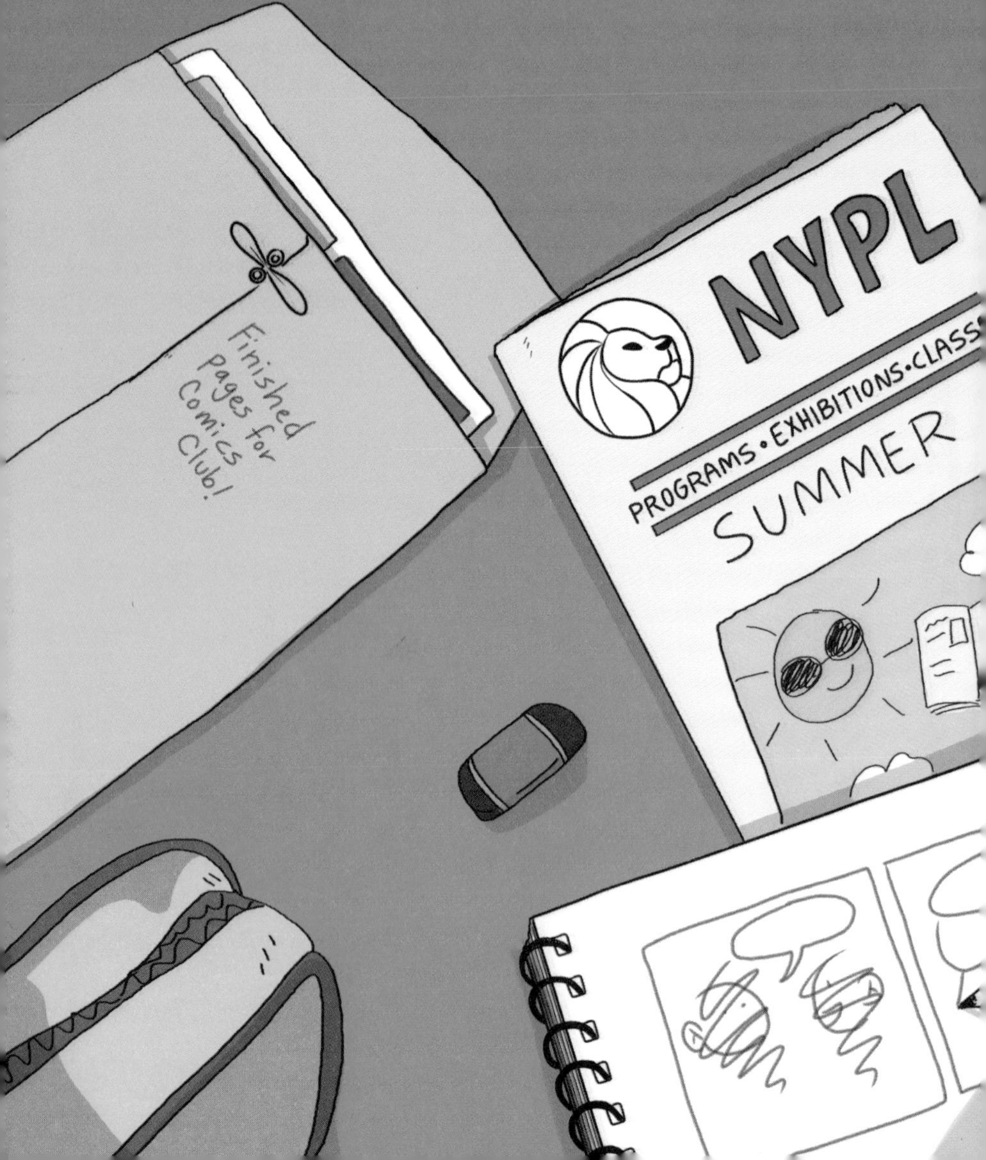
Finished pages for Comics Club!
NYPL
PROGRAMS • EXHIBITIONS • CLASS
SUMMER

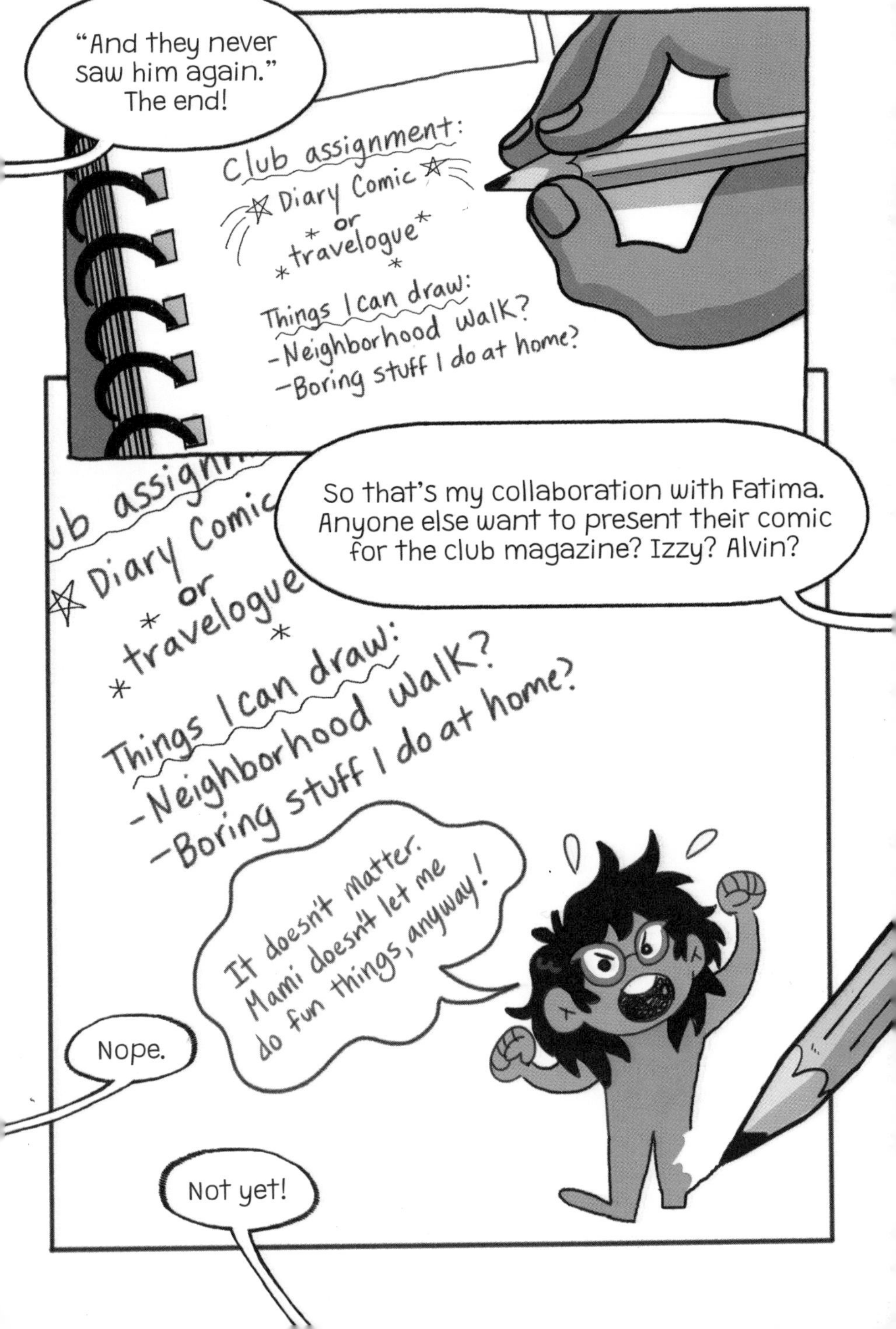

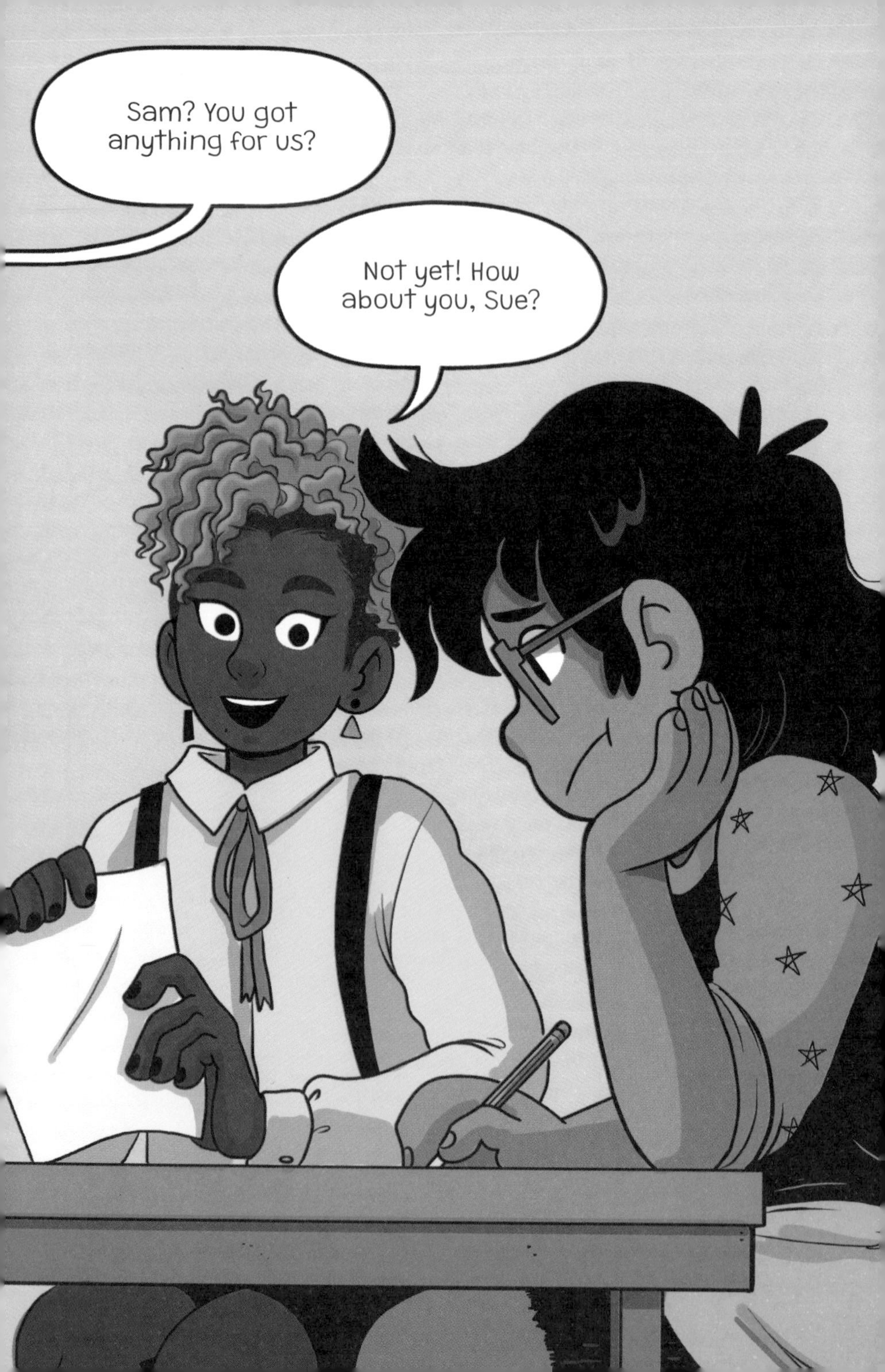
Sam? You got anything for us?
Not yet! How about you, Sue?

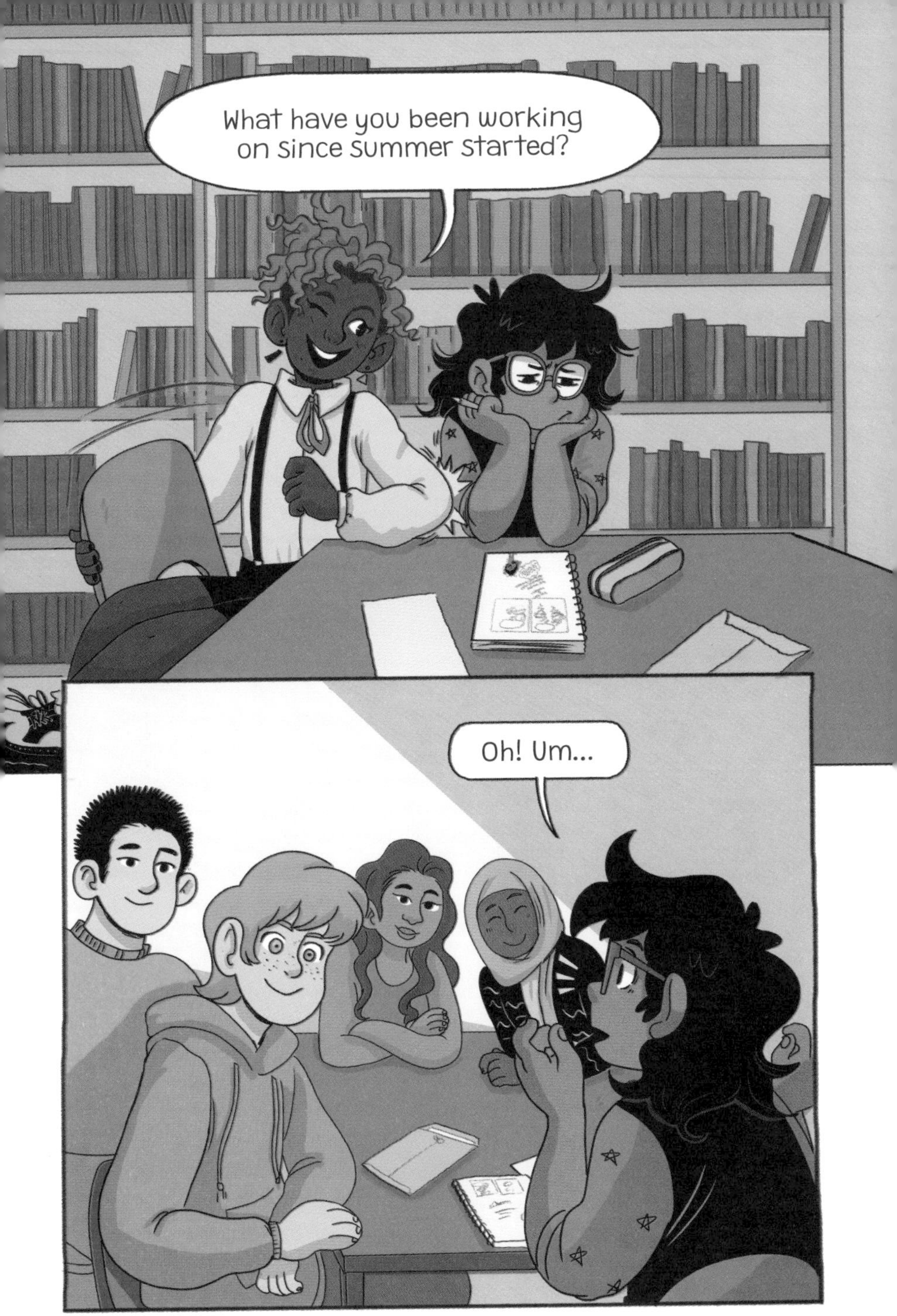
What have you been working on since summer started?
Oh! Um...

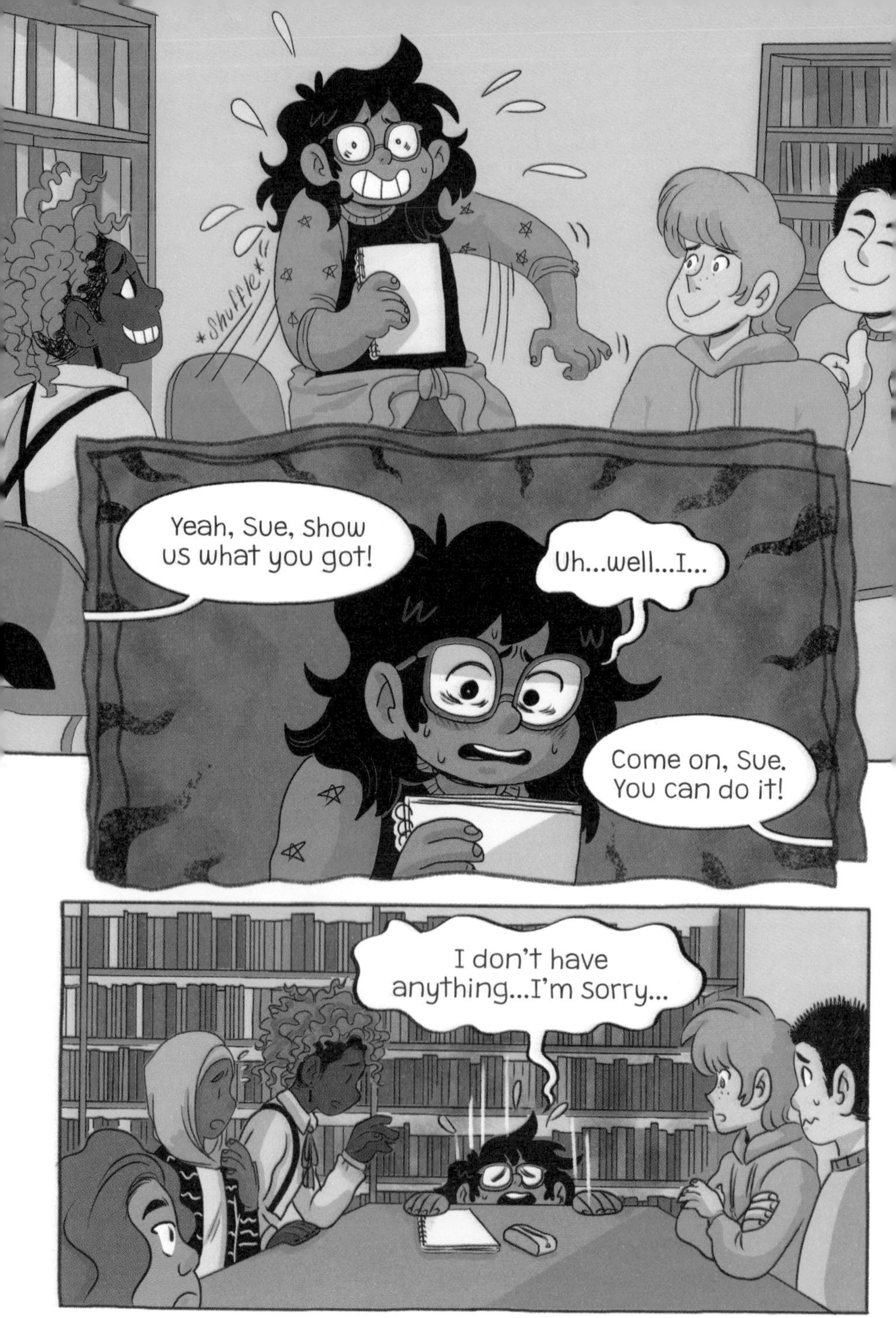
Shuffle
Yeah, Sue, show us what you got!
Uh...well...I...
Come on, Sue. You can do it!
I don't have anything...I'm sorry...

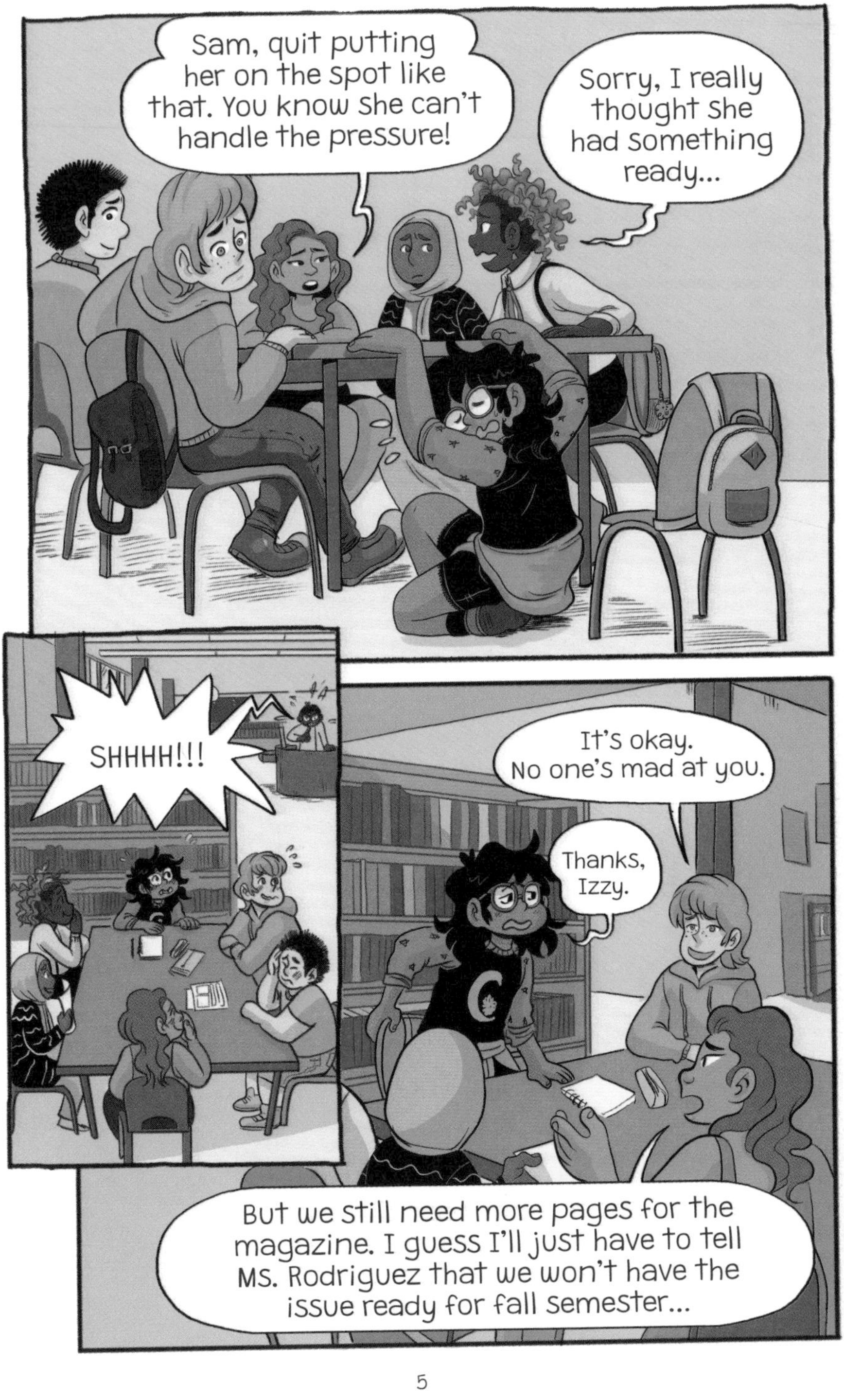
Sam, quit putting her on the spot like that. You know she can't handle the pressure!
Sorry, I really thought she had something ready...
SHHHH!!!
It's okay. No one's mad at you.
Thanks, Izzy.
But we still need more pages for the magazine. I guess I'll just have to tell Ms. Rodriguez that we won't have the issue ready for fall semester...

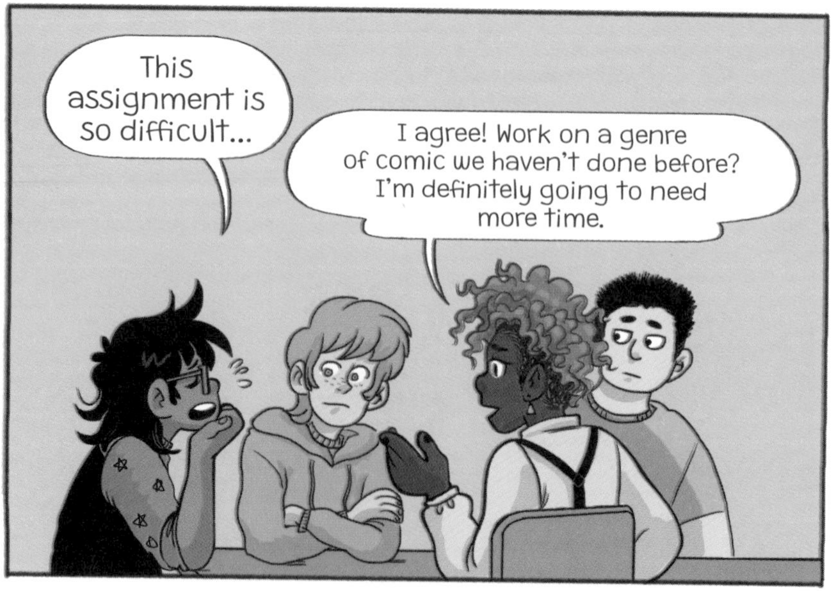
This assignment is so difficult...
I agree! Work on a genre of comic we haven't done before? I'm definitely going to need more time.

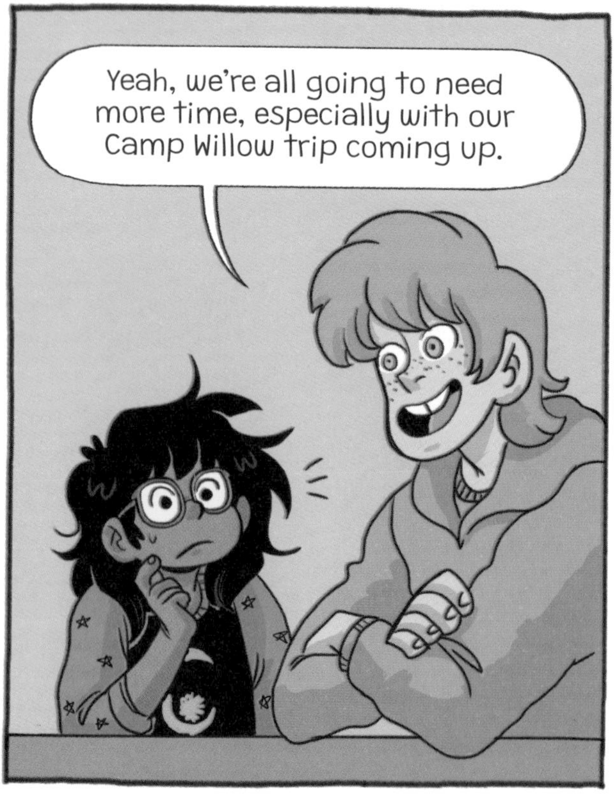
Yeah, we're all going to need more time, especially with our Camp Willow trip coming up.

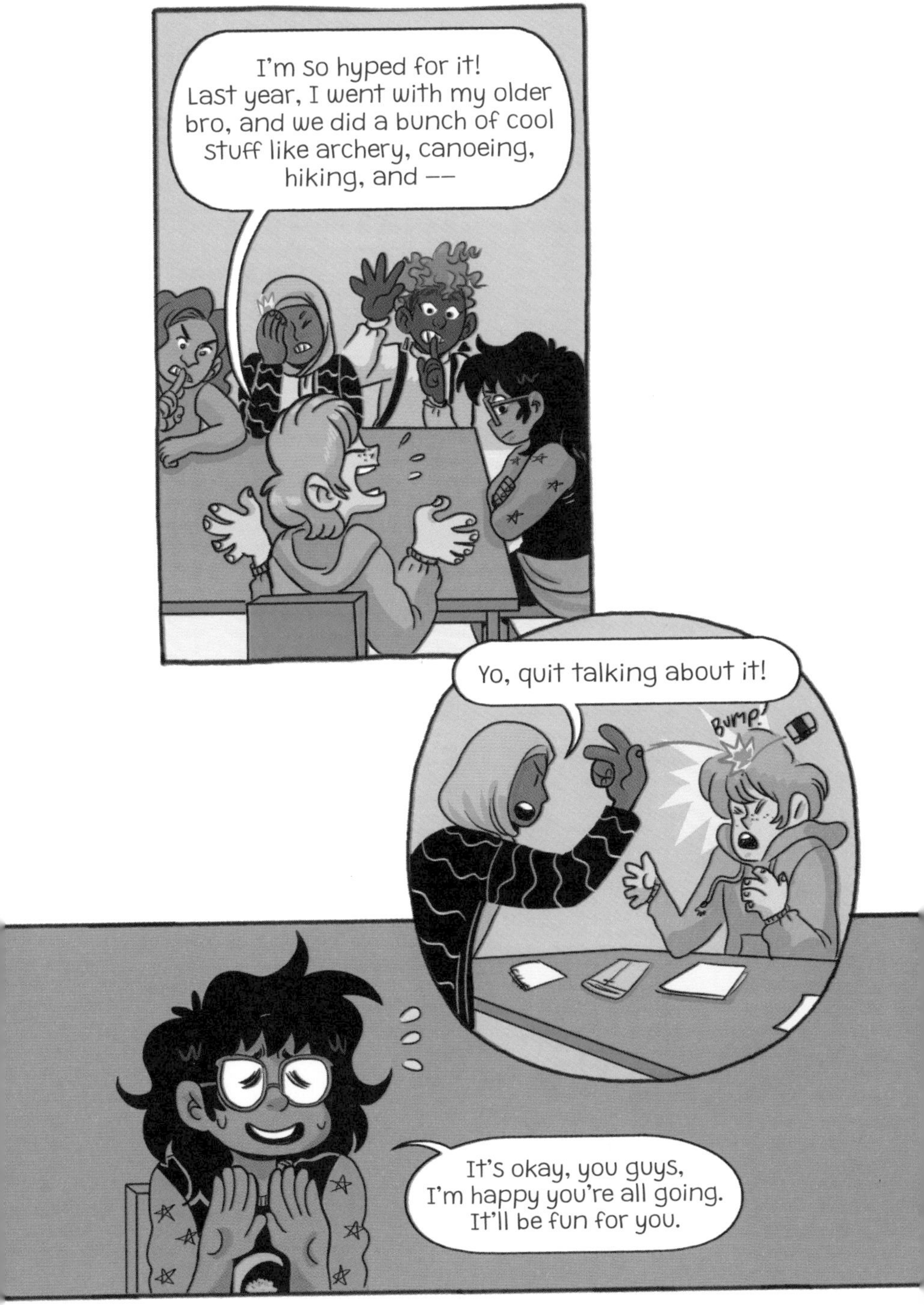
I'm so hyped for it! Last year, I went with my older bro, and we did a bunch of cool stuff like archery, canoeing, hiking, and --
Yo, quit talking about it!
BUMP!
It's okay, you guys, I'm happy you're all going. It'll be fun for you.

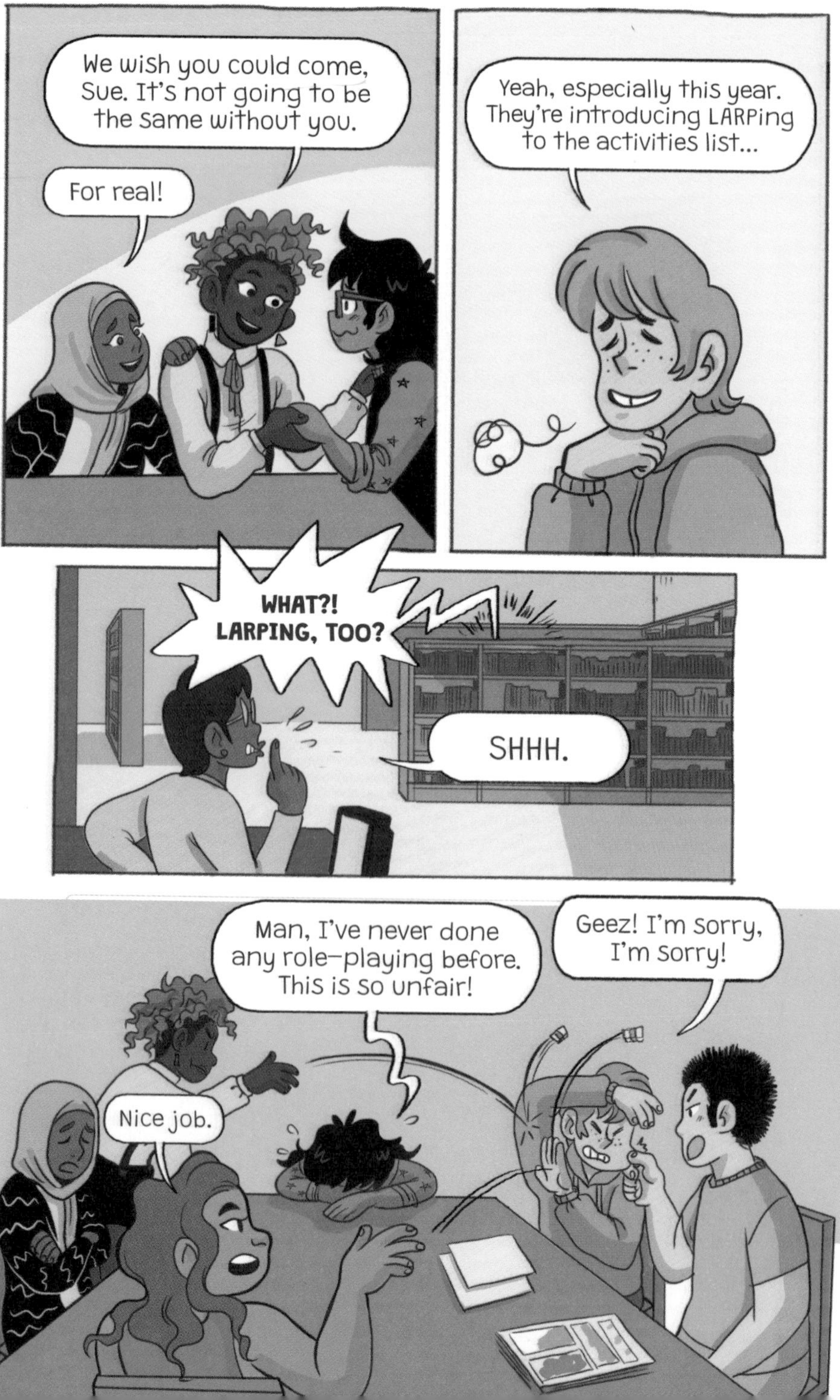
We wish you could come, Sue. It's not going to be the same without you.
For real!
Yeah, especially this year. They're introducing LARPing to the activities list...
WHAT?! LARPING, TOO?
SHHH.
Man, I've never done any role-playing before. This is so unfair!
Geez! I'm sorry, I'm sorry!
Nice job.

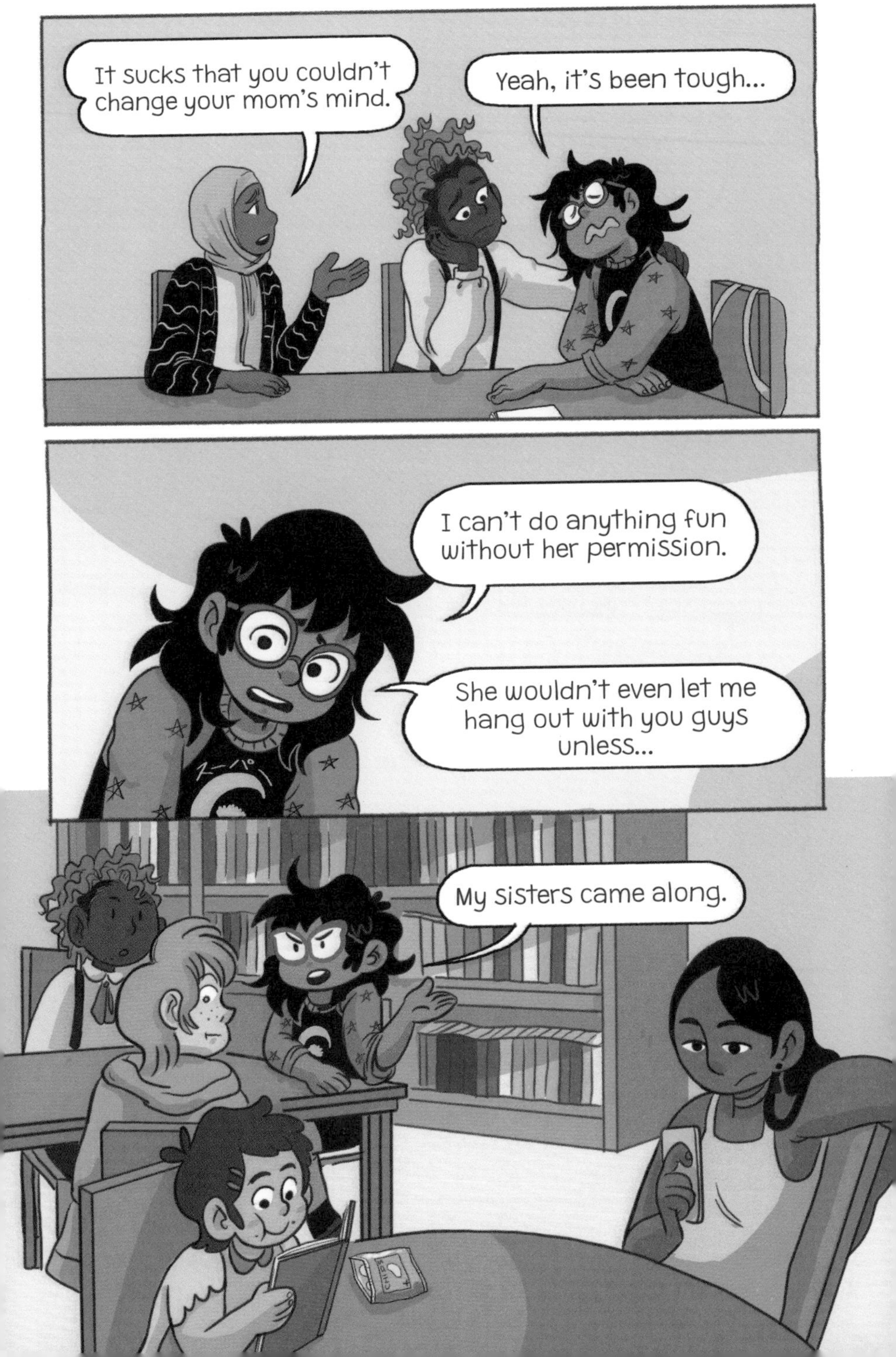
It sucks that you couldn't change your mom's mind.
Yeah, it's been tough...
I can't do anything fun without her permission.
She wouldn't even let me hang out with you guys unless...
My sisters came along.

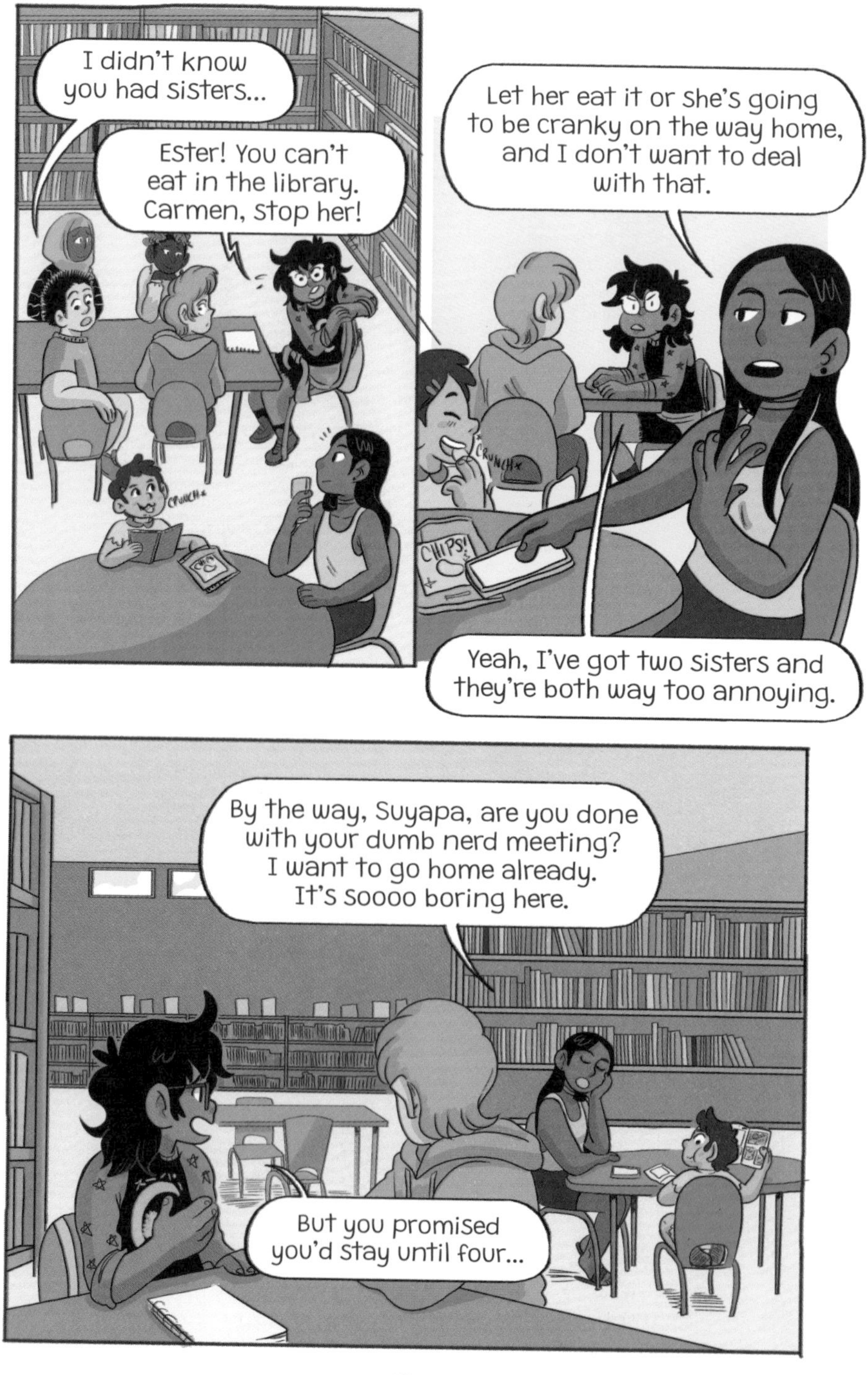
I didn't know you had sisters...
Ester! You can't eat in the library. Carmen, stop her!
CRUNCH
Let her eat it or she's going to be cranky on the way home, and I don't want to deal with that.
CRUNCH
CHIPS!
Yeah, I've got two sisters and they're both way too annoying.
By the way, Suyapa, are you done with your dumb nerd meeting? I want to go home already. It's soooo boring here.
But you promised you'd stay until four...

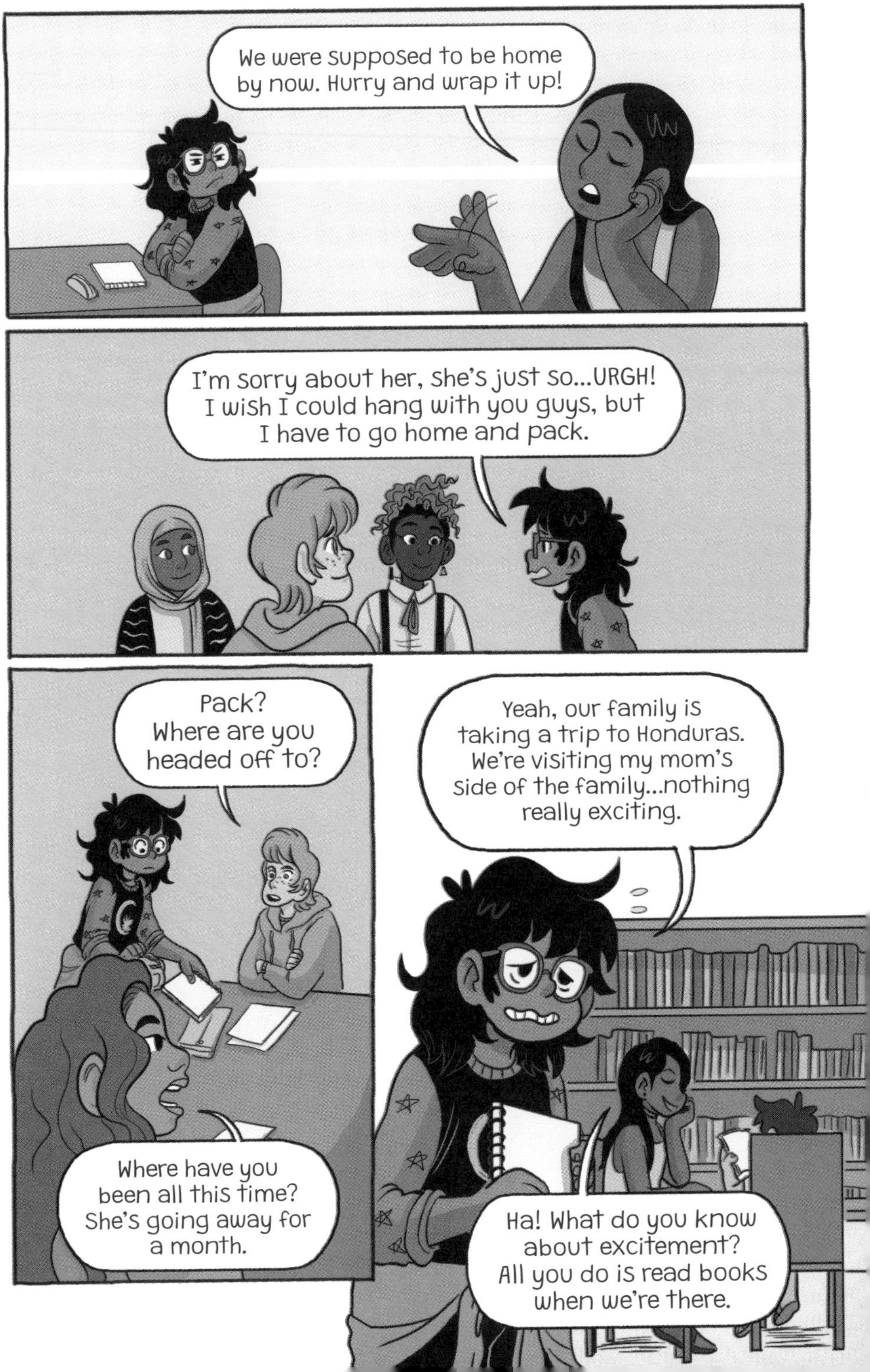
We were supposed to be home by now. Hurry and wrap it up!
I'm sorry about her, she's just so...URGH! I wish I could hang with you guys, but I have to go home and pack.
Pack? Where are you headed off to?
Where have you been all this time? She's going away for a month.
Yeah, our family is taking a trip to Honduras. We're visiting my mom's side of the family...nothing really exciting.
Ha! What do you know about excitement? All you do is read books when we're there.

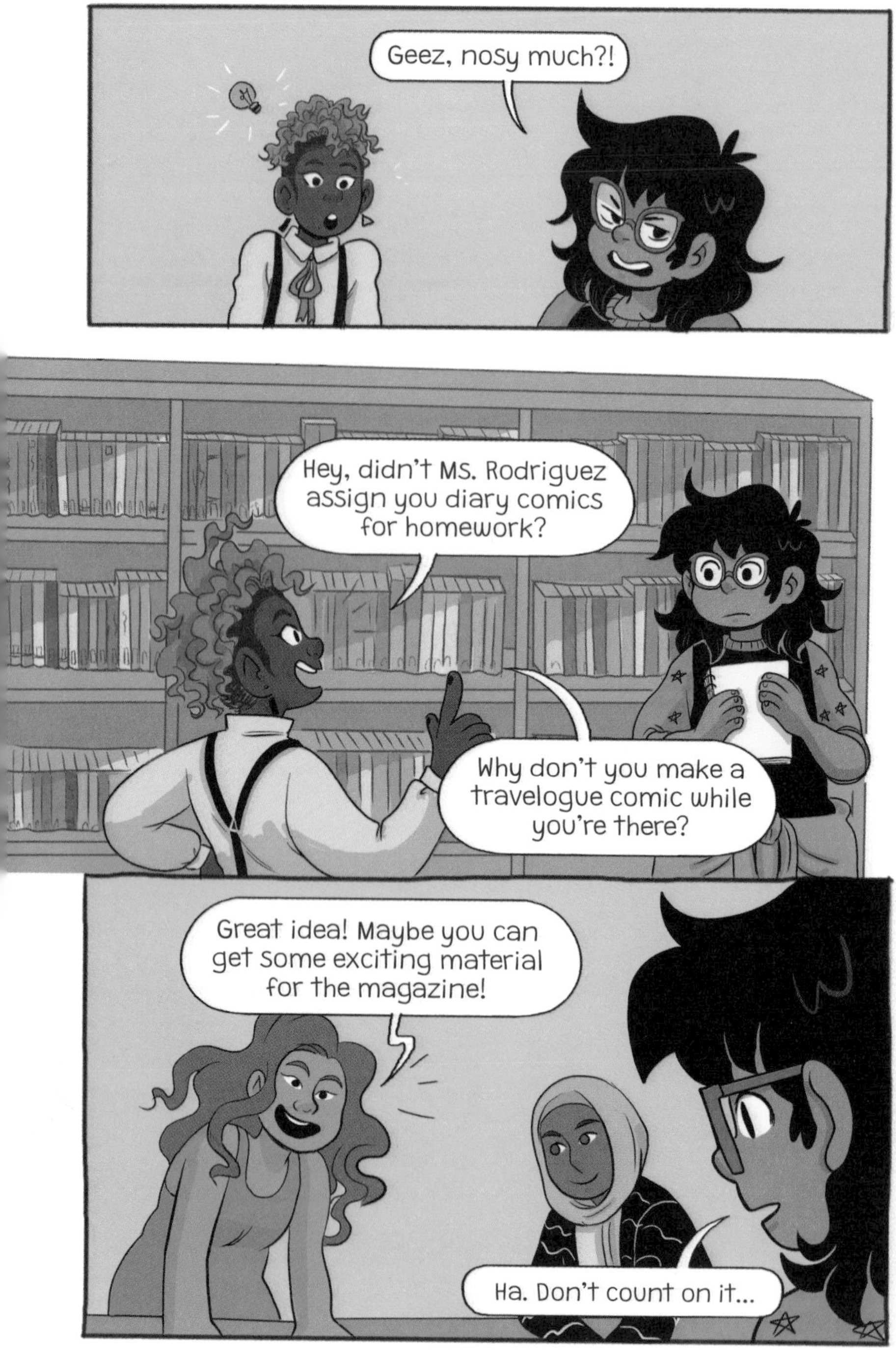
Geez, nosy much?!
Hey, didn't Ms. Rodriguez assign you diary comics for homework?
Why don't you make a travelogue comic while you're there?
Great idea! Maybe you can get some exciting material for the magazine!
Ha. Don't count on it...

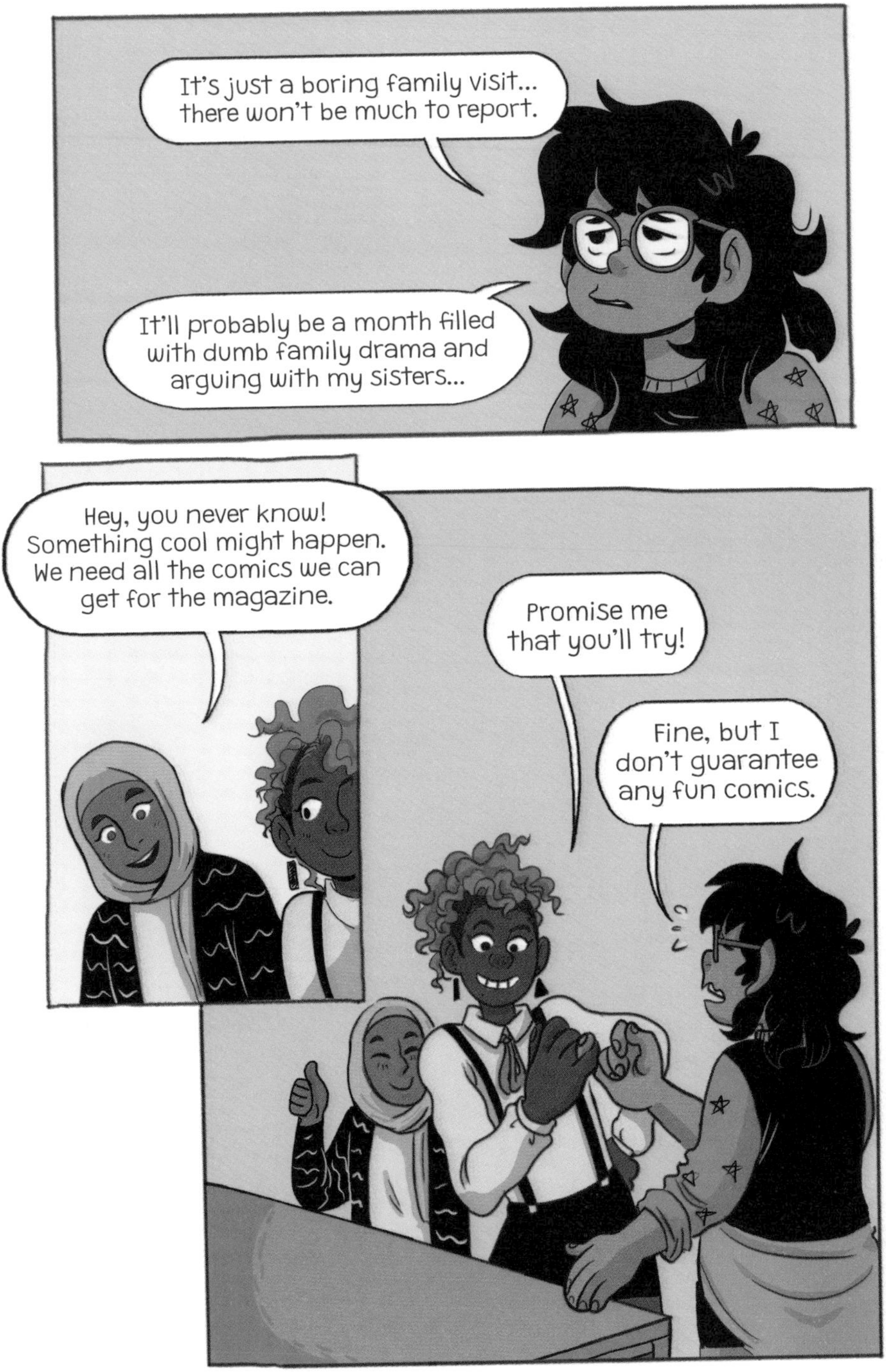
It's just a boring family visit... there won't be much to report.
It'll probably be a month filled with dumb family drama and arguing with my sisters...
Hey, you never know! Something cool might happen. We need all the comics we can get for the magazine.
Promise me that you'll try!
Fine, but I don't guarantee any fun comics.

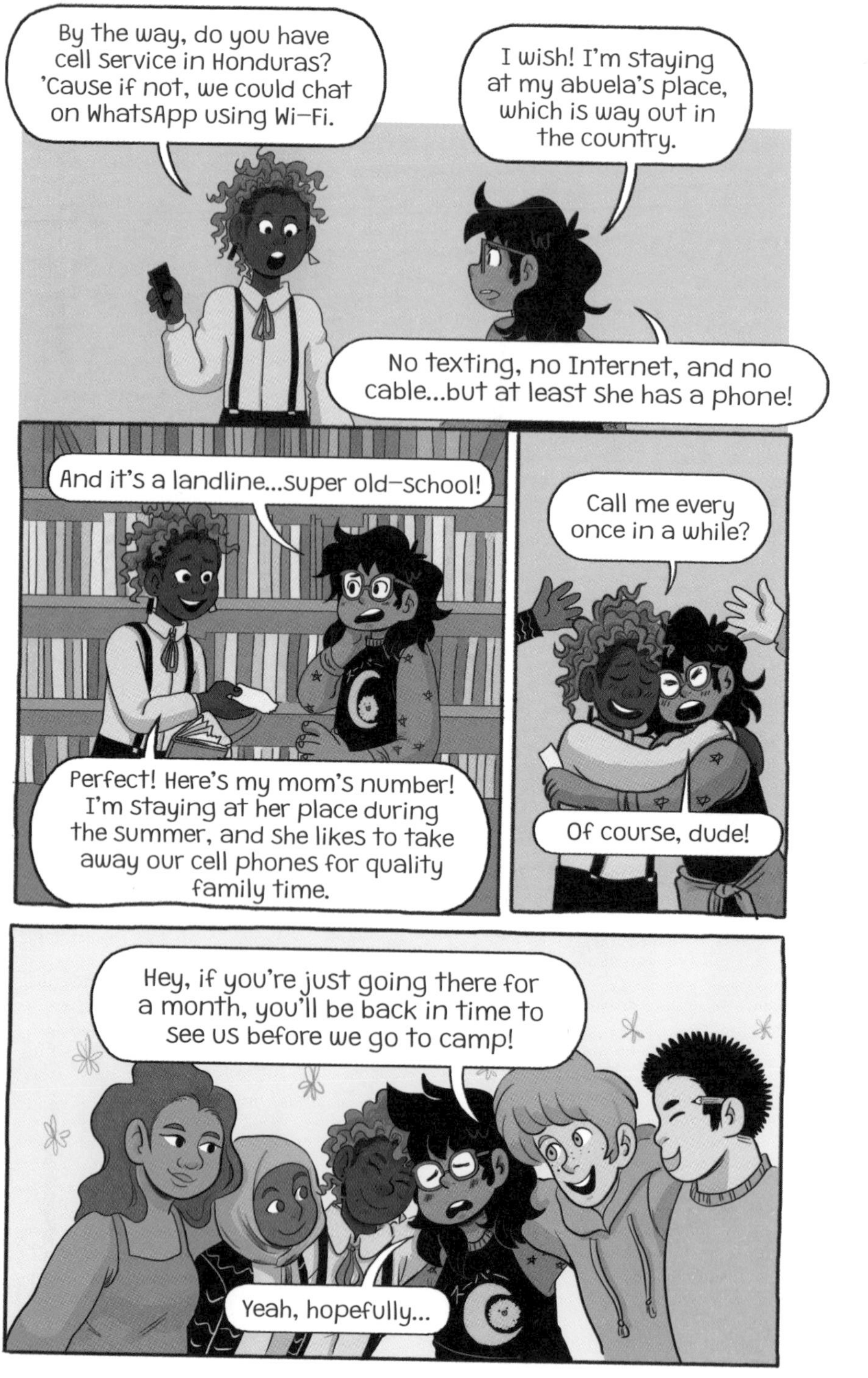
By the way, do you have cell service in Honduras? 'Cause if not, we could chat on WhatsApp using Wi-Fi.
I wish! I'm staying at my abuela's place, which is way out in the country.
No texting, no Internet, and no cable...but at least she has a phone!
And it's a landline...super old-school!
Perfect! Here's my mom's number! I'm staying at her place during the summer, and she likes to take away our cell phones for quality family time.
Call me every once in a while?
Of course, dude!
Hey, if you're just going there for a month, you'll be back in time to see us before we go to camp!
Yeah, hopefully...

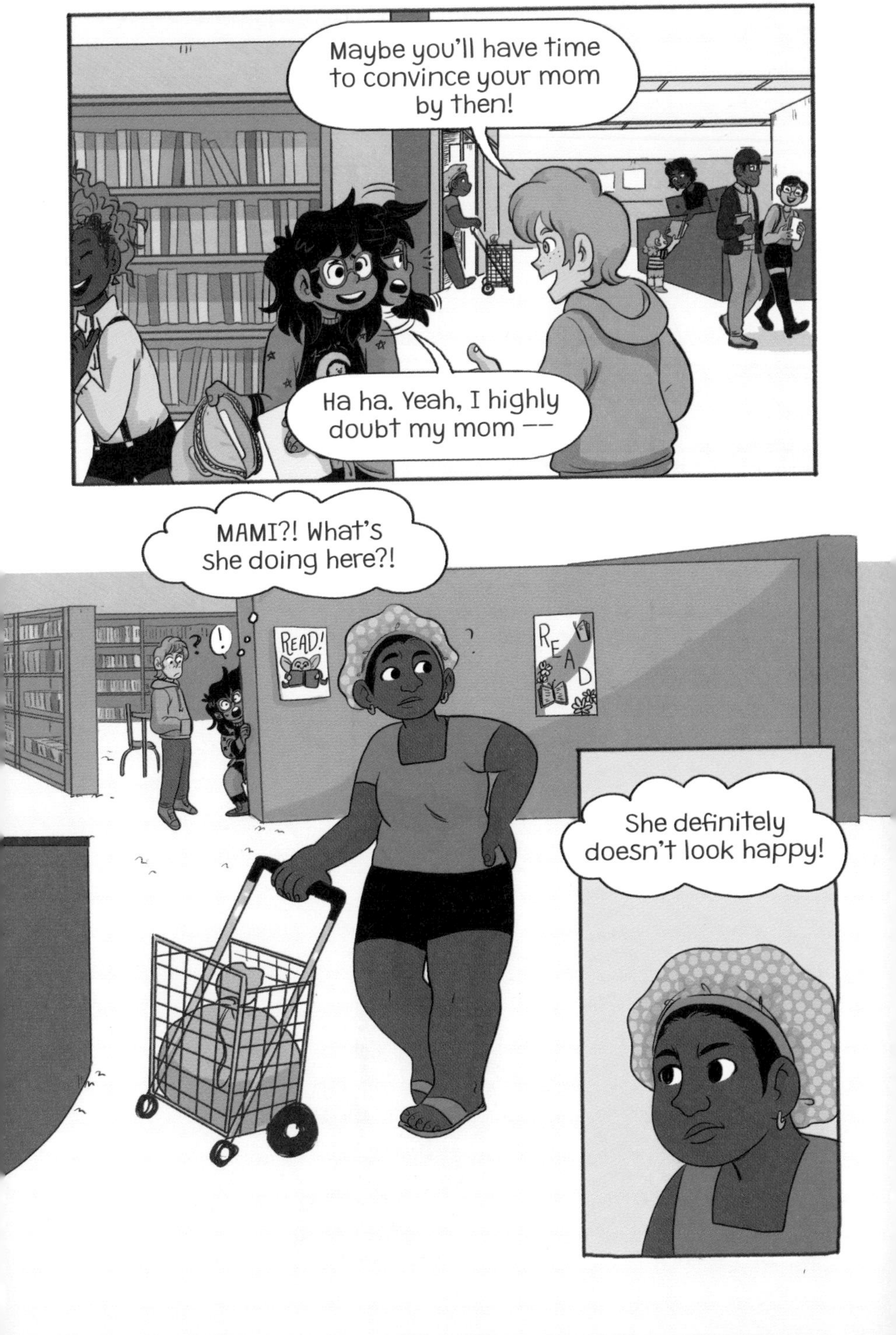
Maybe you'll have time to convince your mom by then!
Ha ha. Yeah, I highly doubt my mom --
READ!
MAMI?! What's she doing here?!
READ
She definitely doesn't look happy!

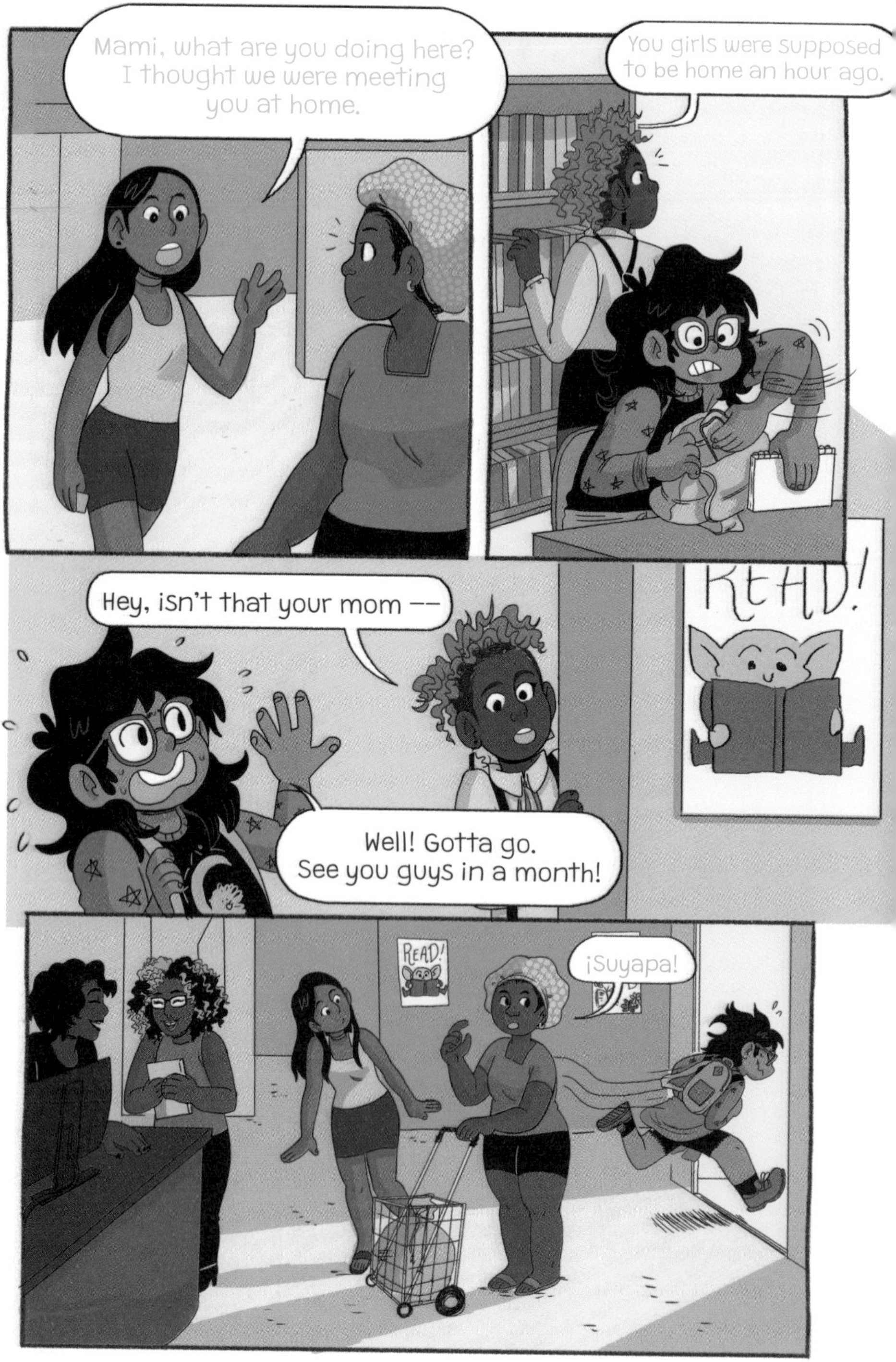
Mami, what are you doing here? I thought we were meeting you at home.
You girls were supposed to be home an hour ago.
Hey, isn't that your mom --
Well! Gotta go. See you guys in a month!
READ!
READ!
¡Suyapa!

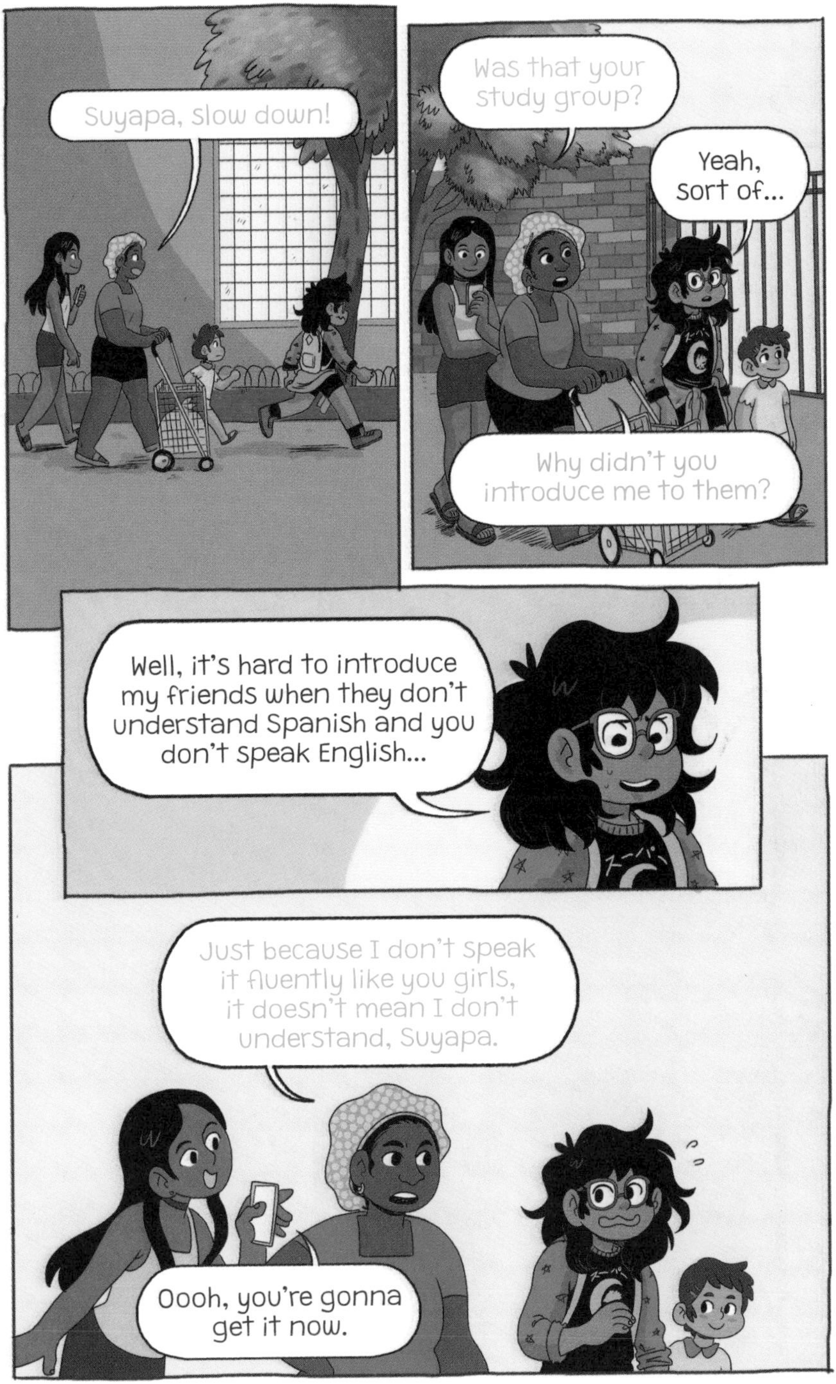

Suyapa, slow down!
Was that your study group?
Yeah, sort of...
Why didn't you introduce me to them?
Well, it's hard to introduce my friends when they don't understand Spanish and you don't speak English...
Just because I don't speak it fluently like you girls, it doesn't mean I don't understand, Suyapa.
Oooh, you're gonna get it now.

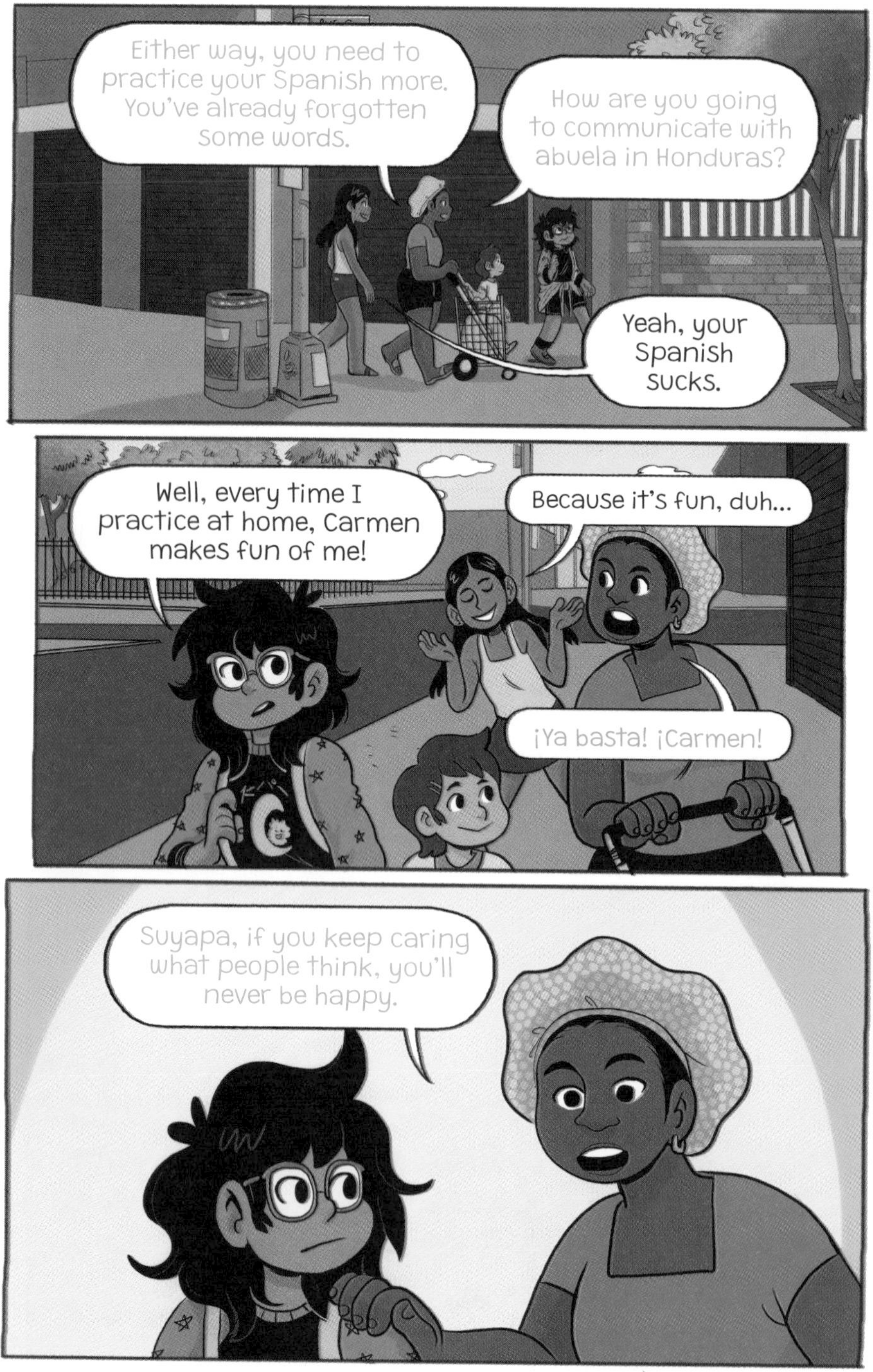
Either way, you need to practice your Spanish more. You've already forgotten some words.
How are you going to communicate with abuela in Honduras?
Yeah, your Spanish sucks.
Well, every time I practice at home, Carmen makes fun of me!
Because it's fun, duh...
¡Ya basta! ¡Carmen!
Suyapa, if you keep caring what people think, you'll never be happy.

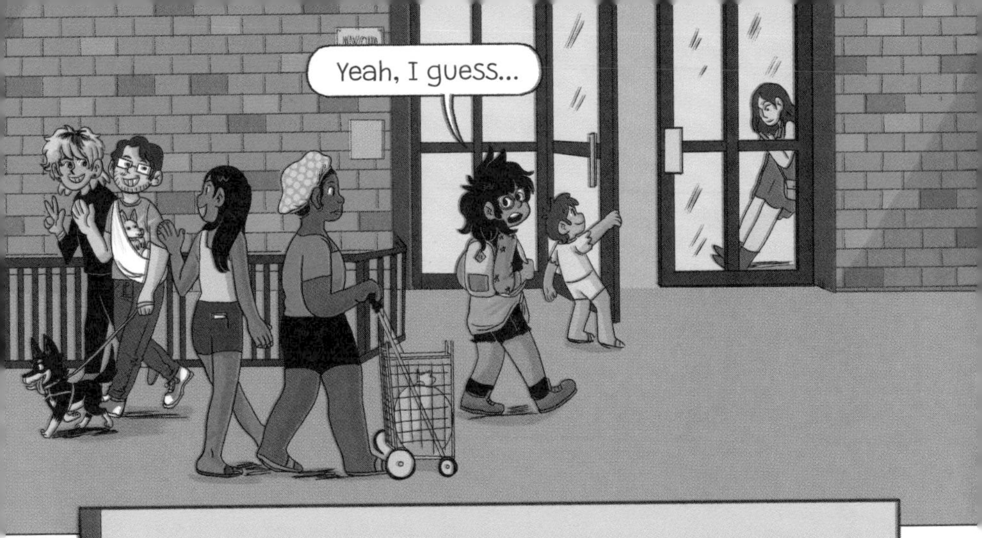
Yeah, I guess...

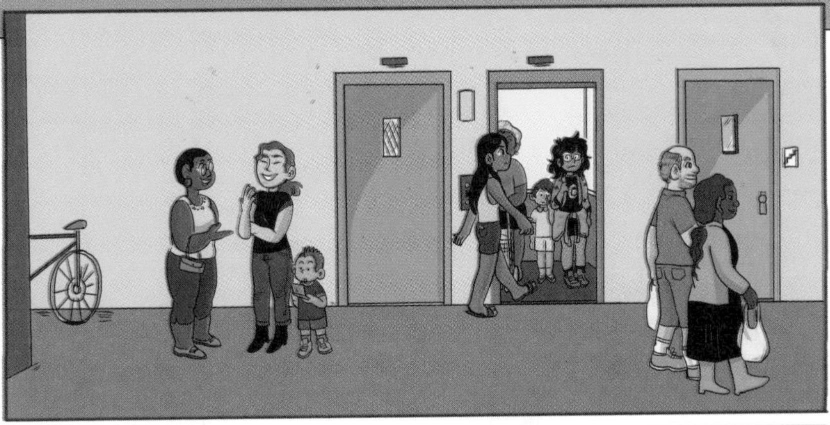

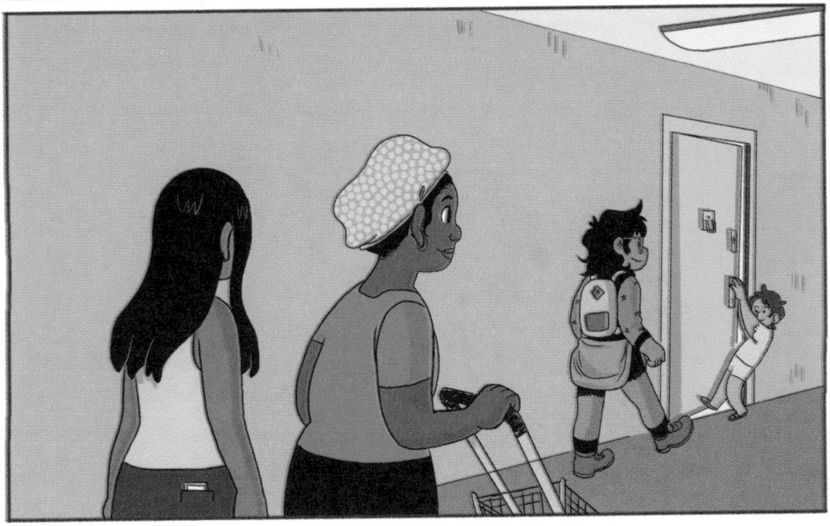

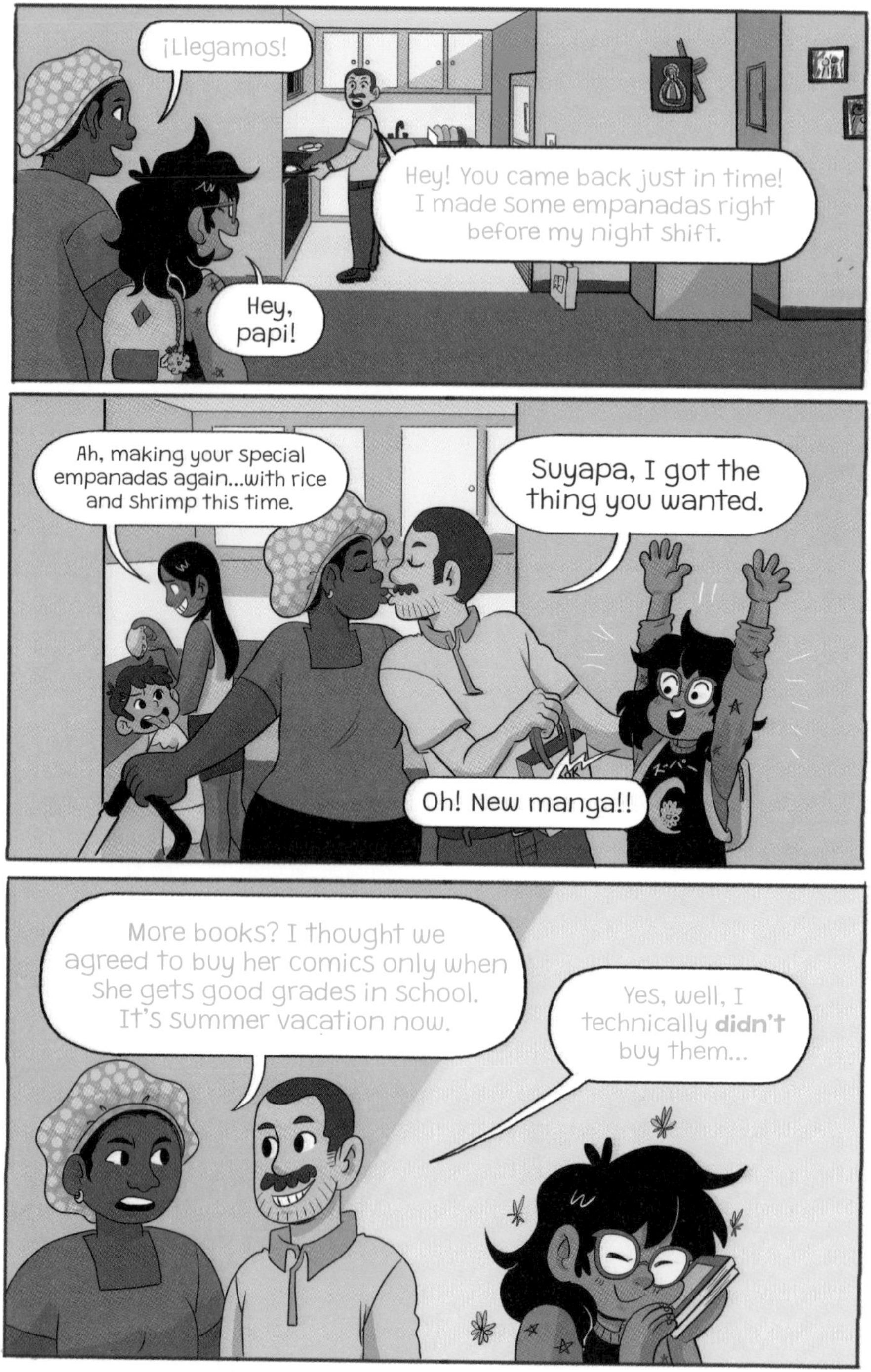
¡Llegamos!
Hey! You came back just in time! I made some empanadas right before my night shift.
Hey, papi!
Ah, making your special empanadas again...with rice and shrimp this time.
Suyapa, I got the thing you wanted.
Oh! New manga!!
More books? I thought we agreed to buy her comics only when she gets good grades in school. It's summer vacation now.
Yes, well, I technically **didn't** buy them...

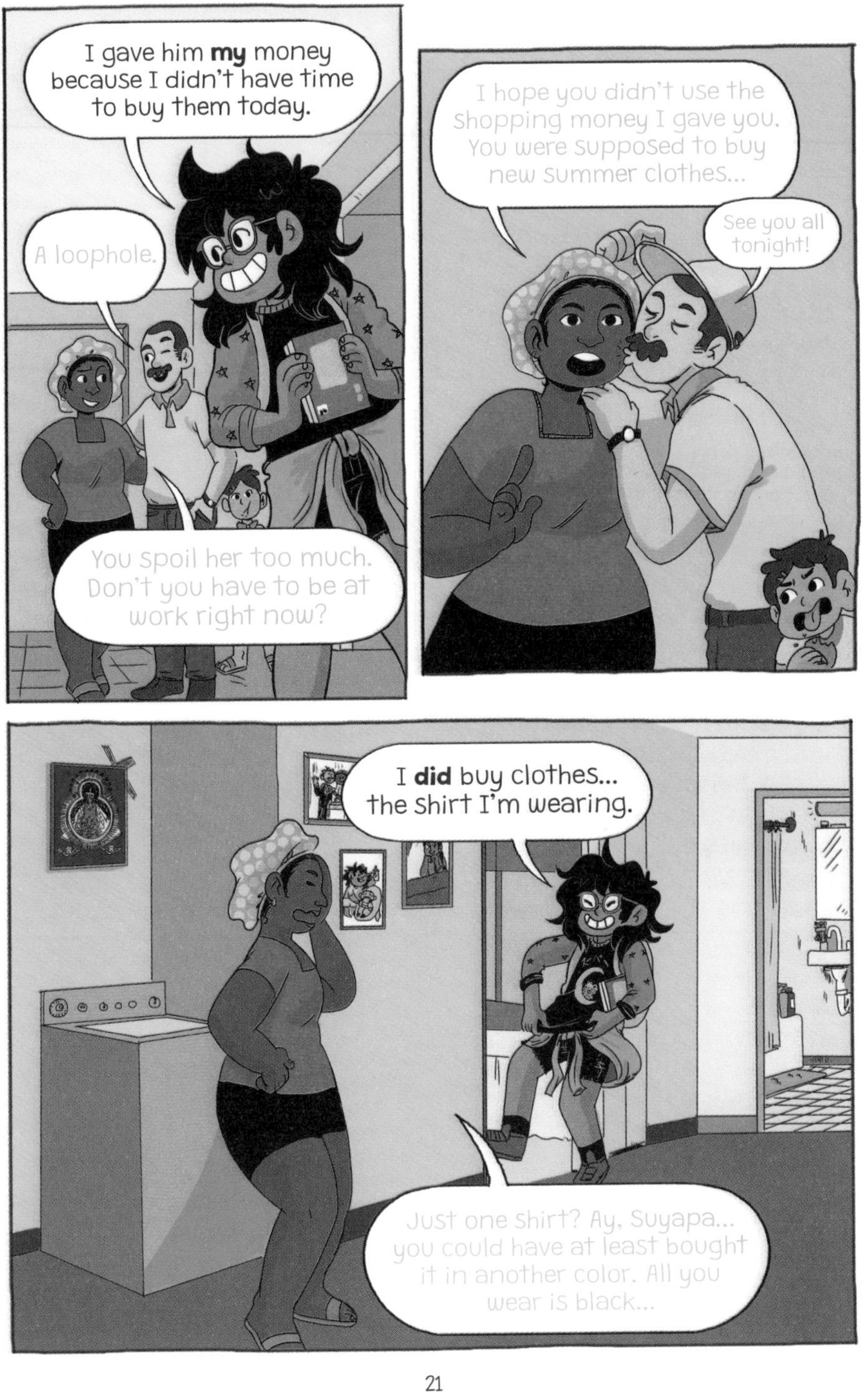
I gave him **my** money because I didn't have time to buy them today.
A loophole.
You spoil her too much. Don't you have to be at work right now?
I hope you didn't use the shopping money I gave you. You were supposed to buy new summer clothes...
See you all tonight!
I **did** buy clothes... the shirt I'm wearing.
Just one shirt? Ay, Suyapa... you could have at least bought it in another color. All you wear is black...

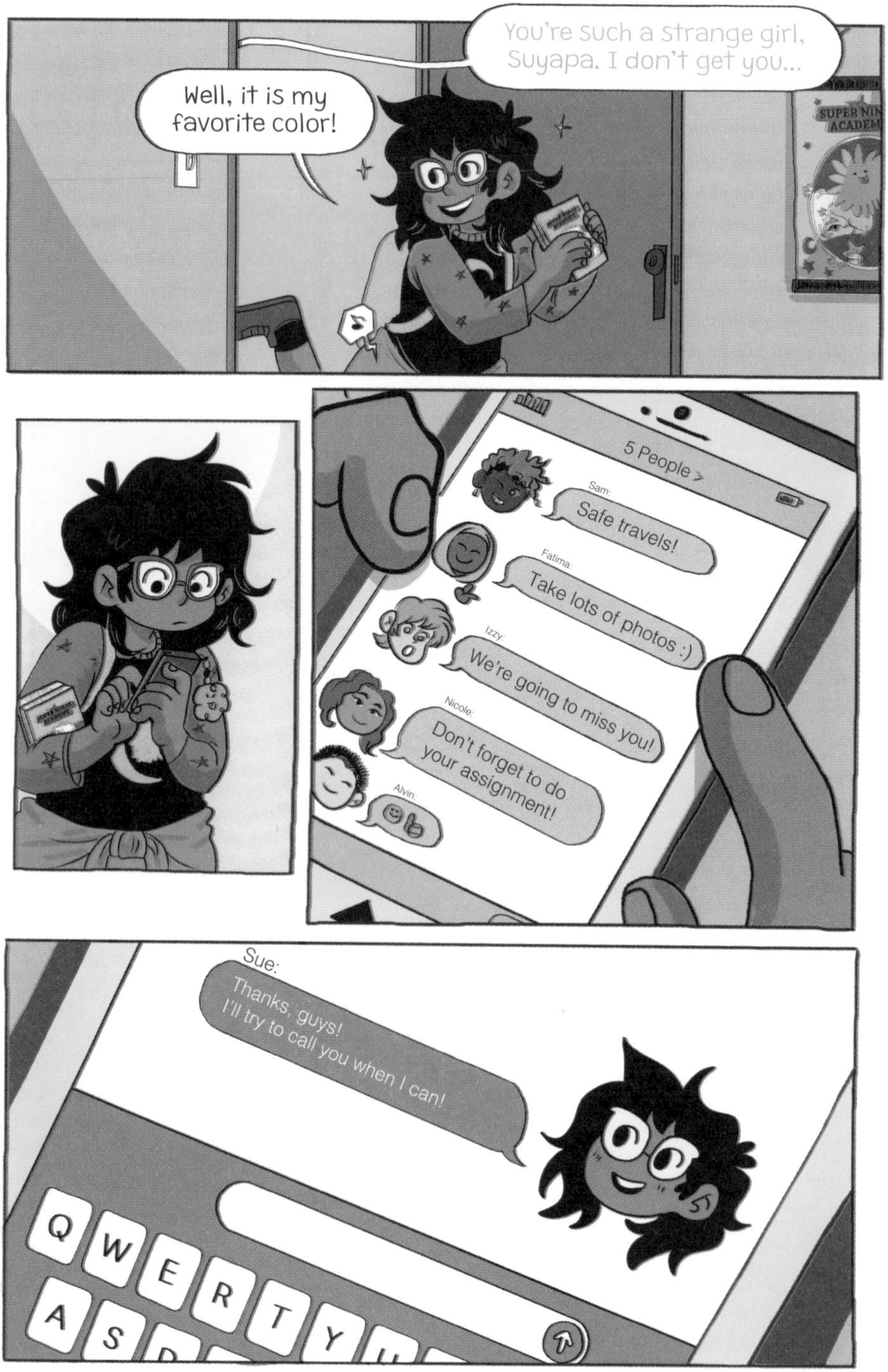

You're such a strange girl, Suyapa. I don't get you...
Well, it is my favorite color!
SUPER NINJA ACADEMY
5 People >
Sam:
Safe travels!
Fatima:
Take lots of photos :)
Izzy:
We're going to miss you!
Nicole:
Don't forget to do your assignment!
Alvin:
Sue:
Thanks, guys!
I'll try to call you when I can!
Q W E R T Y
A S

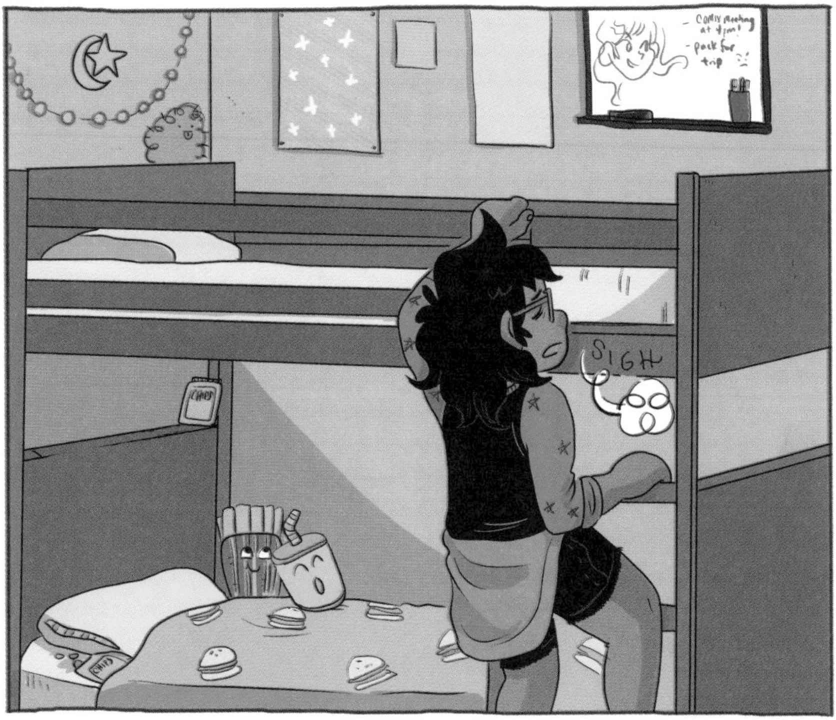
- COMIX meeting at 4pm!
- pack for trip
SIGH

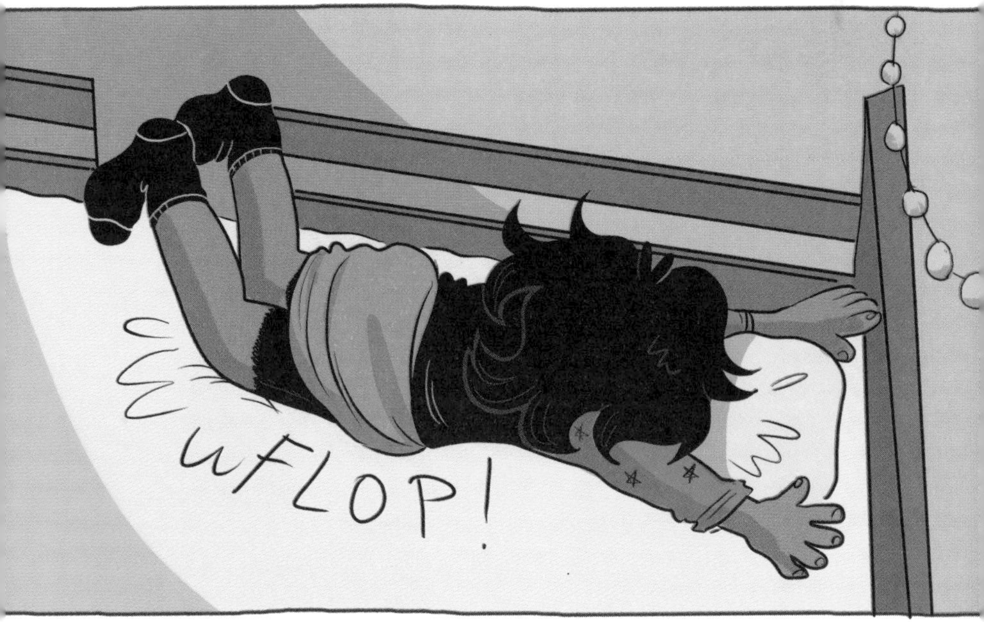
WFLOP!

CHAPTER TWO

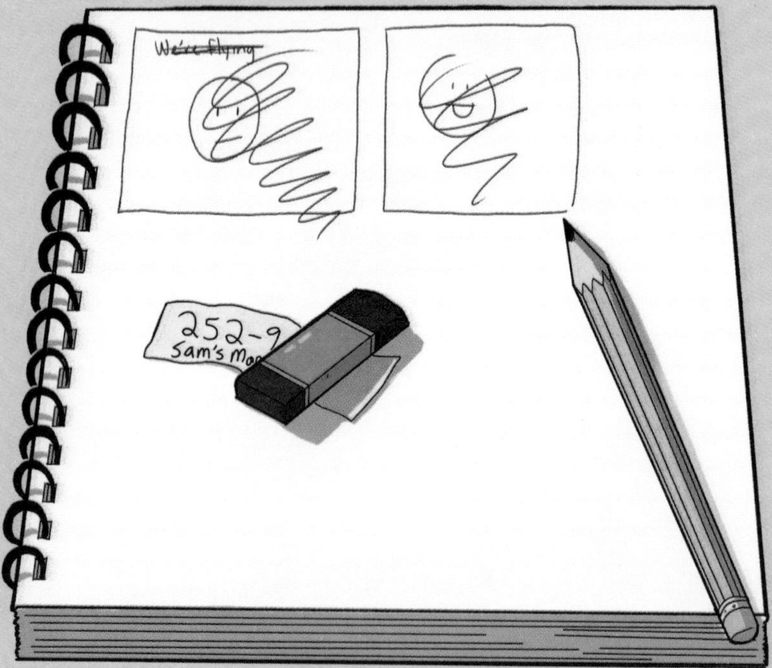

We're flying
252-9
Sam's Mo

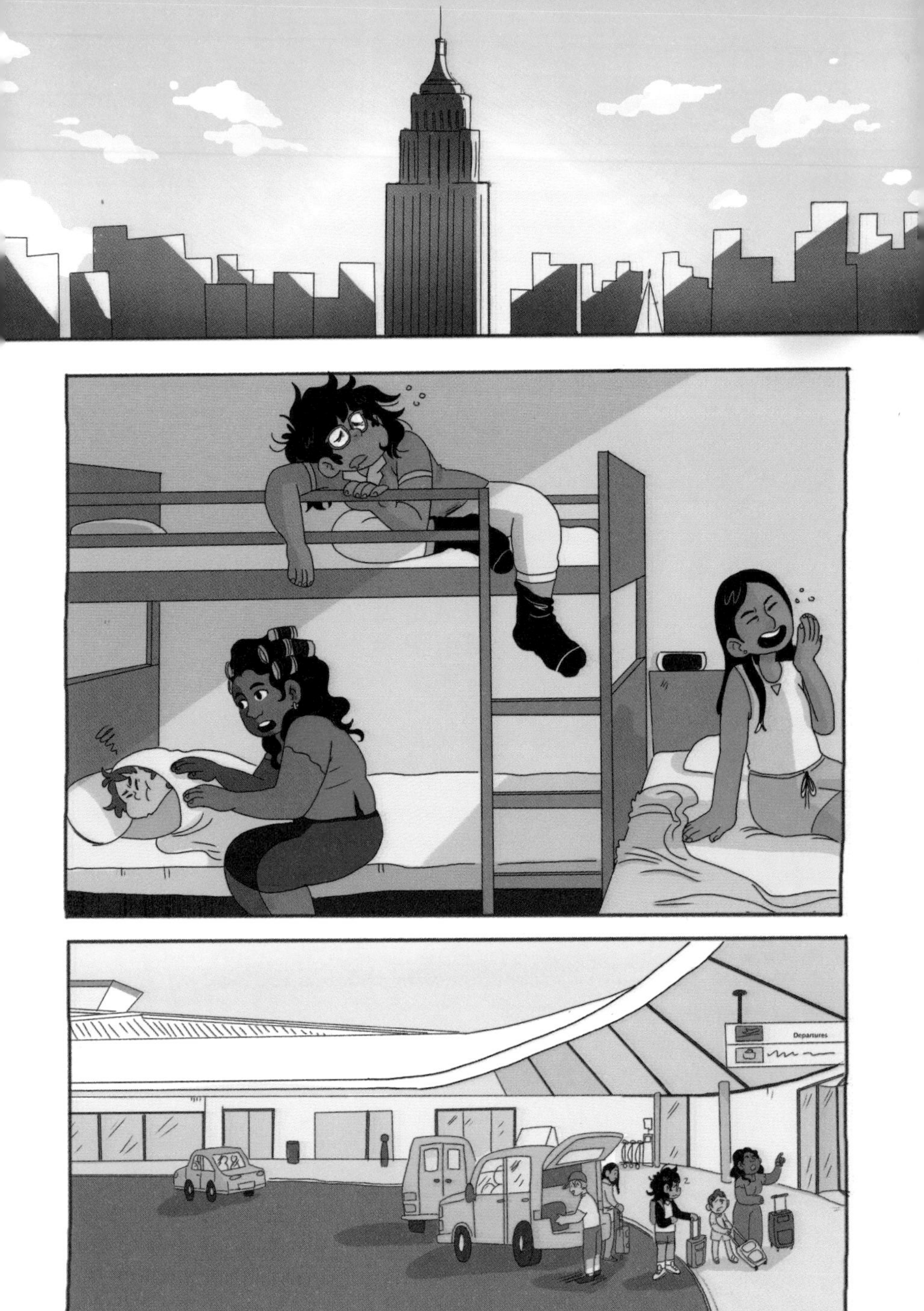
Departures

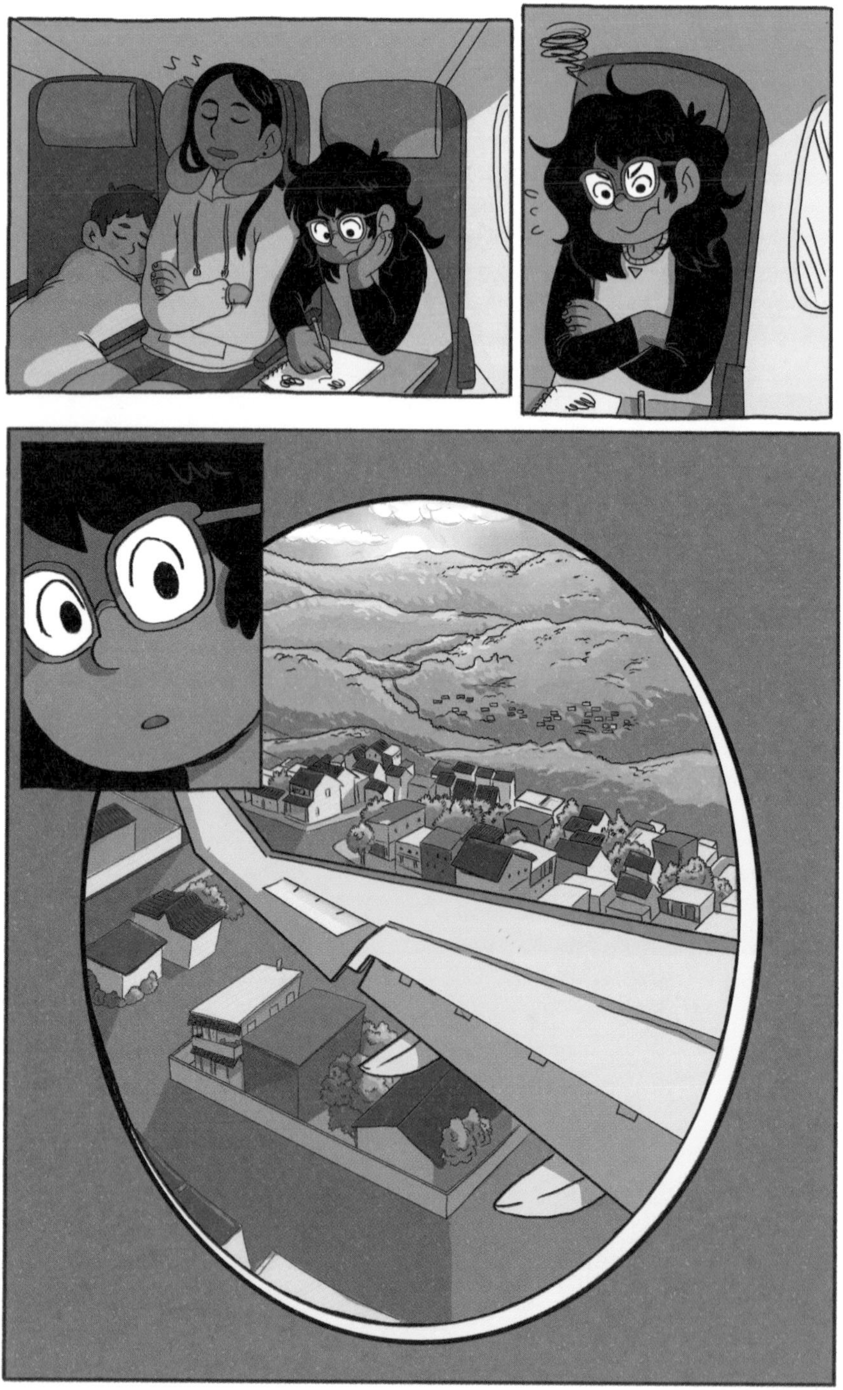

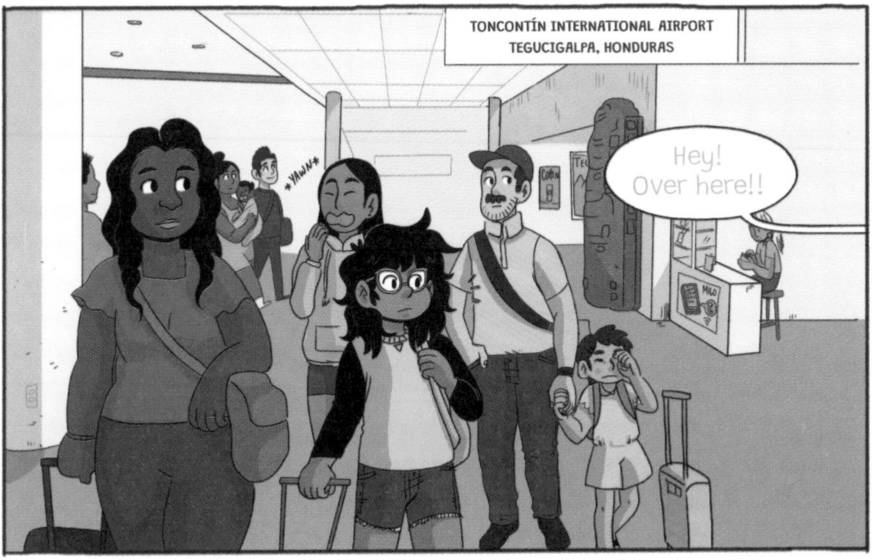
TONCONTÍN INTERNATIONAL AIRPORT
TEGUCIGALPA, HONDURAS
YAWN
Hey! Over here!!

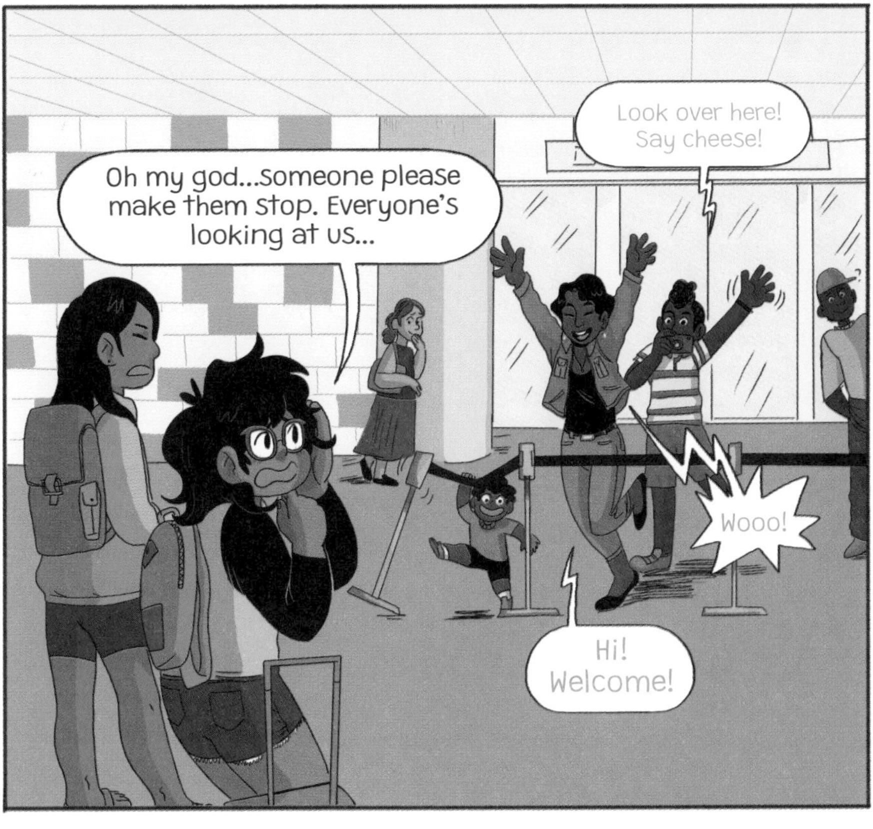
Oh my god...someone please make them stop. Everyone's looking at us...
Look over here! Say cheese!
Wooo!
Hi! Welcome!

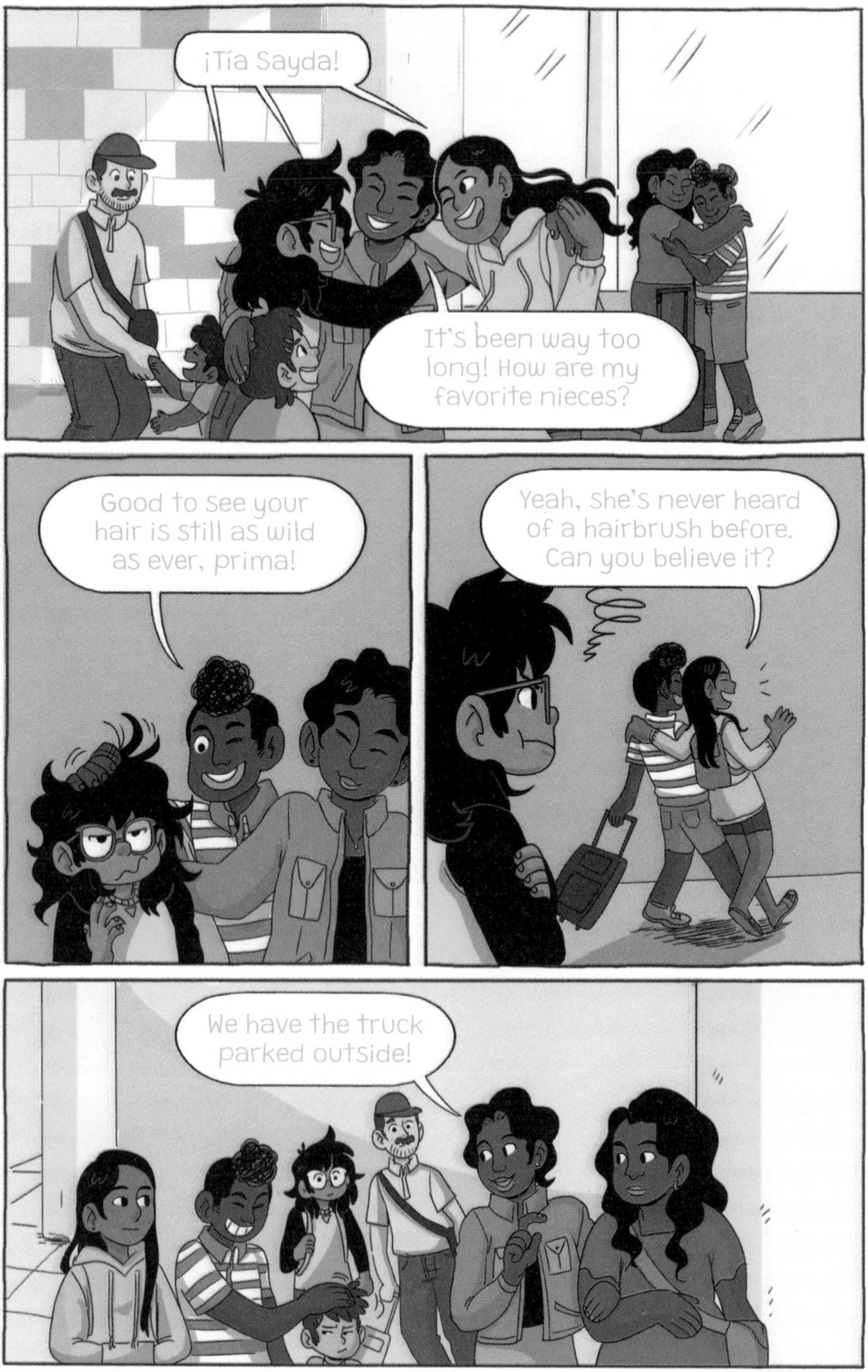
¡Tía Sayda!
It's been way too long! How are my favorite nieces?
Good to see your hair is still as wild as ever, prima!
Yeah, she's never heard of a hairbrush before. Can you believe it?
We have the truck parked outside!

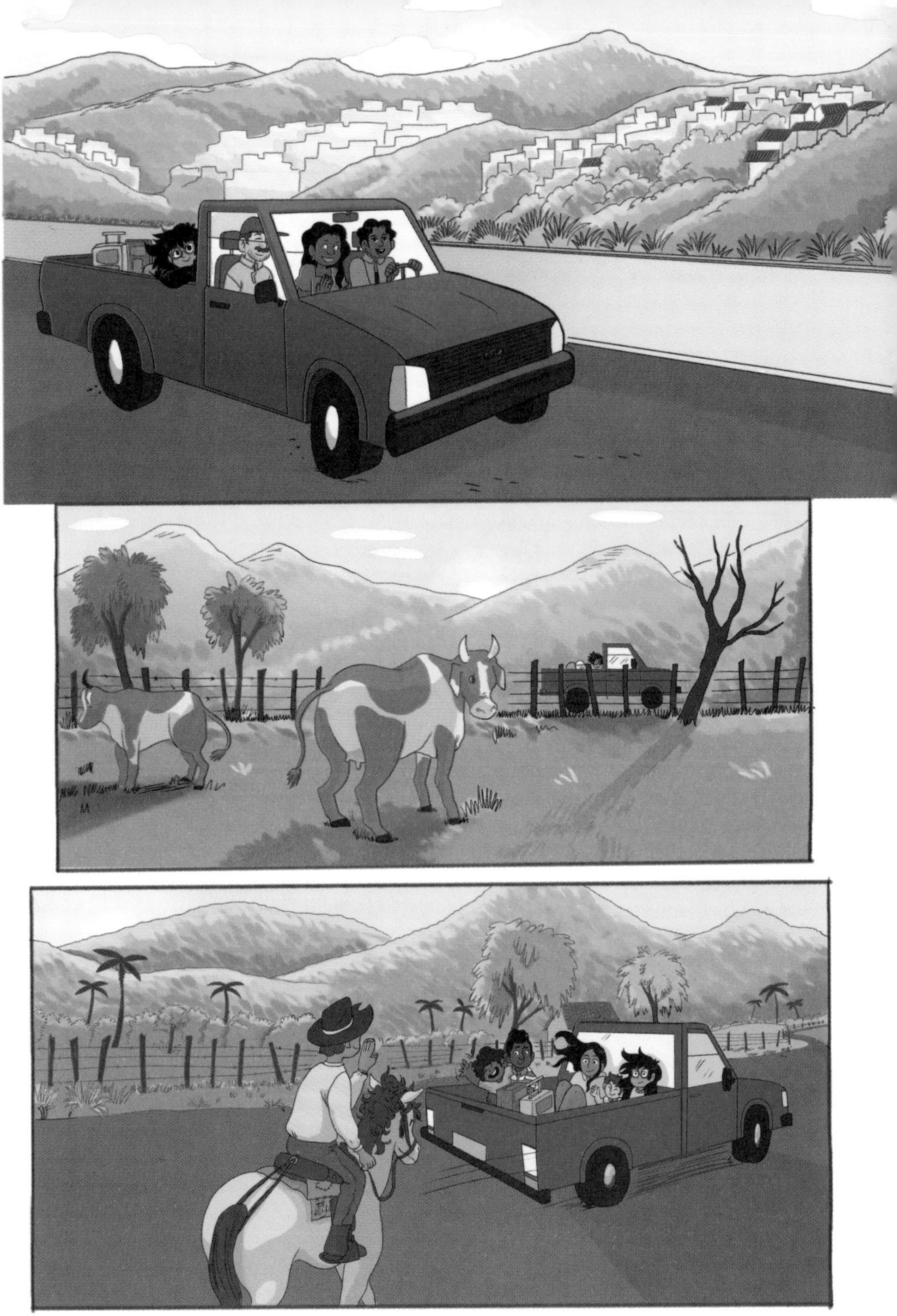

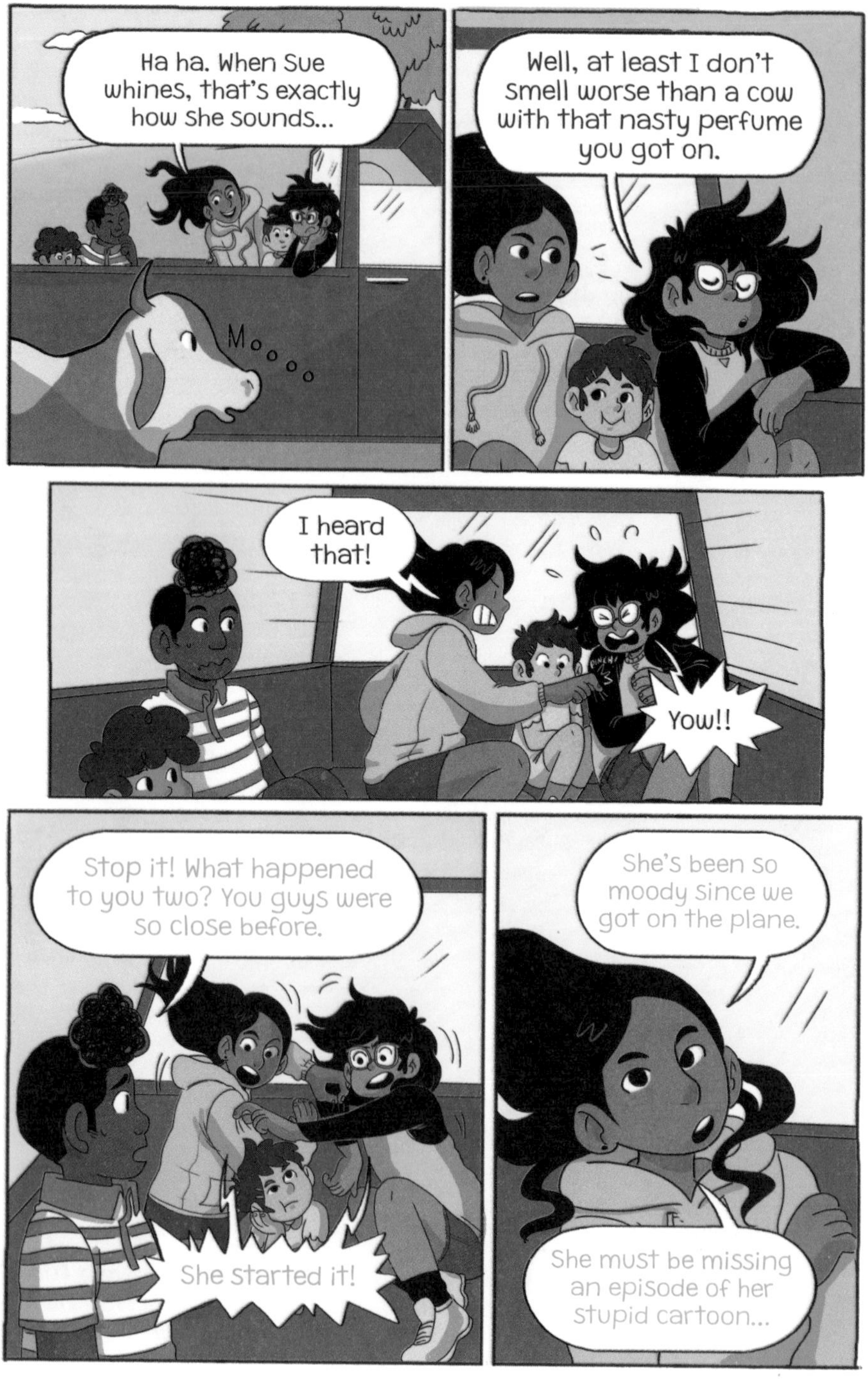
Ha ha. When Sue whines, that's exactly how she sounds...
Moooo
Well, at least I don't smell worse than a cow with that nasty perfume you got on.
I heard that!
PINCH!
YOW!!
Stop it! What happened to you two? You guys were so close before.
She started it!
She's been so moody since we got on the plane.
She must be missing an episode of her stupid cartoon...

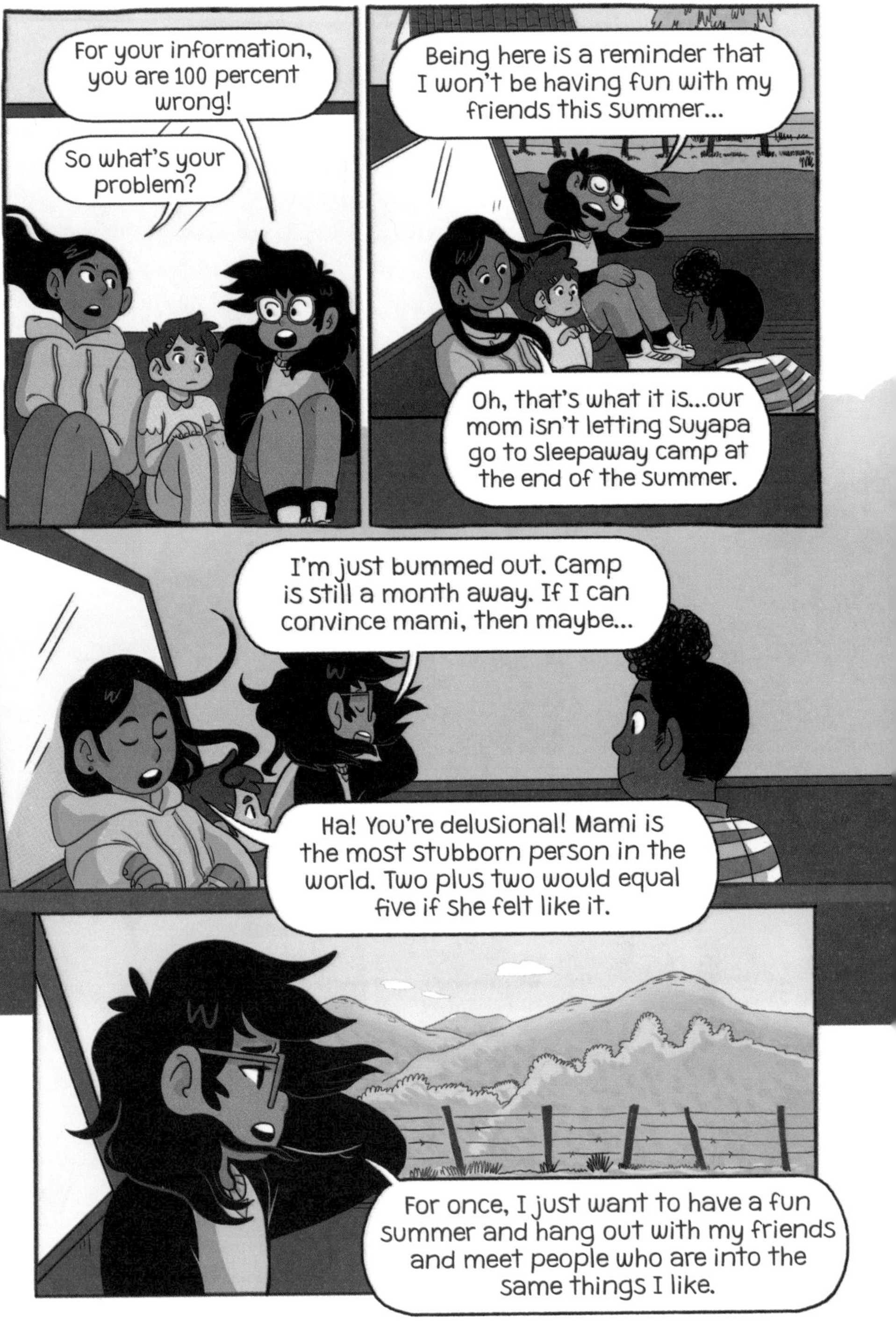
For your information, you are 100 percent wrong!
So what's your problem?
Being here is a reminder that I won't be having fun with my friends this summer...
Oh, that's what it is...our mom isn't letting Suyapa go to sleepaway camp at the end of the summer.
I'm just bummed out. Camp is still a month away. If I can convince mami, then maybe...
Ha! You're delusional! Mami is the most stubborn person in the world. Two plus two would equal five if she felt like it.
For once, I just want to have a fun summer and hang out with my friends and meet people who are into the same things I like.

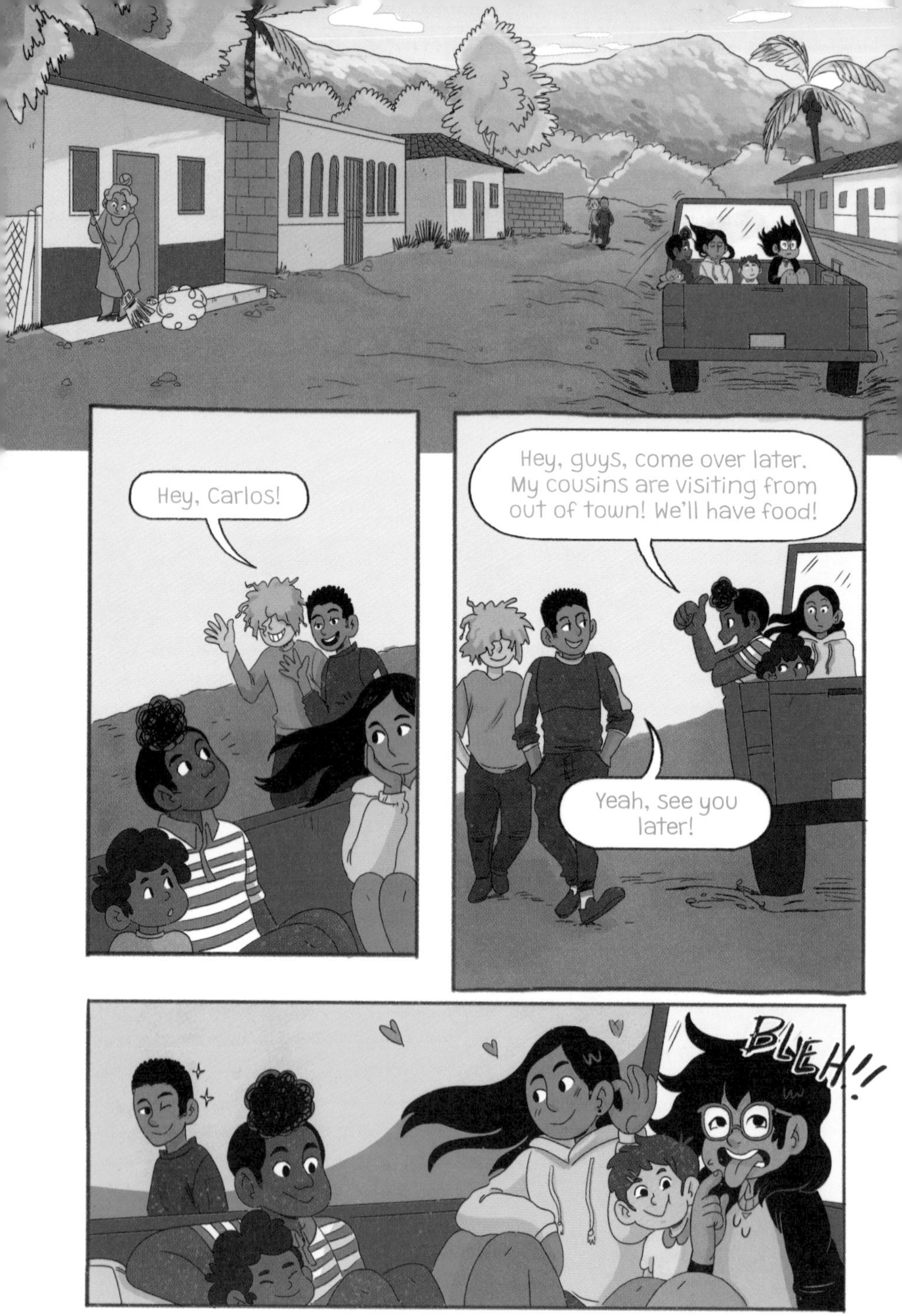
Hey, Carlos!
Hey, guys, come over later. My cousins are visiting from out of town! We'll have food!
Yeah, see you later!
BLEH!!

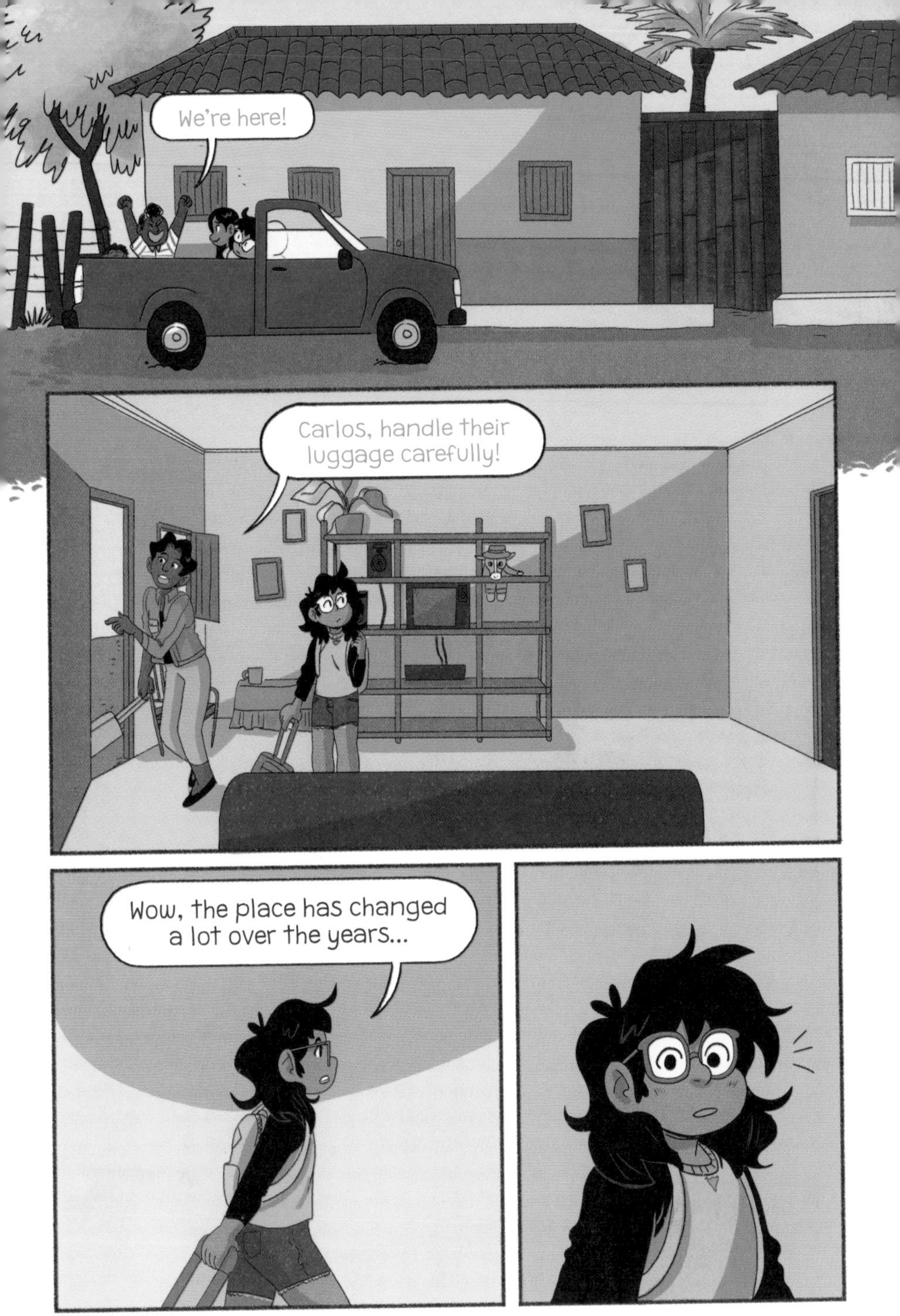
We're here!
Carlos, handle their luggage carefully!
Wow, the place has changed a lot over the years...

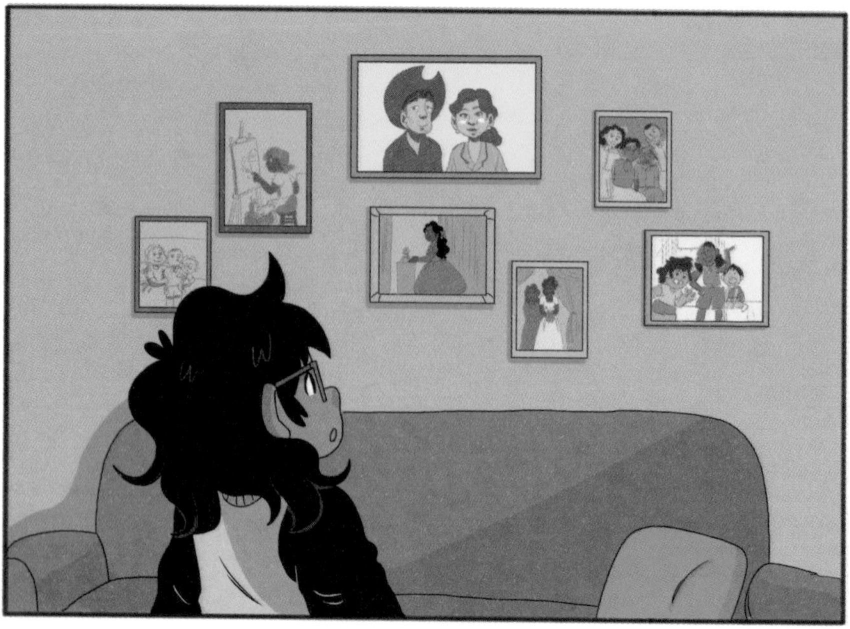

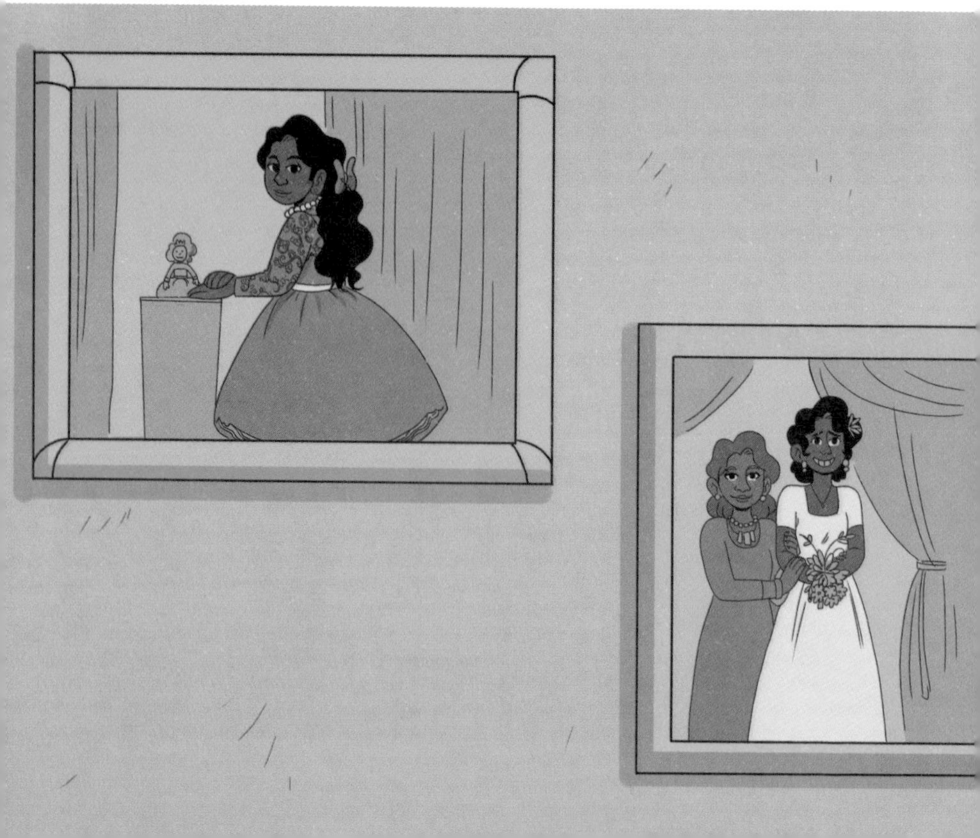

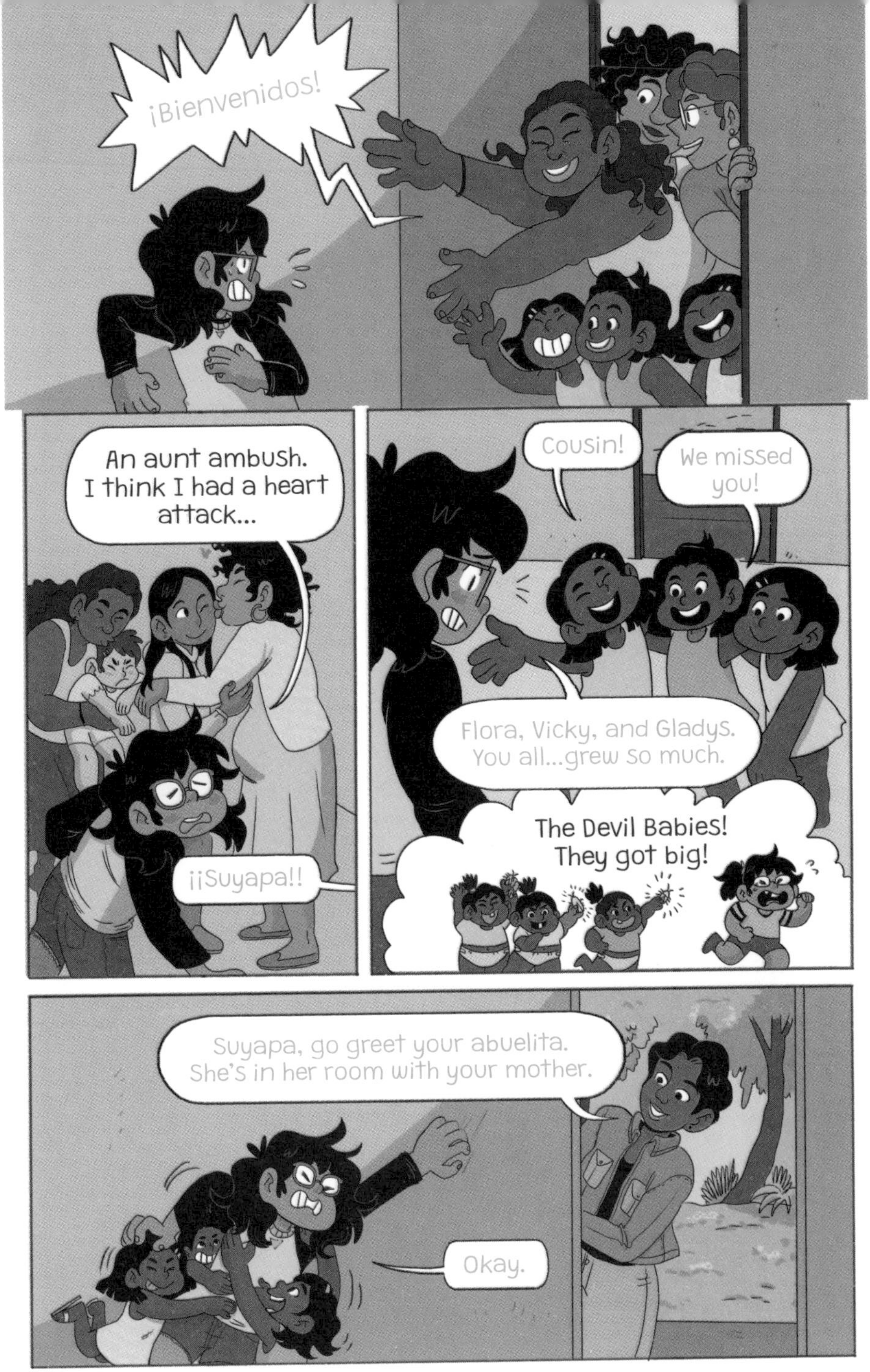
¡Bienvenidos!
An aunt ambush. I think I had a heart attack...
¡¡Suyapa!!
Cousin!
We missed you!
Flora, Vicky, and Gladys. You all...grew so much.
The Devil Babies! They got big!
Suyapa, go greet your abuelita. She's in her room with your mother.
Okay.

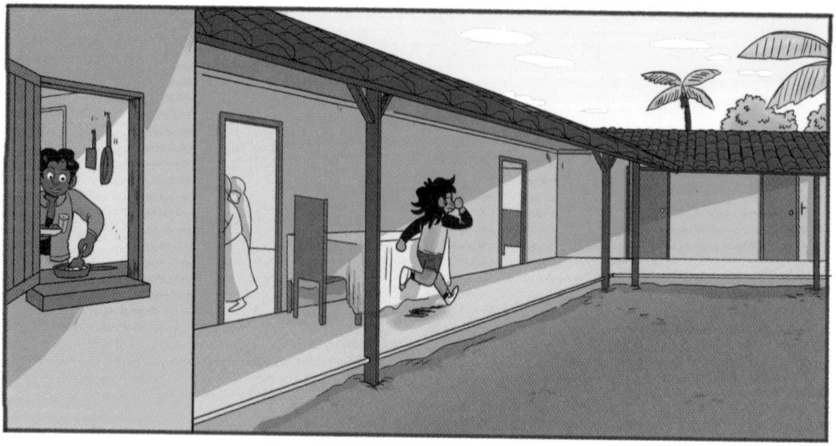

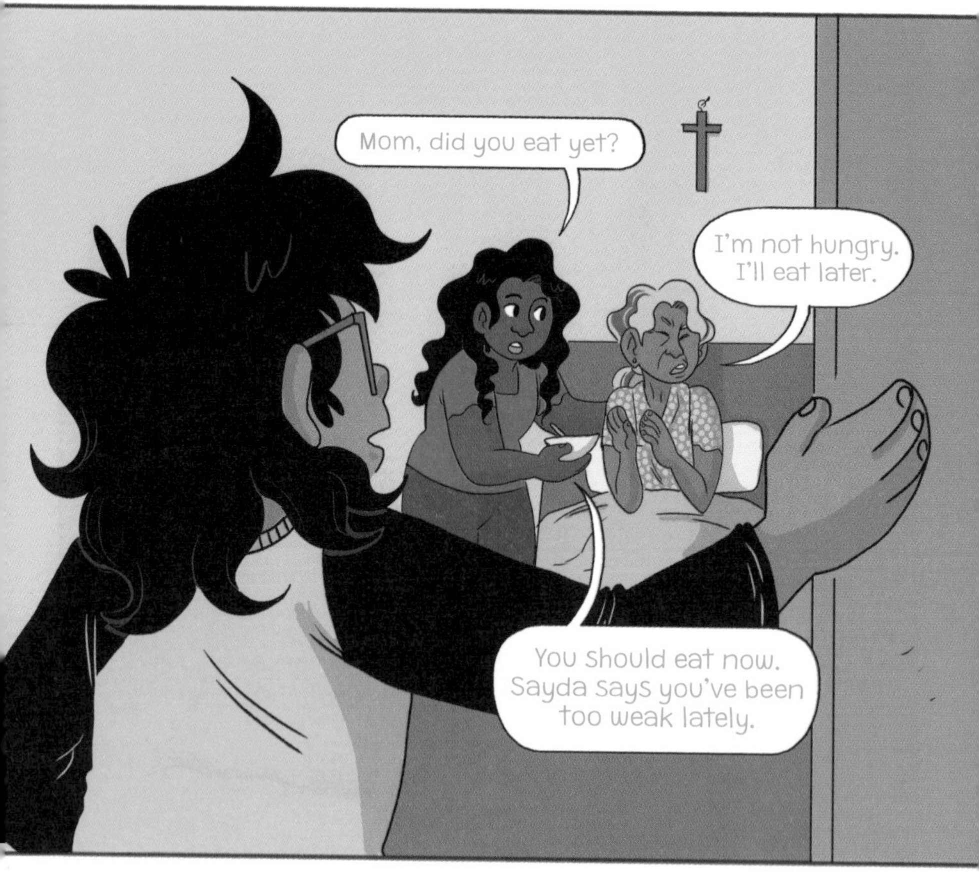
Mom, did you eat yet?
I'm not hungry. I'll eat later.
You should eat now. Sayda says you've been too weak lately.

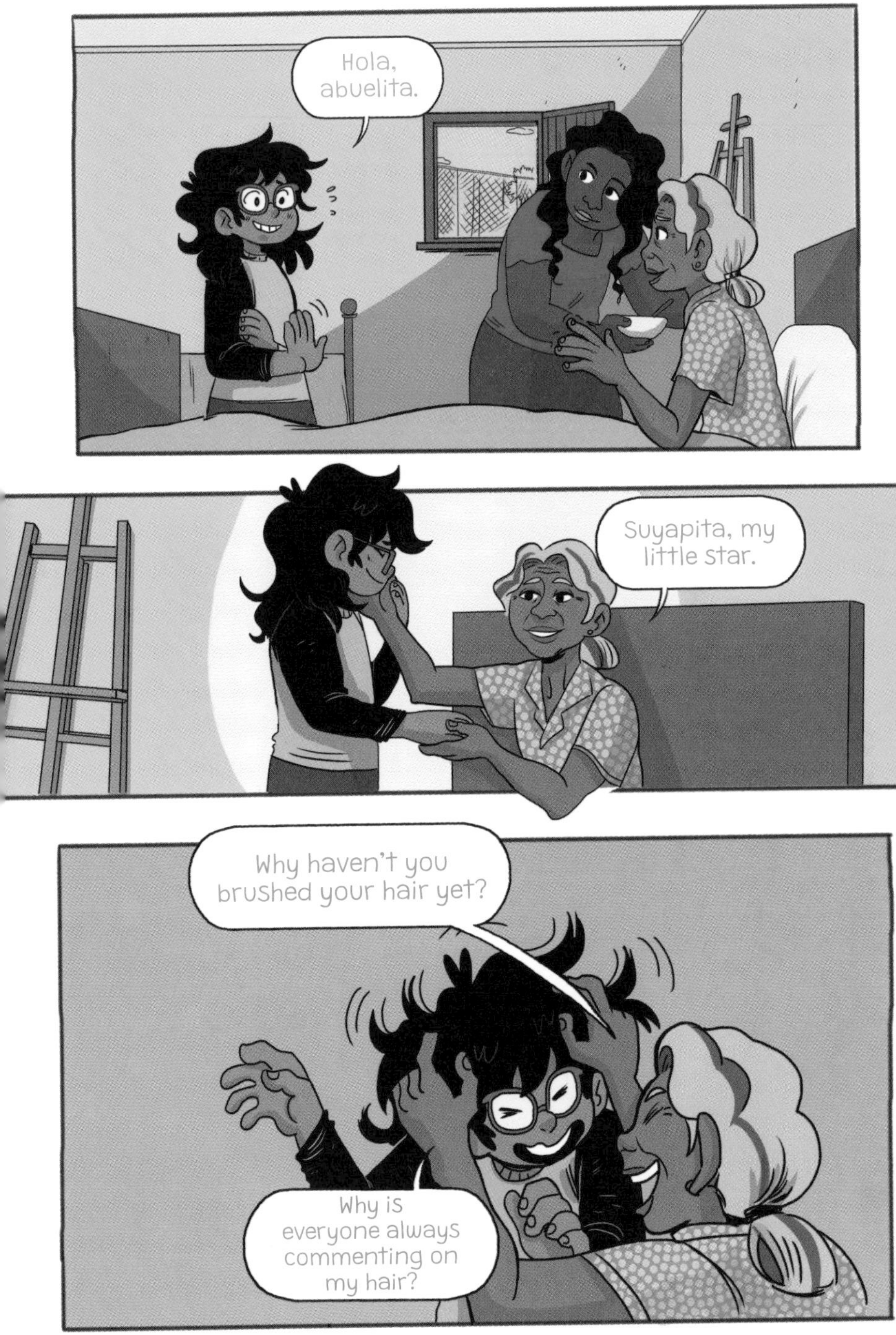
Hola, abuelita.
Suyapita, my little star.
Why haven't you brushed your hair yet?
Why is everyone always commenting on my hair?

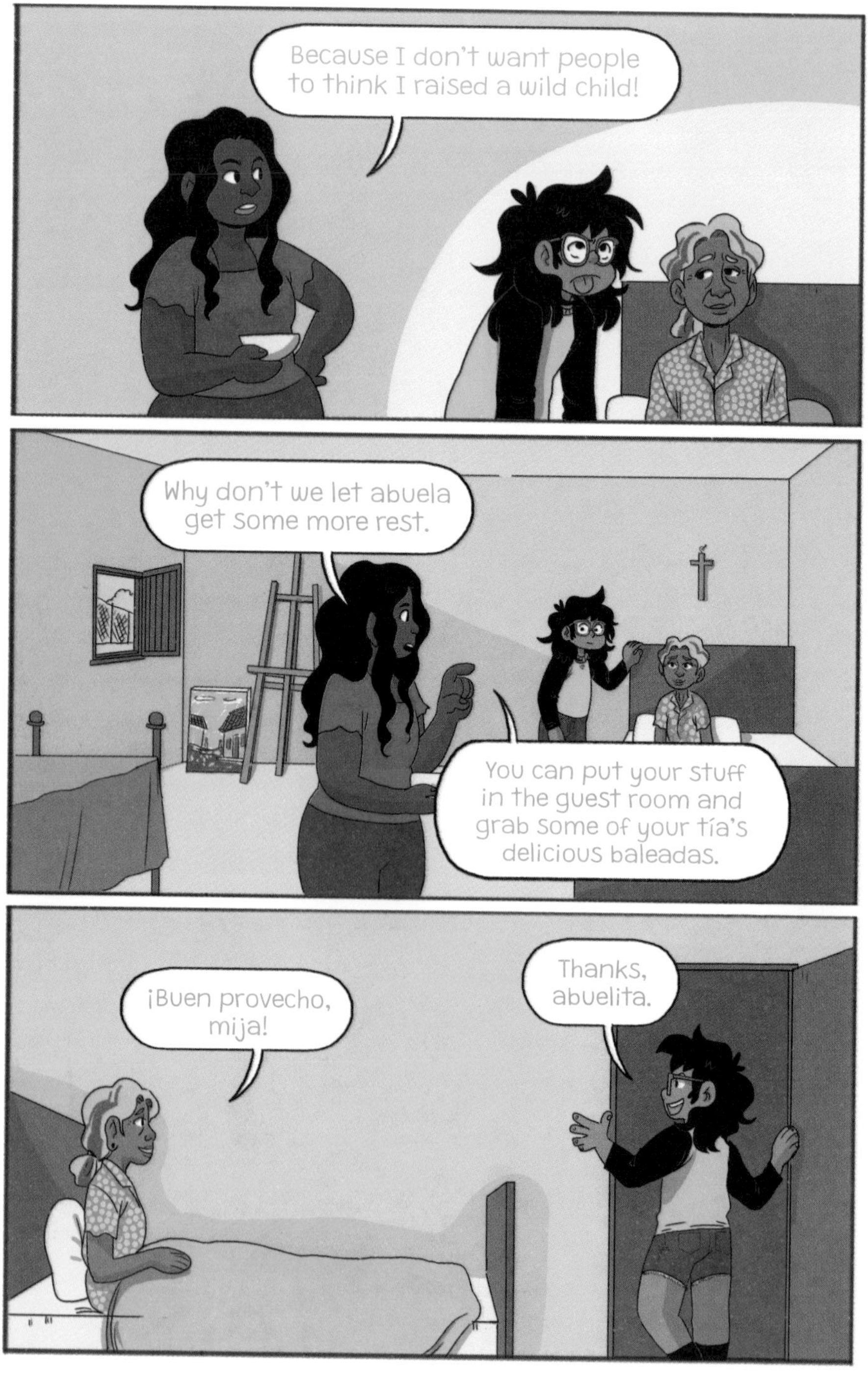
Because I don't want people to think I raised a wild child!
Why don't we let abuela get some more rest.
You can put your stuff in the guest room and grab some of your tía's delicious baleadas.
¡Buen provecho, mija!
Thanks, abuelita.

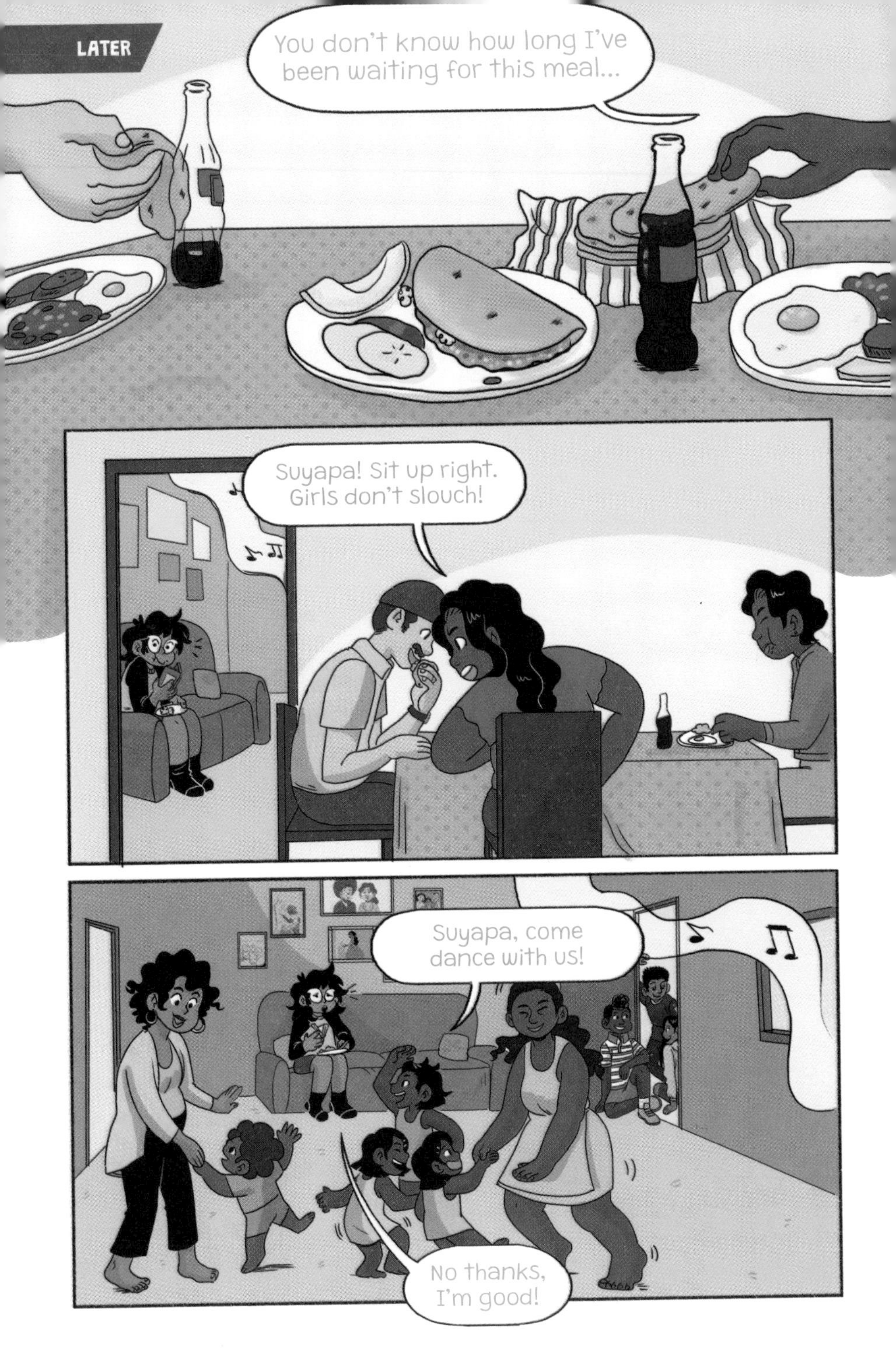
LATER
You don't know how long I've been waiting for this meal...
Suyapa! Sit up right. Girls don't slouch!
Suyapa, come dance with us!
No thanks, I'm good!

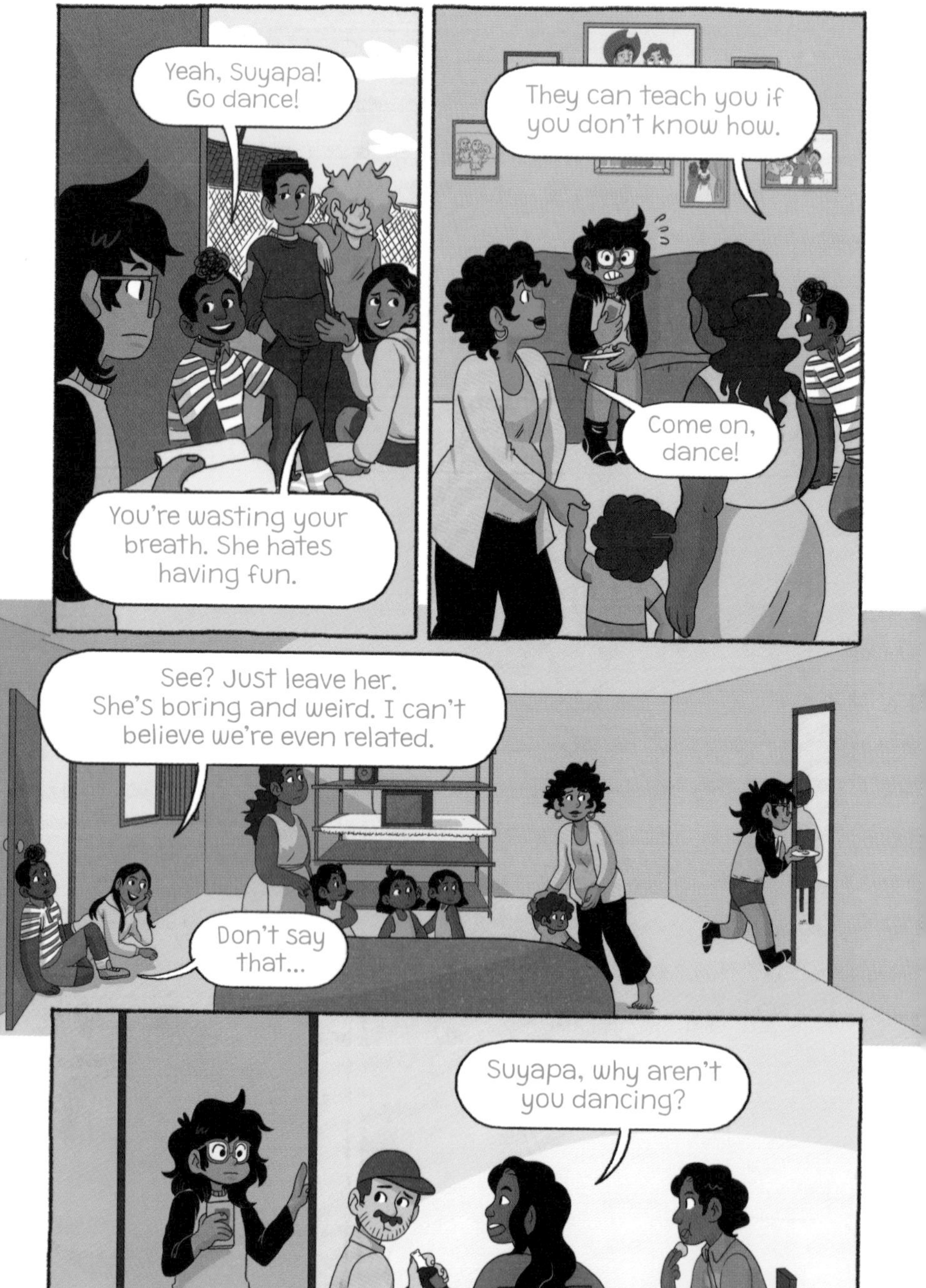
Yeah, Suyapa! Go dance!
You're wasting your breath. She hates having fun.
They can teach you if you don't know how.
Come on, dance!
See? Just leave her. She's boring and weird. I can't believe we're even related.
Don't say that...
Suyapa, why aren't you dancing?

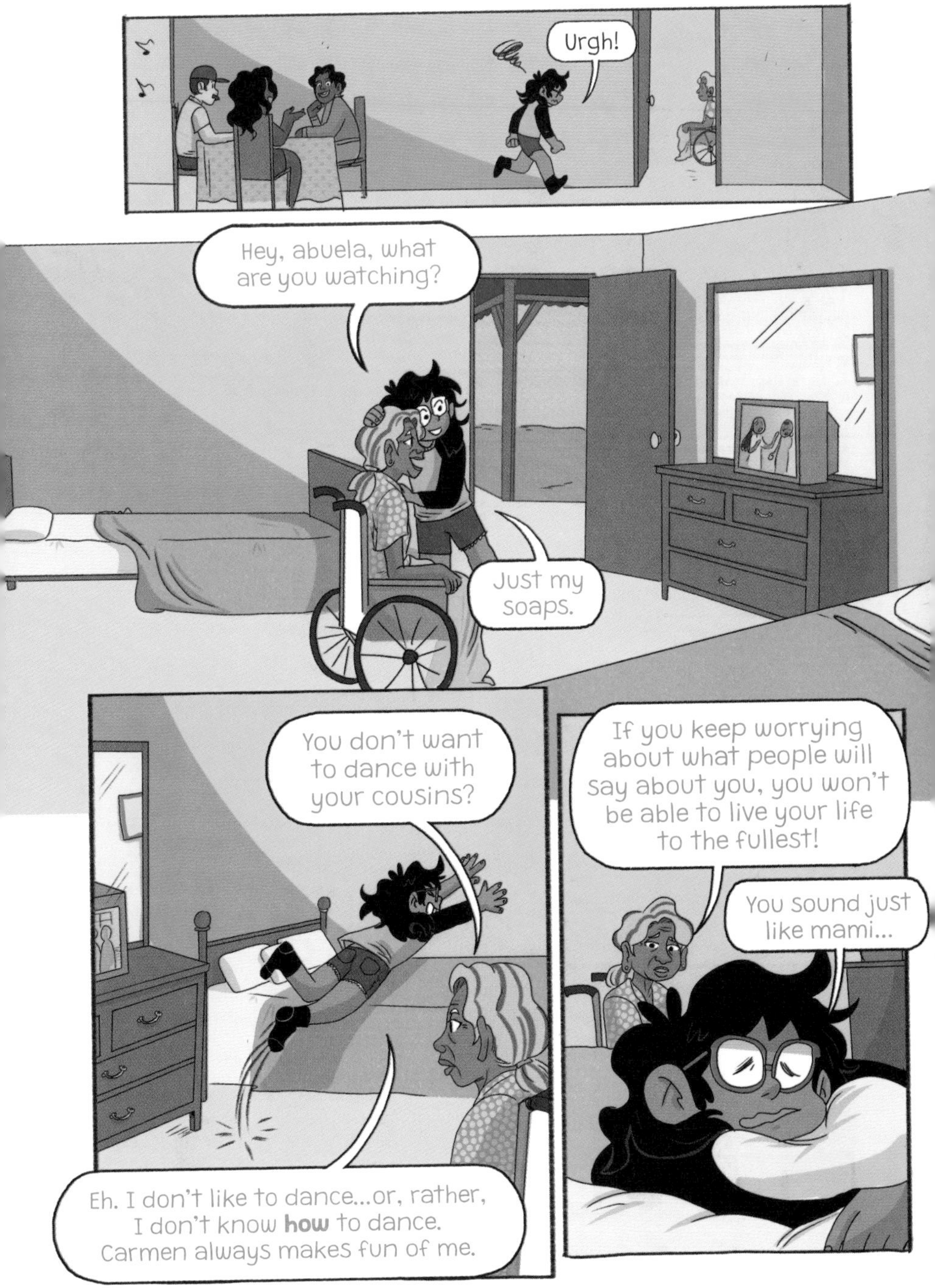
Urgh!
Hey, abuela, what are you watching?
Just my soaps.
You don't want to dance with your cousins?
Eh. I don't like to dance...or, rather, I don't know **how** to dance. Carmen always makes fun of me.
If you keep worrying about what people will say about you, you won't be able to live your life to the fullest!
You sound just like mami...

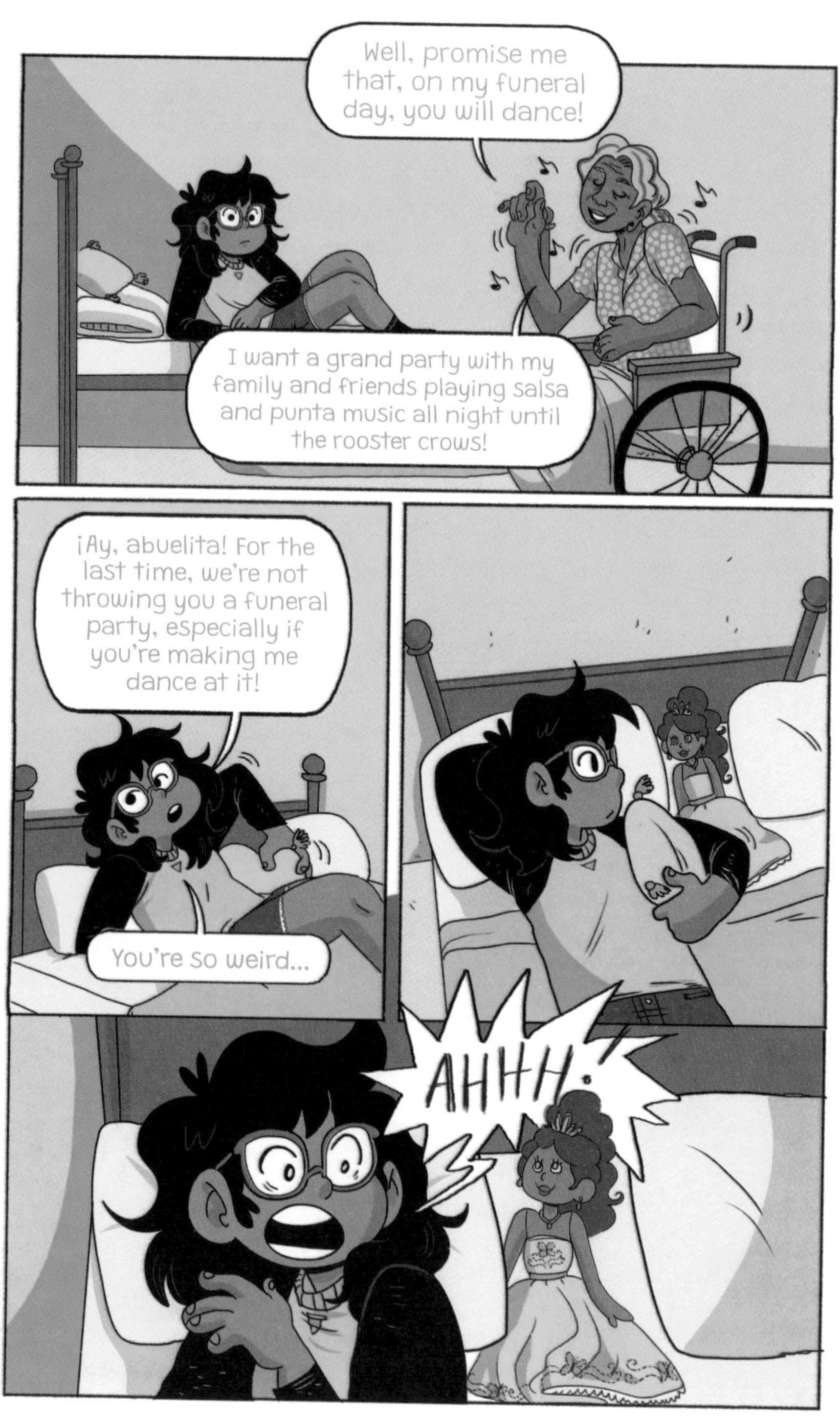
Well, promise me that, on my funeral day, you will dance!
I want a grand party with my family and friends playing salsa and punta music all night until the rooster crows!
¡Ay, abuelita! For the last time, we're not throwing you a funeral party, especially if you're making me dance at it!
You're so weird...
AHHH!

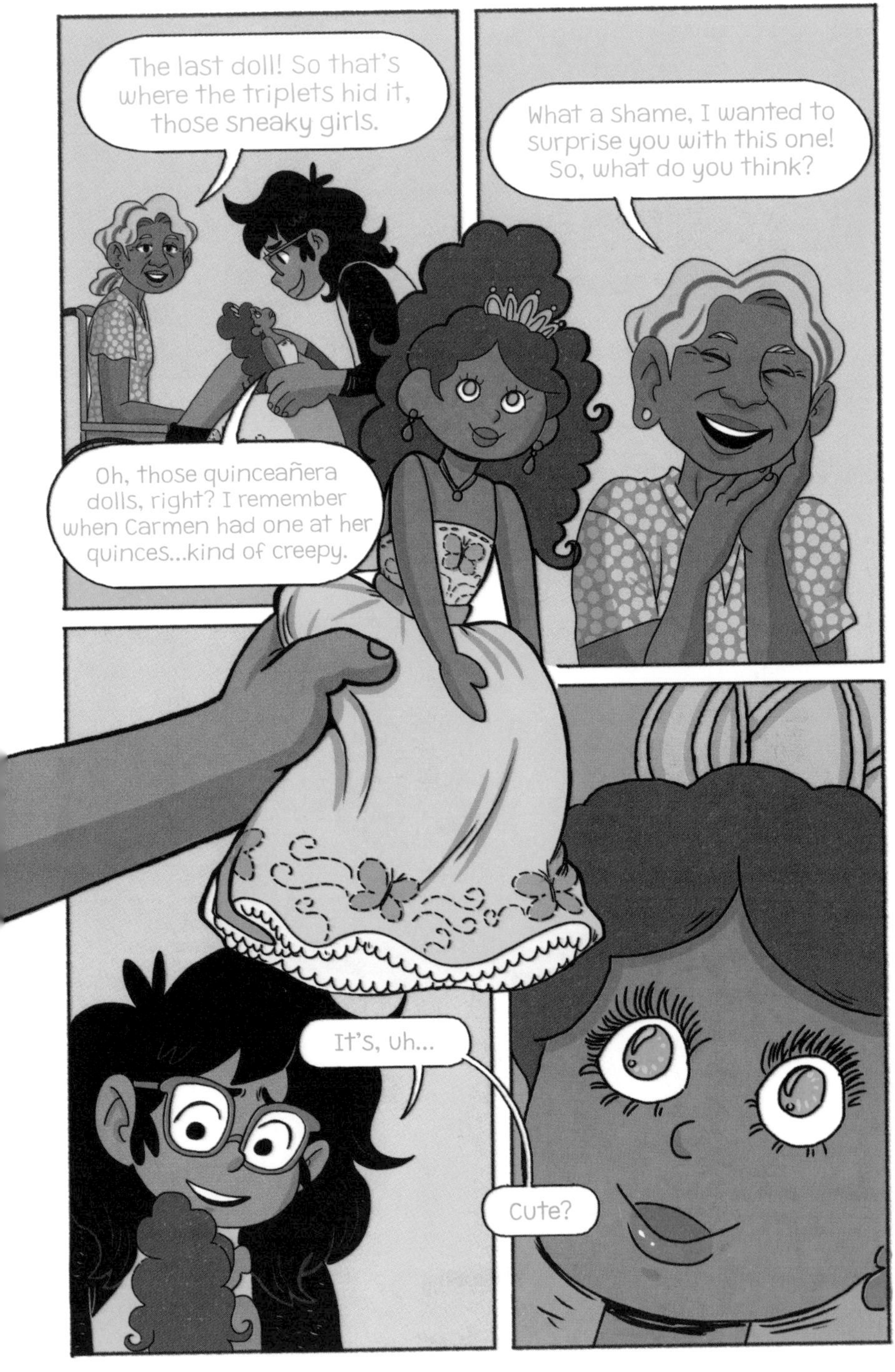
The last doll! So that's where the triplets hid it, those sneaky girls.
Oh, those quinceañera dolls, right? I remember when Carmen had one at her quinces...kind of creepy.
What a shame, I wanted to surprise you with this one! So, what do you think?
It's, uh...
Cute?

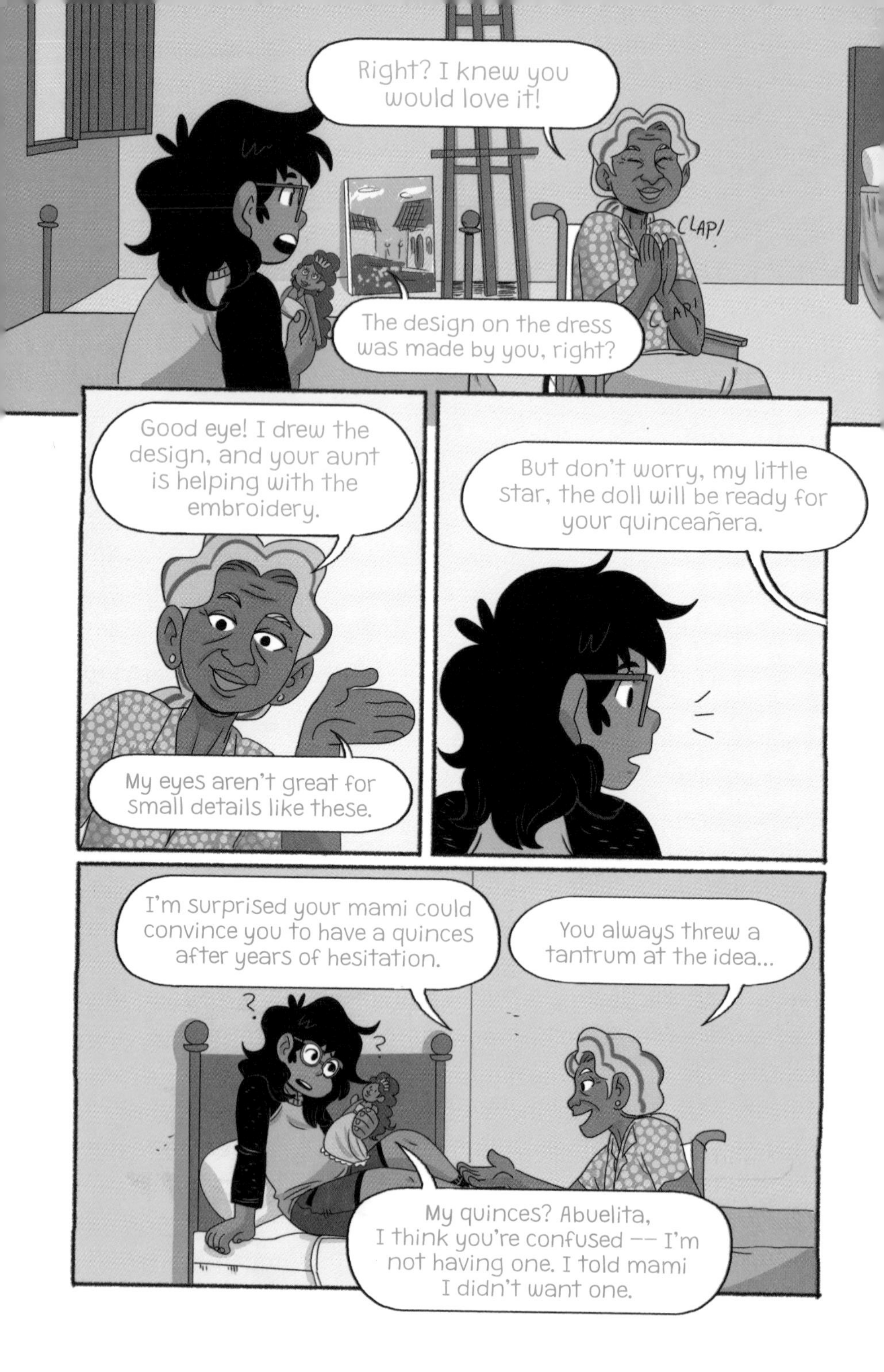

Right? I knew you would love it!
CLAP!
CLAP!
The design on the dress was made by you, right?
Good eye! I drew the design, and your aunt is helping with the embroidery.
My eyes aren't great for small details like these.
But don't worry, my little star, the doll will be ready for your quinceañera.
I'm surprised your mami could convince you to have a quinces after years of hesitation.
You always threw a tantrum at the idea...
?
?
My quinces? Abuelita, I think you're confused -- I'm not having one. I told mami I didn't want one.

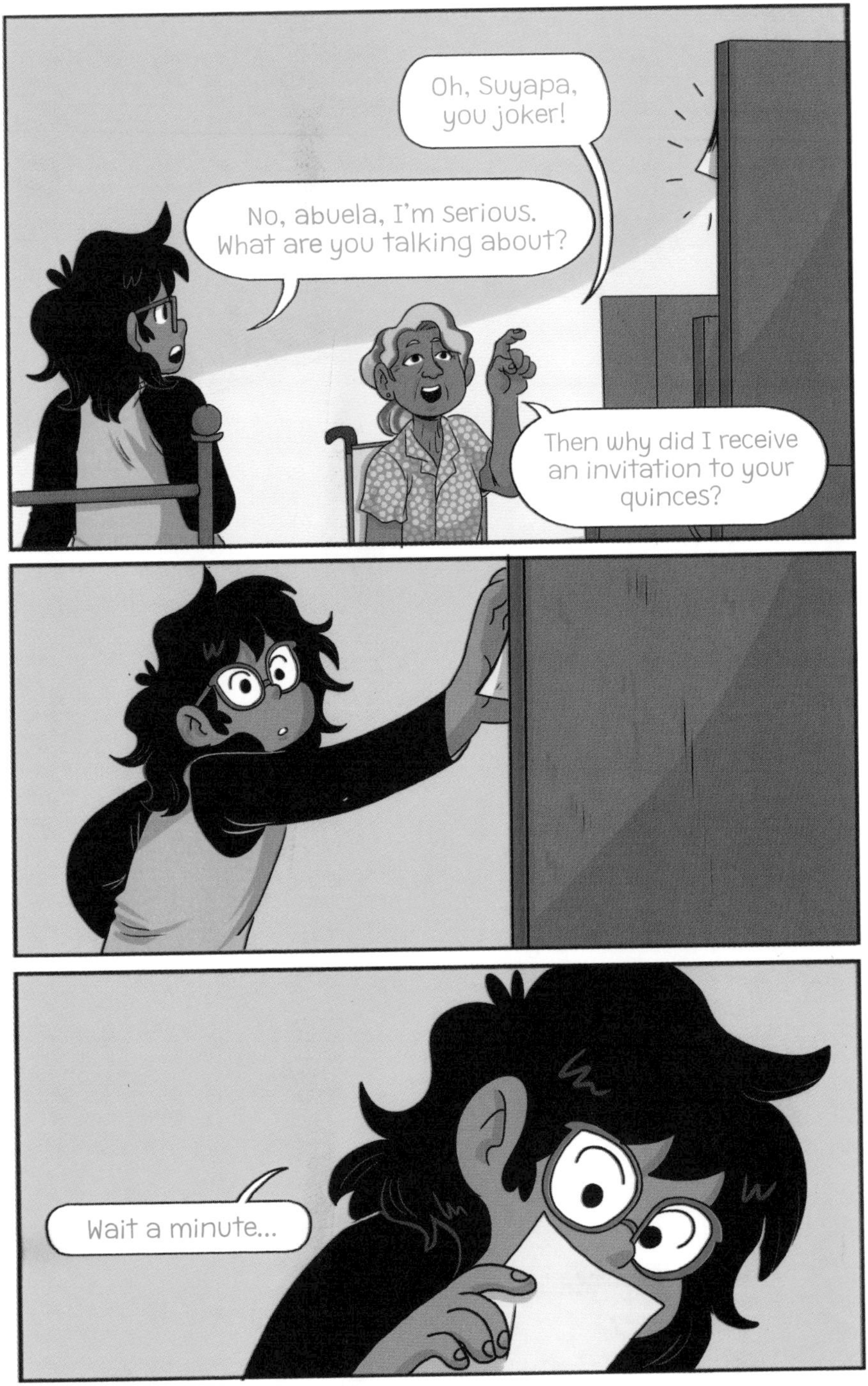
Oh, Suyapa, you joker!
No, abuela, I'm serious. What are you talking about?
Then why did I receive an invitation to your quinces?
Wait a minute...

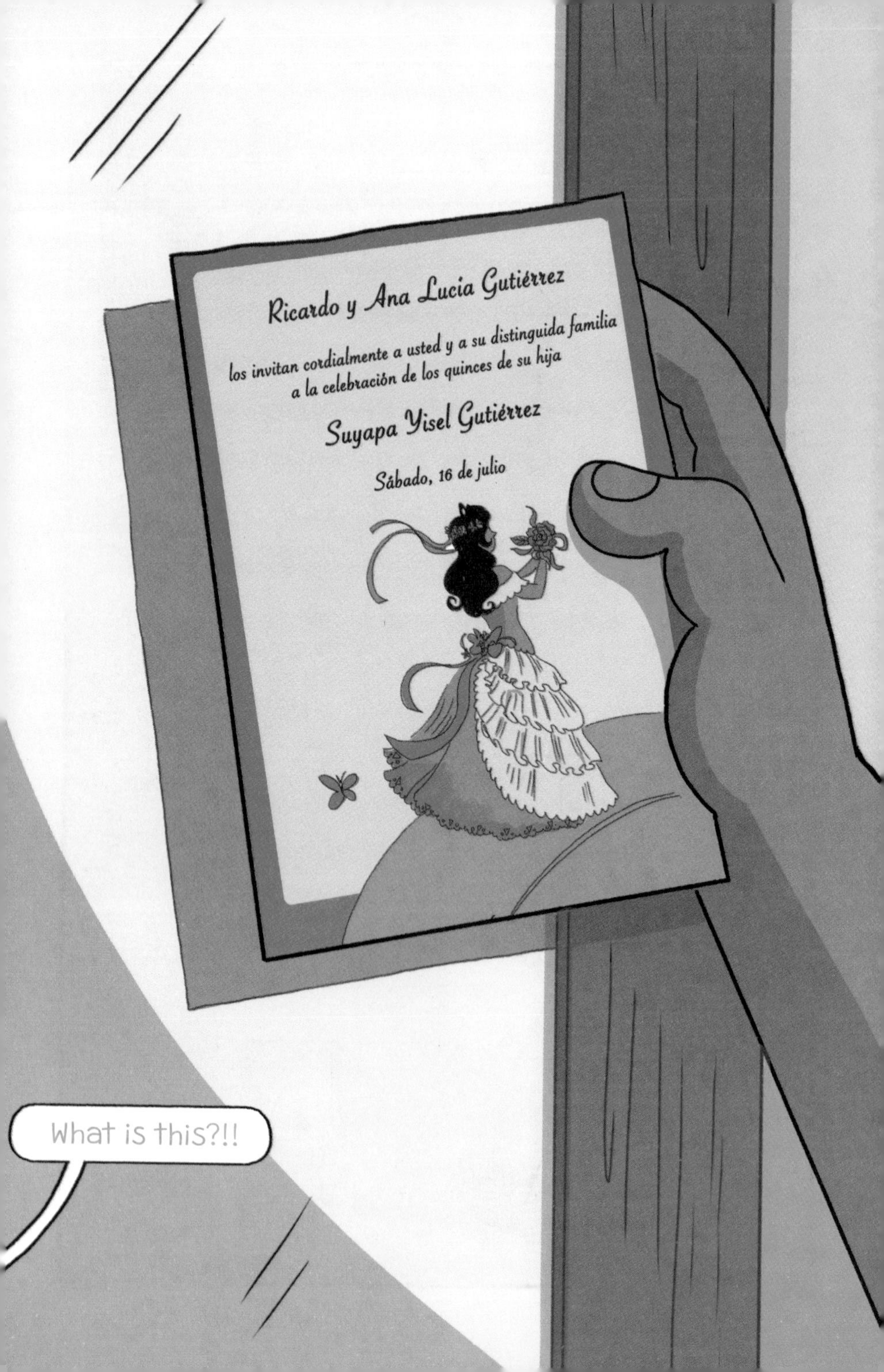
Ricardo y Ana Lucia Gutiérrez
los invitan cordialmente a usted y a su distinguida familia
a la celebración de los quinces de su hija
Suyapa Yisel Gutiérrez
Sábado, 16 de julio
What is this?!!

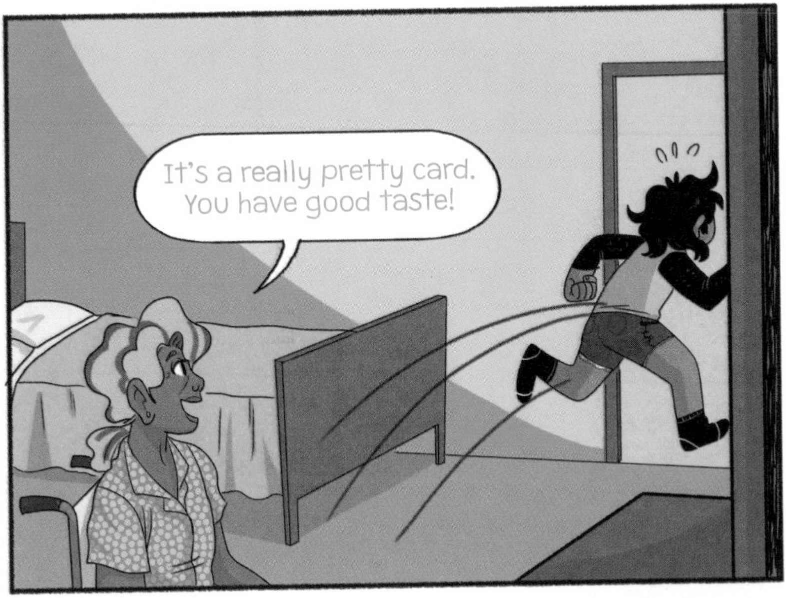
It's a really pretty card.
You have good taste!

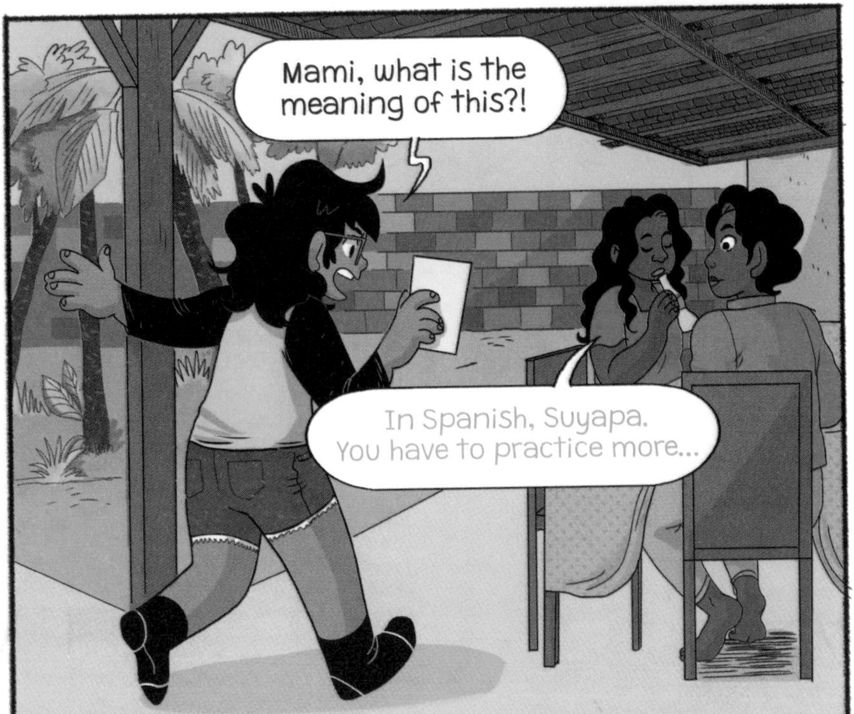
Mami, what is the meaning of this?!
In Spanish, Suyapa.
You have to practice more...

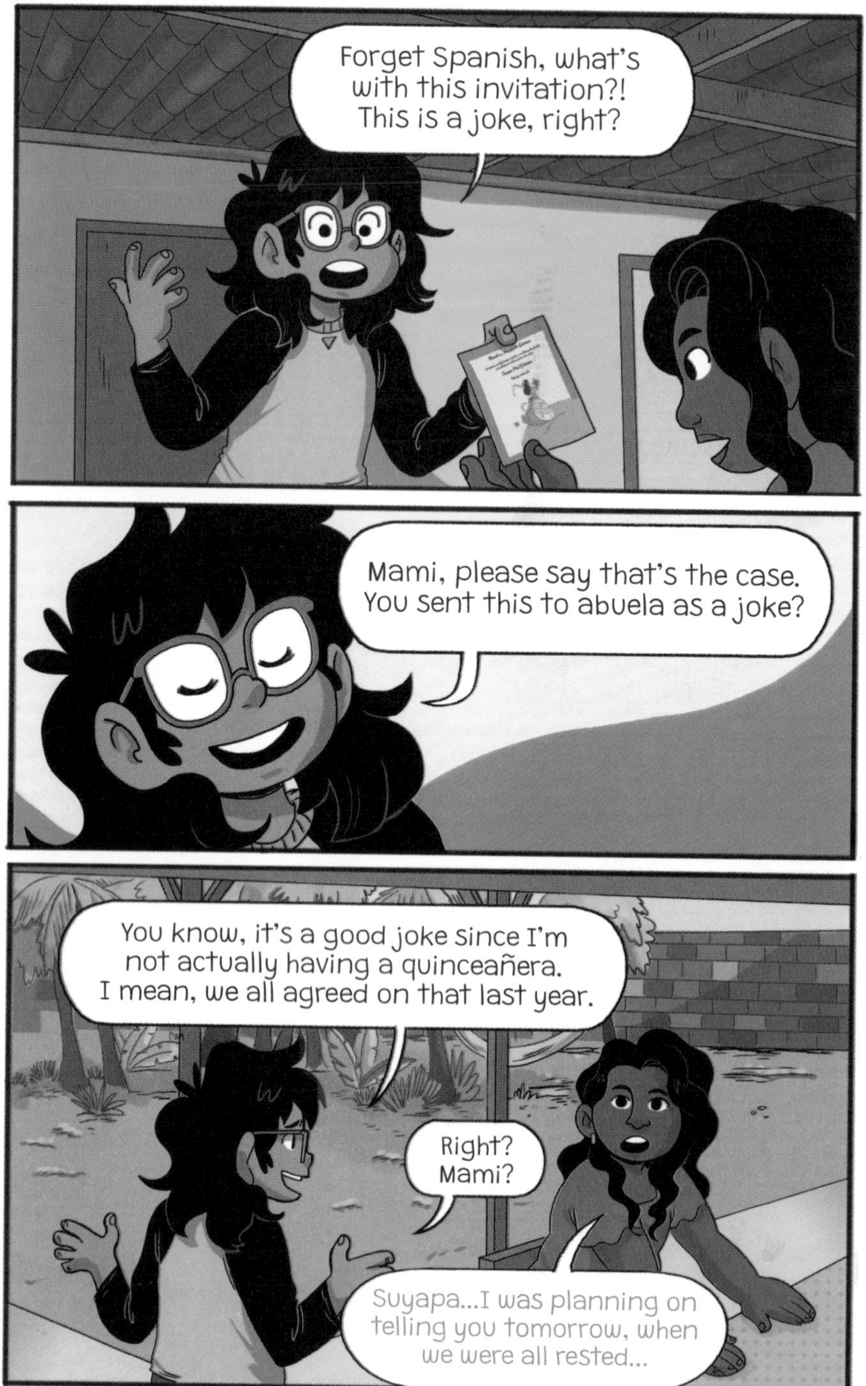
Forget Spanish, what's with this invitation?! This is a joke, right?
Mami, please say that's the case. You sent this to abuela as a joke?
You know, it's a good joke since I'm not actually having a quinceañera. I mean, we all agreed on that last year.
Right? Mami?
Suyapa...I was planning on telling you tomorrow, when we were all rested...

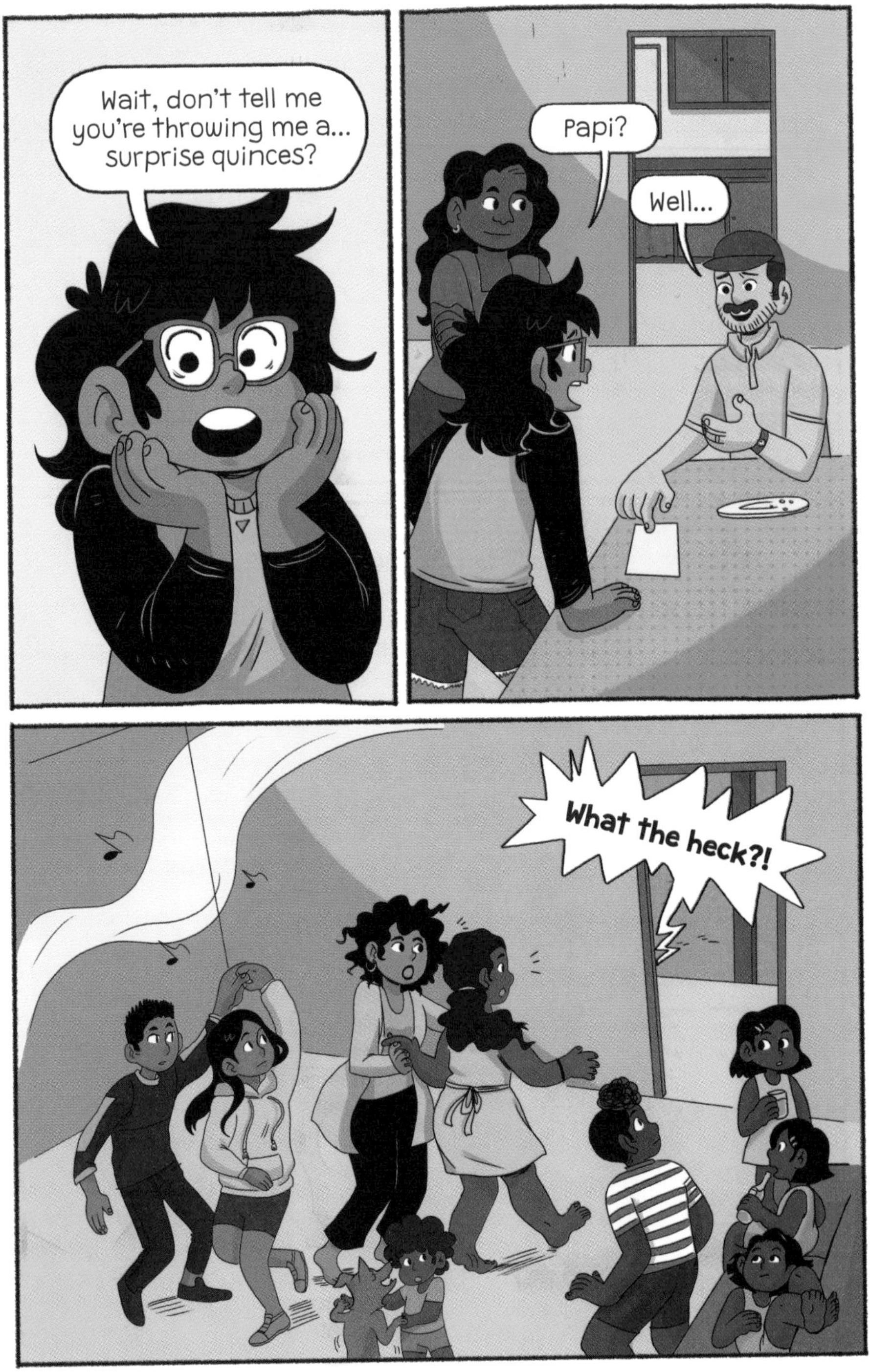
Wait, don't tell me you're throwing me a... surprise quinces?
Papi?
Well...
What the heck?!

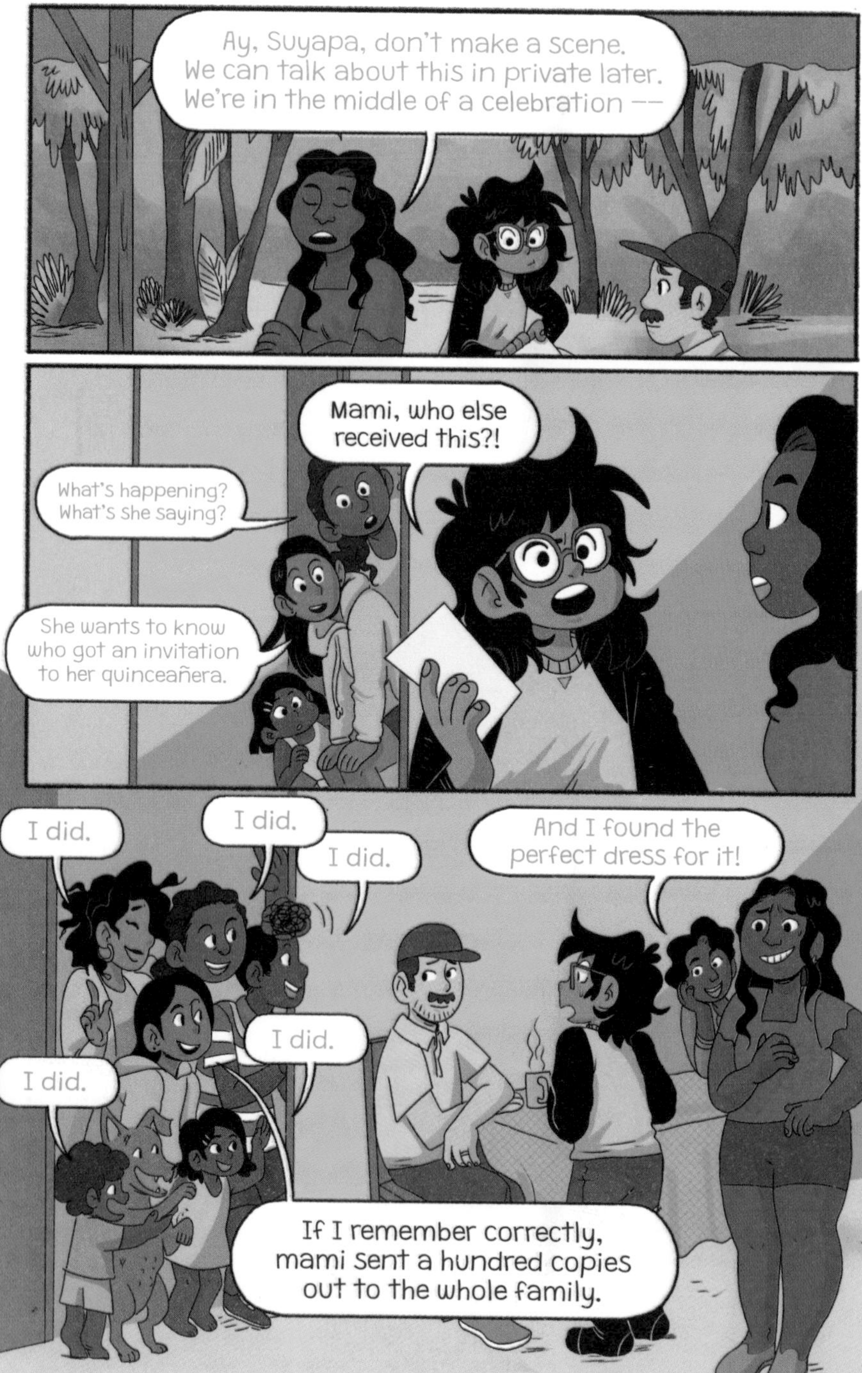
Ay, Suyapa, don't make a scene. We can talk about this in private later. We're in the middle of a celebration --
Mami, who else received this?!
What's happening? What's she saying?
She wants to know who got an invitation to her quinceañera.
I did.
I did.
I did.
And I found the perfect dress for it!
I did.
I did.
If I remember correctly, mami sent a hundred copies out to the whole family.

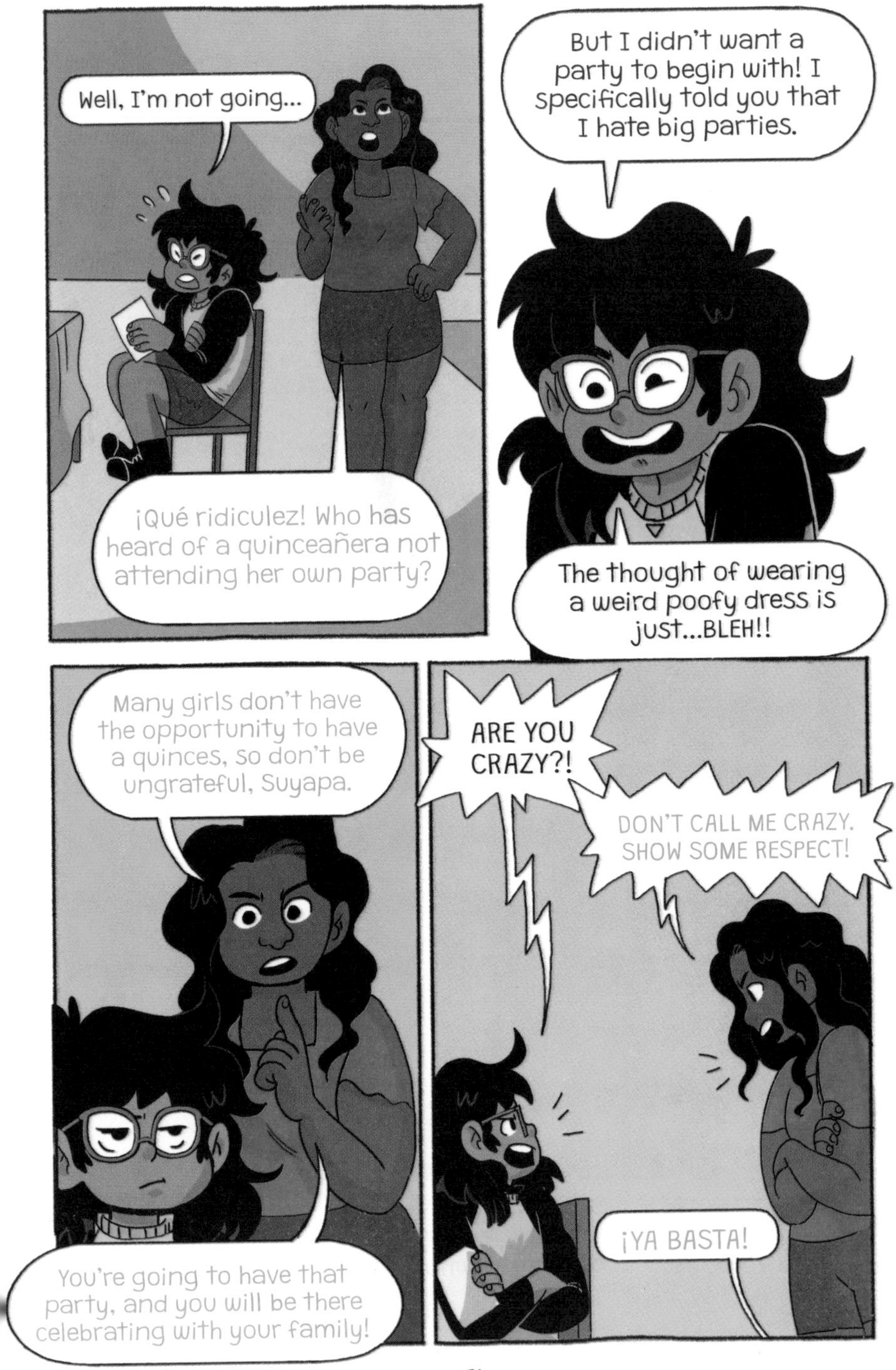
Well, I'm not going...
¡Qué ridiculez! Who has heard of a quinceañera not attending her own party?
But I didn't want a party to begin with! I specifically told you that I hate big parties.
The thought of wearing a weird poofy dress is just...BLEH!!
Many girls don't have the opportunity to have a quinces, so don't be ungrateful, Suyapa.
You're going to have that party, and you will be there celebrating with your family!
ARE YOU CRAZY?!
DON'T CALL ME CRAZY. SHOW SOME RESPECT!
¡YA BASTA!

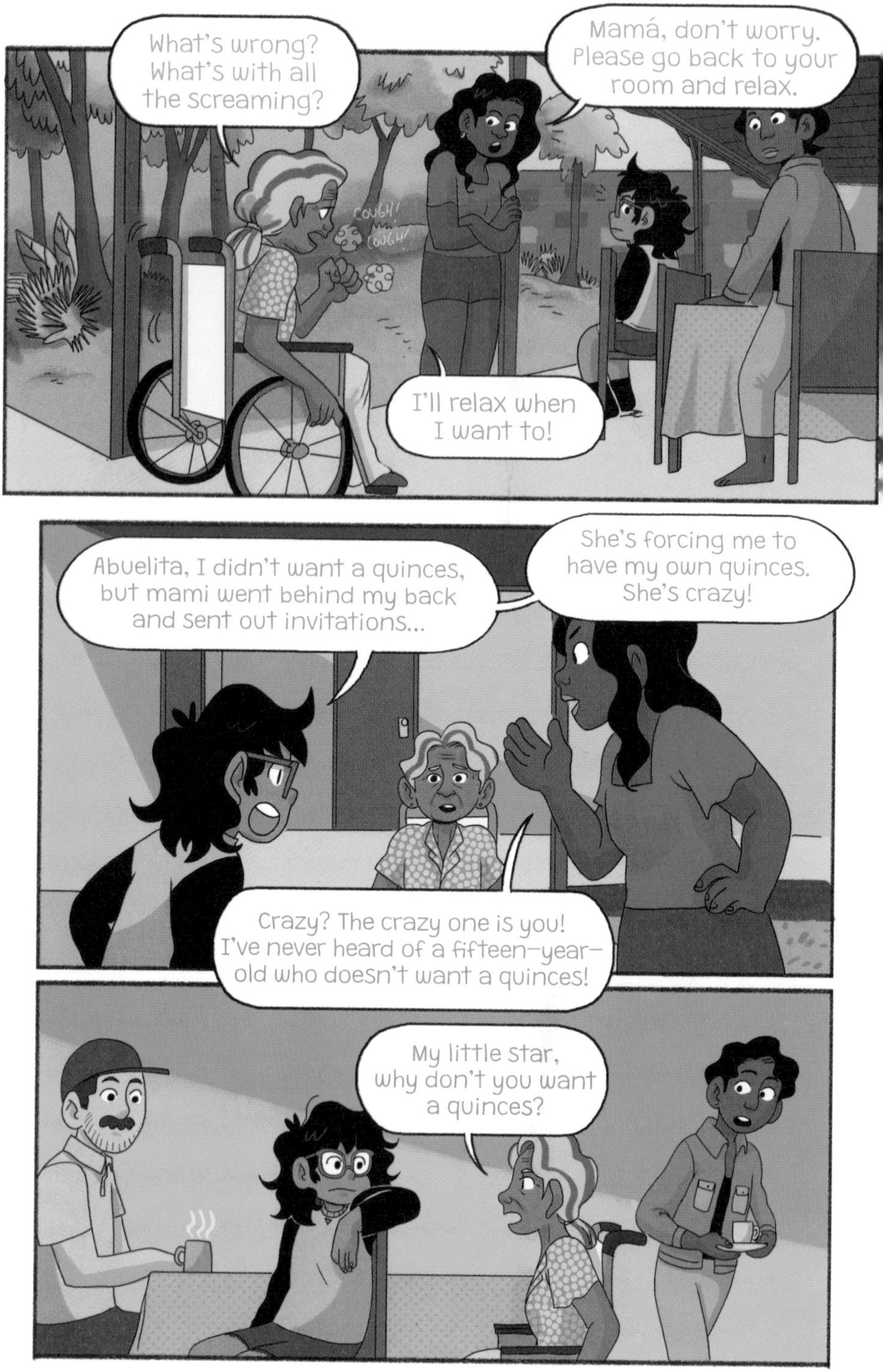
What's wrong? What's with all the screaming?
Mamá, don't worry. Please go back to your room and relax.
COUGH! COUGH!
I'll relax when I want to!
Abuelita, I didn't want a quinces, but mami went behind my back and sent out invitations...
She's forcing me to have my own quinces. She's crazy!
Crazy? The crazy one is you! I've never heard of a fifteen-year-old who doesn't want a quinces!
My little star, why don't you want a quinces?

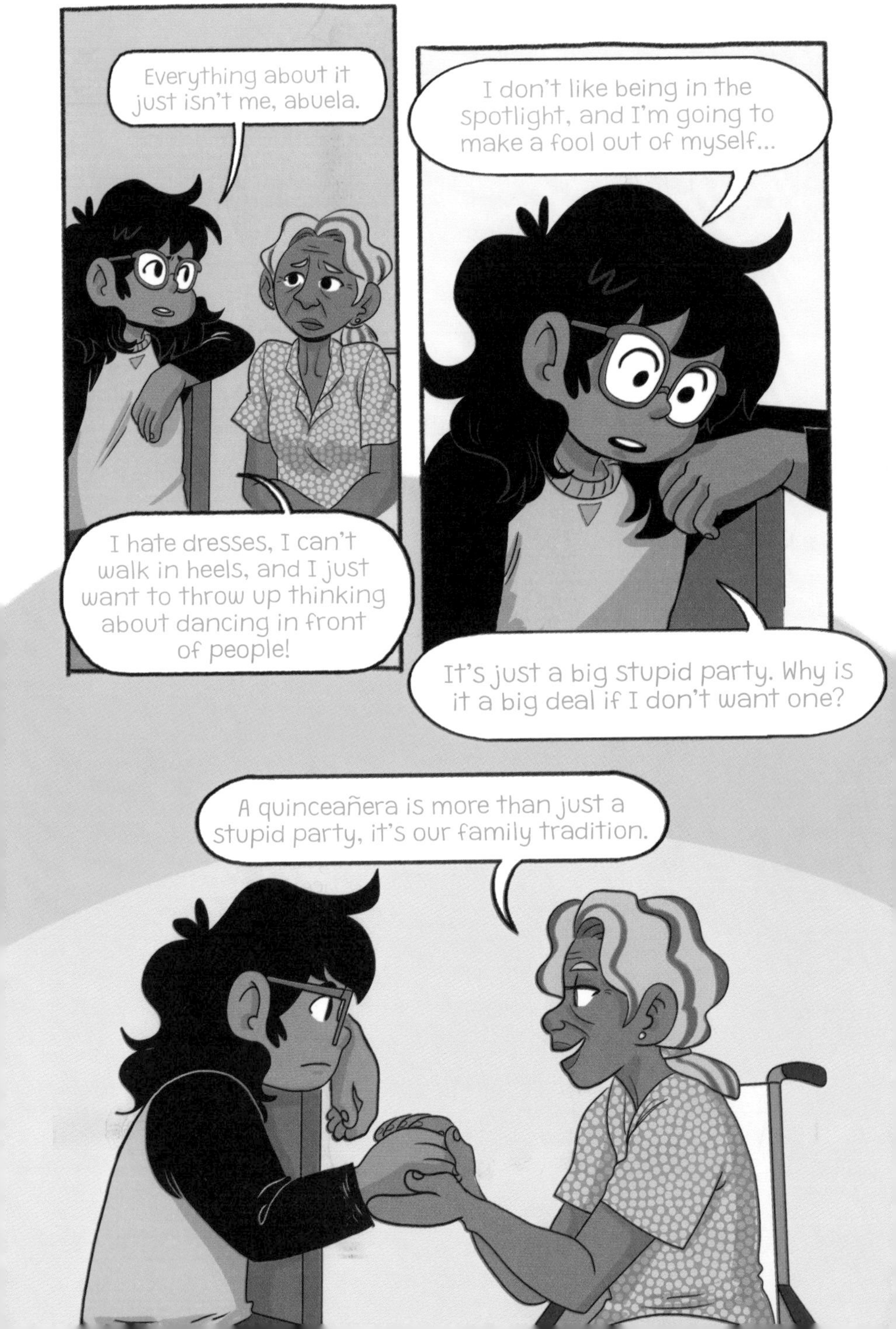
Everything about it just isn't me, abuela.
I hate dresses, I can't walk in heels, and I just want to throw up thinking about dancing in front of people!
I don't like being in the spotlight, and I'm going to make a fool out of myself...
It's just a big stupid party. Why is it a big deal if I don't want one?
A quinceañera is more than just a stupid party, it's our family tradition.

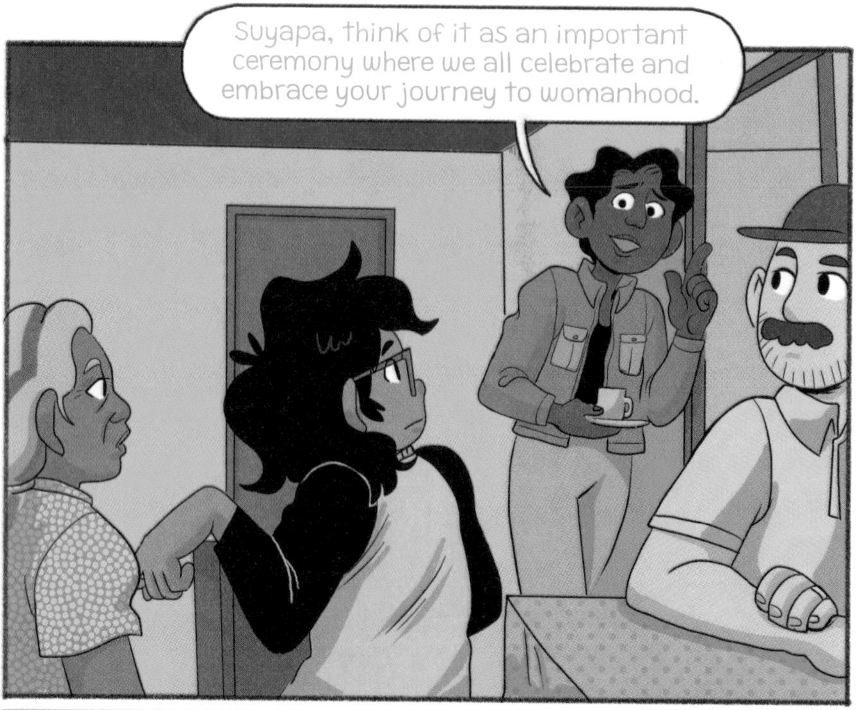
Suyapa, think of it as an important ceremony where we all celebrate and embrace your journey to womanhood.

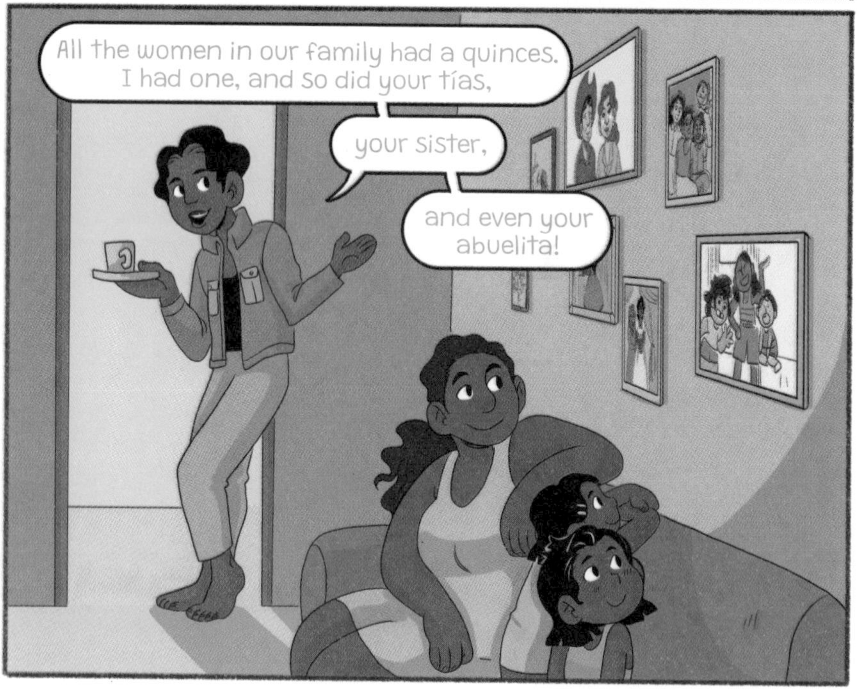
All the women in our family had a quinces. I had one, and so did your tías,
your sister,
and even your abuelita!

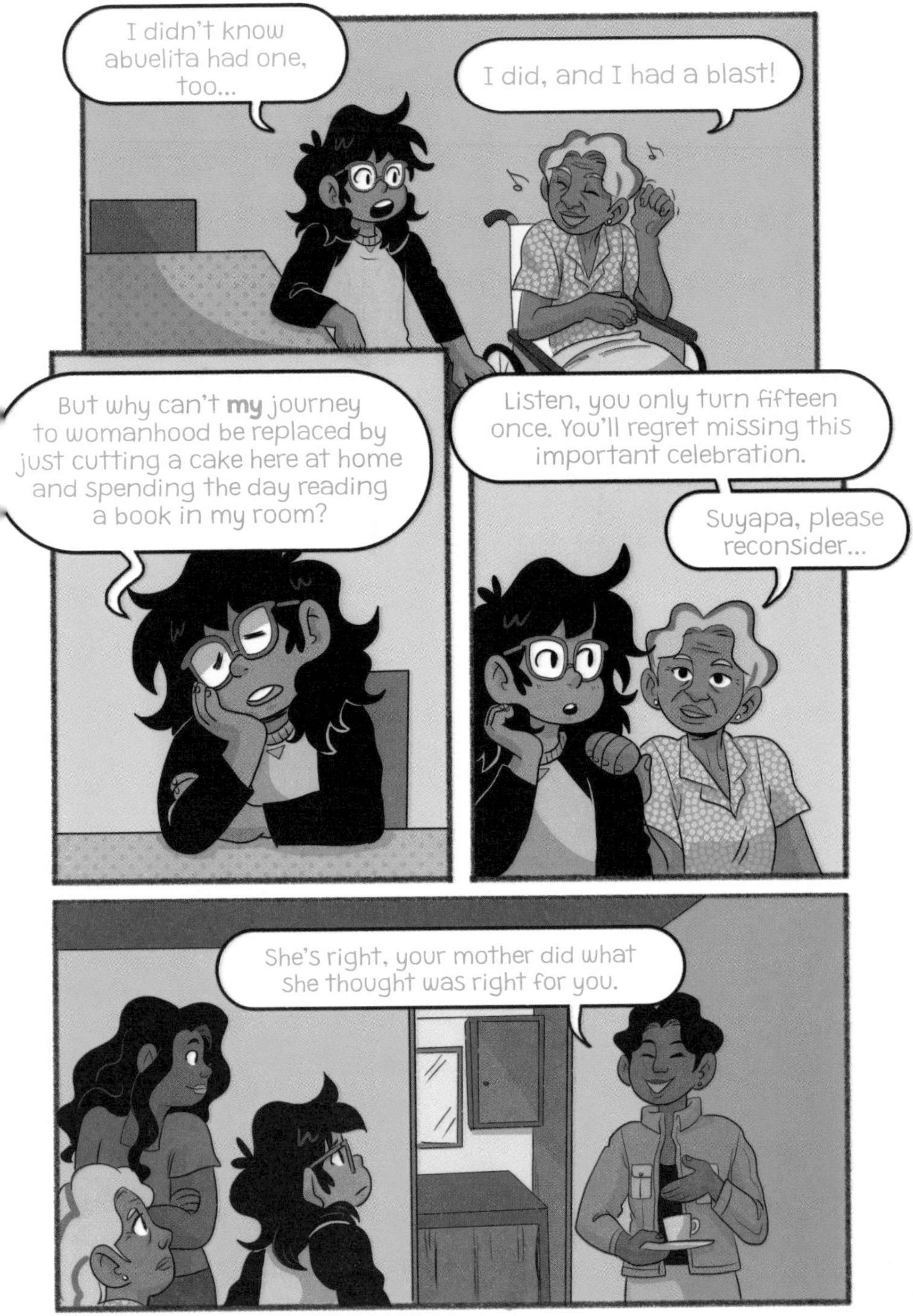
I didn't know abuelita had one, too...
I did, and I had a blast!
But why can't **my** journey to womanhood be replaced by just cutting a cake here at home and spending the day reading a book in my room?
Listen, you only turn fifteen once. You'll regret missing this important celebration.
Suyapa, please reconsider...
She's right, your mother did what she thought was right for you.

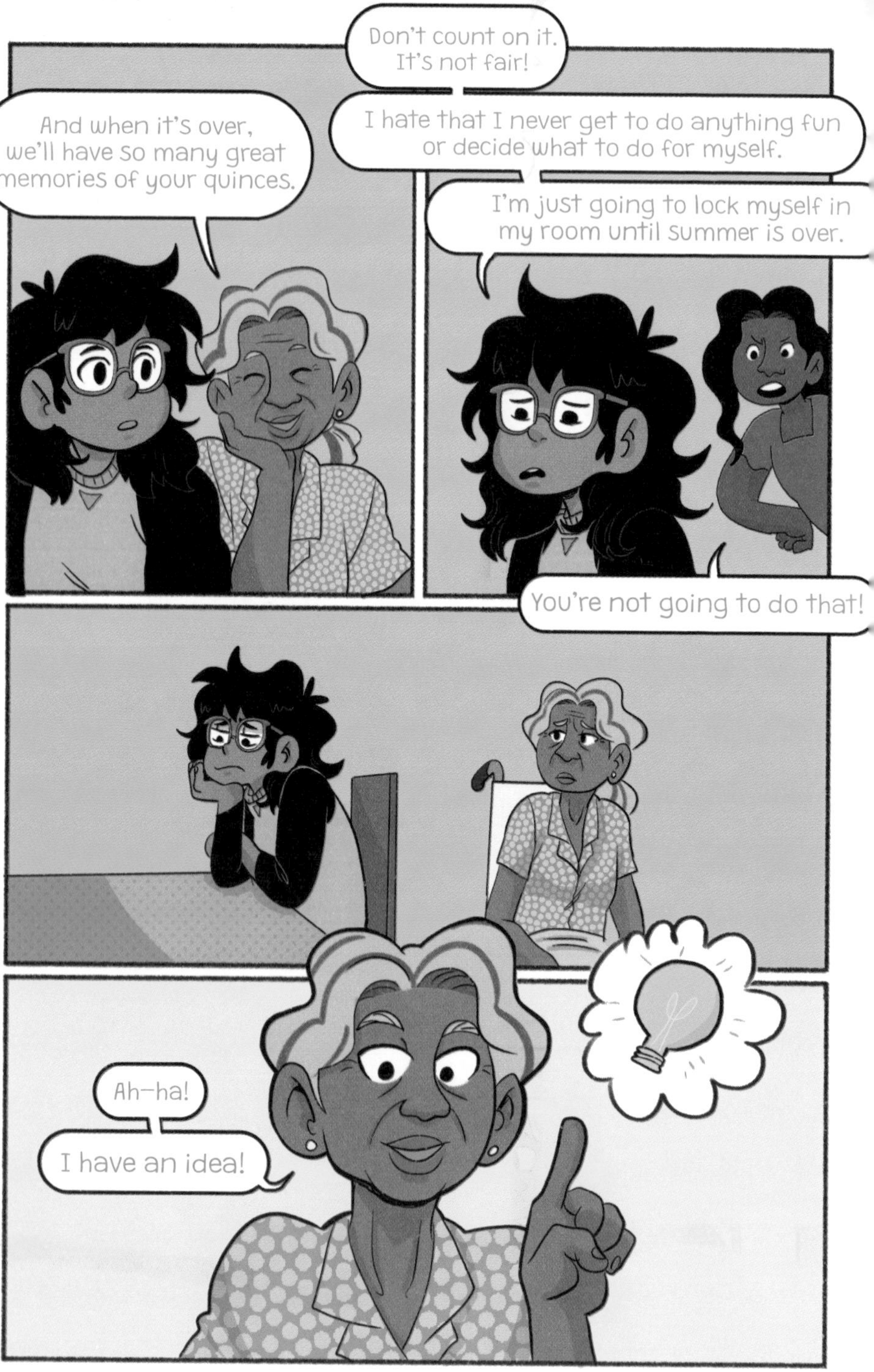
And when it's over, we'll have so many great memories of your quinces.
Don't count on it. It's not fair!
I hate that I never get to do anything fun or decide what to do for myself.
I'm just going to lock myself in my room until summer is over.
You're not going to do that!
Ah-ha!
I have an idea!

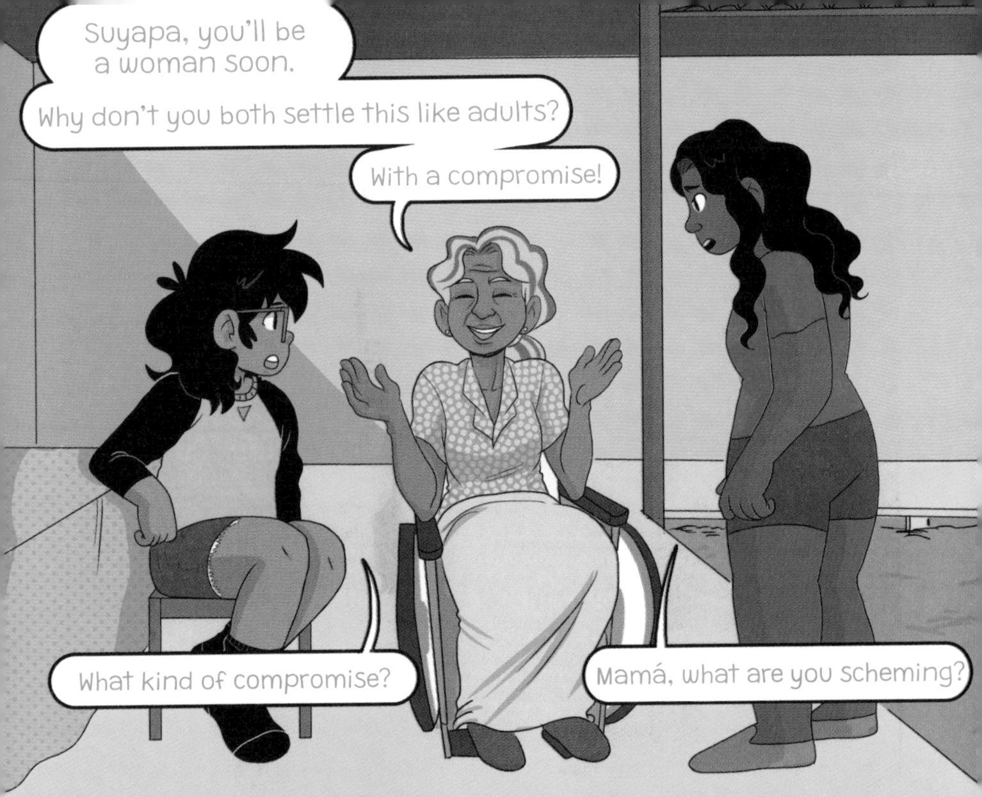
Suyapa, you'll be a woman soon.
Why don't you both settle this like adults?
With a compromise!
What kind of compromise?
Mamá, what are you scheming?

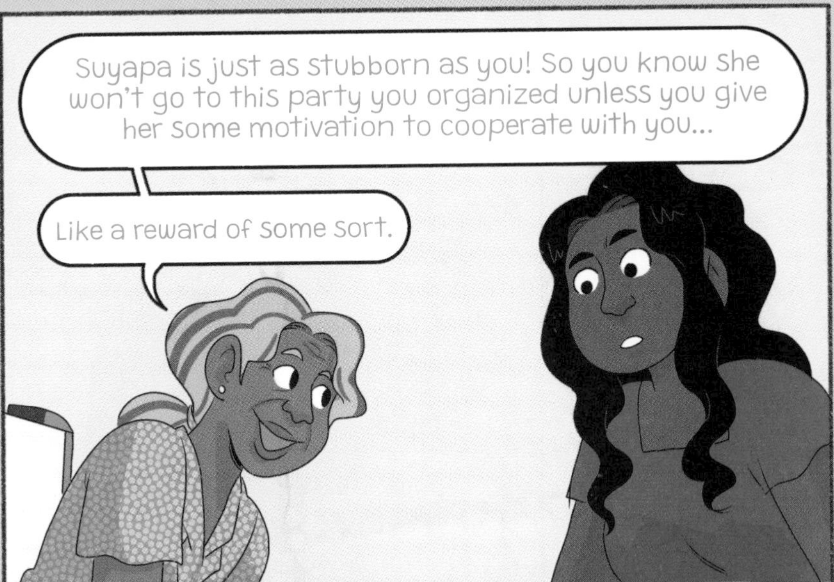
Suyapa is just as stubborn as you! So you know she won't go to this party you organized unless you give her some motivation to cooperate with you...
Like a reward of some sort.

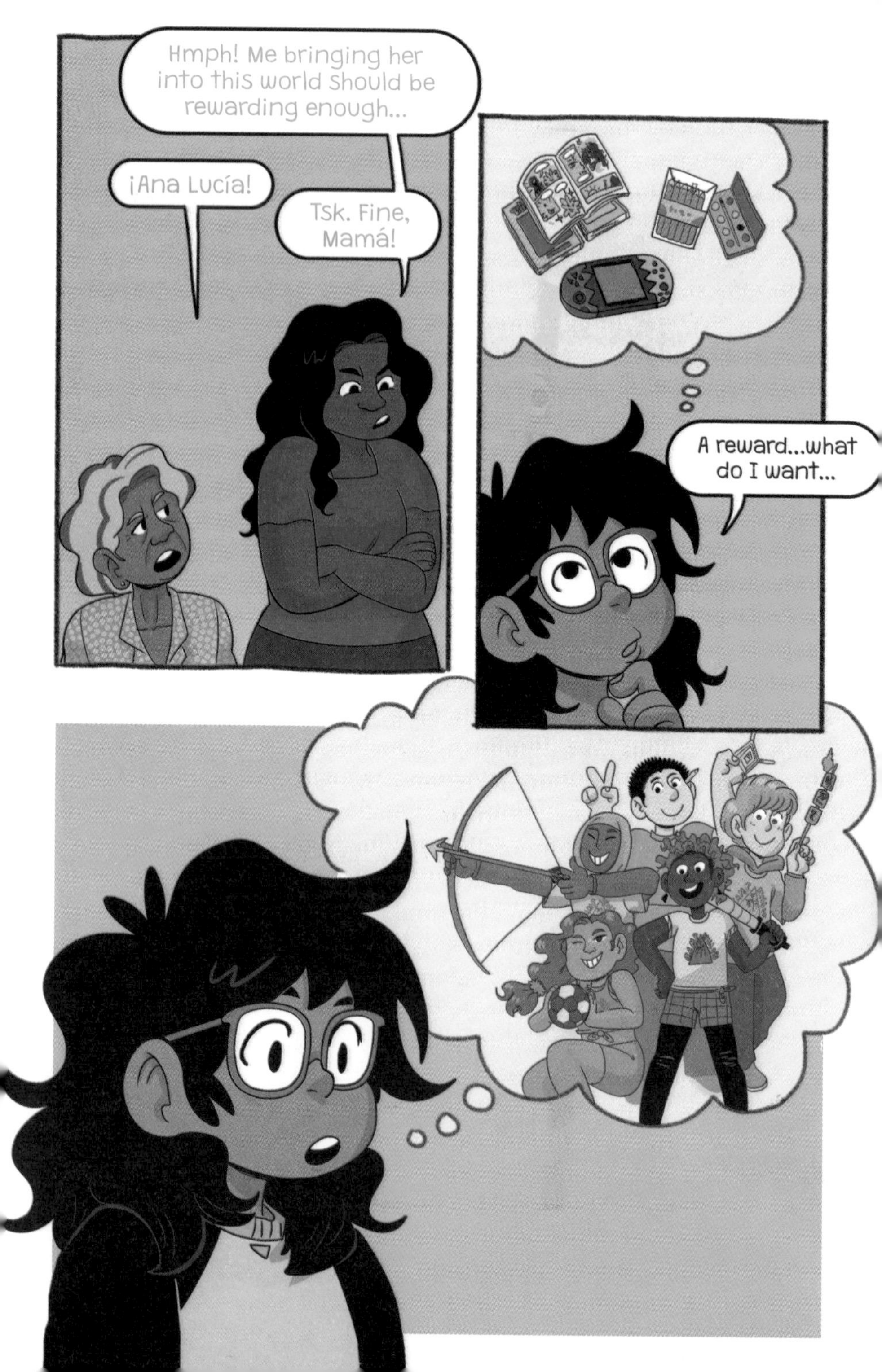
Hmph! Me bringing her into this world should be rewarding enough...
¡Ana Lucía!
Tsk. Fine, Mamá!
A reward...what do I want...

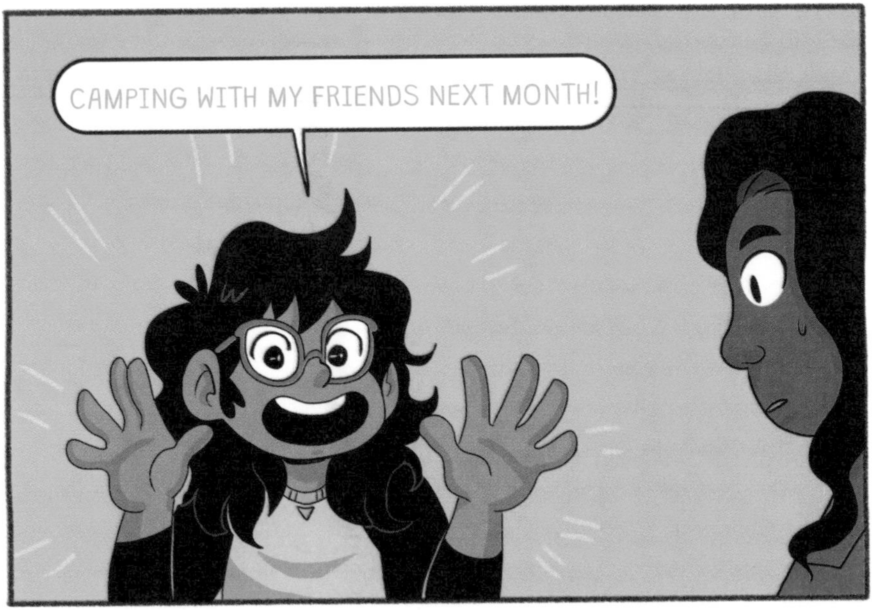
CAMPING WITH MY FRIENDS NEXT MONTH!

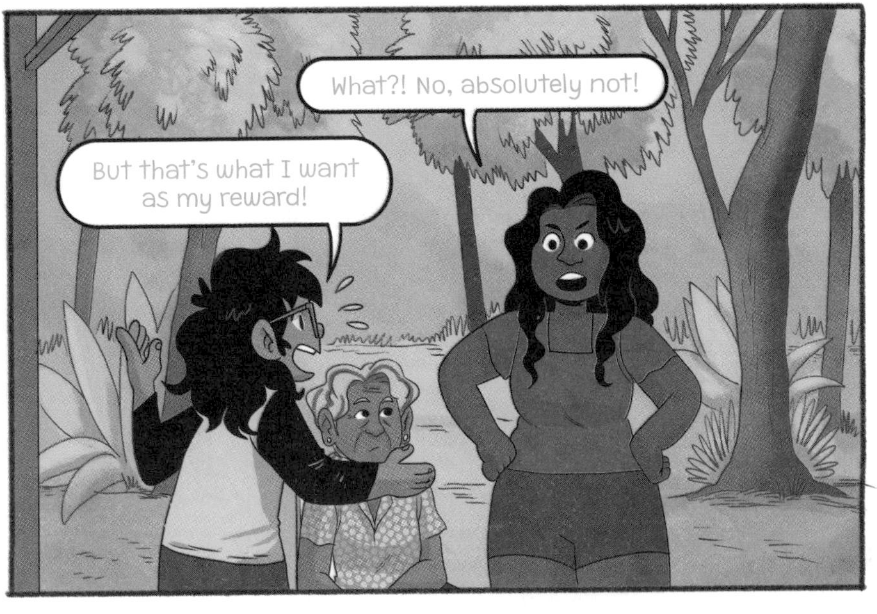
What?! No, absolutely not!
But that's what I want as my reward!

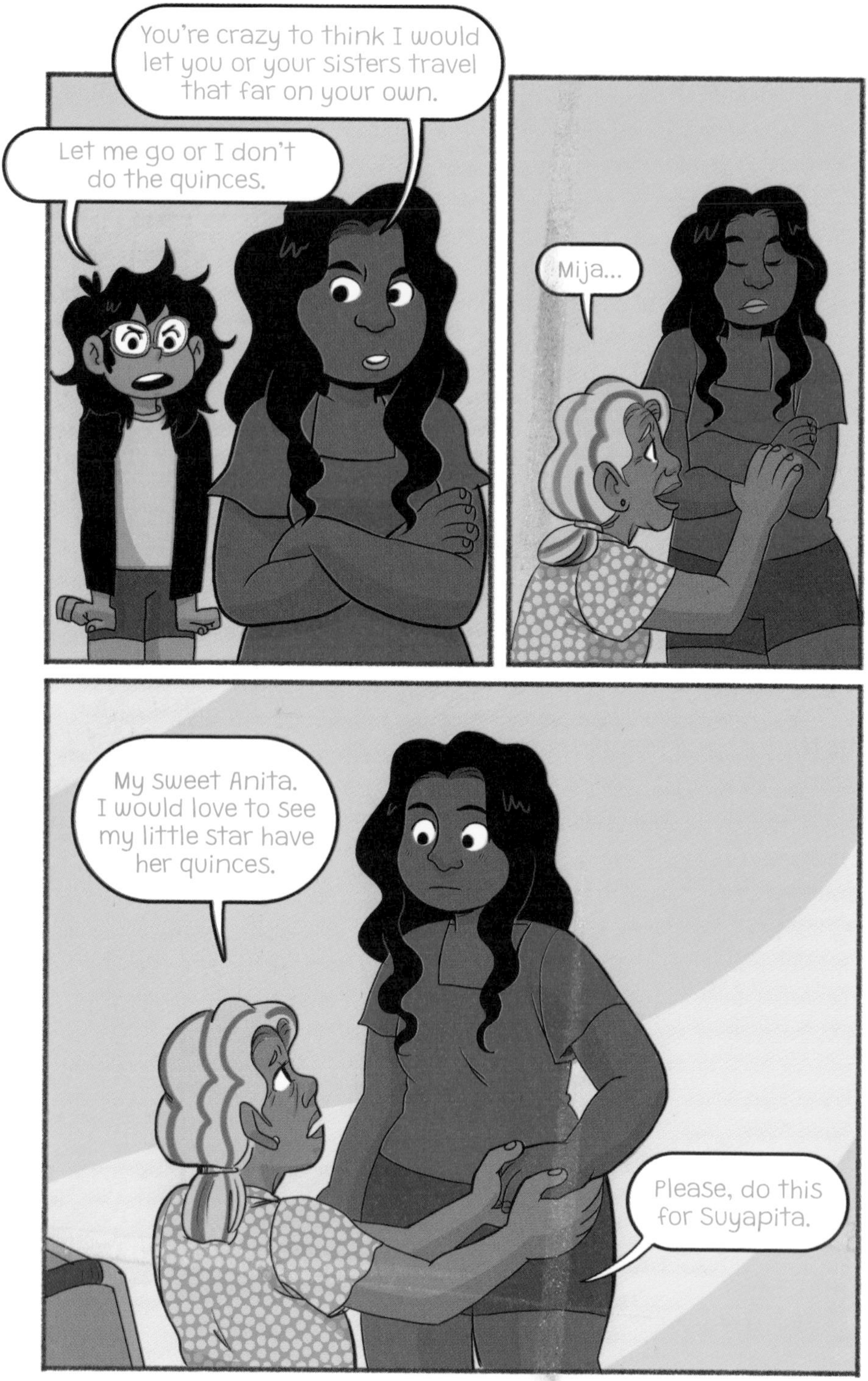
You're crazy to think I would let you or your sisters travel that far on your own.
Let me go or I don't do the quinces.
Mija...
My sweet Anita. I would love to see my little star have her quinces.
Please, do this for Suyapita.

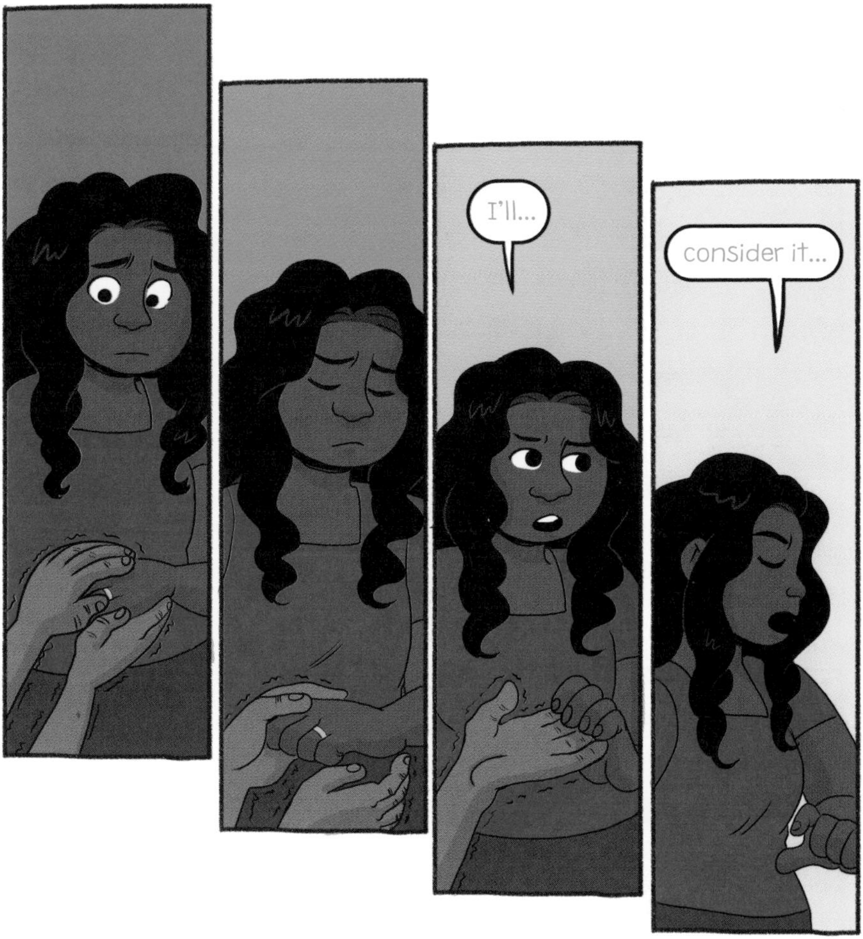
I'll...
consider it...

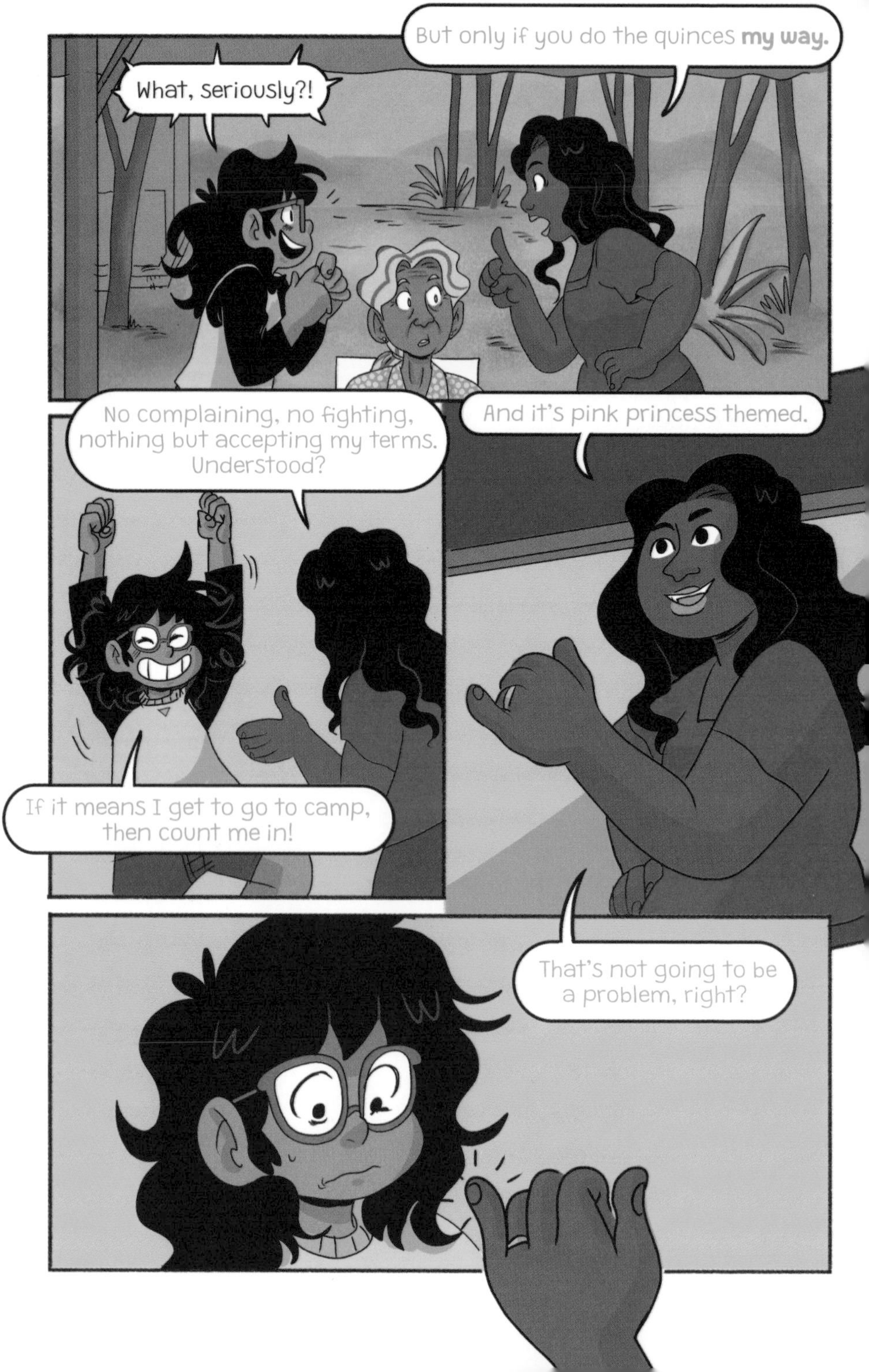
What, seriously?!
But only if you do the quinces **my way.**
No complaining, no fighting, nothing but accepting my terms. Understood?
If it means I get to go to camp, then count me in!
And it's pink princess themed.
That's not going to be a problem, right?

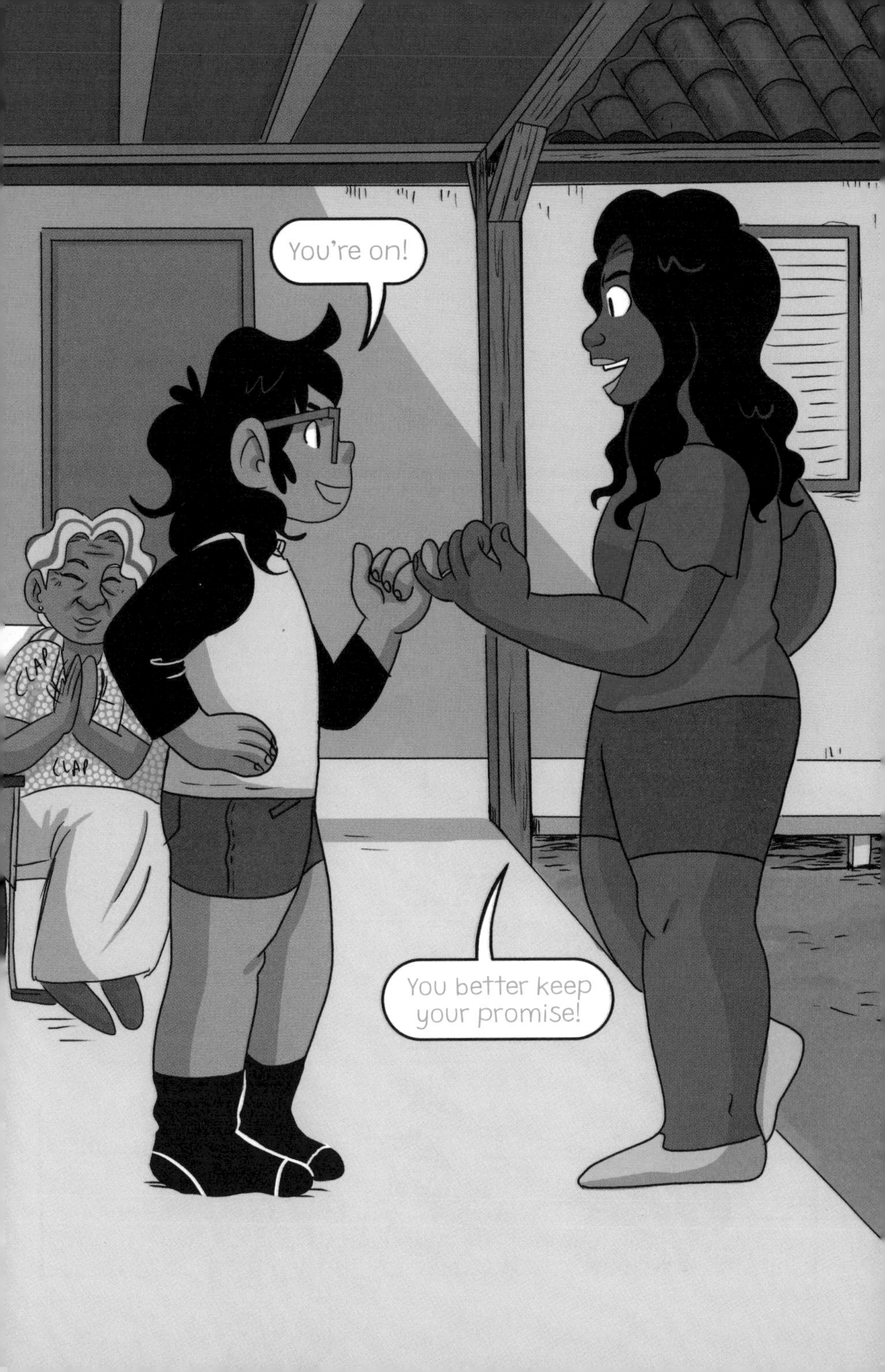
You're on!
CLAP
CLAP
You better keep your promise!

CHAPTER THREE

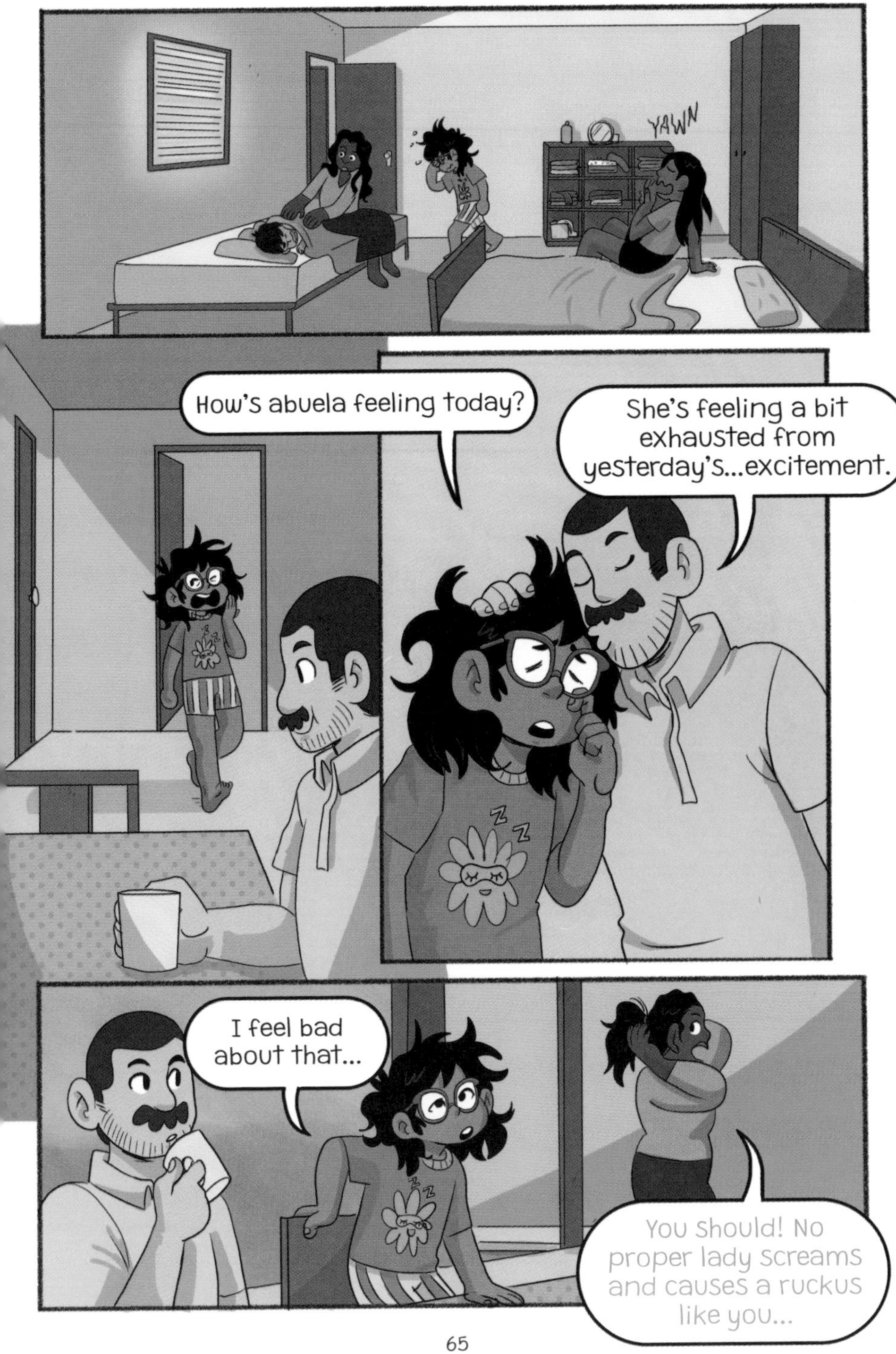
YAWN
How's abuela feeling today?
She's feeling a bit exhausted from yesterday's...excitement.
I feel bad about that...
You should! No proper lady screams and causes a ruckus like you...

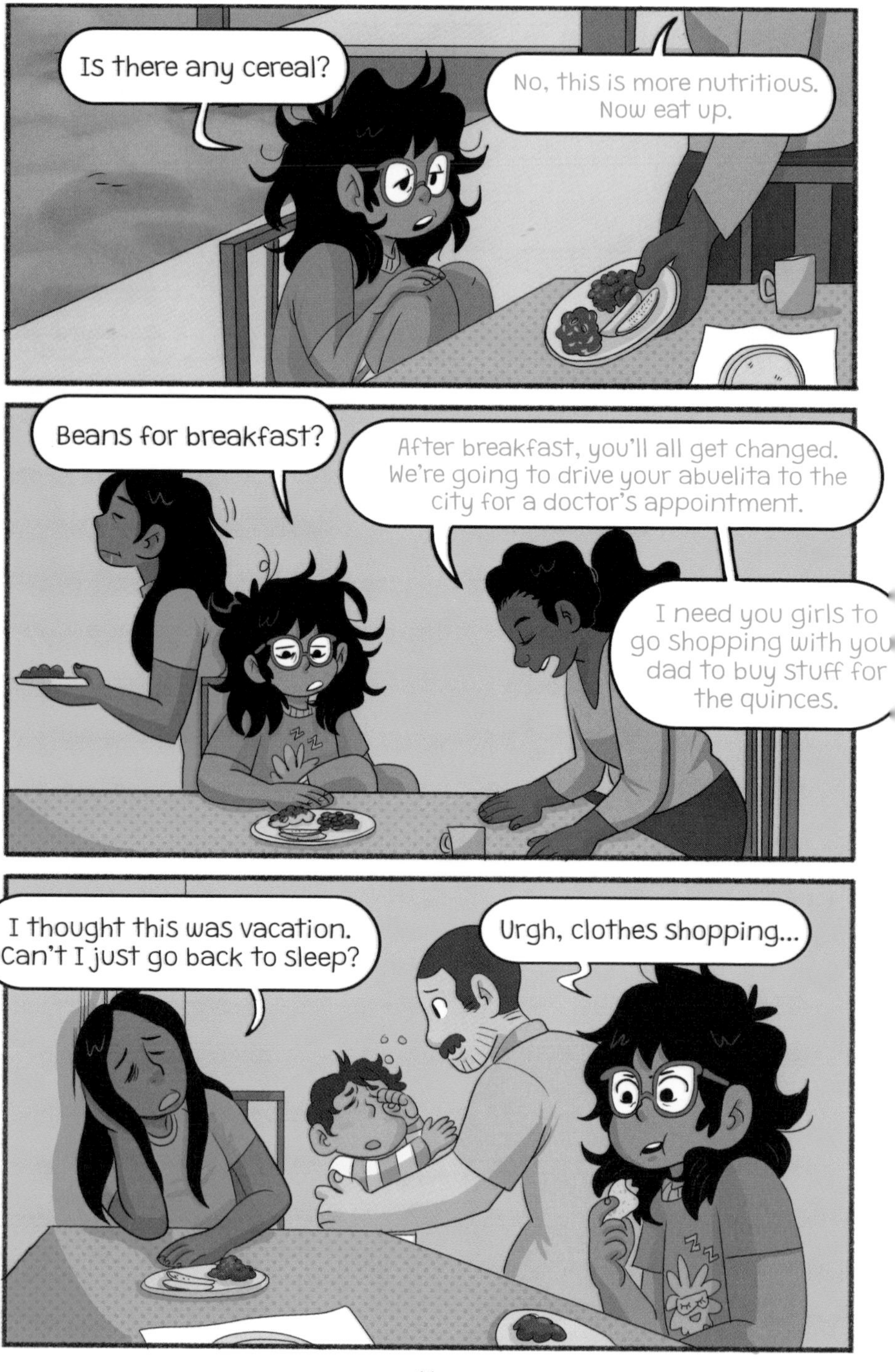
Is there any cereal?
No, this is more nutritious. Now eat up.
Beans for breakfast?
After breakfast, you'll all get changed. We're going to drive your abuelita to the city for a doctor's appointment.
I need you girls to go shopping with you dad to buy stuff for the quinces.
I thought this was vacation. Can't I just go back to sleep?
Urgh, clothes shopping...

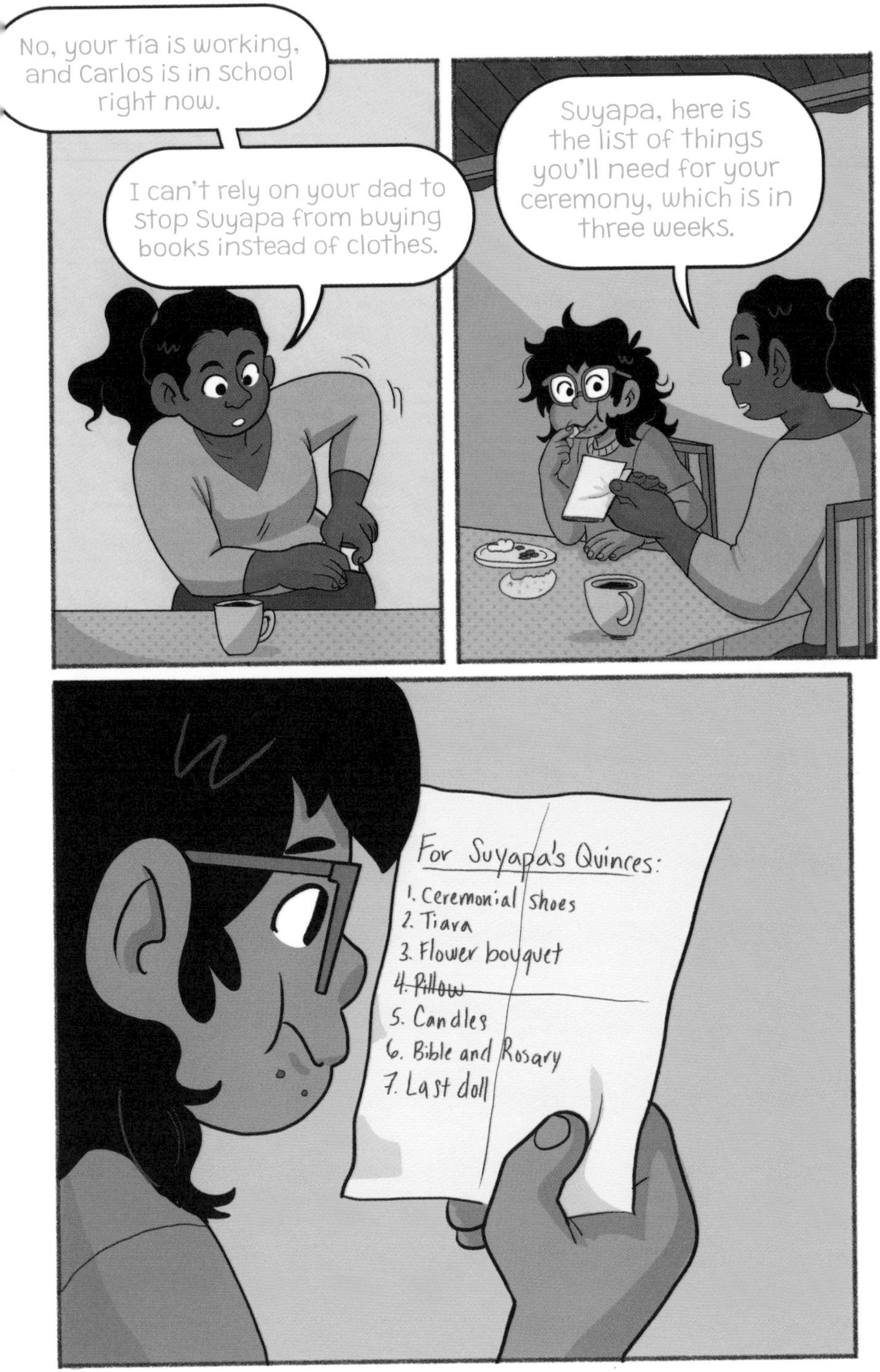
No, your tía is working, and Carlos is in school right now.
I can't rely on your dad to stop Suyapa from buying books instead of clothes.
Suyapa, here is the list of things you'll need for your ceremony, which is in three weeks.
For Suyapa's Quinces:
1. Ceremonial shoes
2. Tiara
3. Flower bouquet
4. Pillow
5. Candles
6. Bible and Rosary
7. Last doll

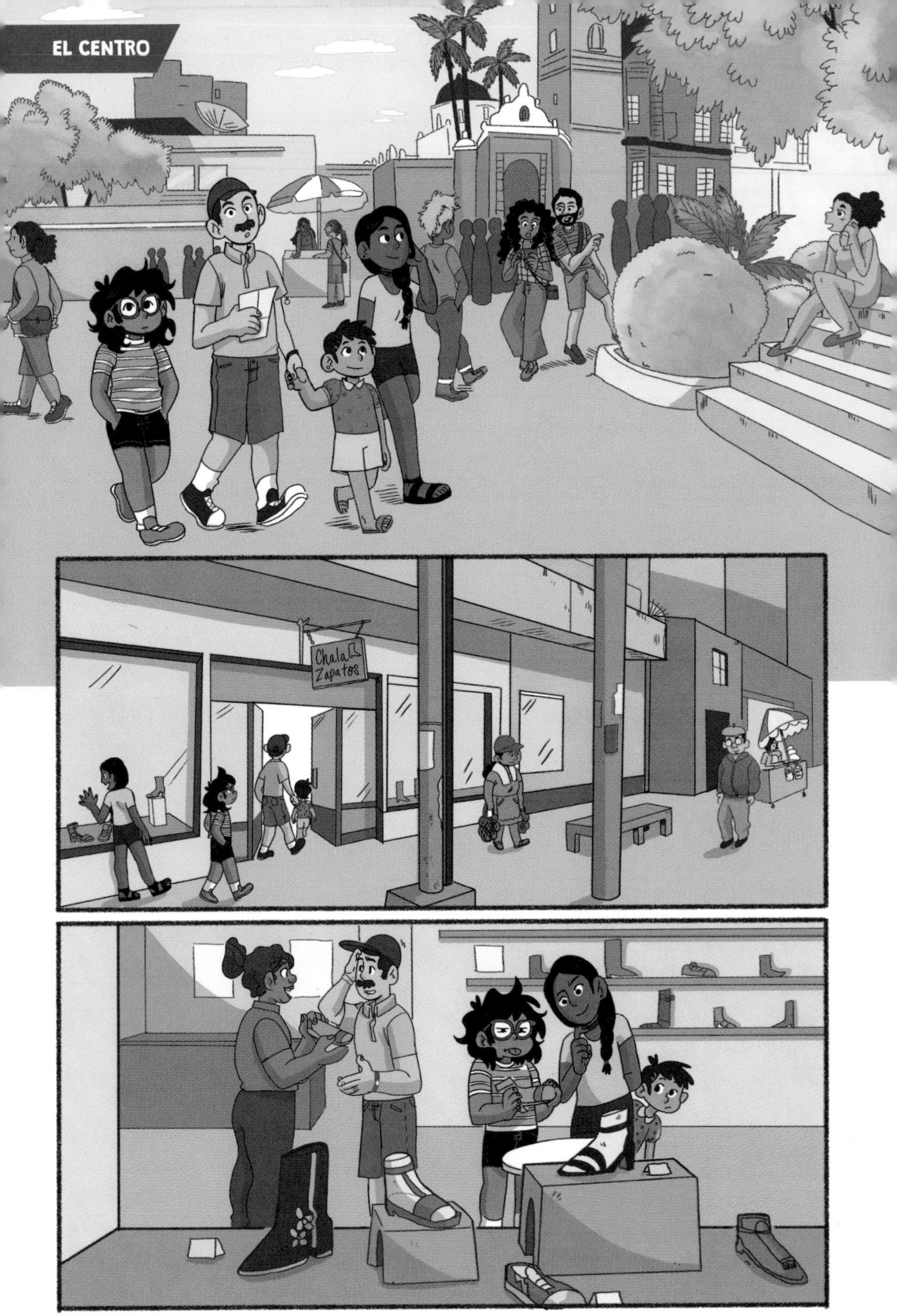
EL CENTRO
Chala Zapatos

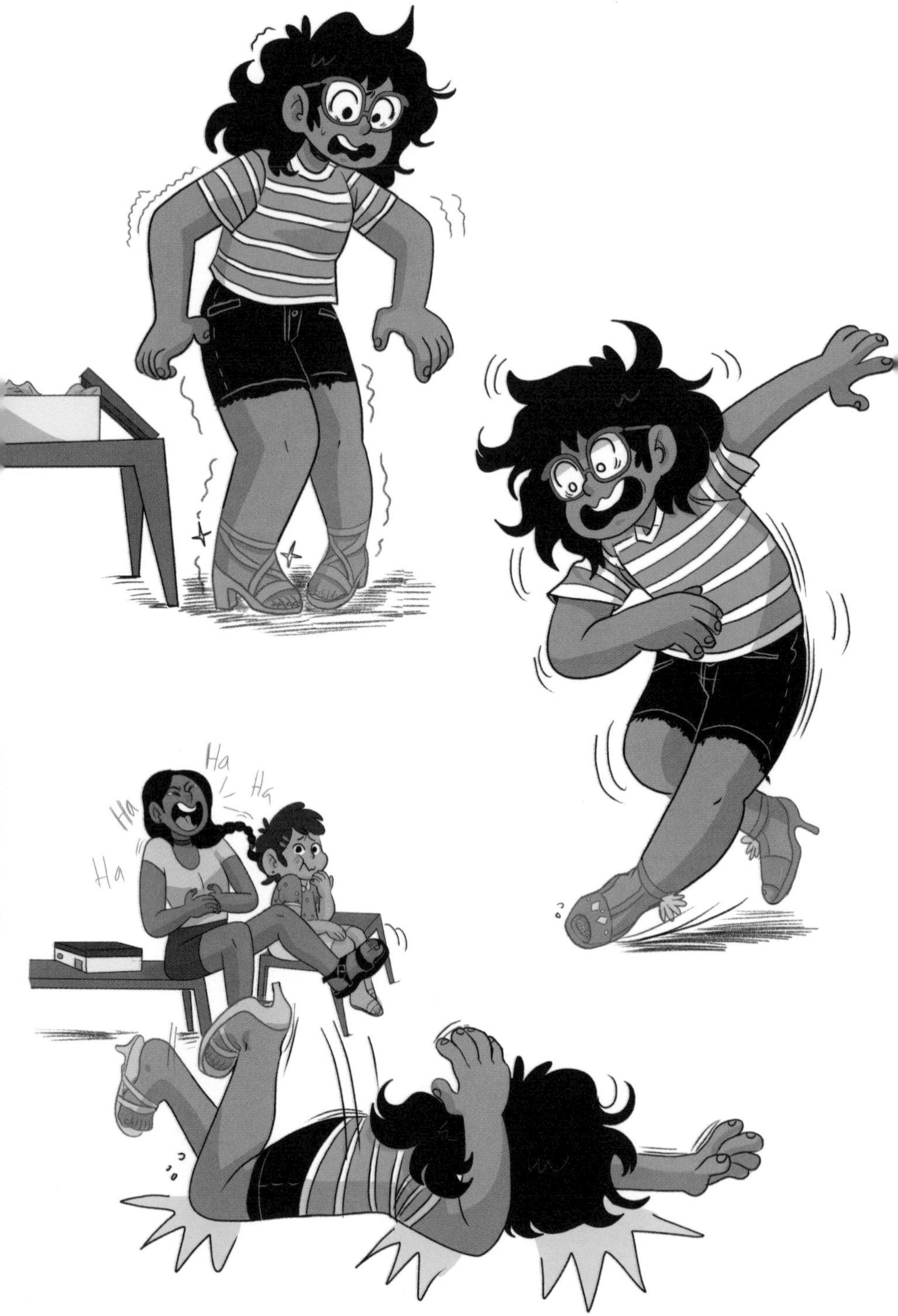

Ha
Ha
Ha
Ha

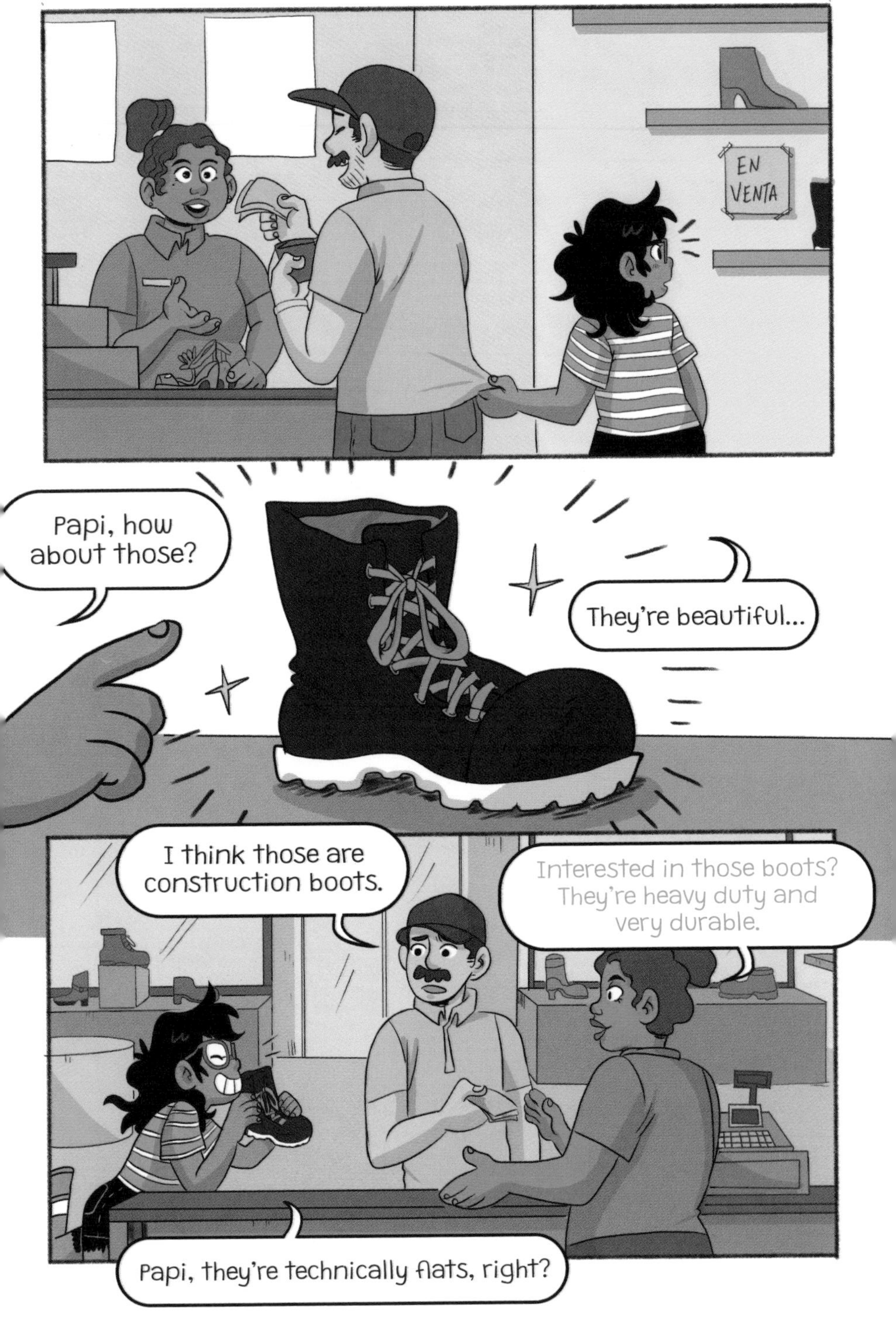
EN VENTA
Papi, how about those?
They're beautiful...
I think those are construction boots.
Interested in those boots? They're heavy duty and very durable.
Papi, they're technically flats, right?

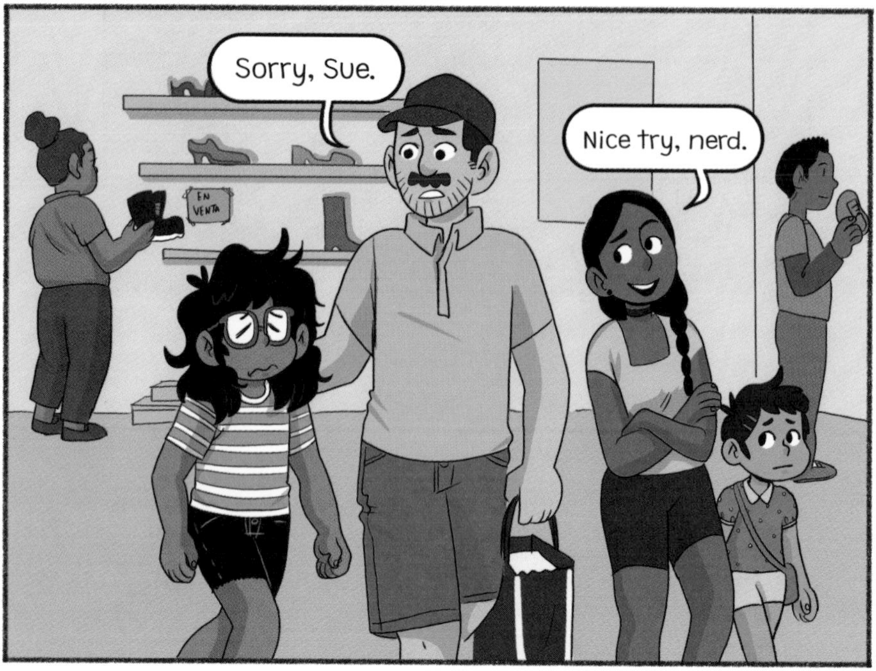
Sorry, Sue.
Nice try, nerd.
EN VENTA

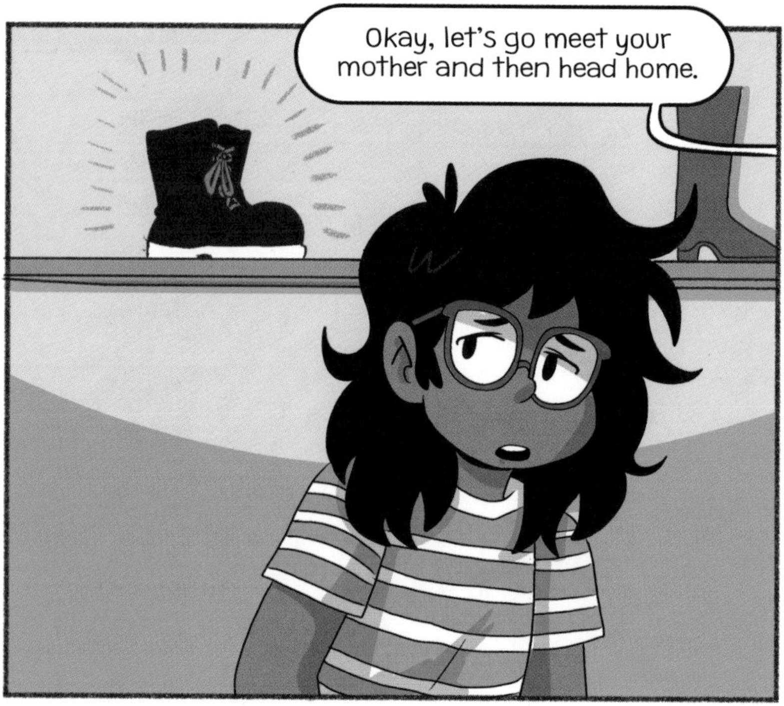
Okay, let's go meet your mother and then head home.

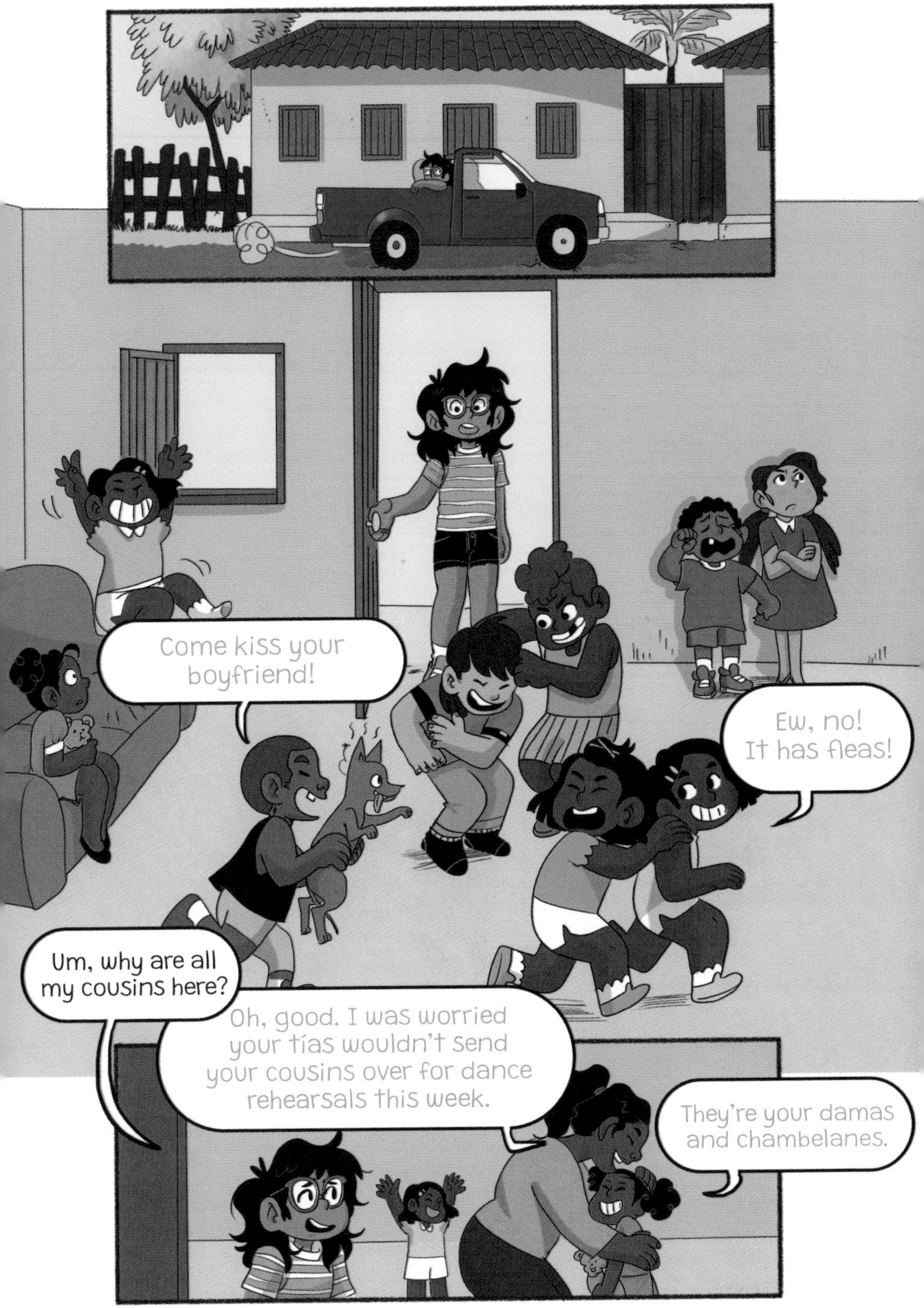
Come kiss your boyfriend!
Ew, no! It has fleas!
Um, why are all my cousins here?
Oh, good. I was worried your tías wouldn't send your cousins over for dance rehearsals this week.
They're your damas and chambelanes.

74

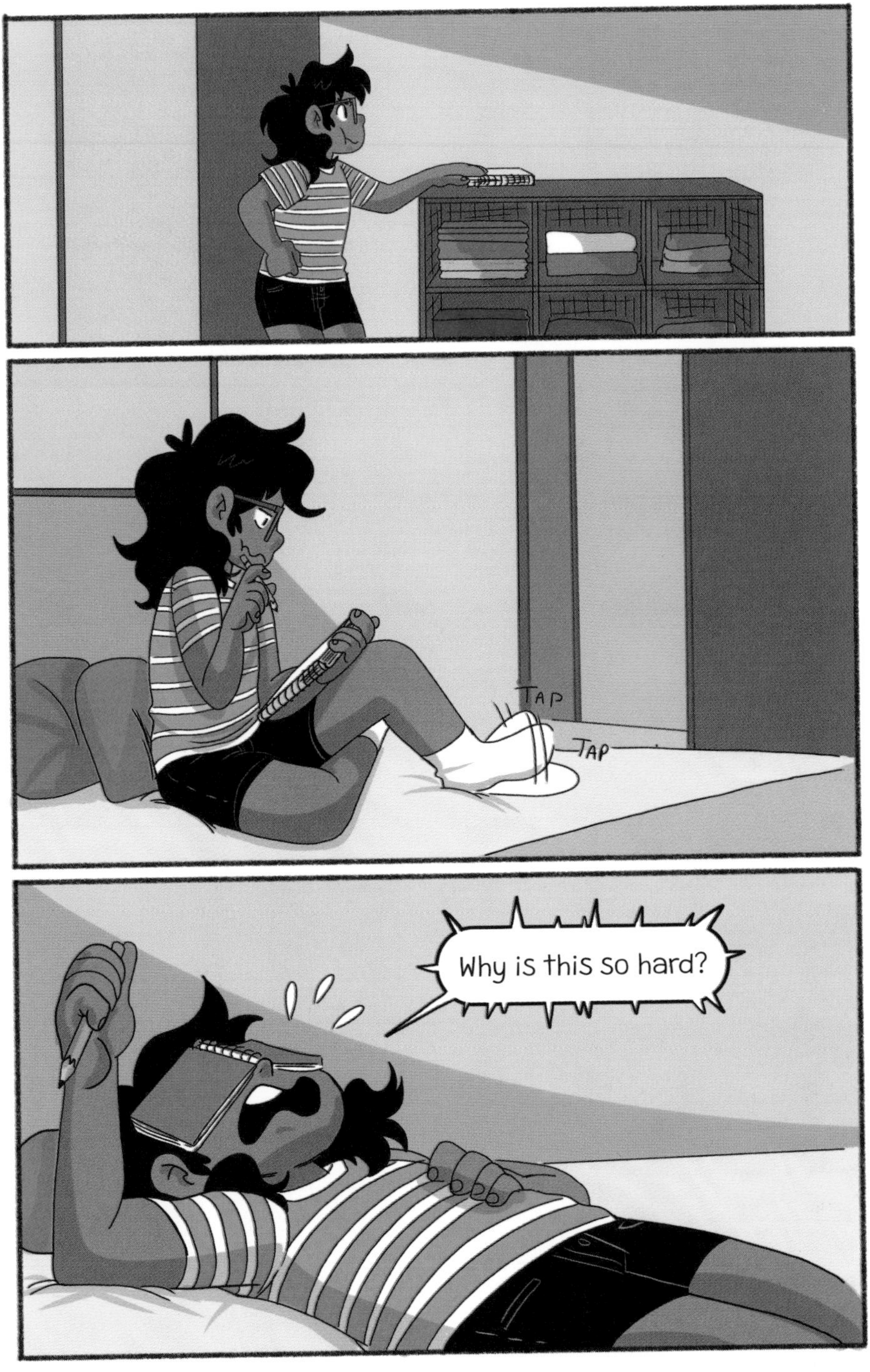
TAP
TAP
Why is this so hard?

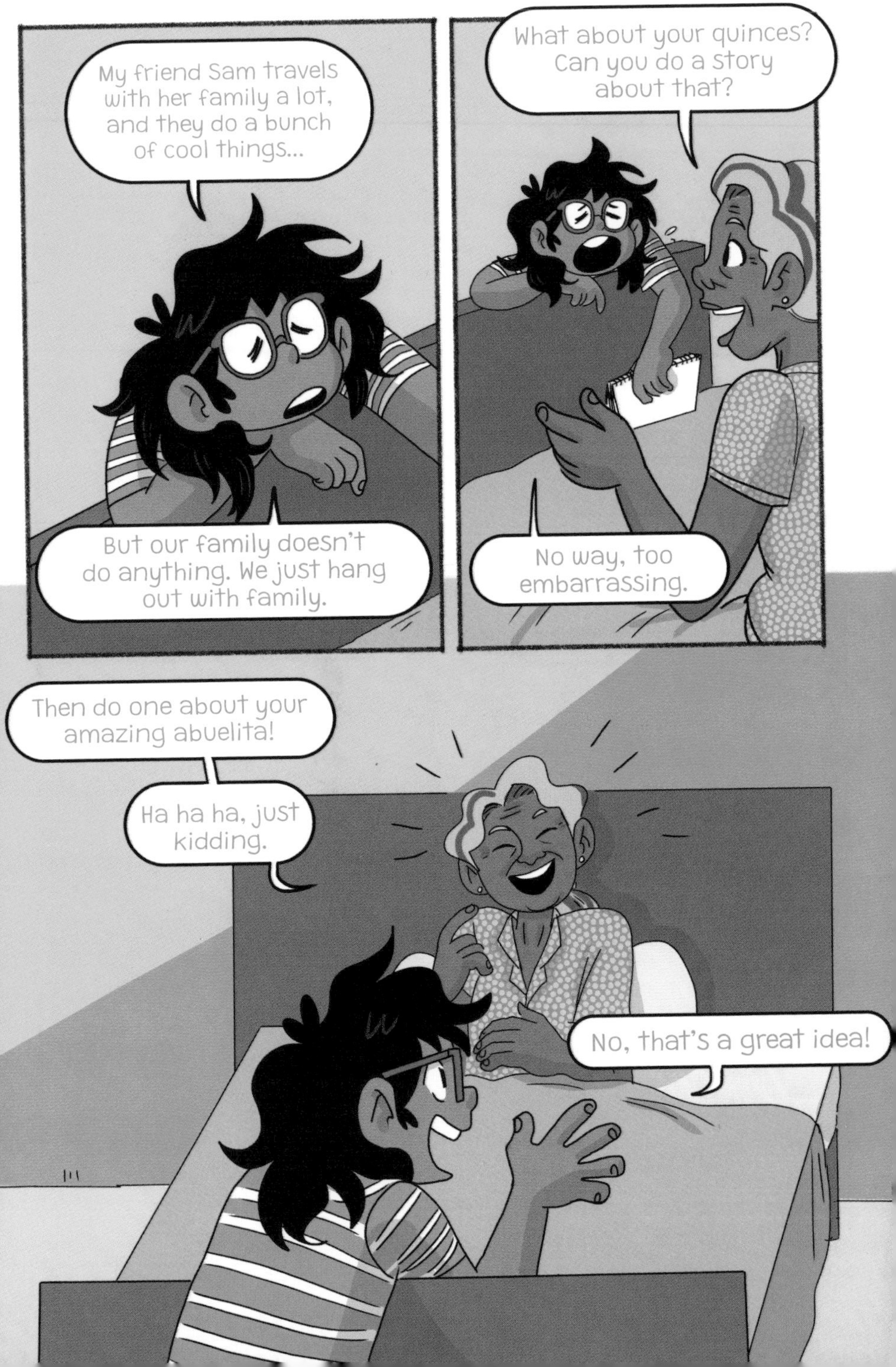
My friend Sam travels with her family a lot, and they do a bunch of cool things...
But our family doesn't do anything. We just hang out with family.
What about your quinces? Can you do a story about that?
No way, too embarrassing.
Then do one about your amazing abuelita!
Ha ha ha, just kidding.
No, that's a great idea!

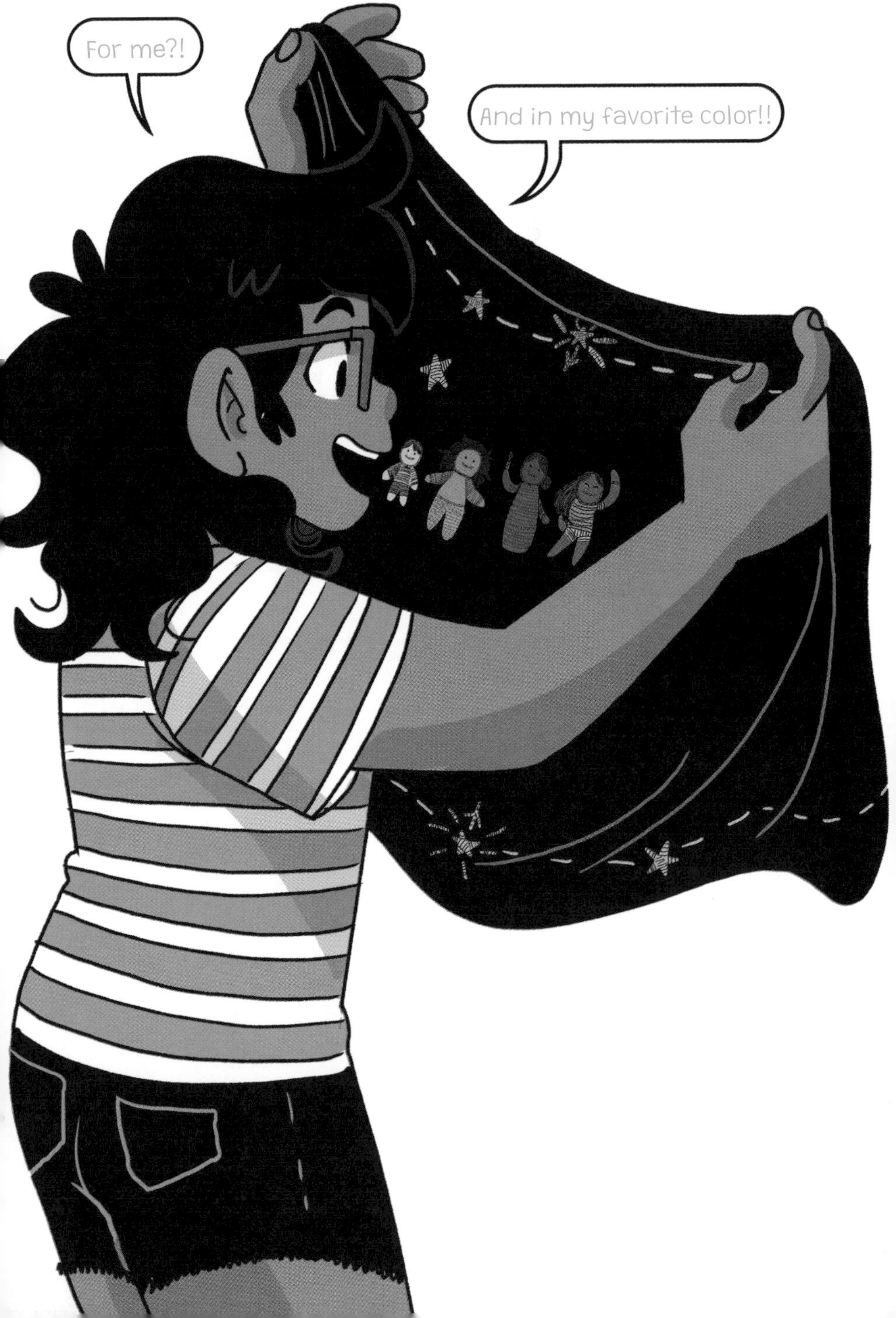
For me?!
And in my favorite color!!

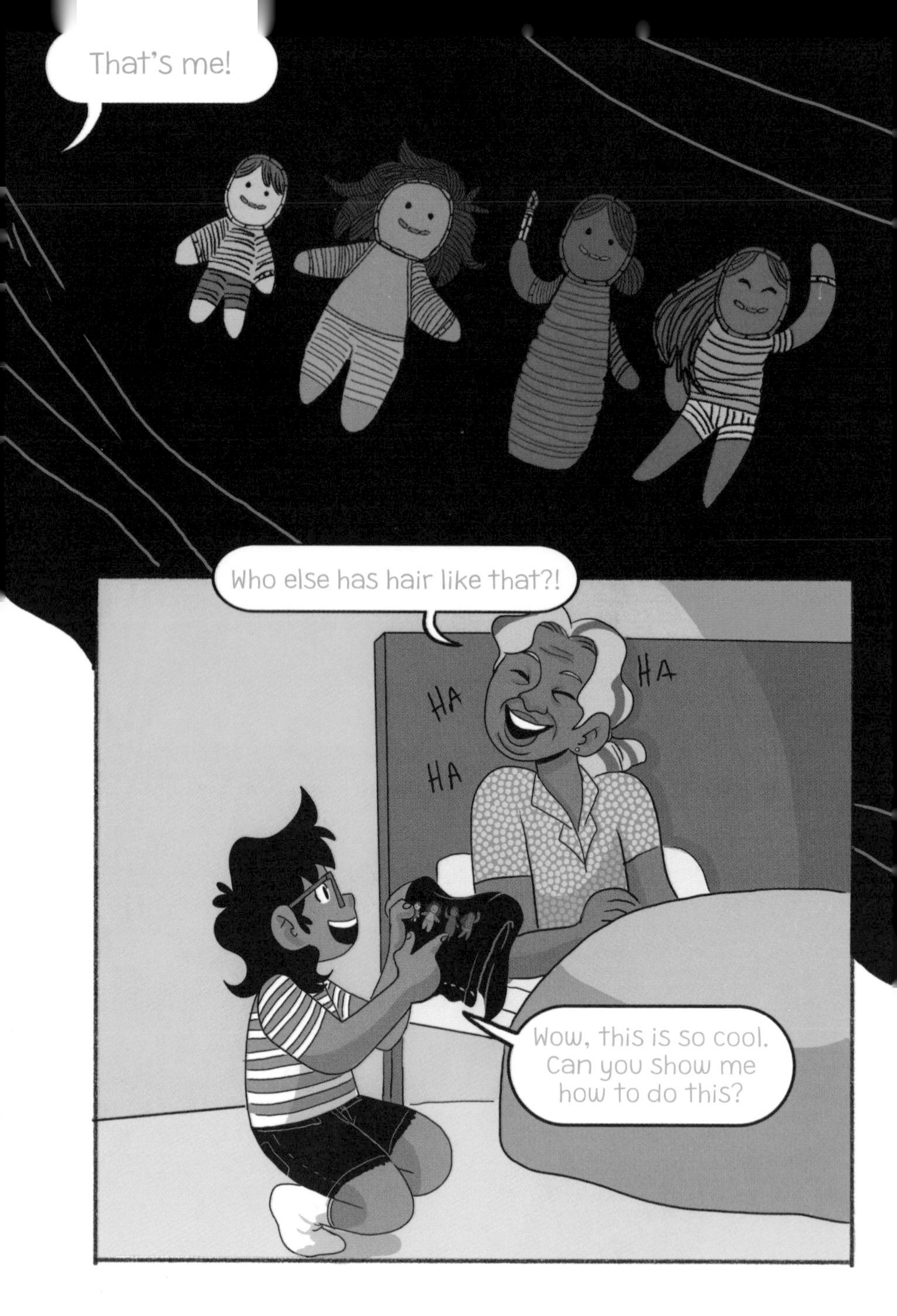
That's me!
Who else has hair like that?!
HA
HA
HA
HA
Wow, this is so cool. Can you show me how to do this?

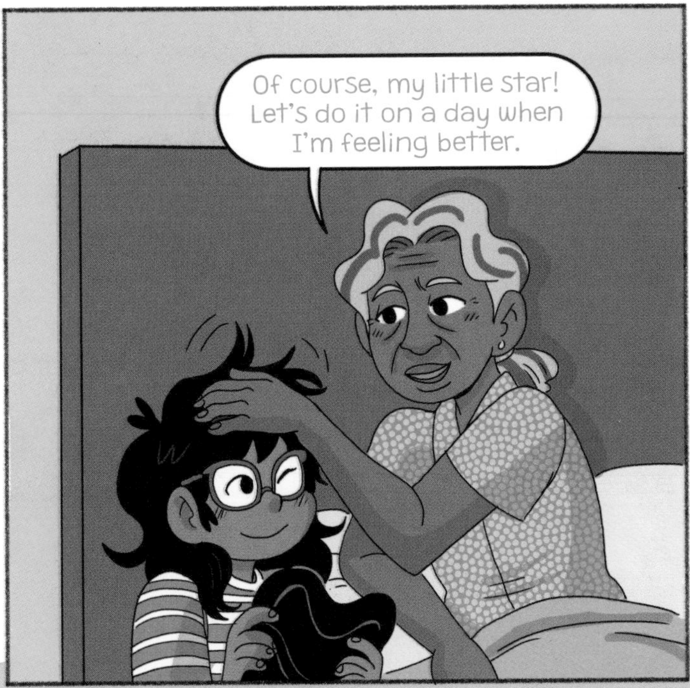
Of course, my little star! Let's do it on a day when I'm feeling better.

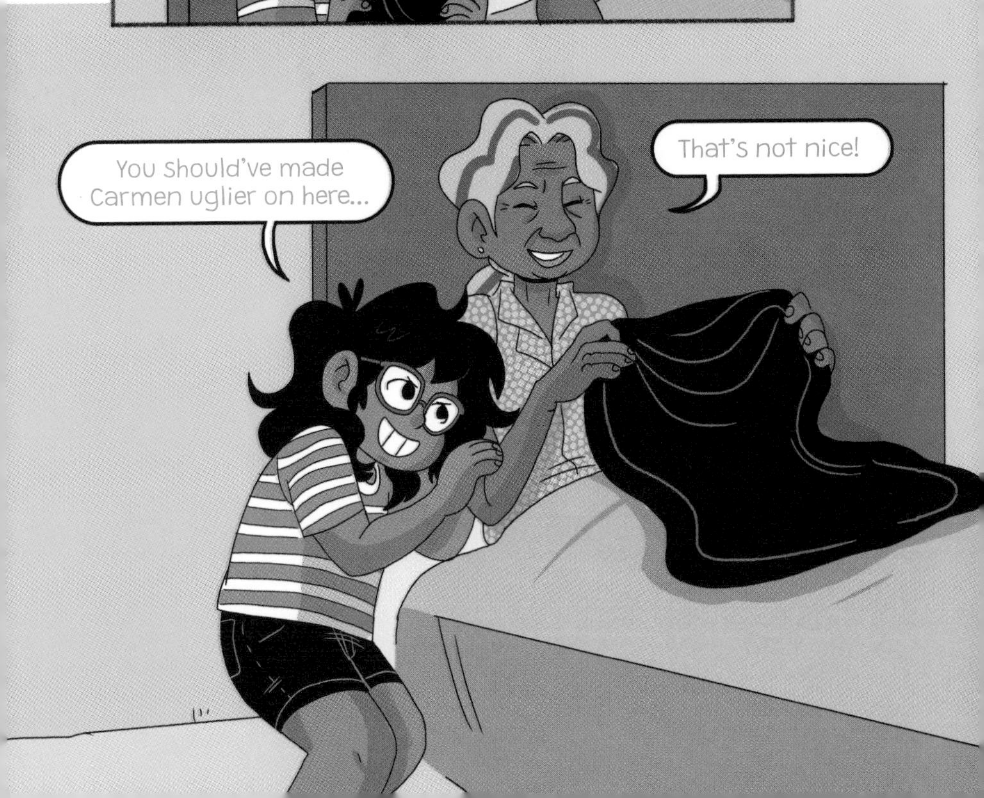
You should've made Carmen uglier on here...
That's not nice!

CHAPTER FOUR

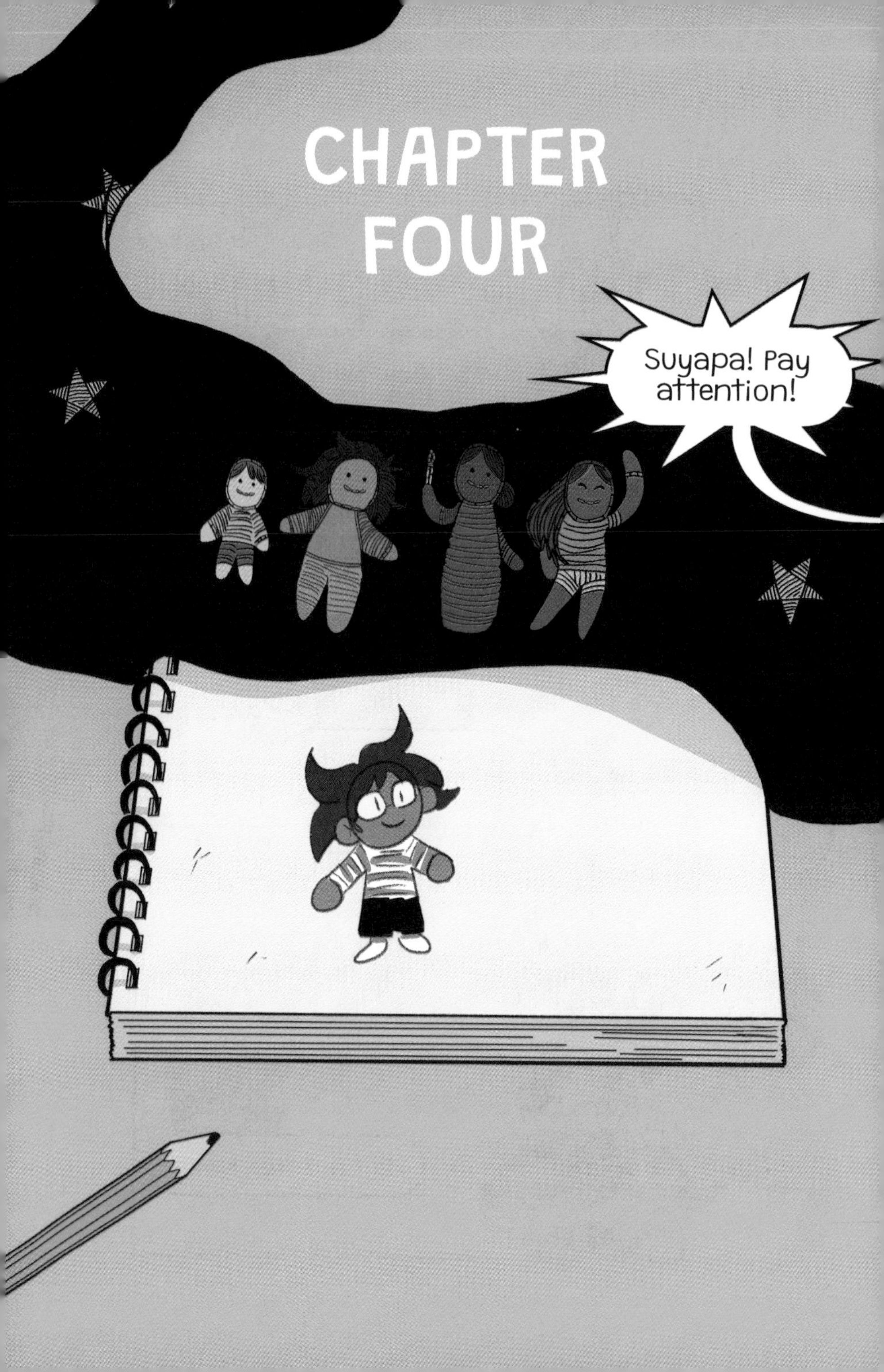
Suyapa! Pay attention!

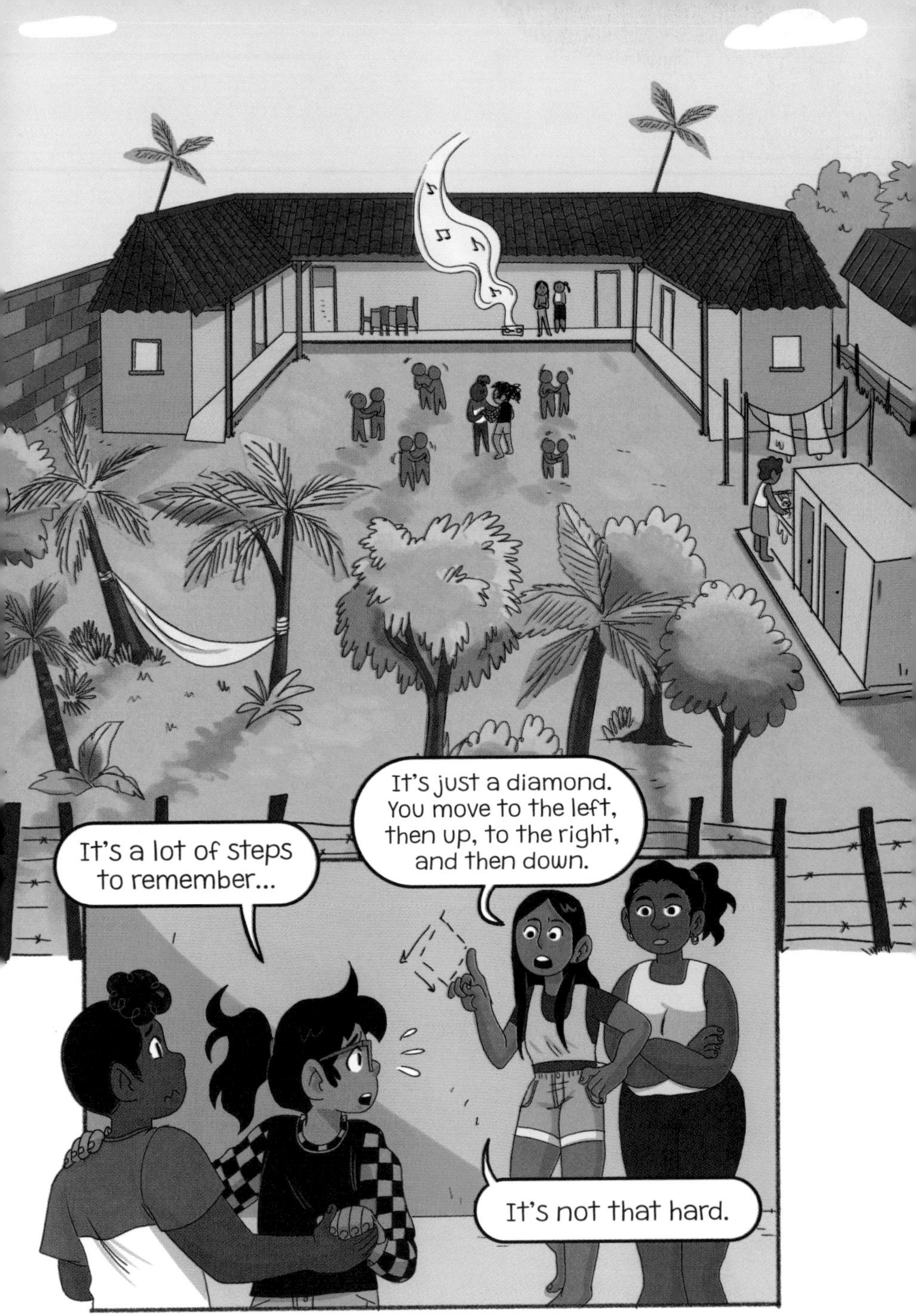
It's a lot of steps to remember...
It's just a diamond. You move to the left, then up, to the right, and then down.
It's not that hard.

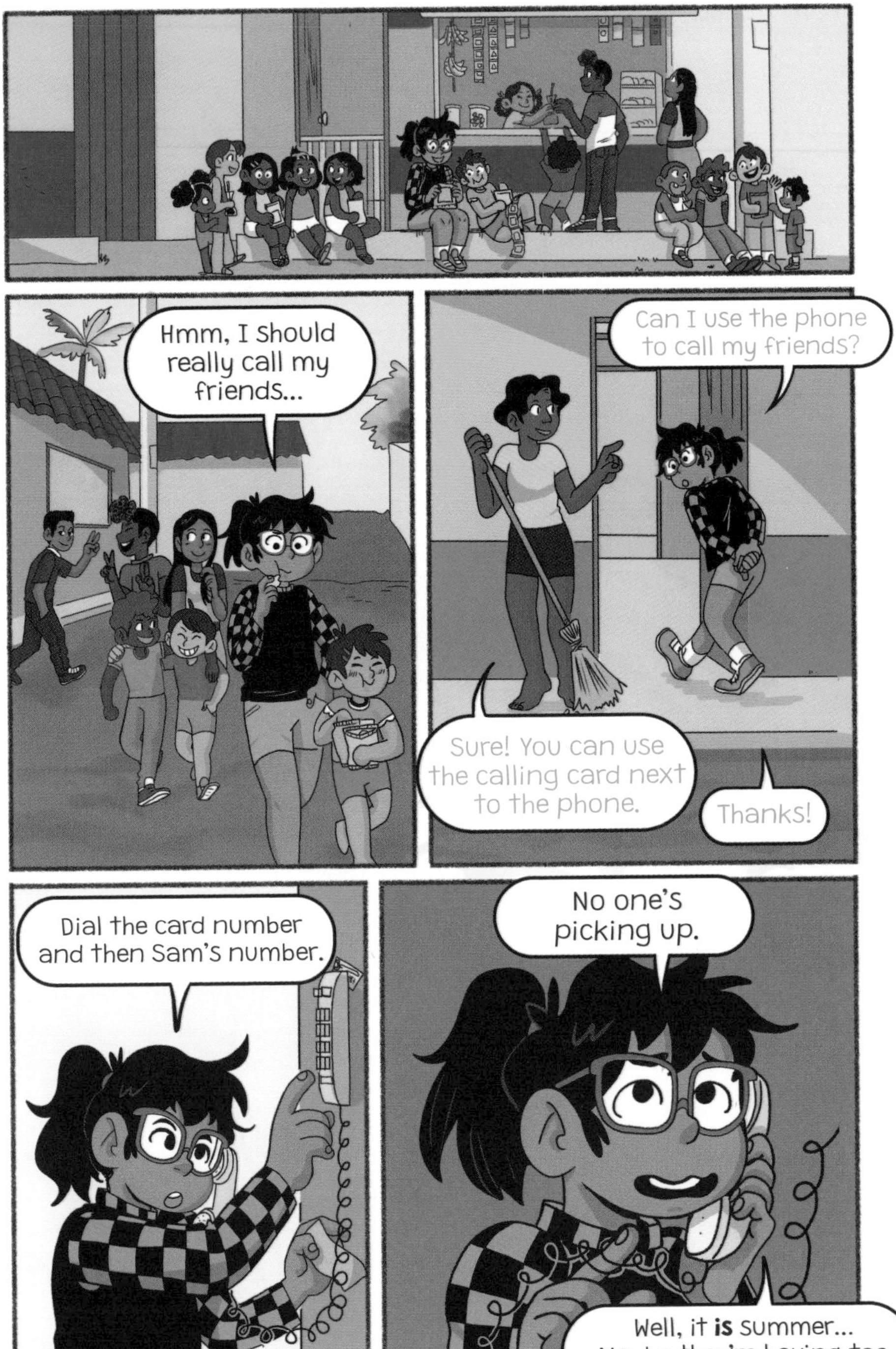
Hmm, I should really call my friends...
Can I use the phone to call my friends?
Sure! You can use the calling card next to the phone.
Thanks!
Dial the card number and then Sam's number.
No one's picking up.
Well, it **is** summer... Maybe they're having too much fun without me?

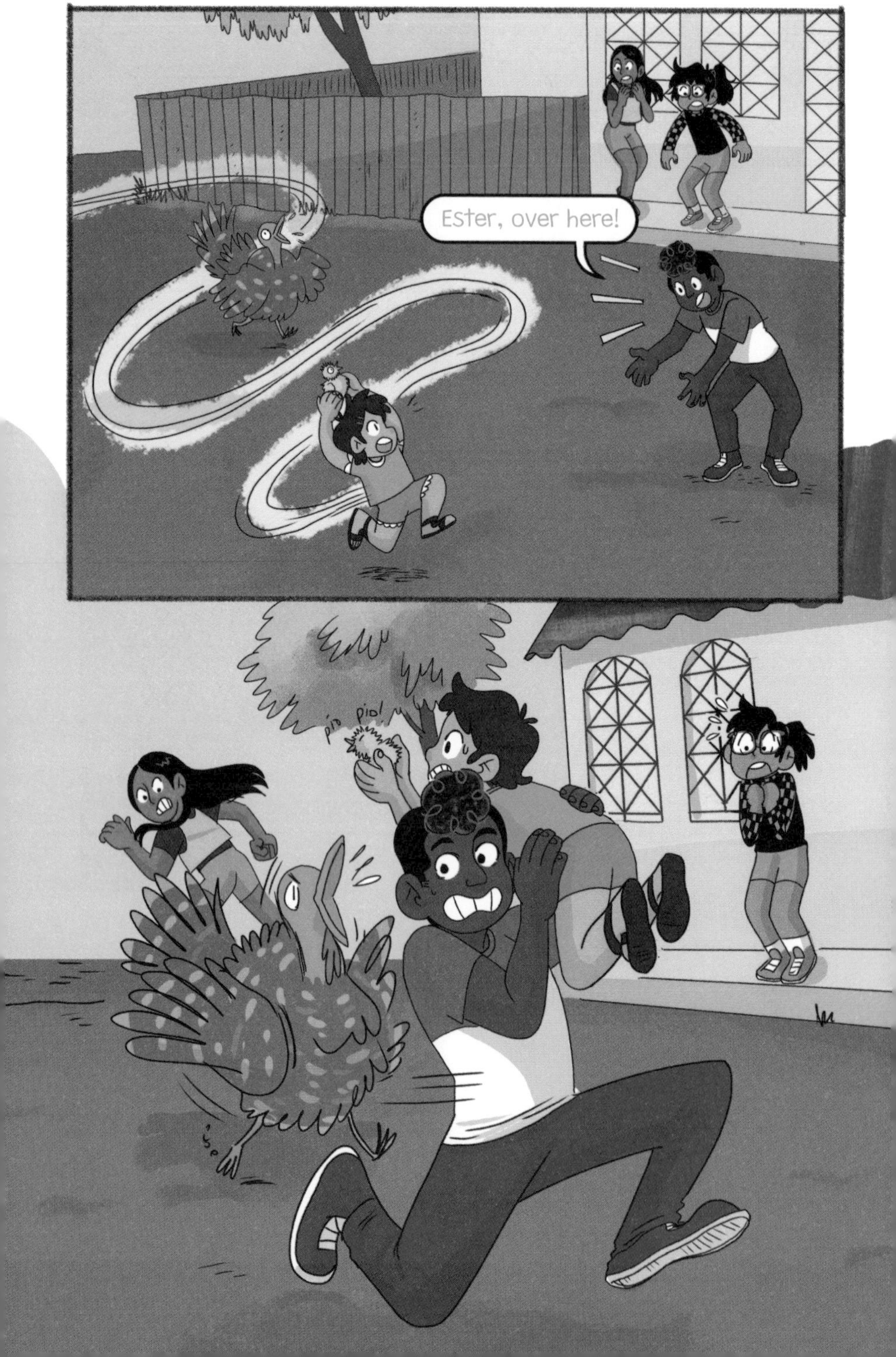
Ester, over here!
pio pio!

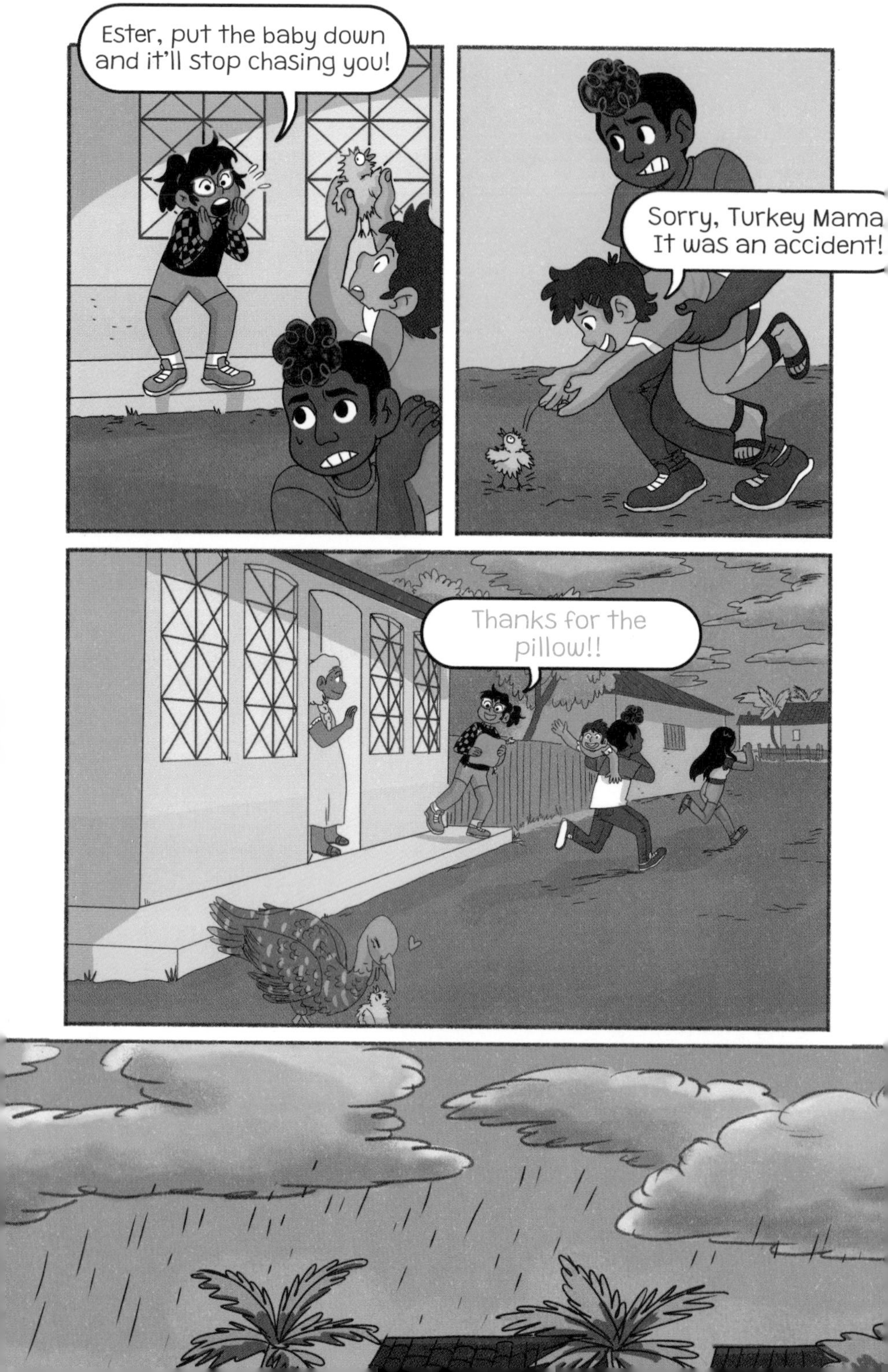
Ester, put the baby down and it'll stop chasing you!
Sorry, Turkey Mama It was an accident!
Thanks for the pillow!!

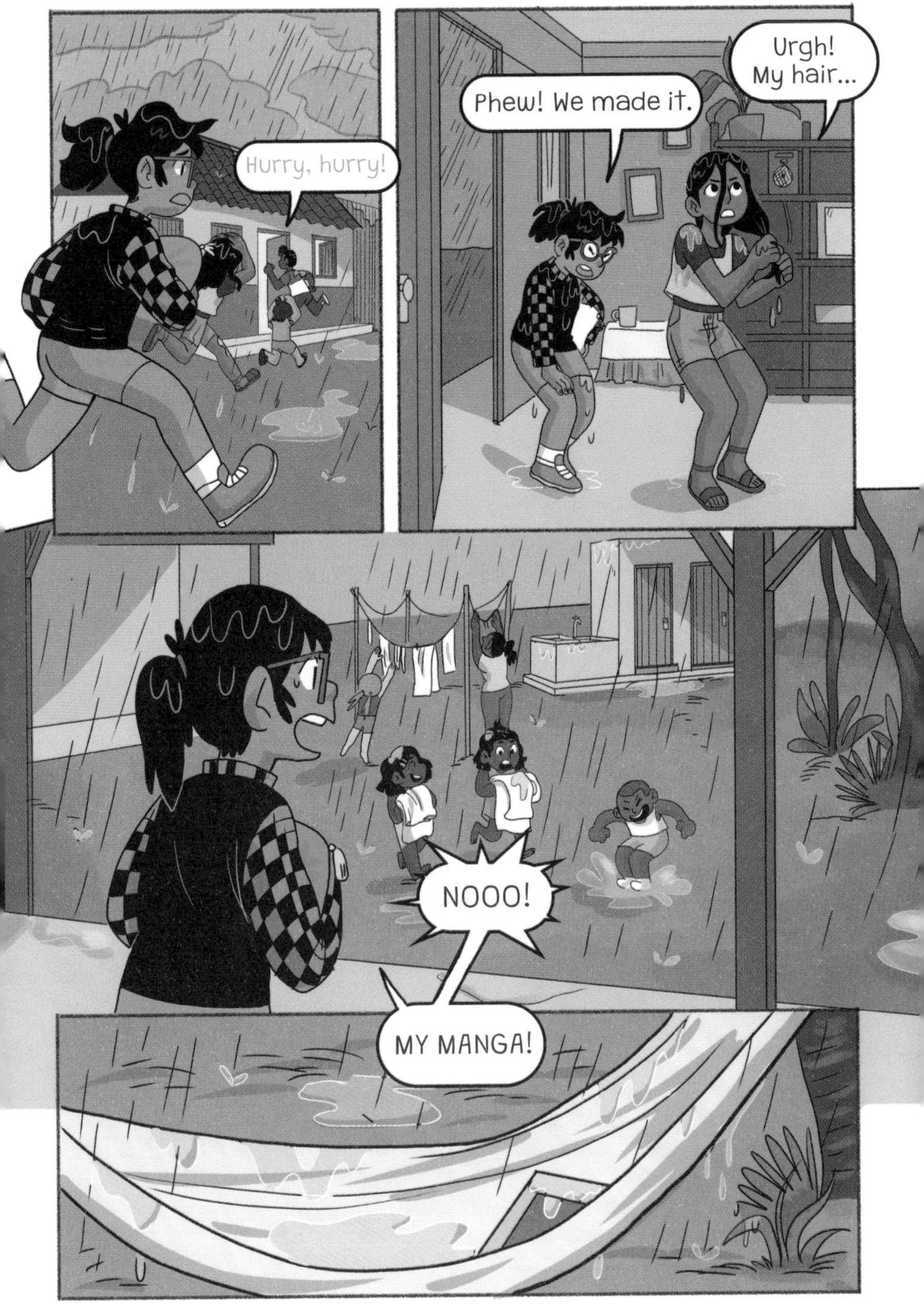
Hurry, hurry!
Phew! We made it.
Urgh! My hair...
NOOO!
MY MANGA!

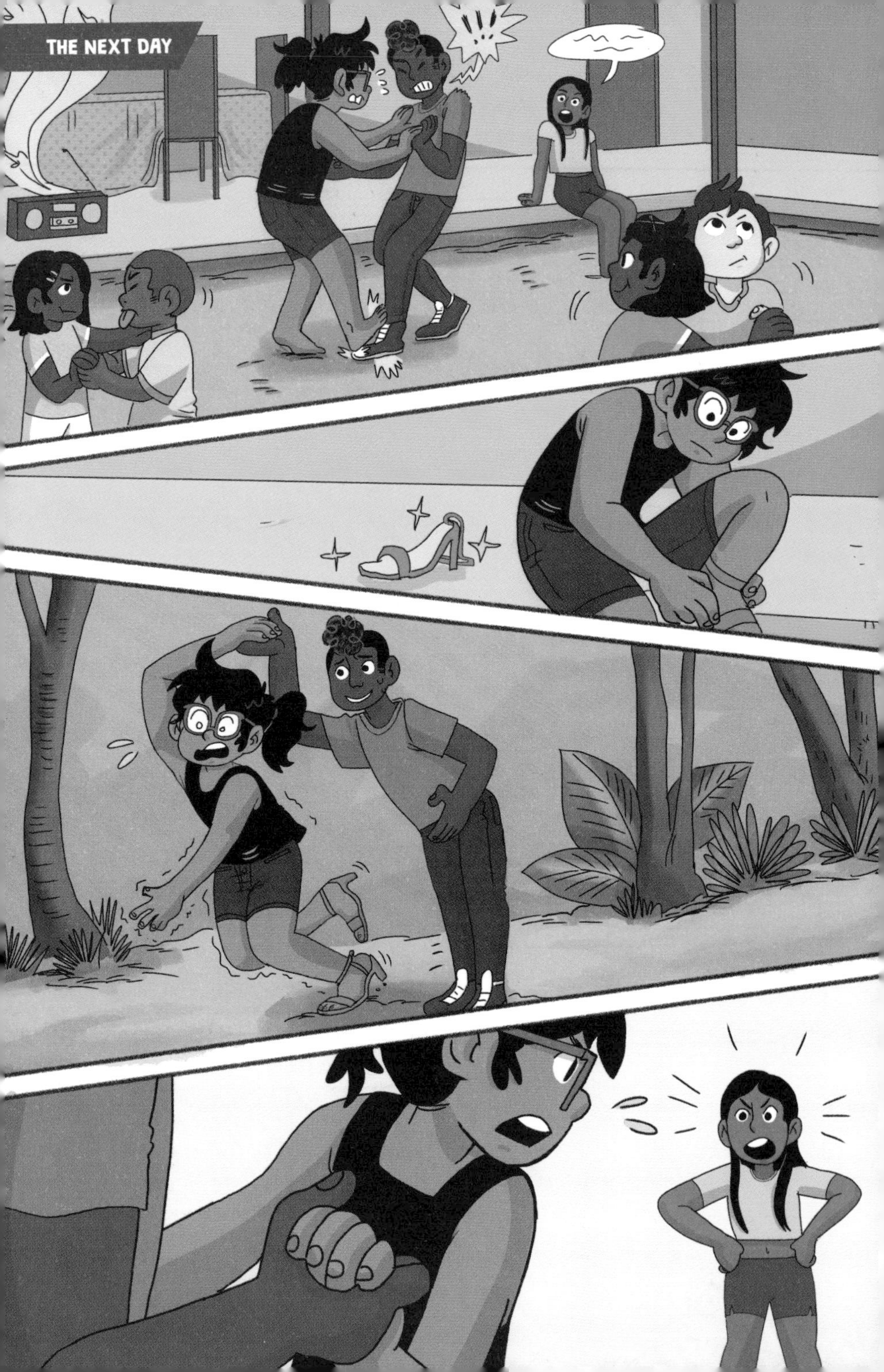
THE NEXT DAY
!!!

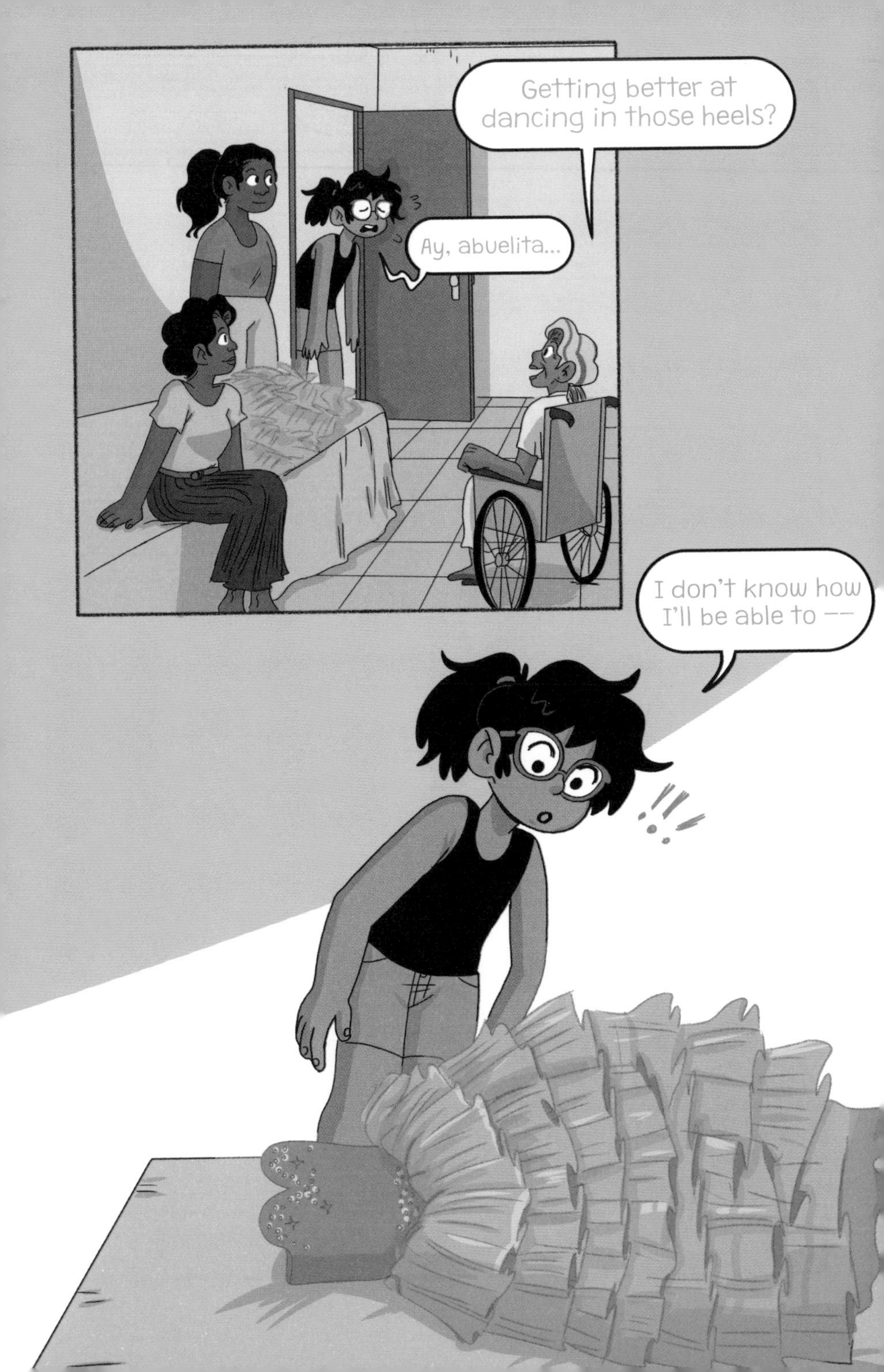
Getting better at dancing in those heels?
Ay, abuelita...
I don't know how I'll be able to --

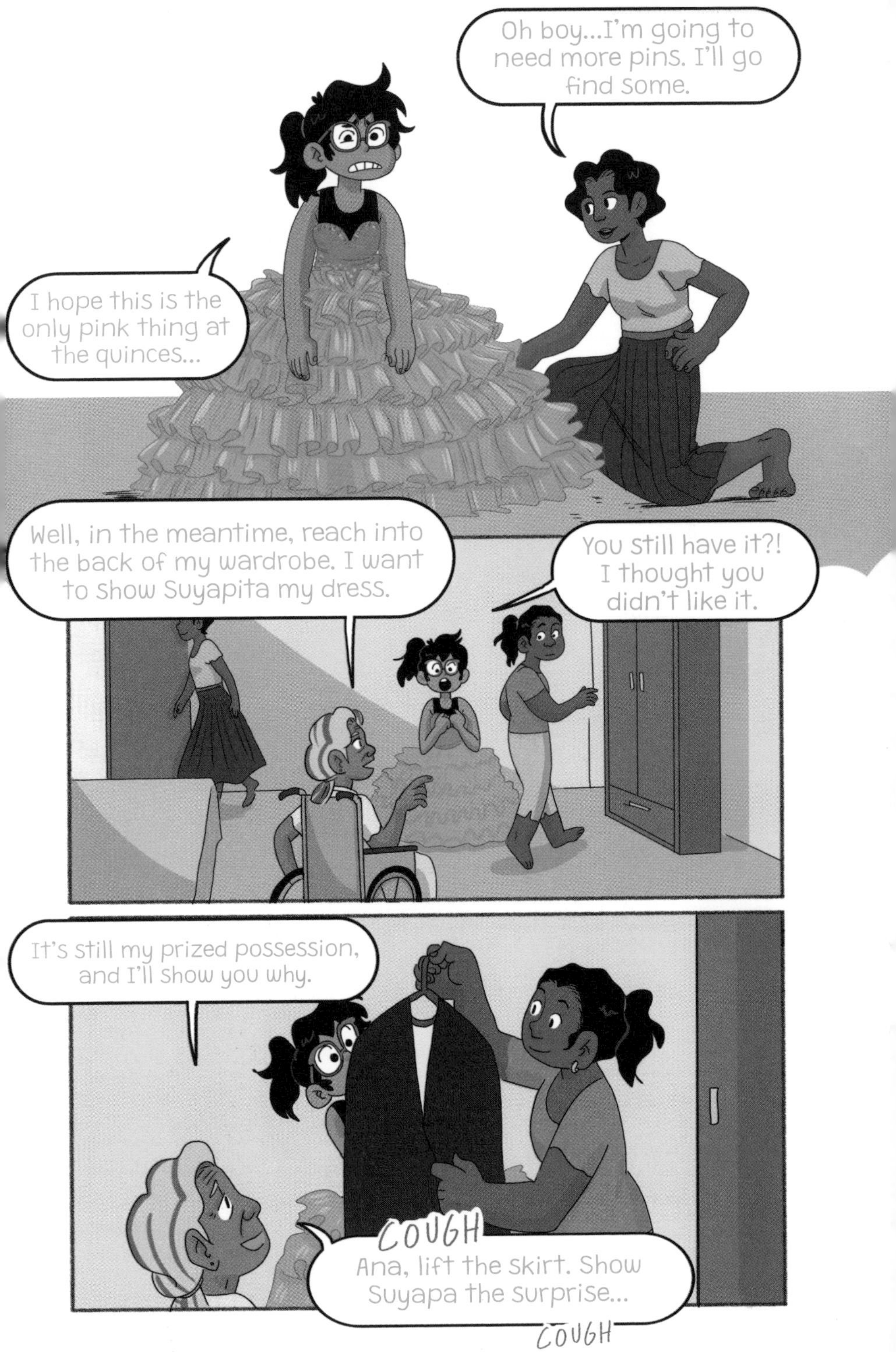
Oh boy...I'm going to need more pins. I'll go find some.
I hope this is the only pink thing at the quinces...
Well, in the meantime, reach into the back of my wardrobe. I want to show Suyapita my dress.
You still have it?! I thought you didn't like it.
It's still my prized possession, and I'll show you why.
COUGH
Ana, lift the skirt. Show Suyapa the surprise...
COUGH

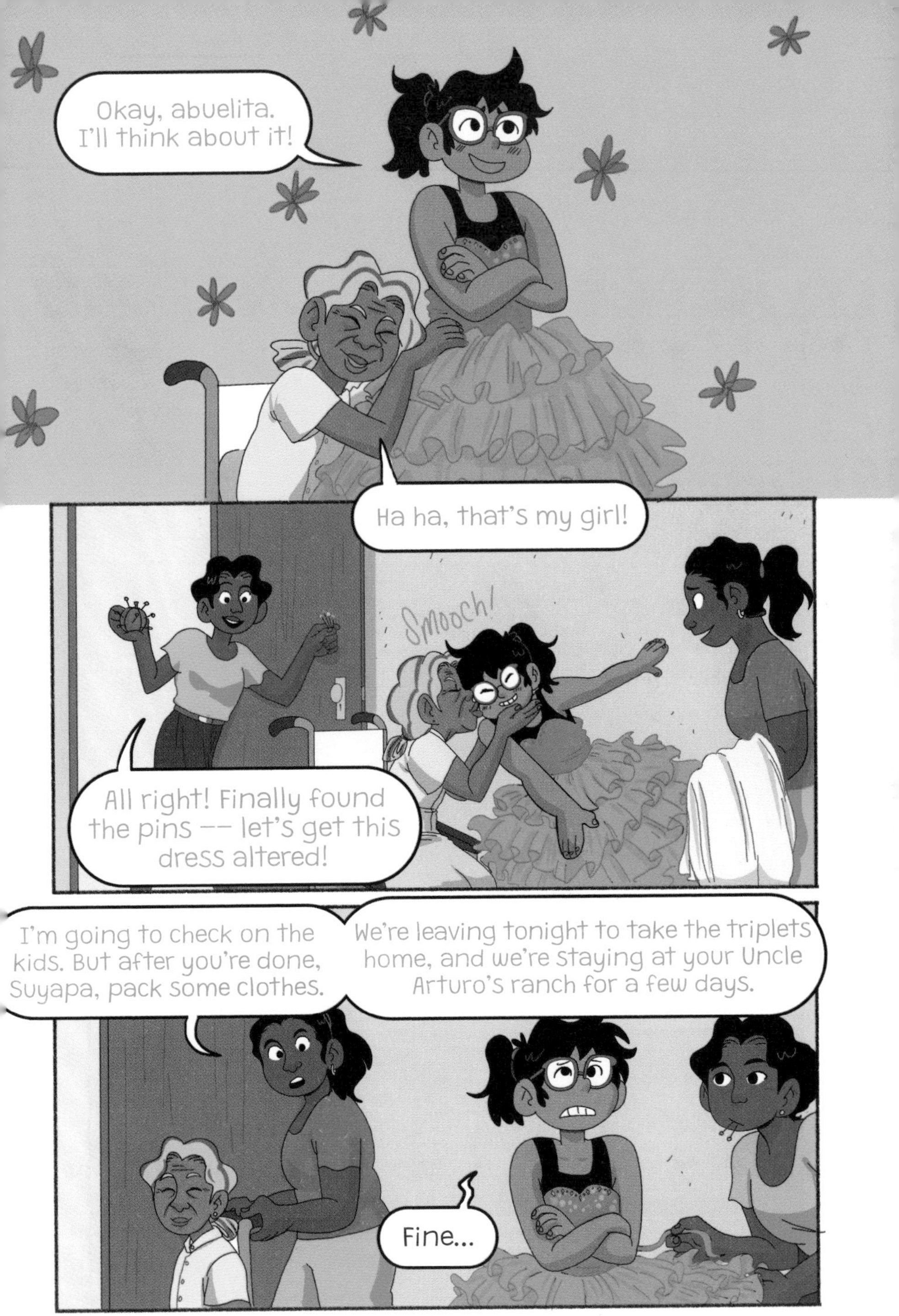
Okay, abuelita. I'll think about it!
Ha ha, that's my girl!
Smooch!
All right! Finally found the pins -- let's get this dress altered!
I'm going to check on the kids. But after you're done, Suyapa, pack some clothes.
We're leaving tonight to take the triplets home, and we're staying at your Uncle Arturo's ranch for a few days.
Fine...

CHAPTER FIVE

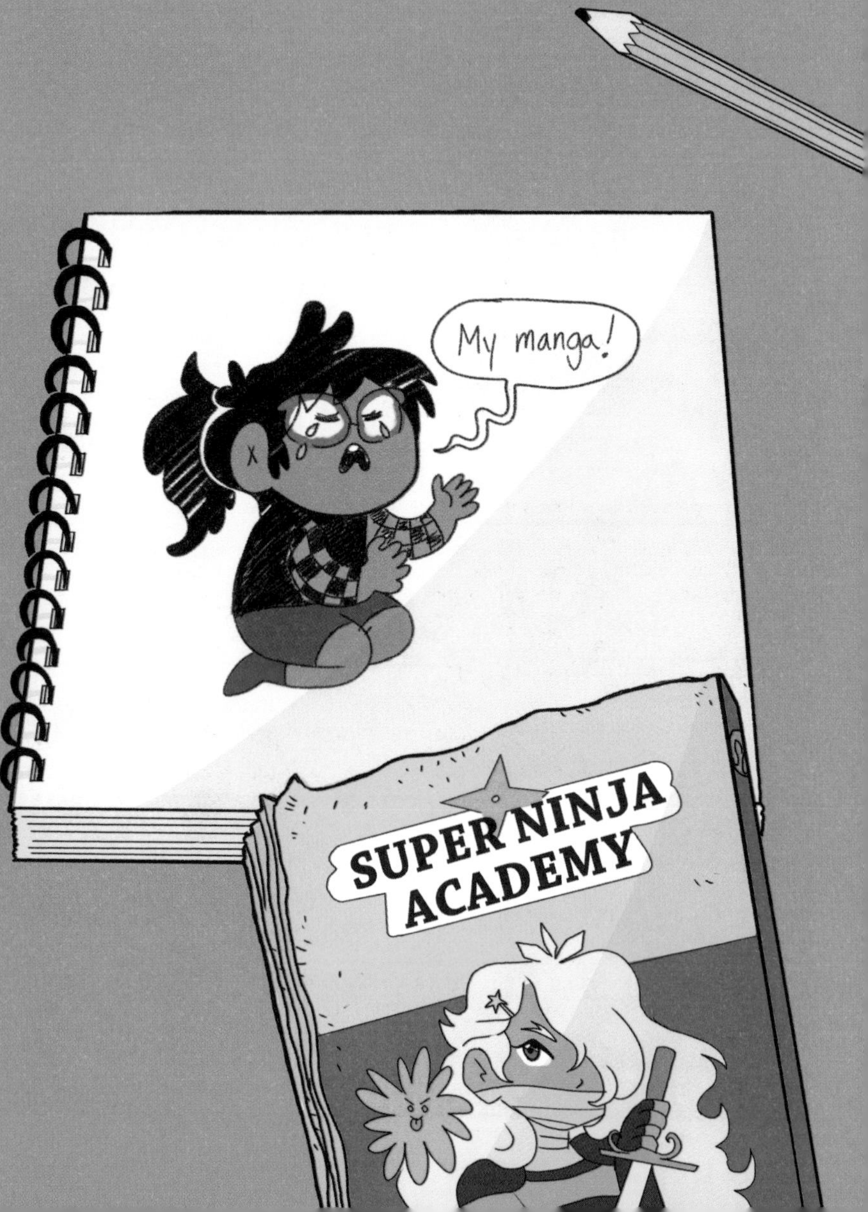
My manga!
SUPER NINJA ACADEMY

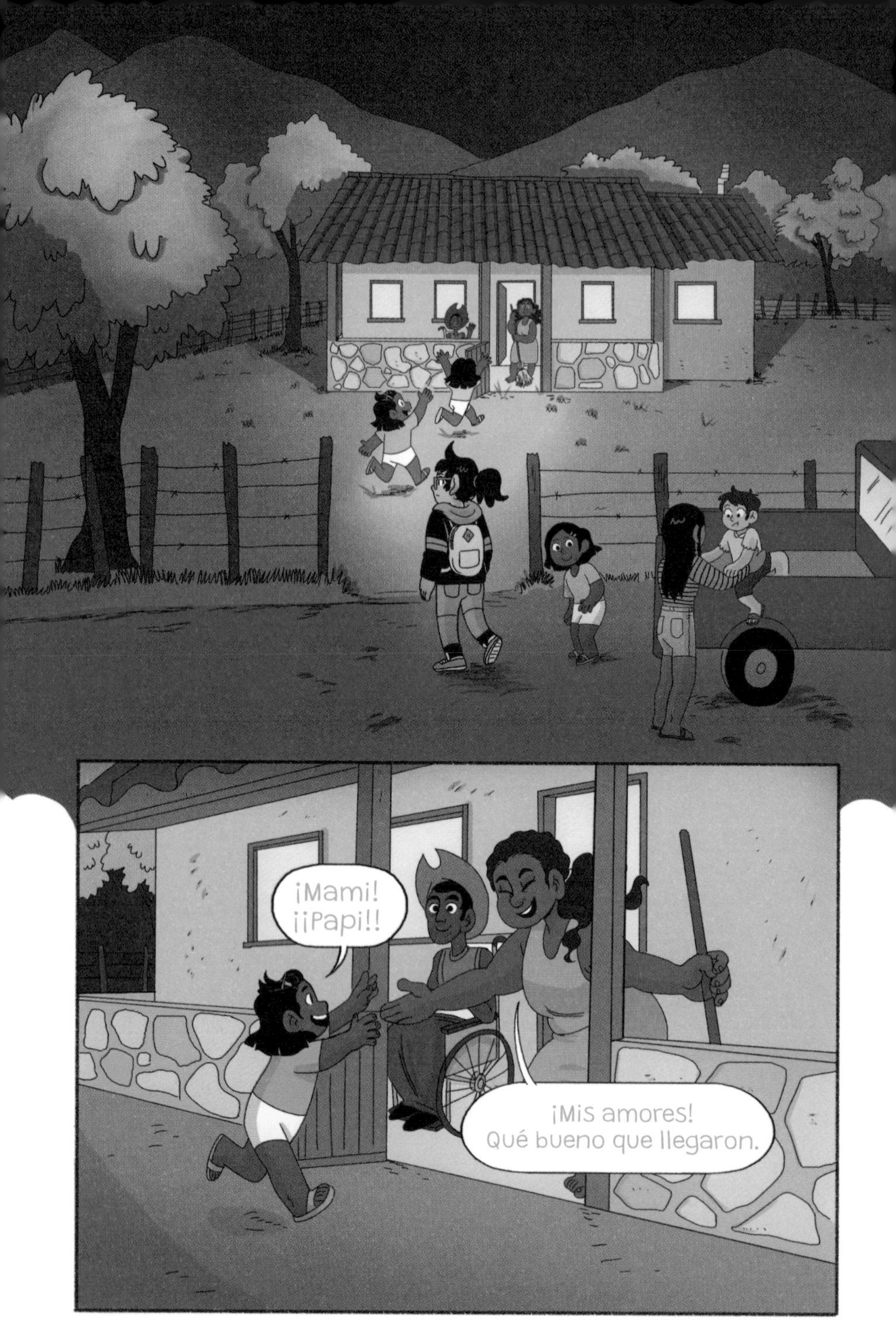
¡Mami!
¡¡Papi!!
¡Mis amores!
Qué bueno que llegaron.

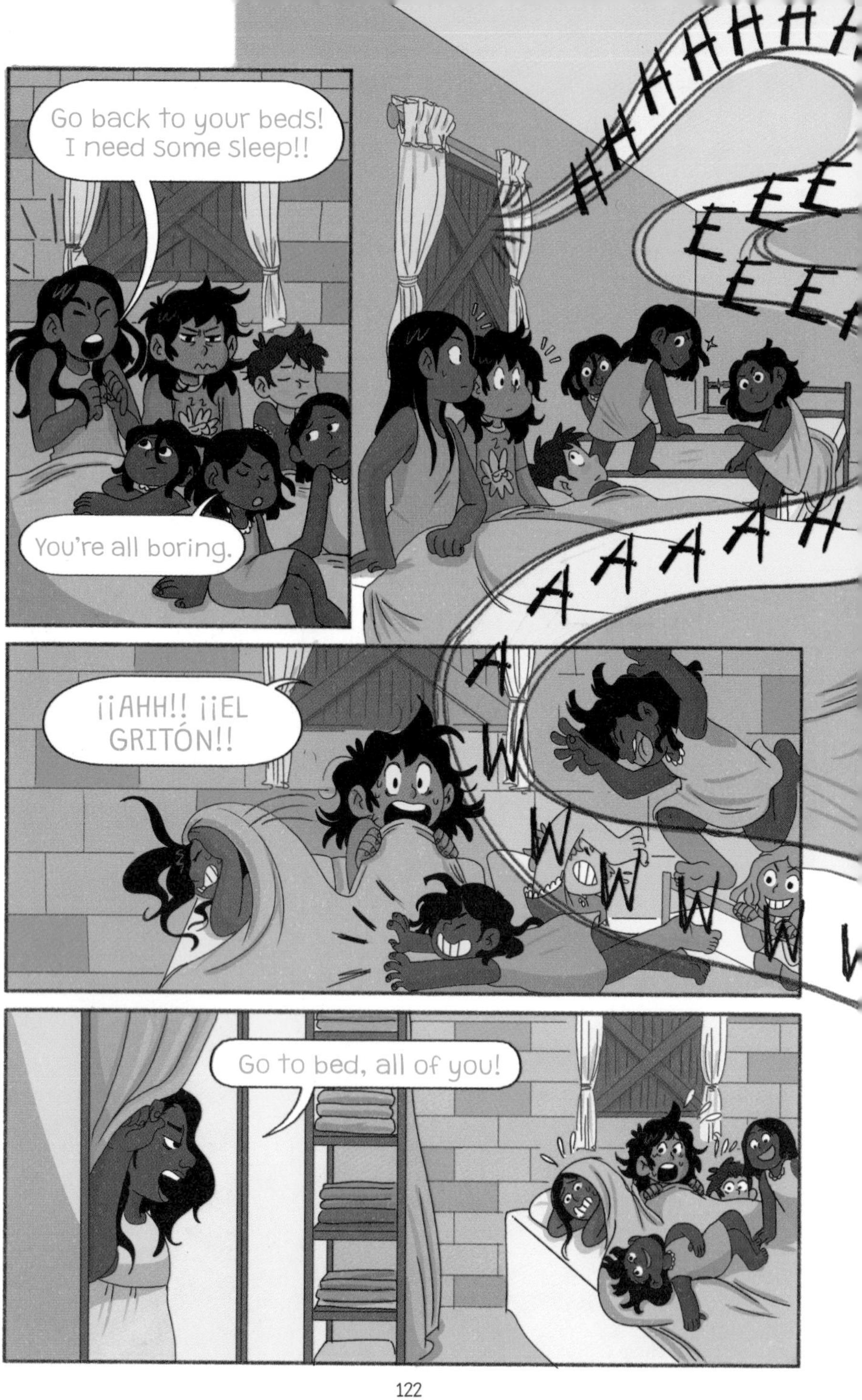
Go back to your beds! I need some sleep!!
You're all boring.
AHHHHHHHHEEEEEEEAAAAAAAAWWWWWW
¡¡AHH!! ¡¡EL GRITÓN!!
Go to bed, all of you!

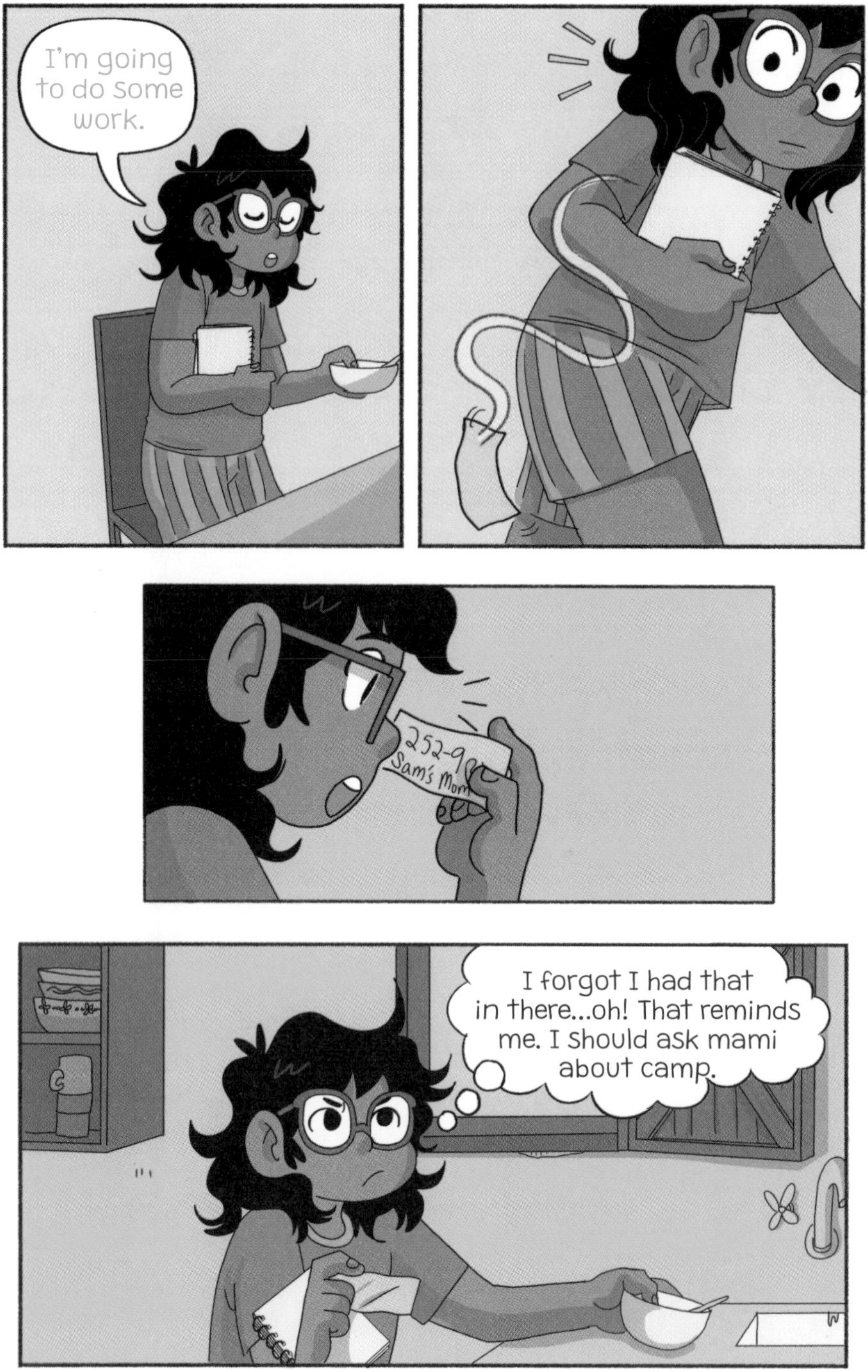
I'm going to do some work.
252-9
Sam's Mom
I forgot I had that in there...oh! That reminds me. I should ask mami about camp.

126

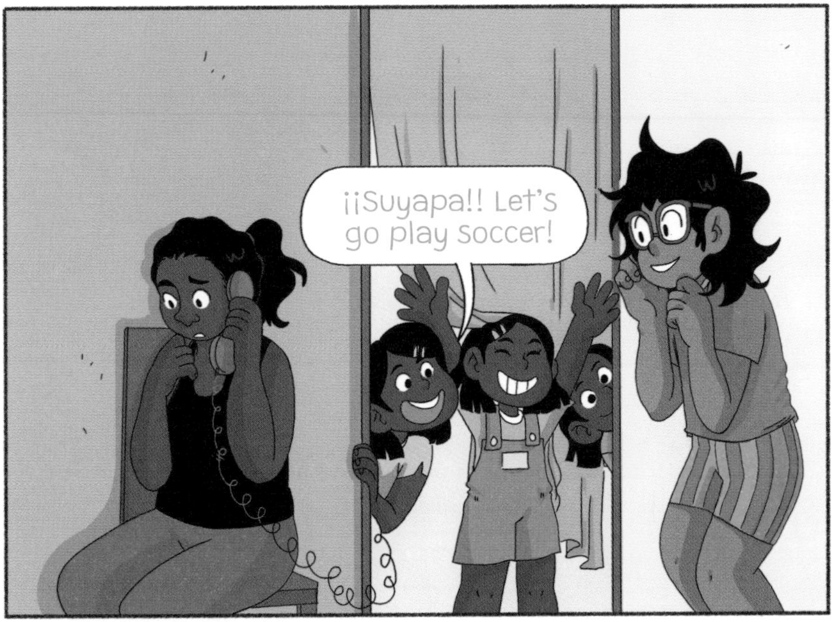

¡¡Suyapa!! Let's go play soccer!

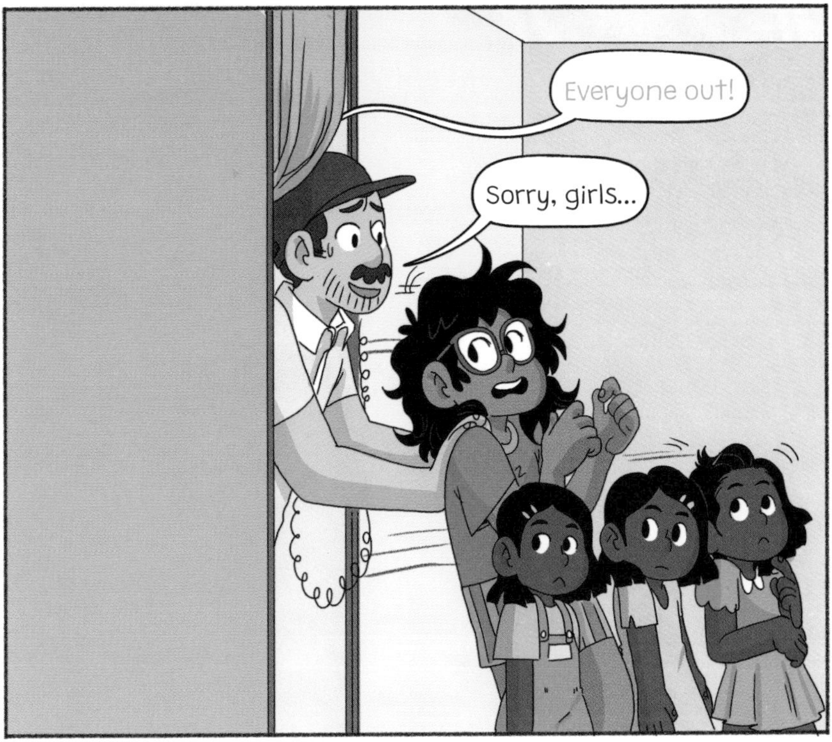

Everyone out!
Sorry, girls...

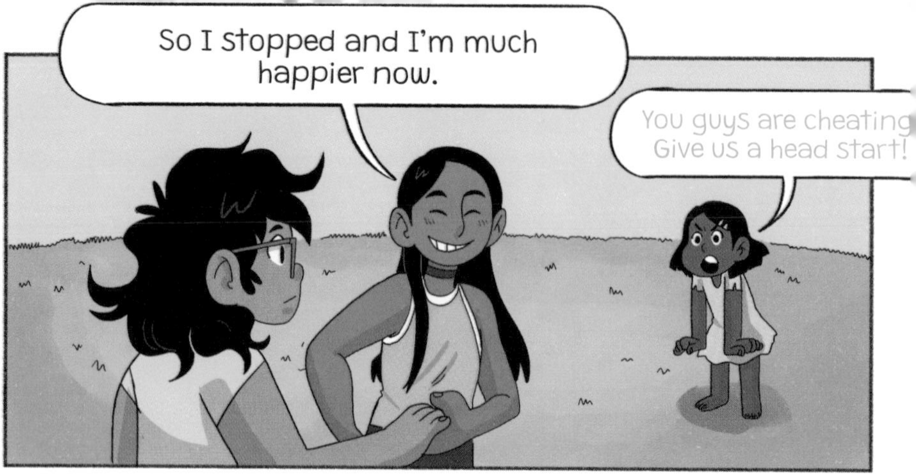
So I stopped and I'm much happier now.
You guys are cheating! Give us a head start!

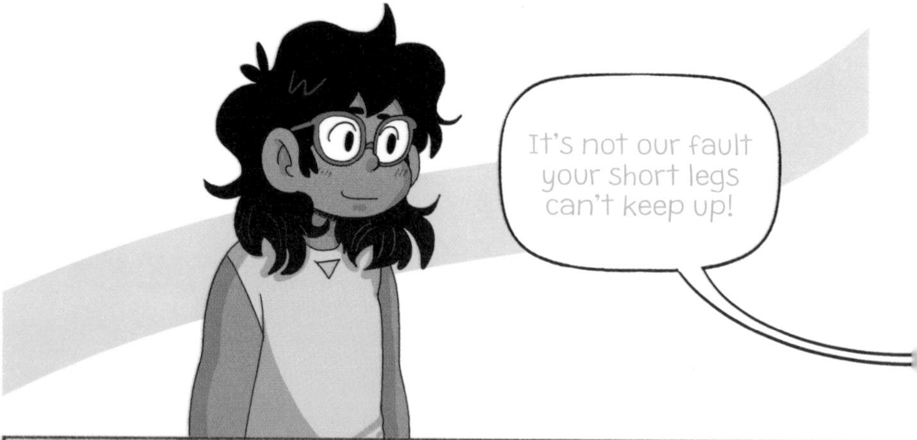
It's not our fault your short legs can't keep up!

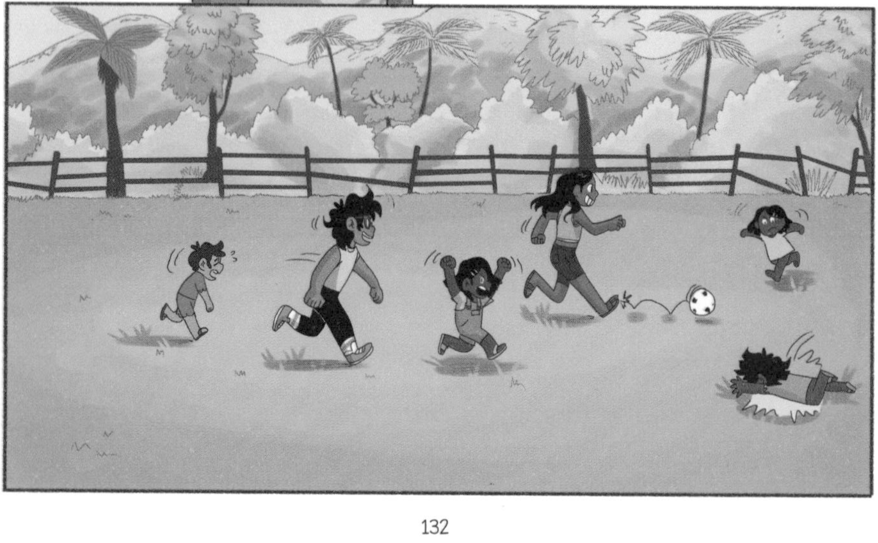

133

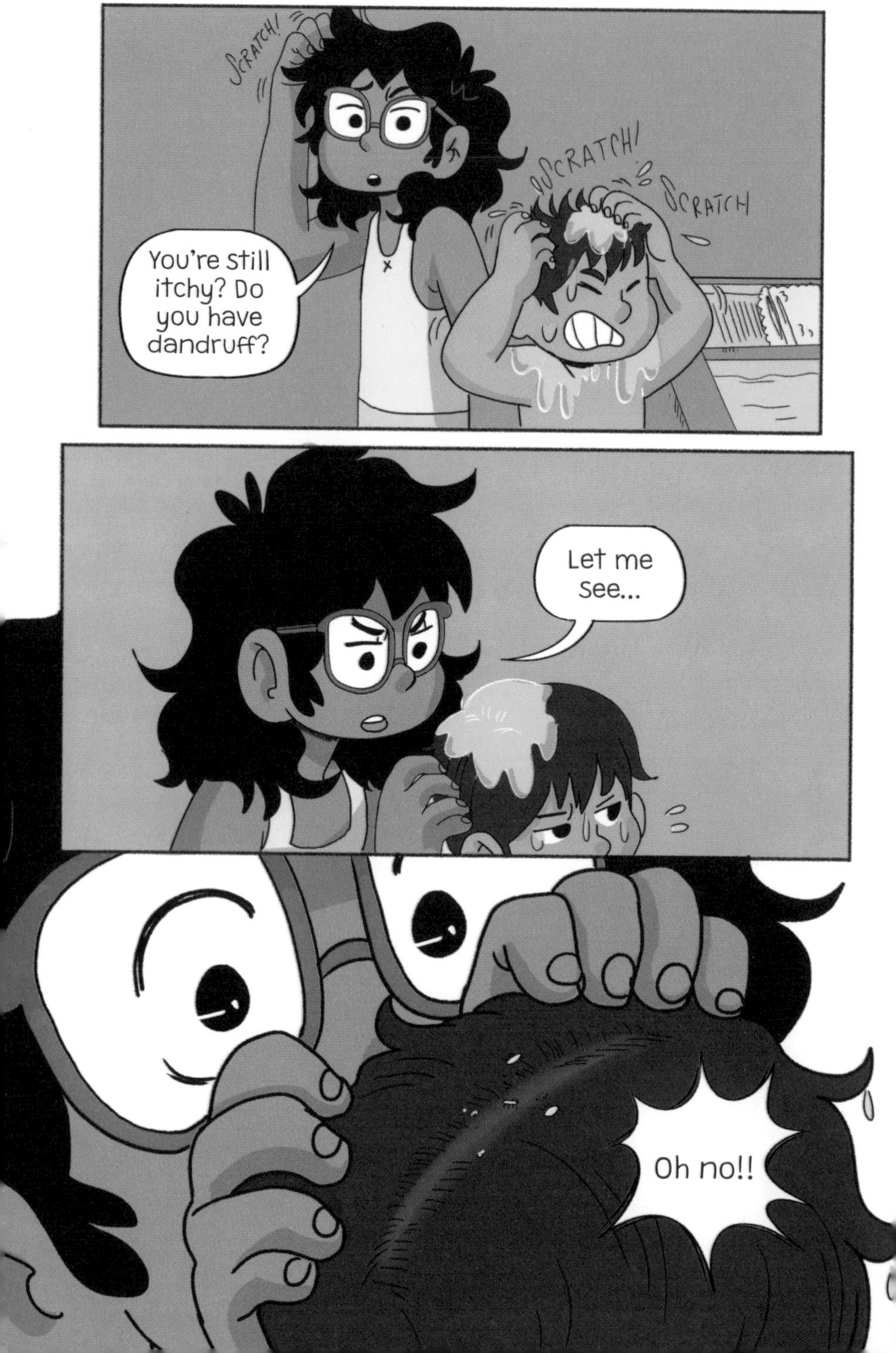

SCRATCH!
SCRATCH!
SCRATCH
You're still itchy? Do you have dandruff?
Let me see...
Oh no!!

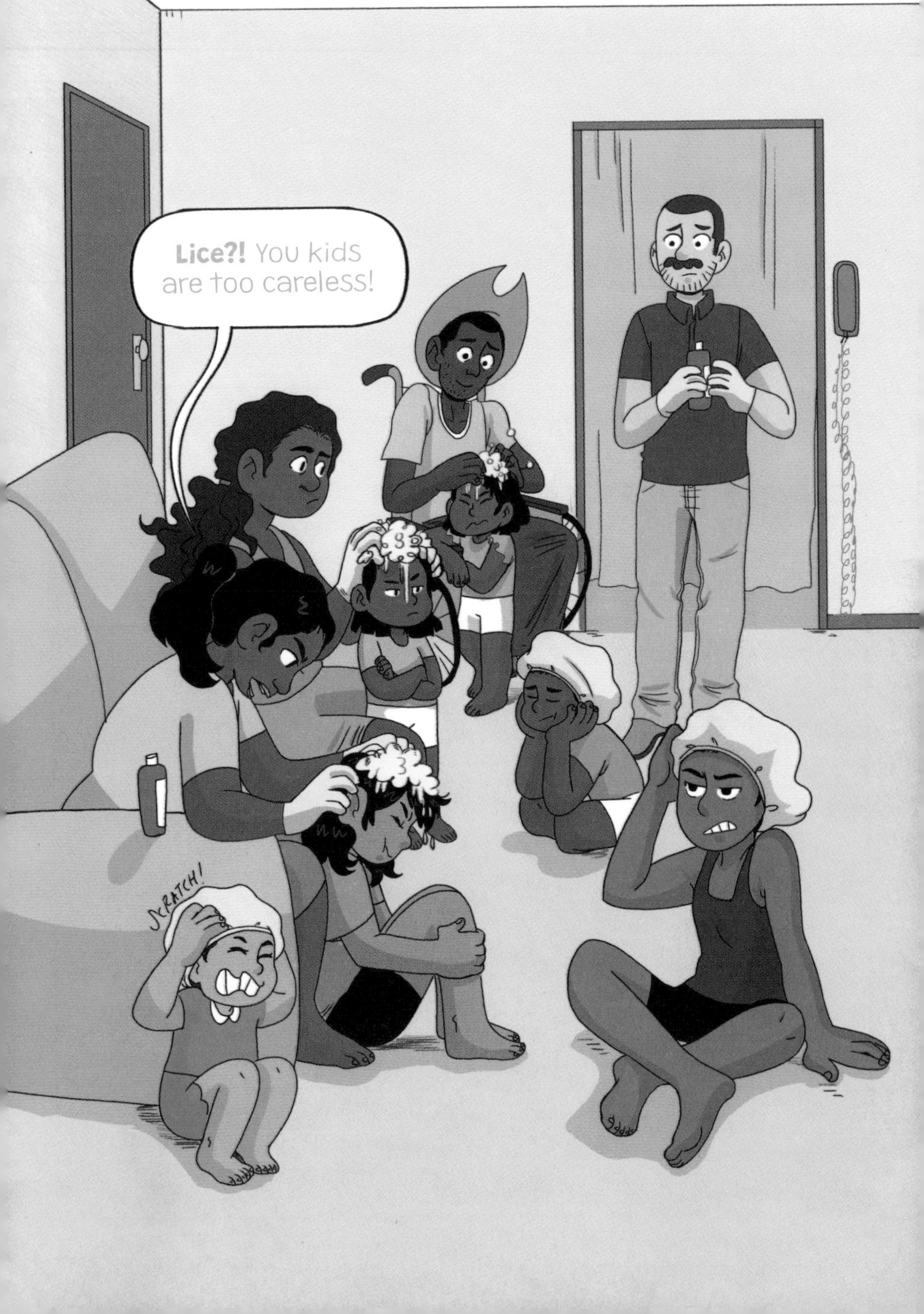

Lice?! You kids are too careless!
SCRATCH!

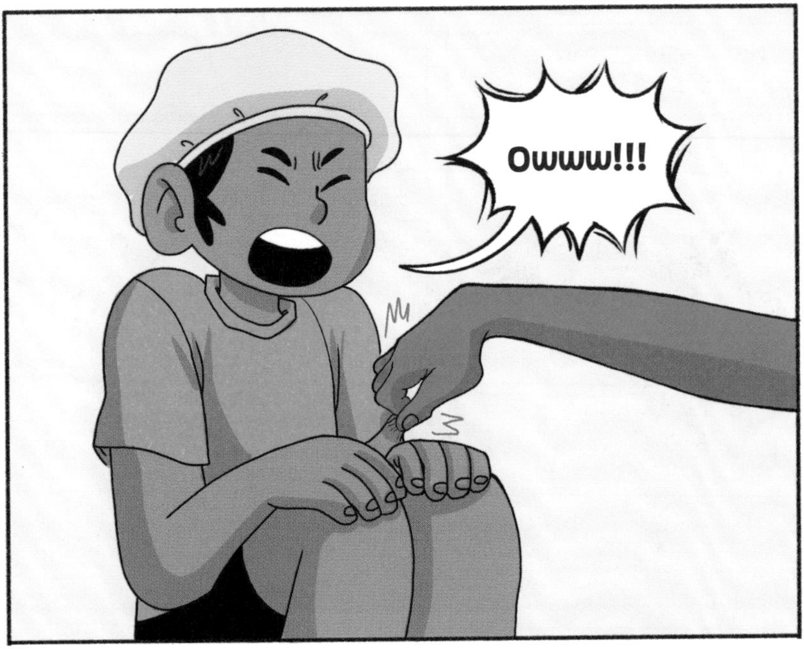
Owww!!!

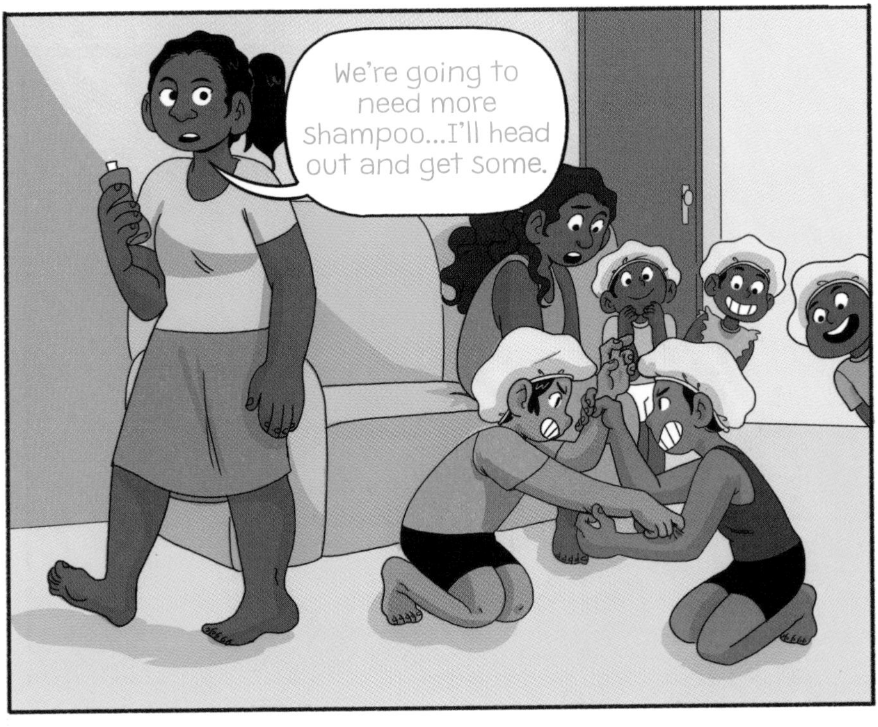
We're going to need more shampoo...I'll head out and get some.

141

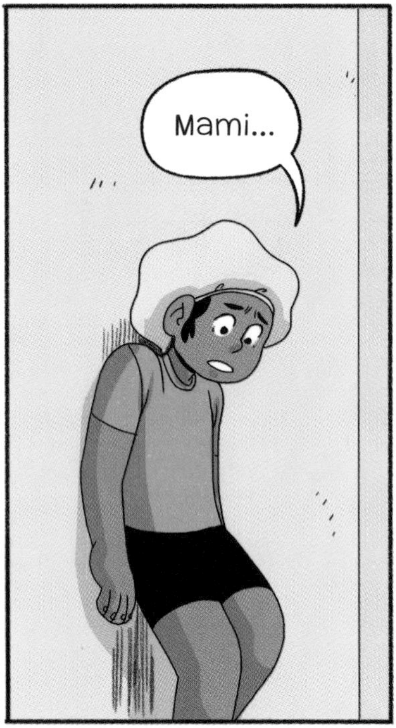
Mami...

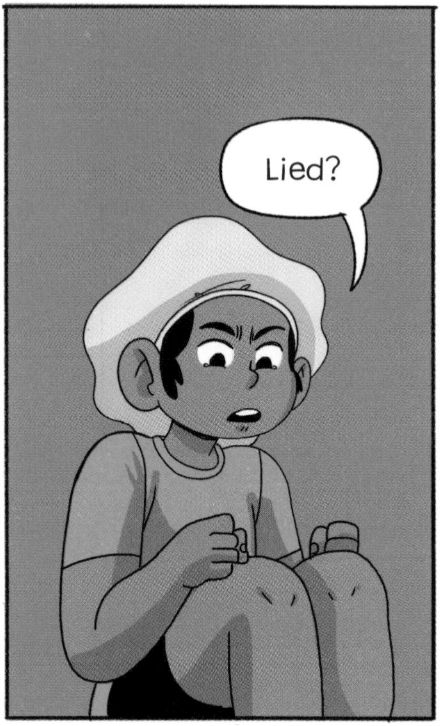
Lied?

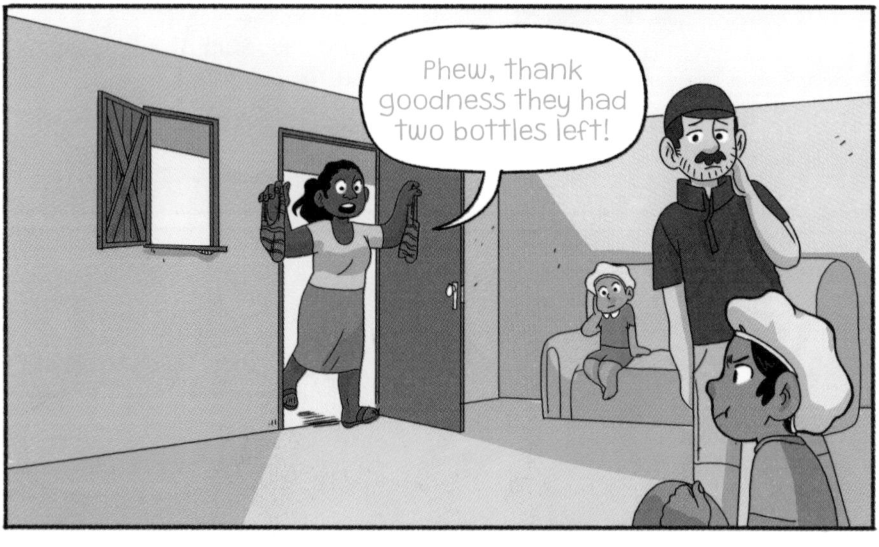
Phew, thank goodness they had two bottles left!

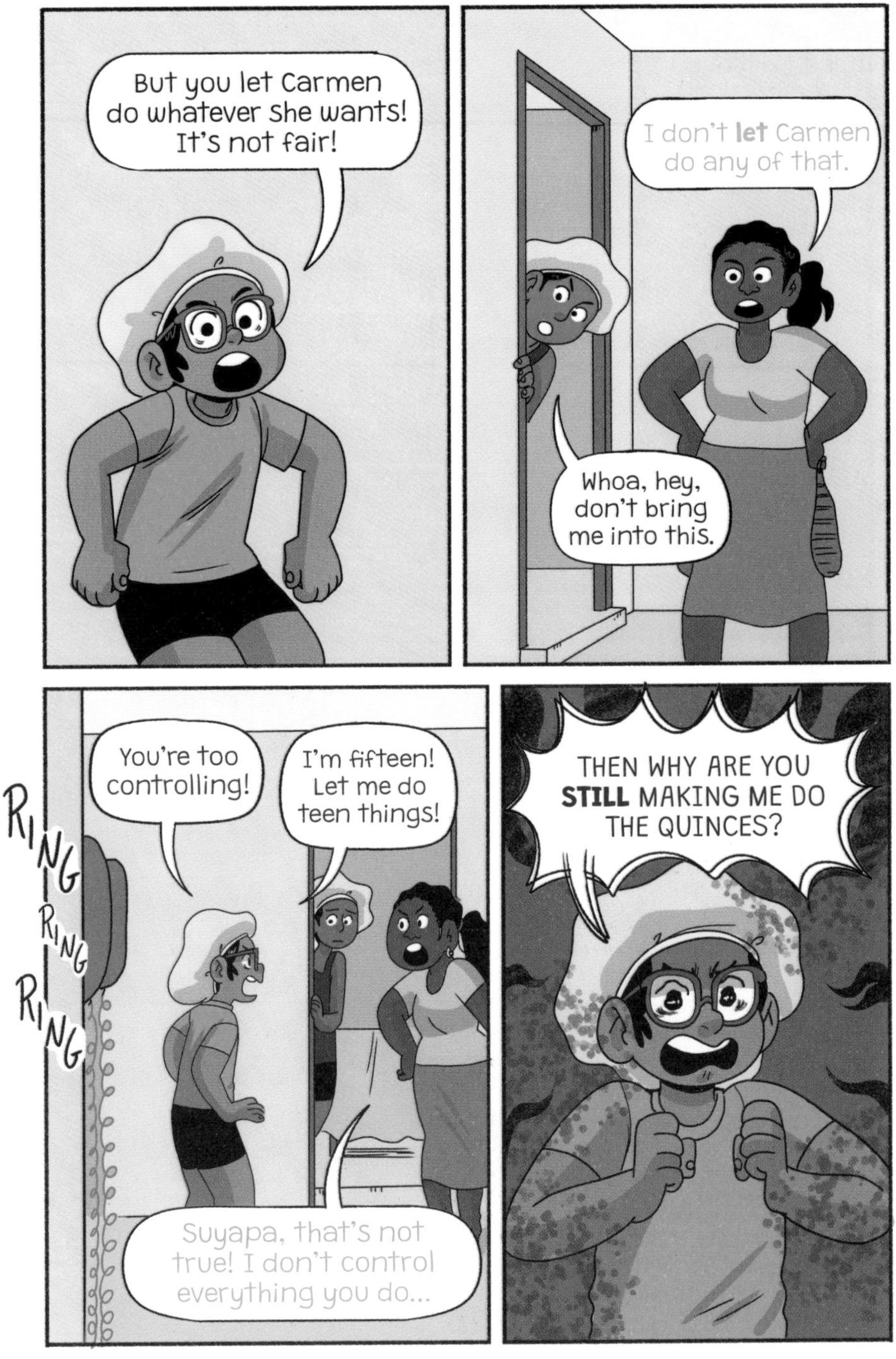
But you let Carmen do whatever she wants! It's not fair!
I don't **let** Carmen do any of that.
Whoa, hey, don't bring me into this.
You're too controlling!
I'm fifteen! Let me do teen things!
RING RING RING
Suyapa, that's not true! I don't control everything you do...
THEN WHY ARE YOU **STILL** MAKING ME DO THE QUINCES?

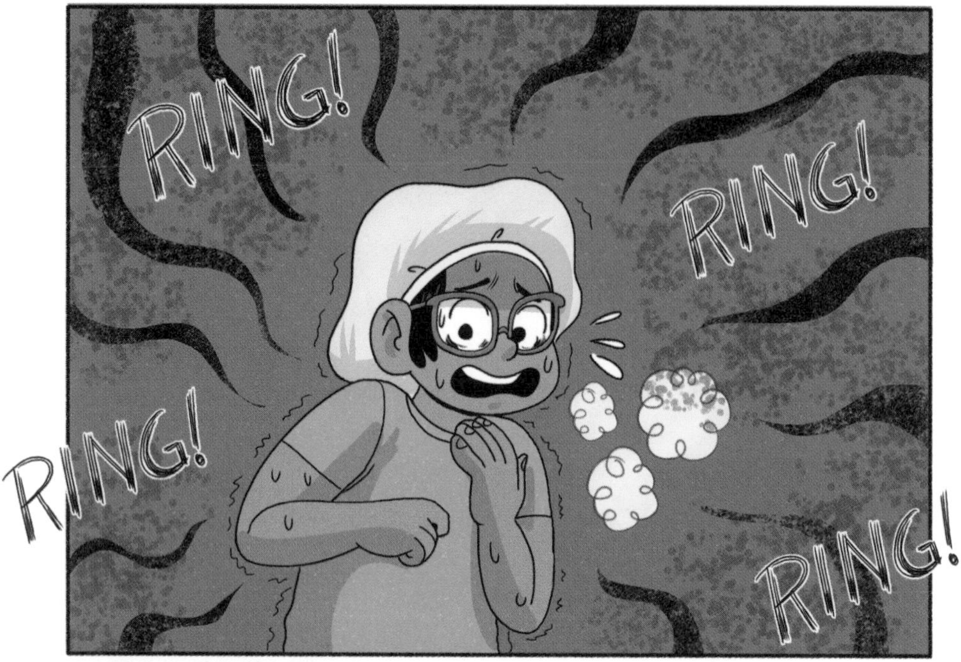
RING!
RING!
RING!
RING!

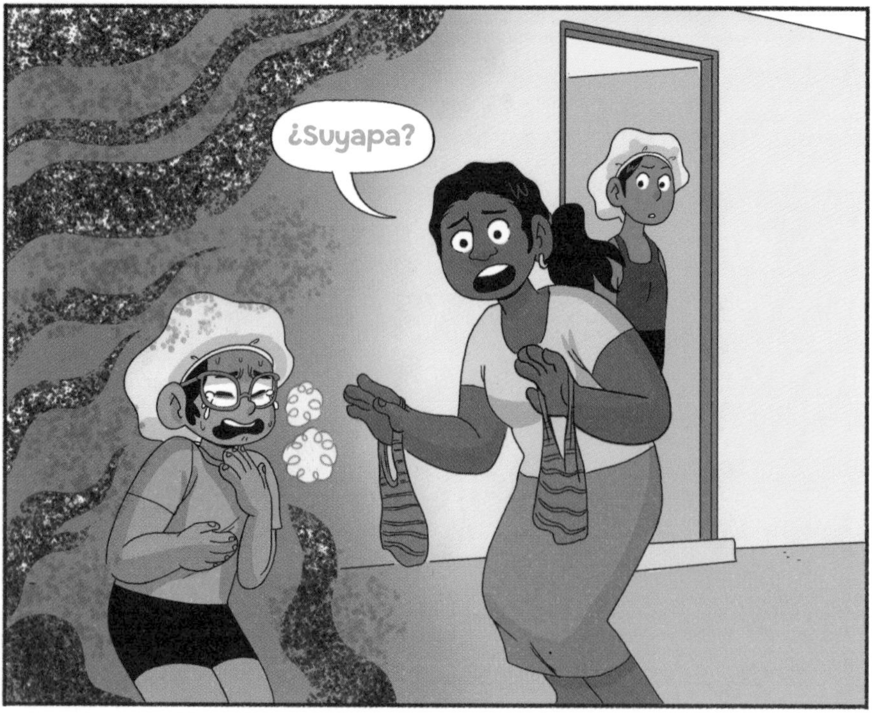
¿Suyapa?

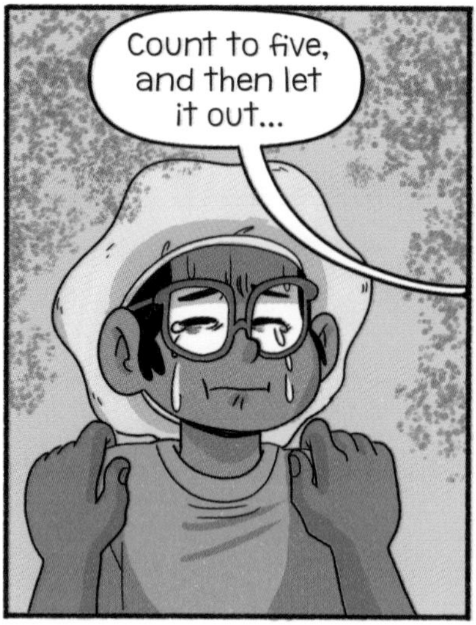
Count to five, and then let it out...

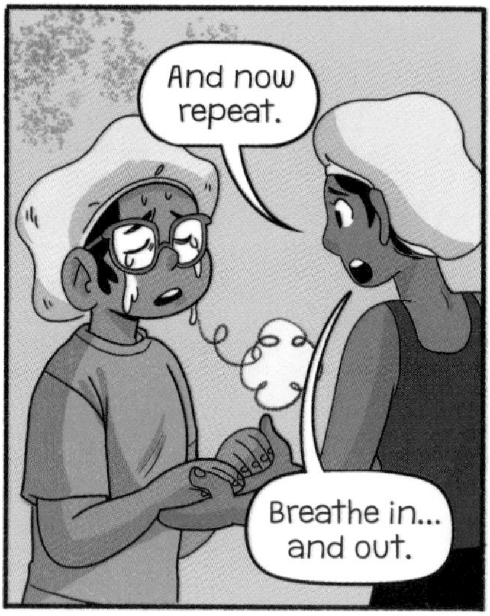
And now repeat.
Breathe in... and out.

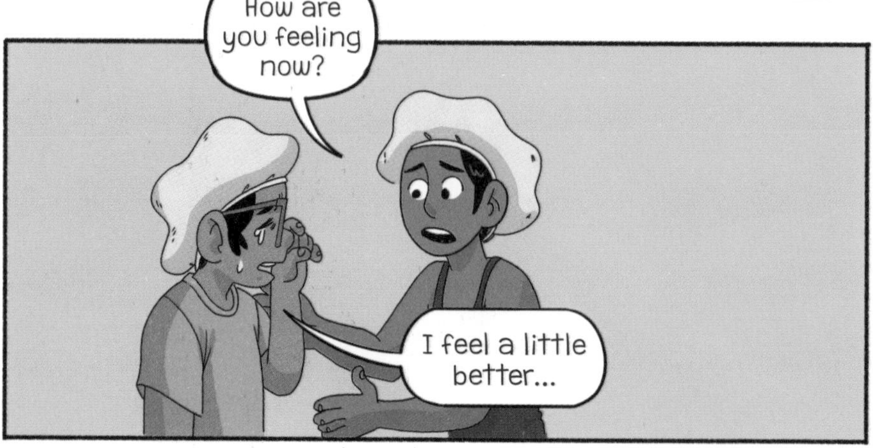
How are you feeling now?
I feel a little better...

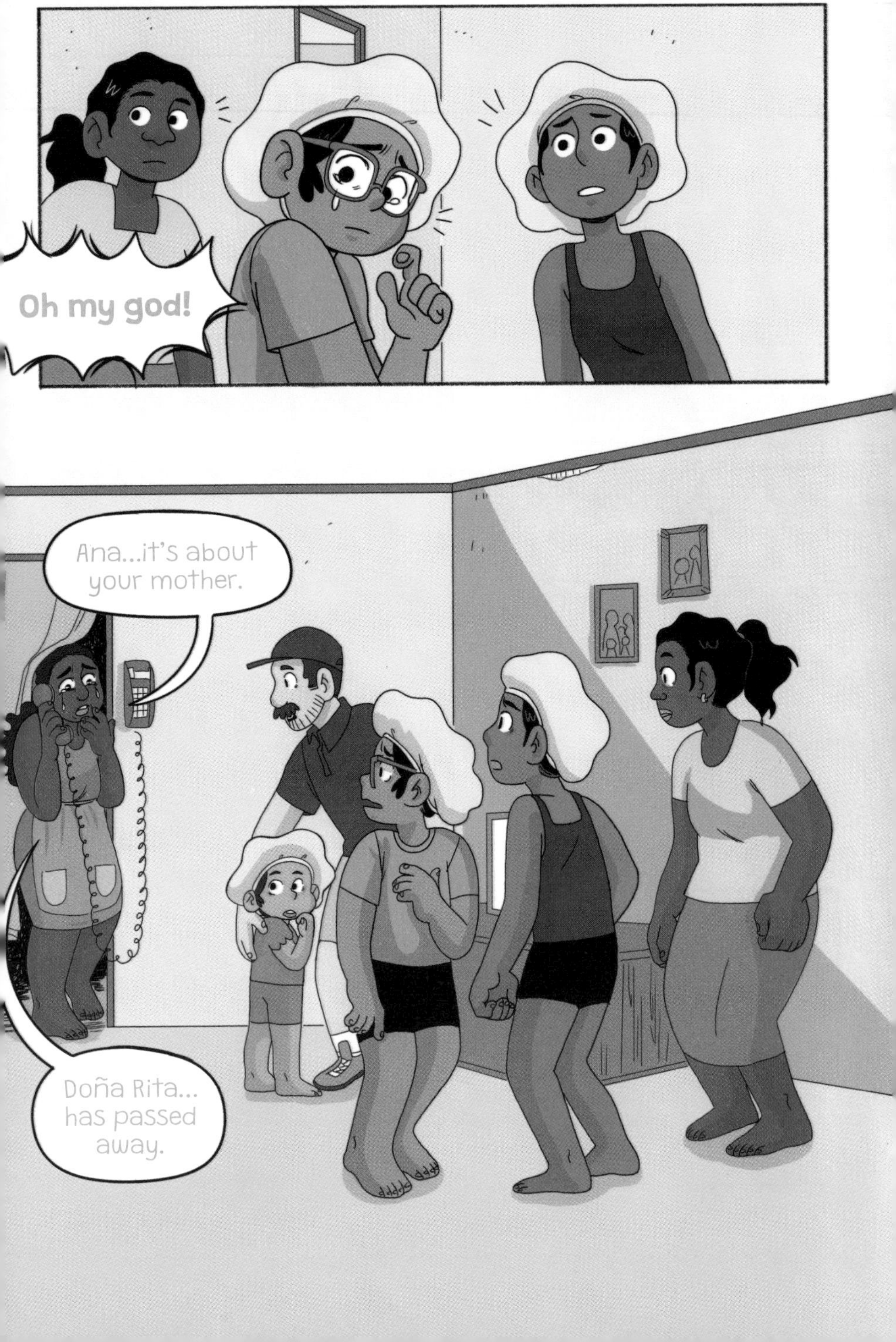
Oh my god!
Ana...it's about your mother.
Doña Rita... has passed away.

CHAPTER SIX

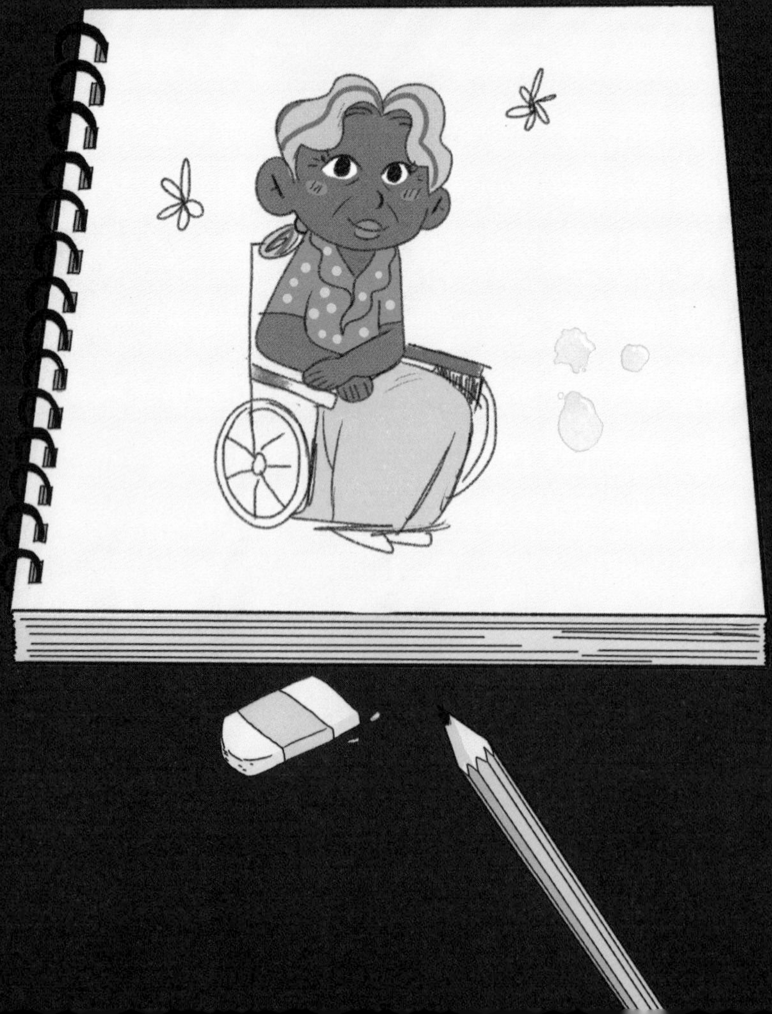

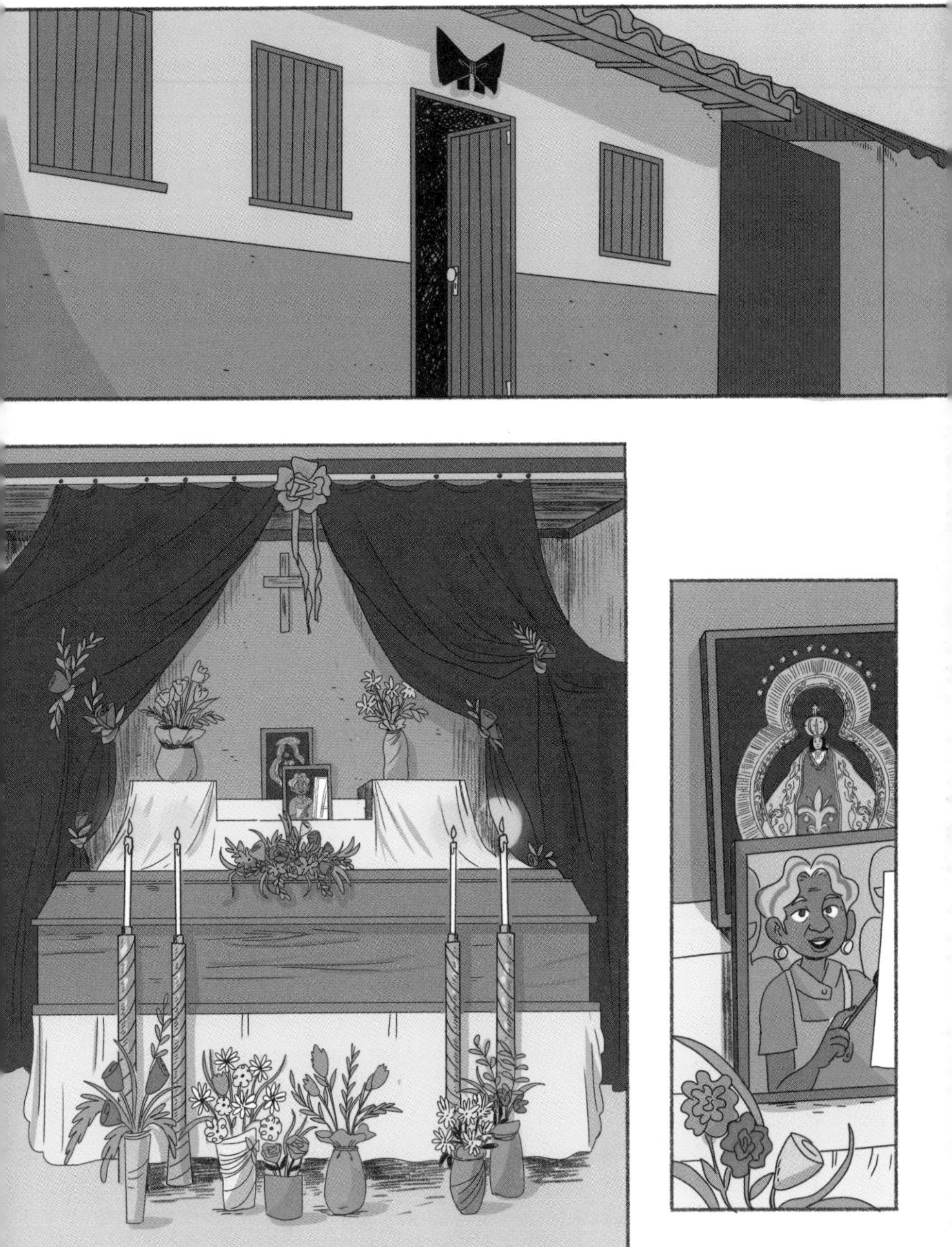

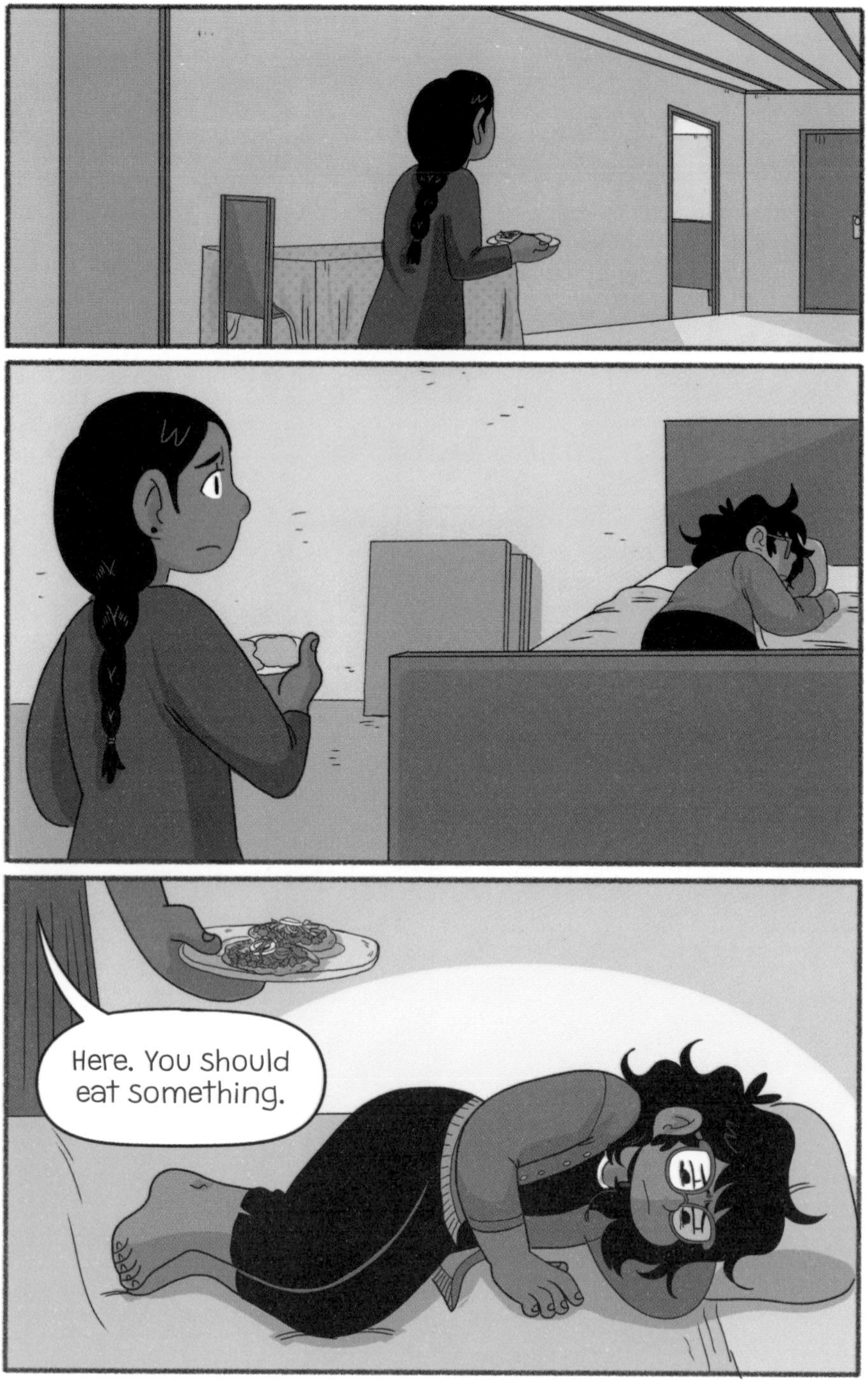
Here. You should eat something.

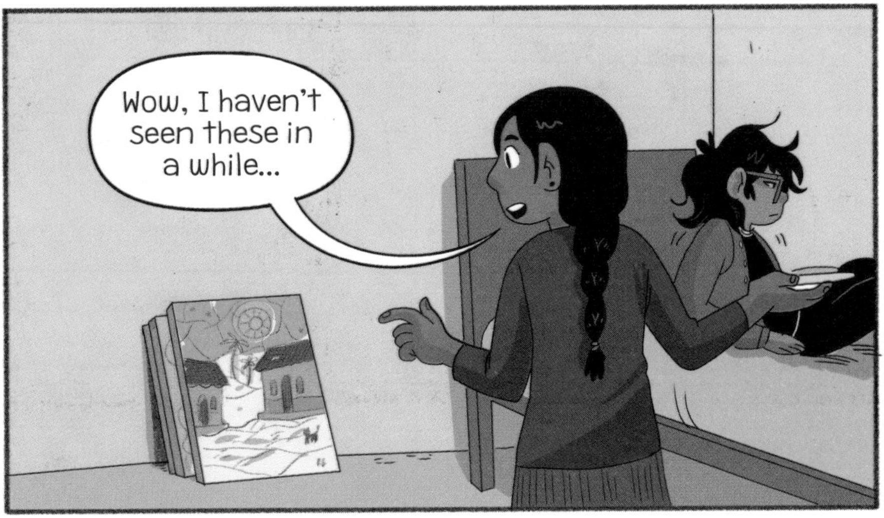
Wow, I haven't seen these in a while...

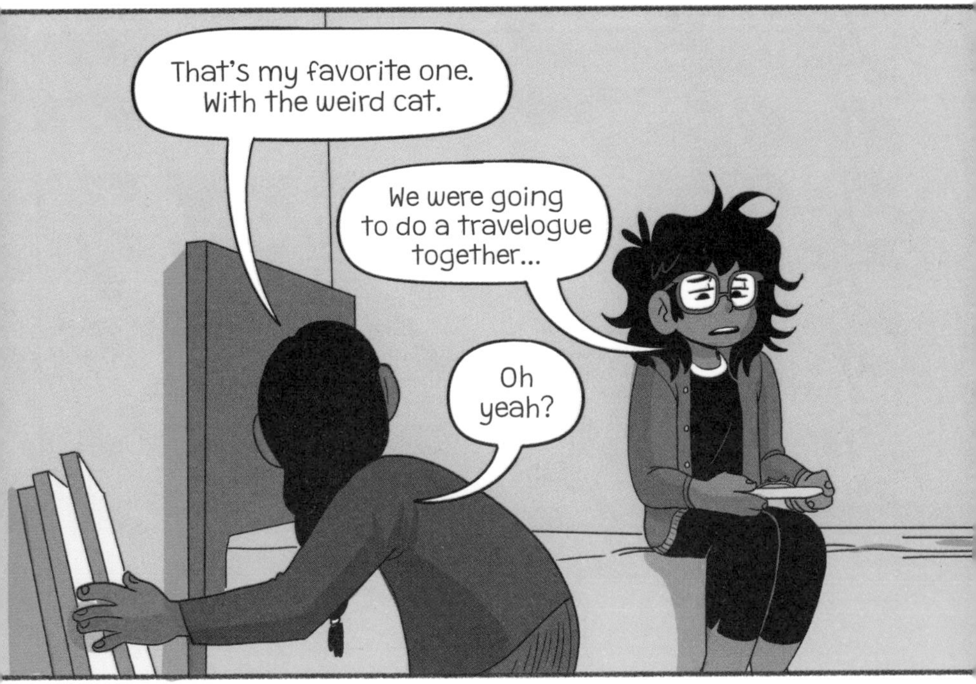
That's my favorite one. With the weird cat.
We were going to do a travelogue together...
Oh yeah?

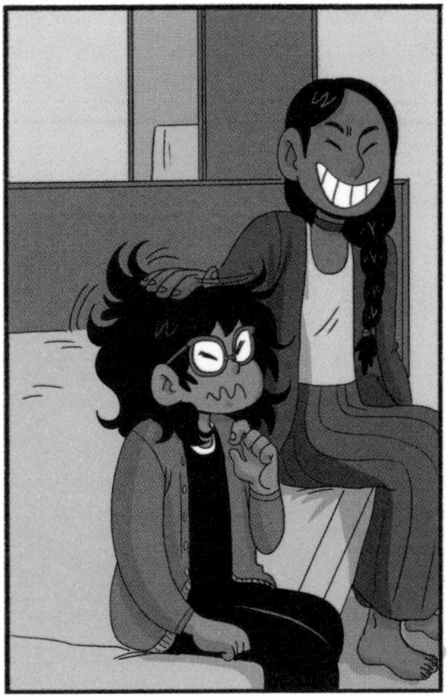

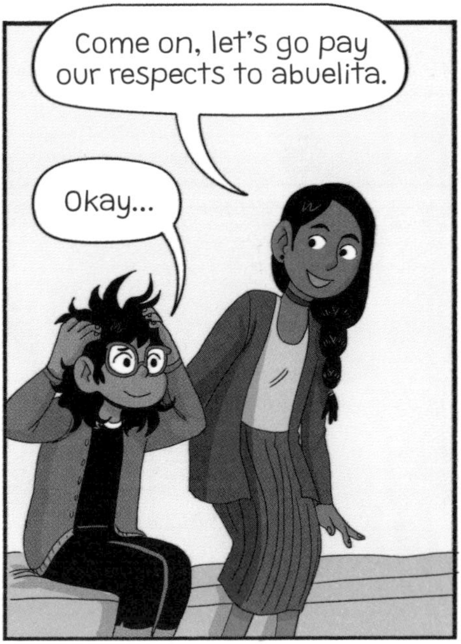
Come on, let's go pay our respects to abuelita.
Okay...

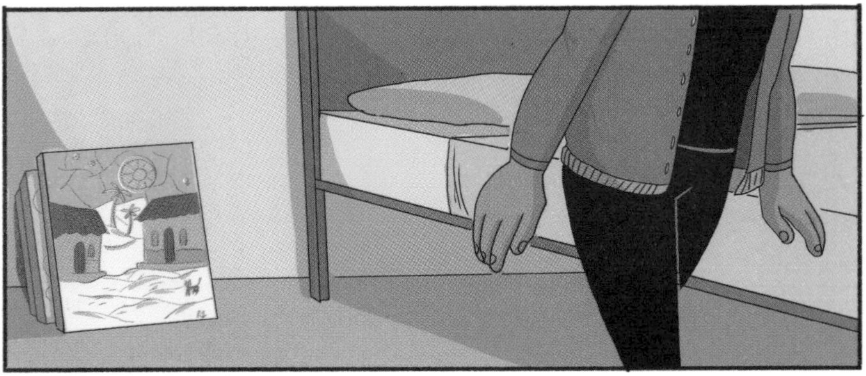

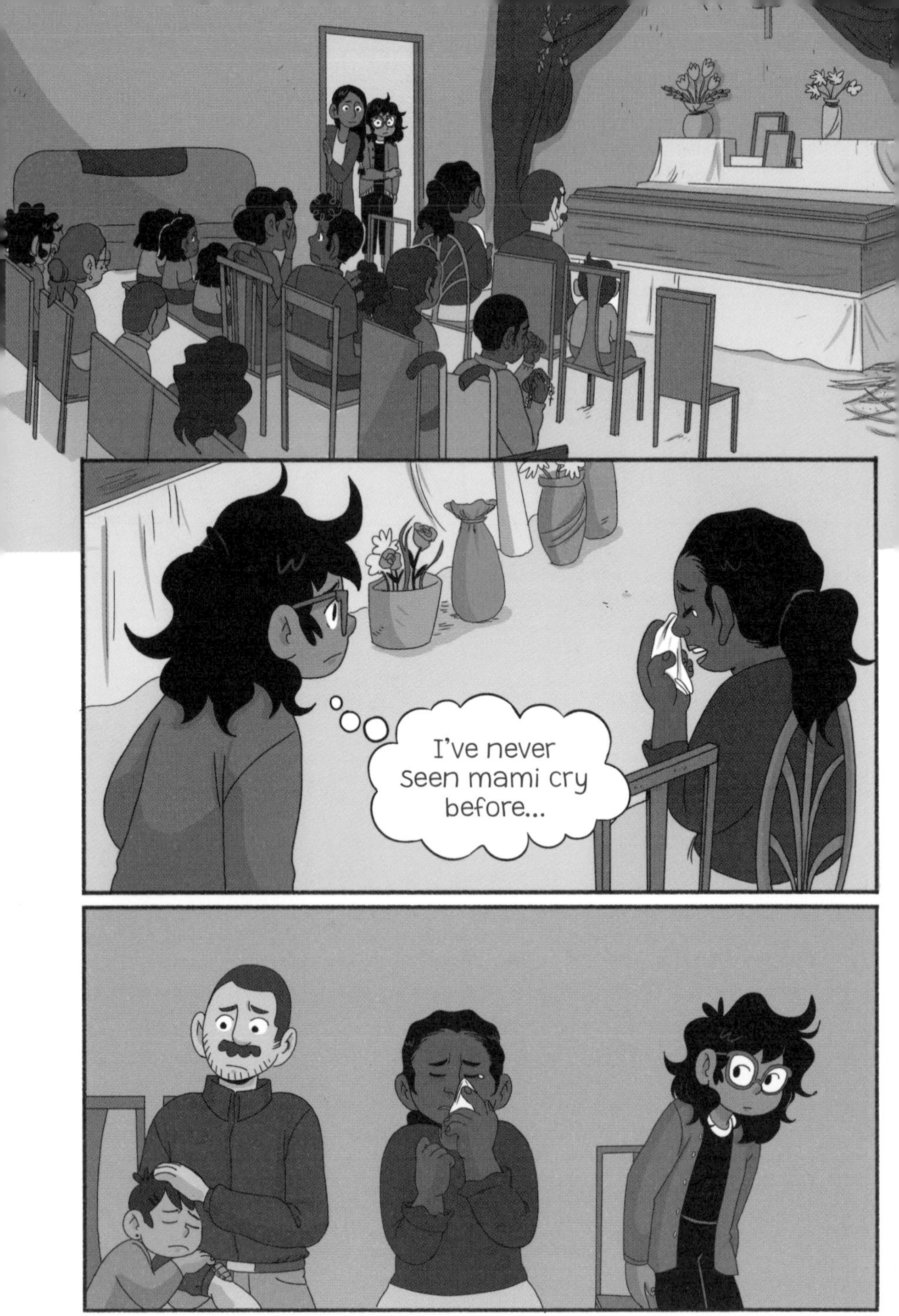
I've never seen mami cry before...

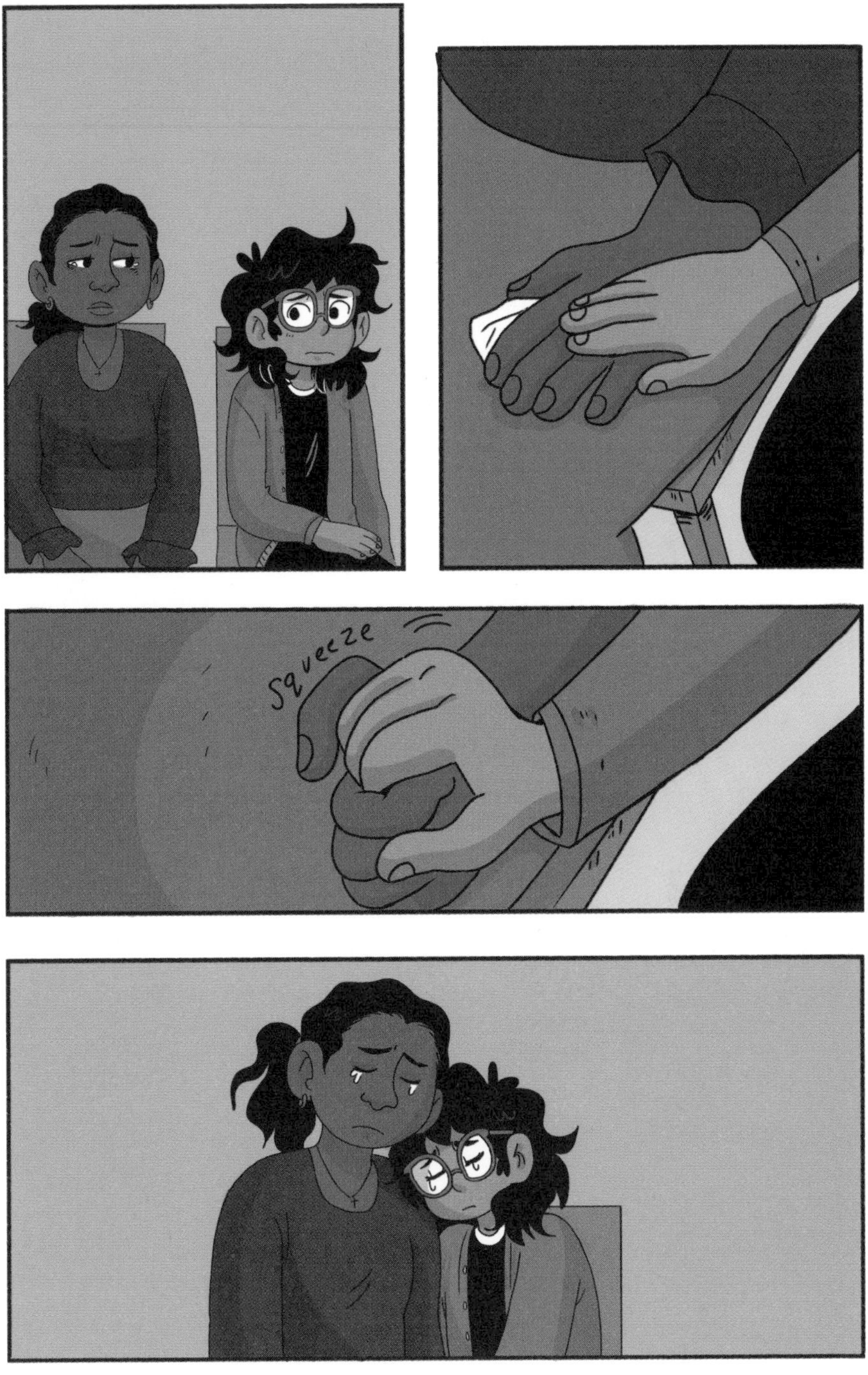
squeeze

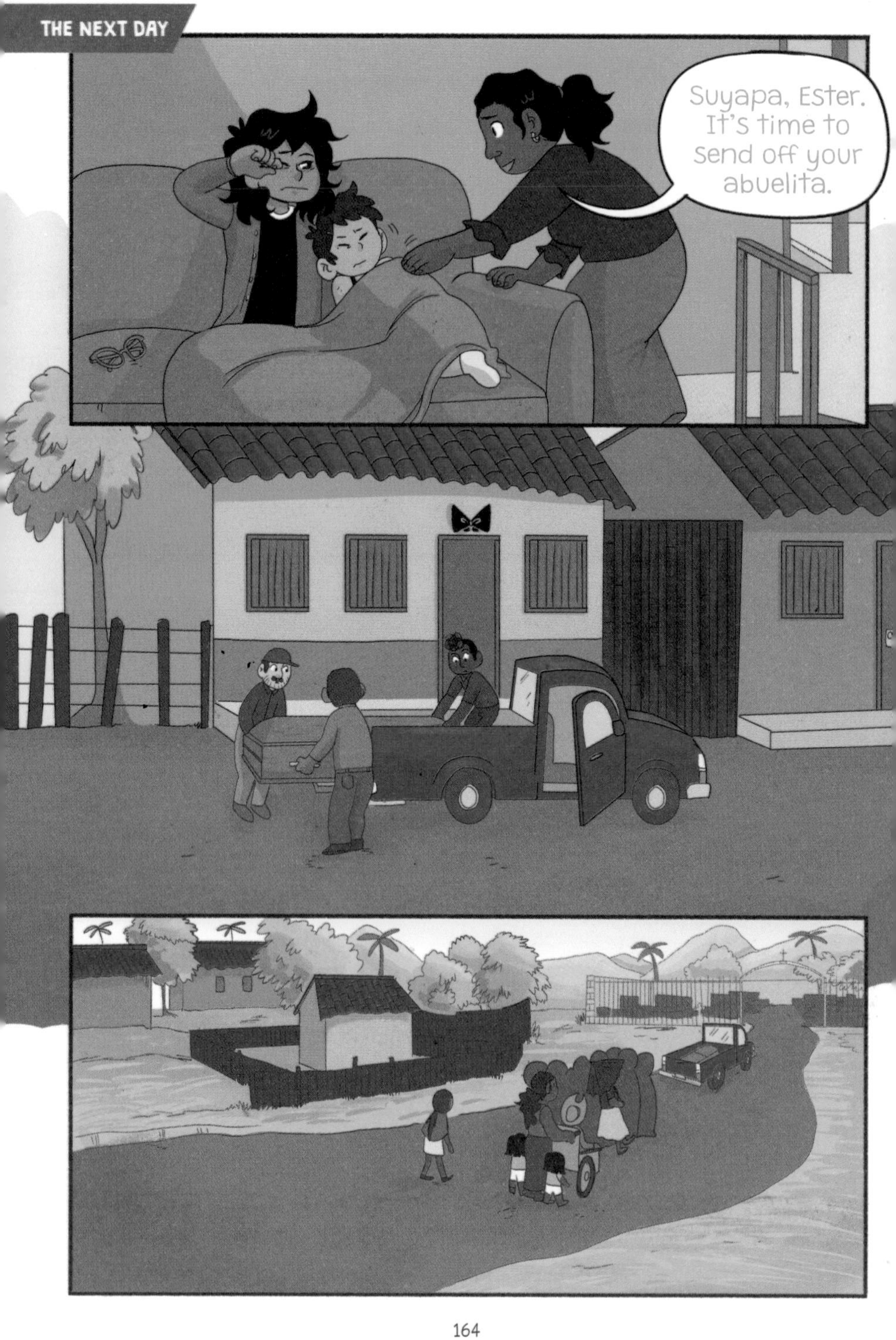
THE NEXT DAY
Suyapa, Ester. It's time to send off your abuelita.

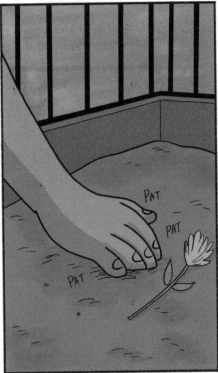

PAT
PAT
PAT

CHAPTER SEVEN

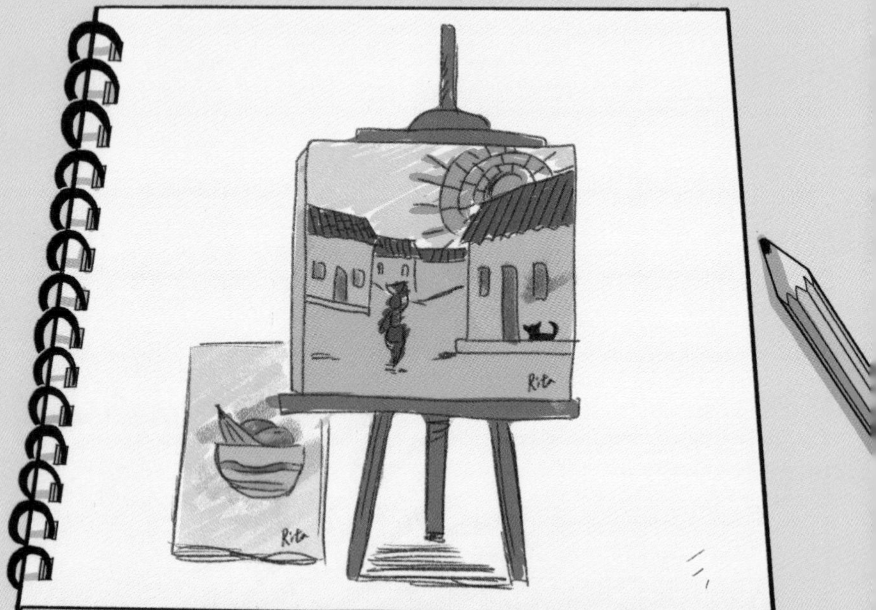

Rita
Rita

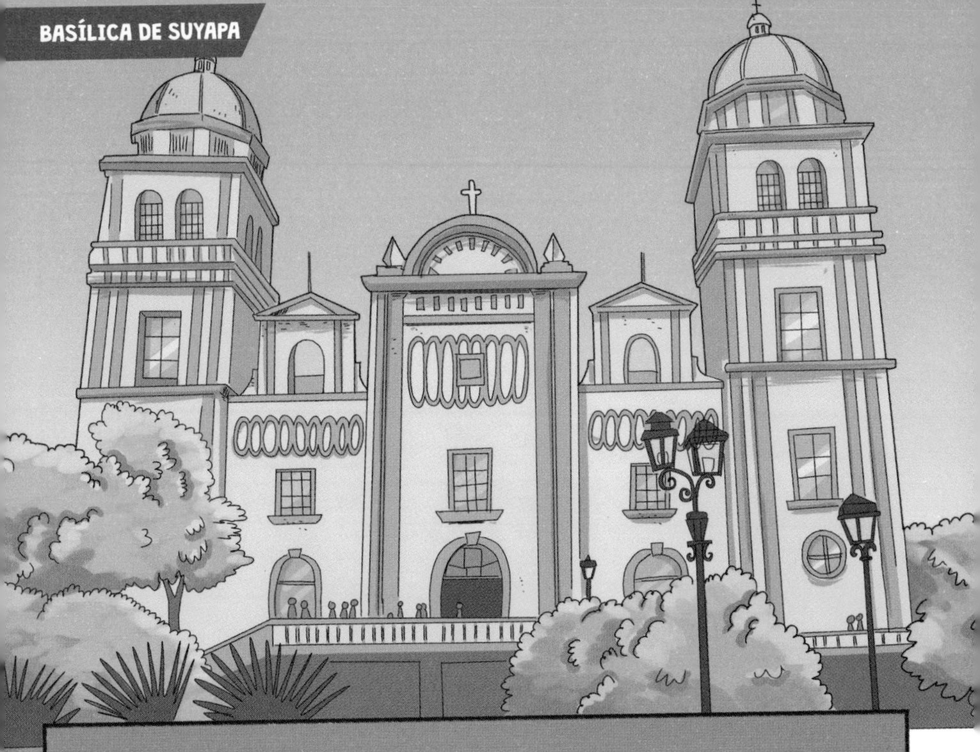
BASÍLICA DE SUYAPA

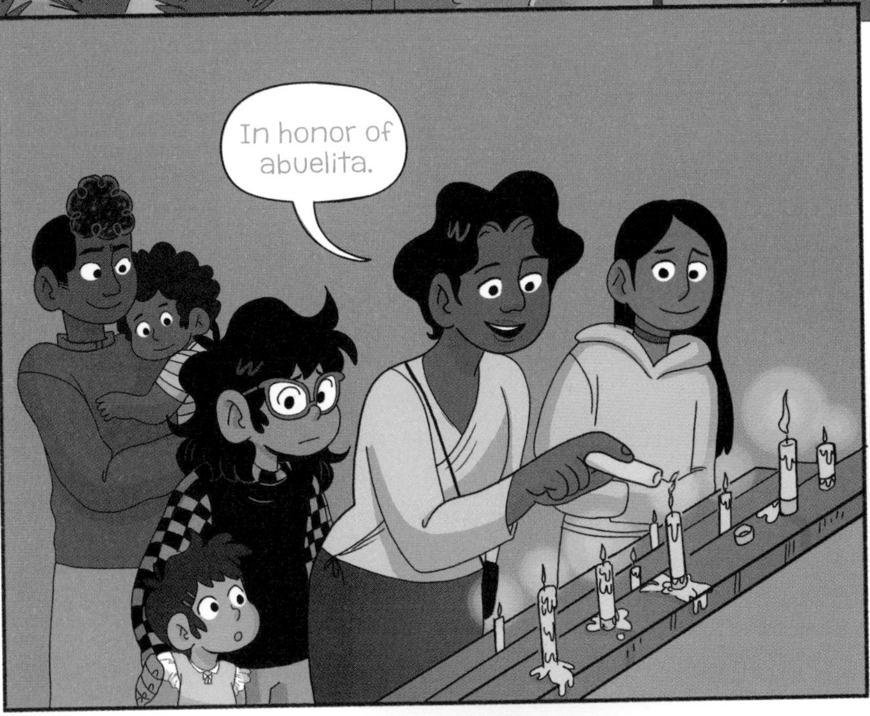
In honor of abuelita.

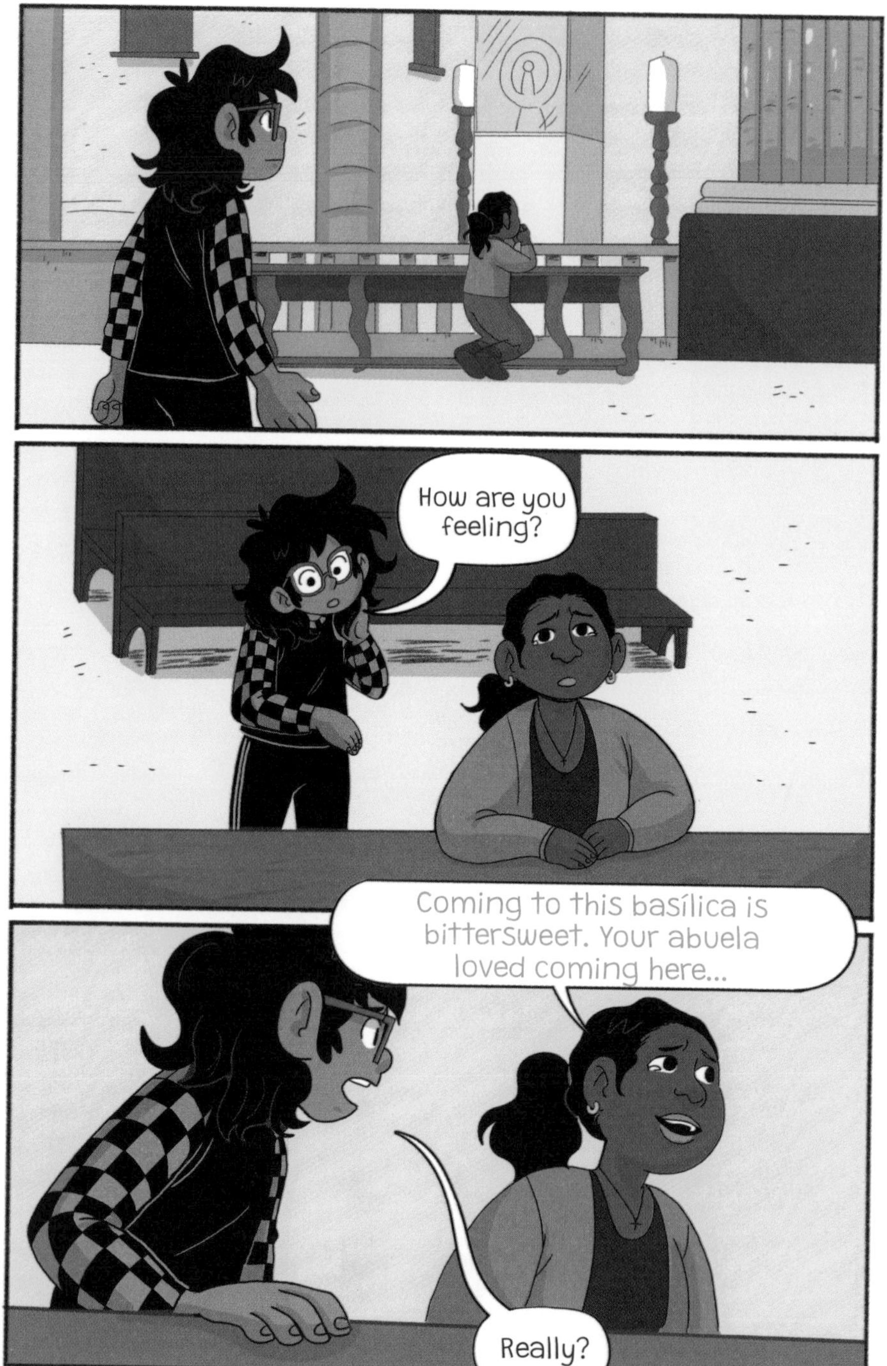
How are you feeling?
Coming to this basílica is bittersweet. Your abuela loved coming here...
Really?

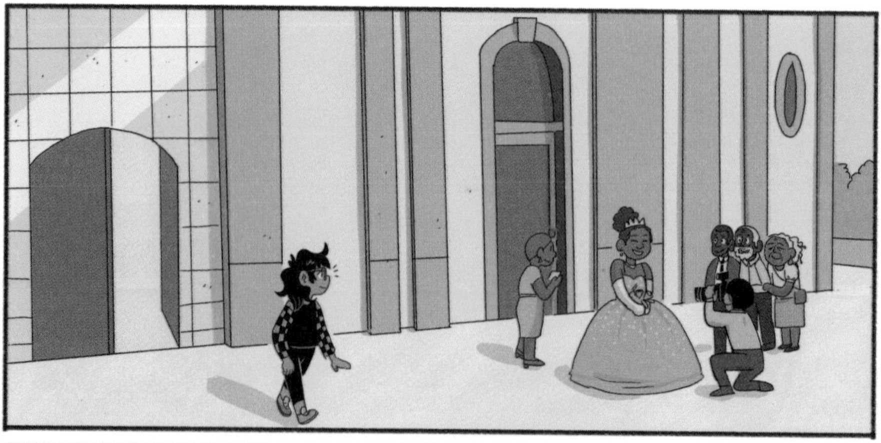

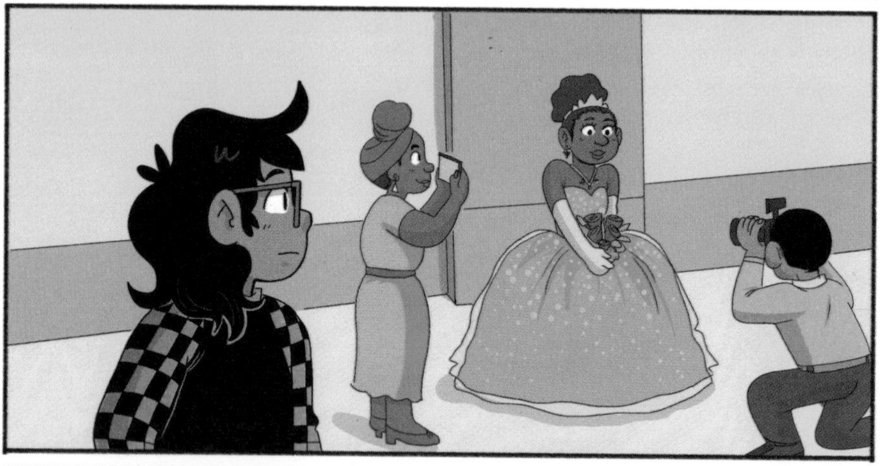

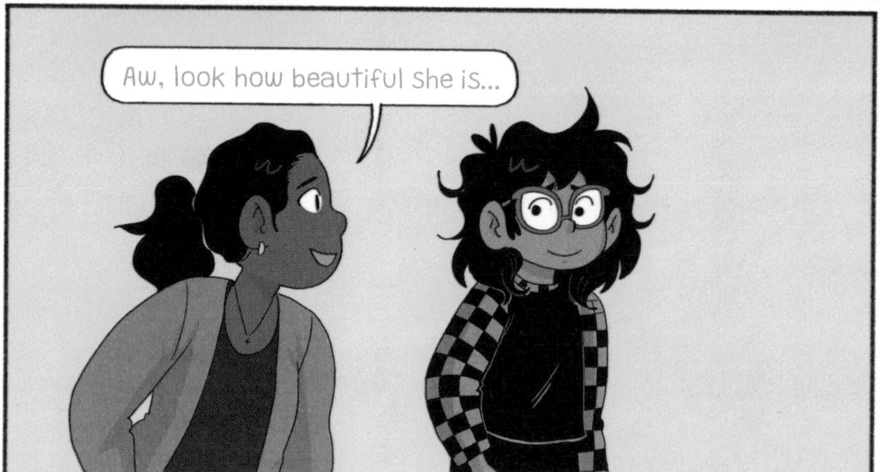
Aw, look how beautiful she is...

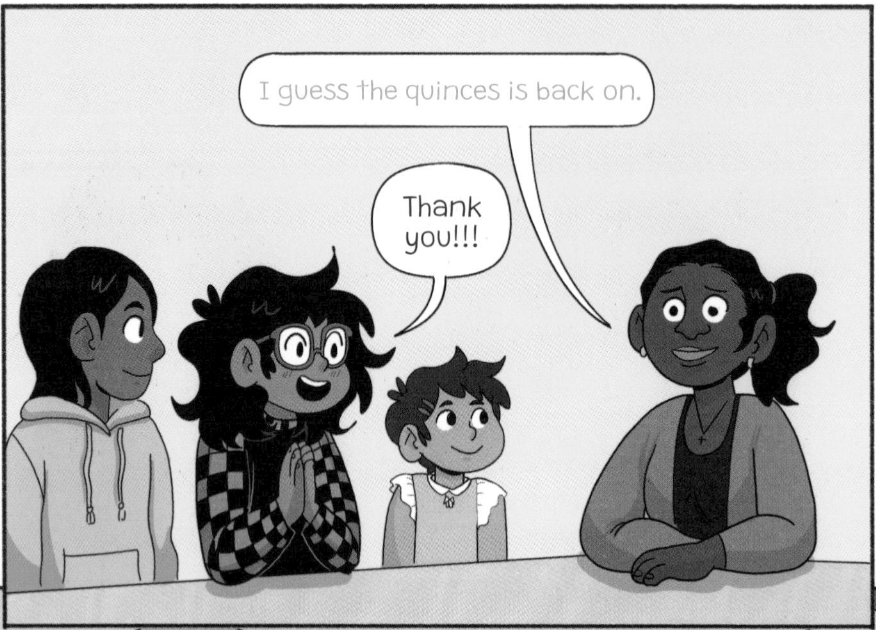
I guess the quinces is back on.
Thank you!!!

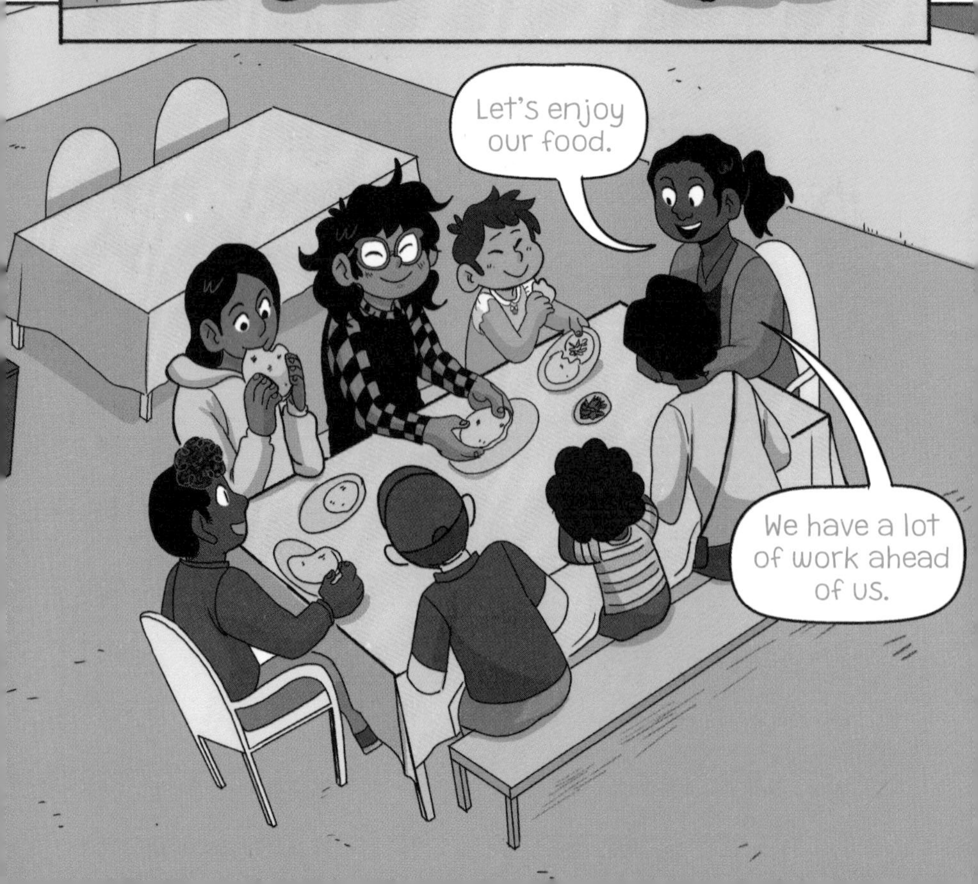
Let's enjoy our food.
We have a lot of work ahead of us.

CHAPTER EIGHT

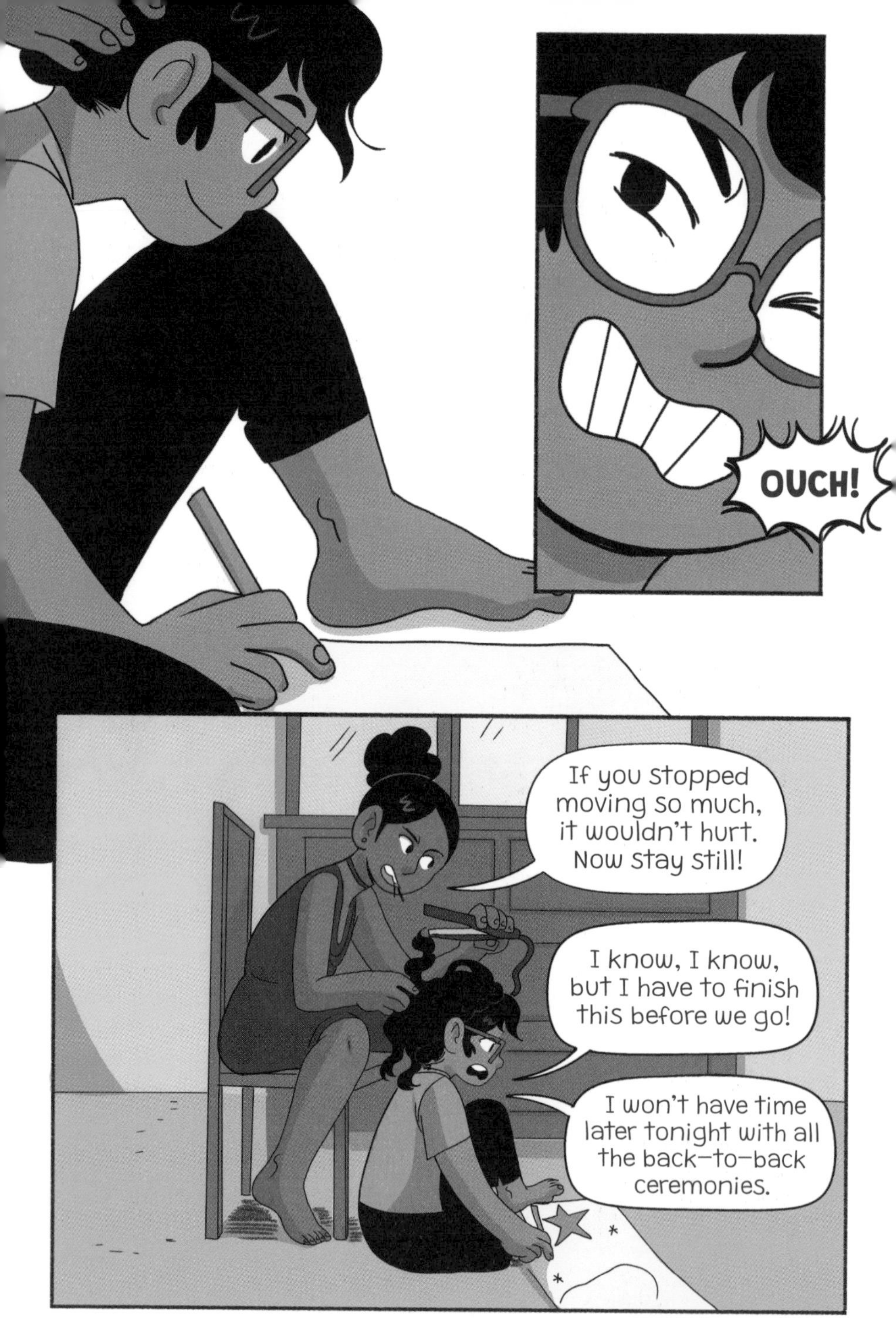
OUCH!
If you stopped moving so much, it wouldn't hurt. Now stay still!
I know, I know, but I have to finish this before we go!
I won't have time later tonight with all the back-to-back ceremonies.

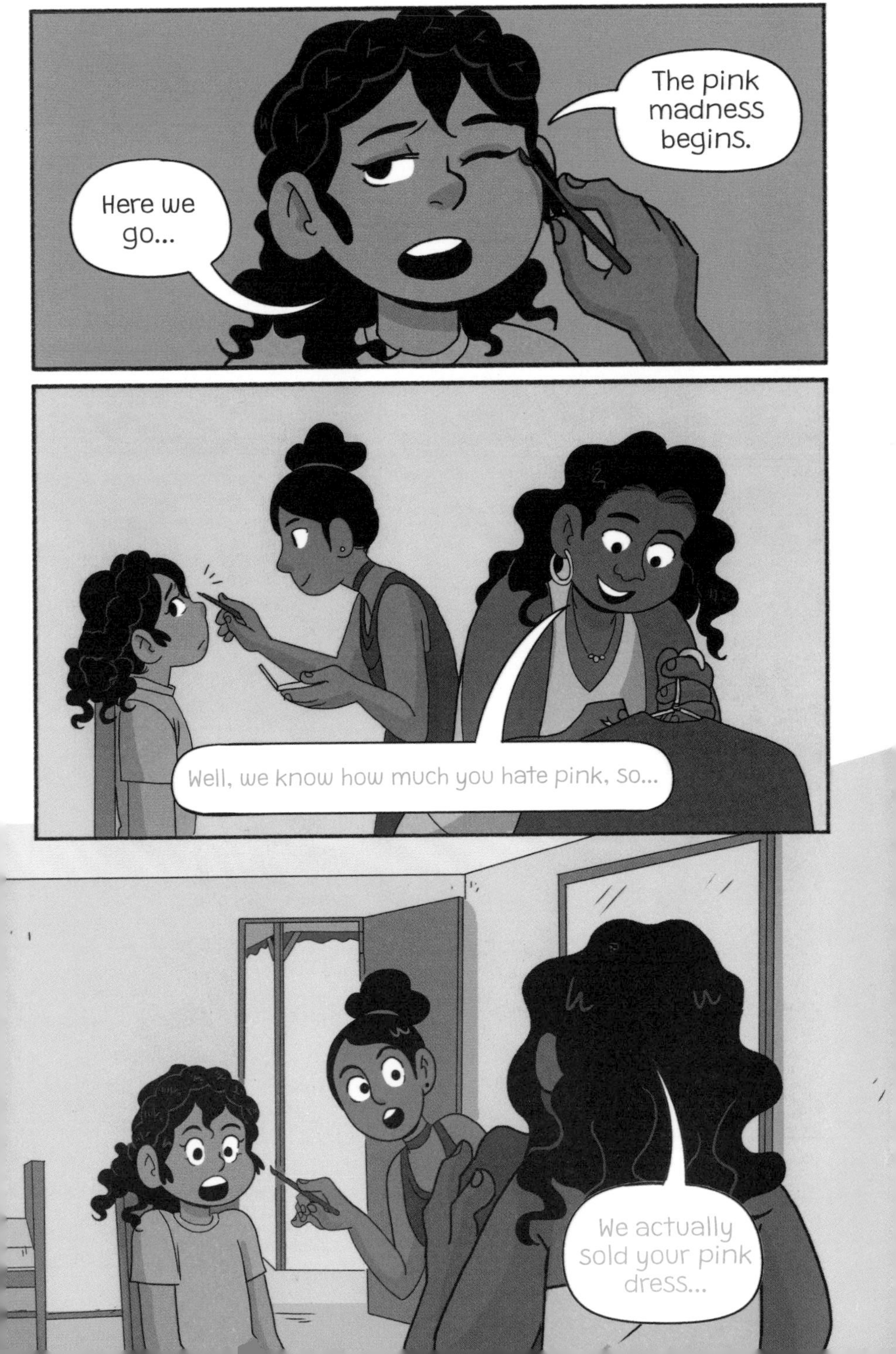
The pink madness begins.
Here we go...
Well, we know how much you hate pink, so...
We actually sold your pink dress...

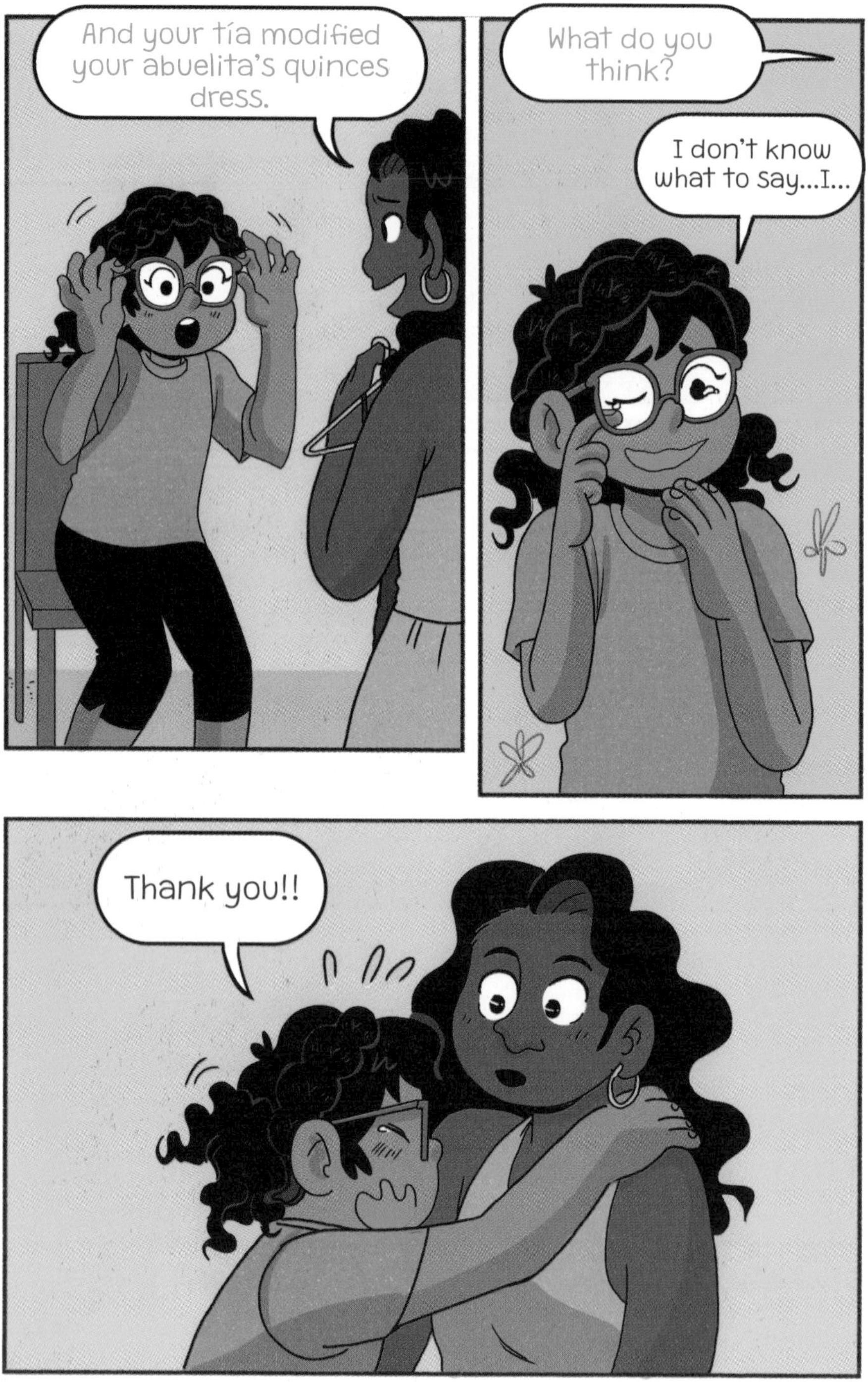
And your tía modified your abuelita's quinces dress.
What do you think?
I don't know what to say...I...
Thank you!!

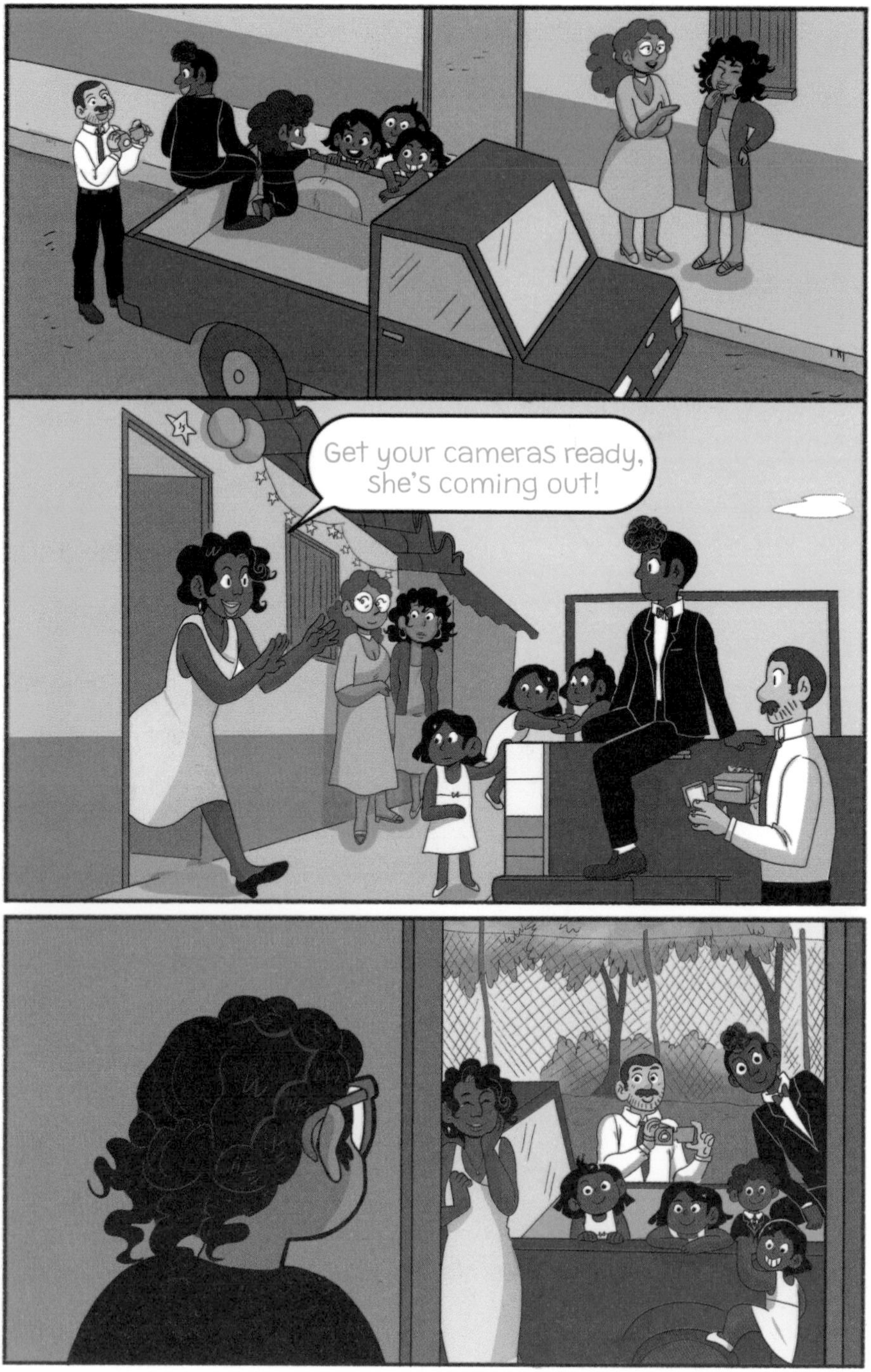
Get your cameras ready, she's coming out!

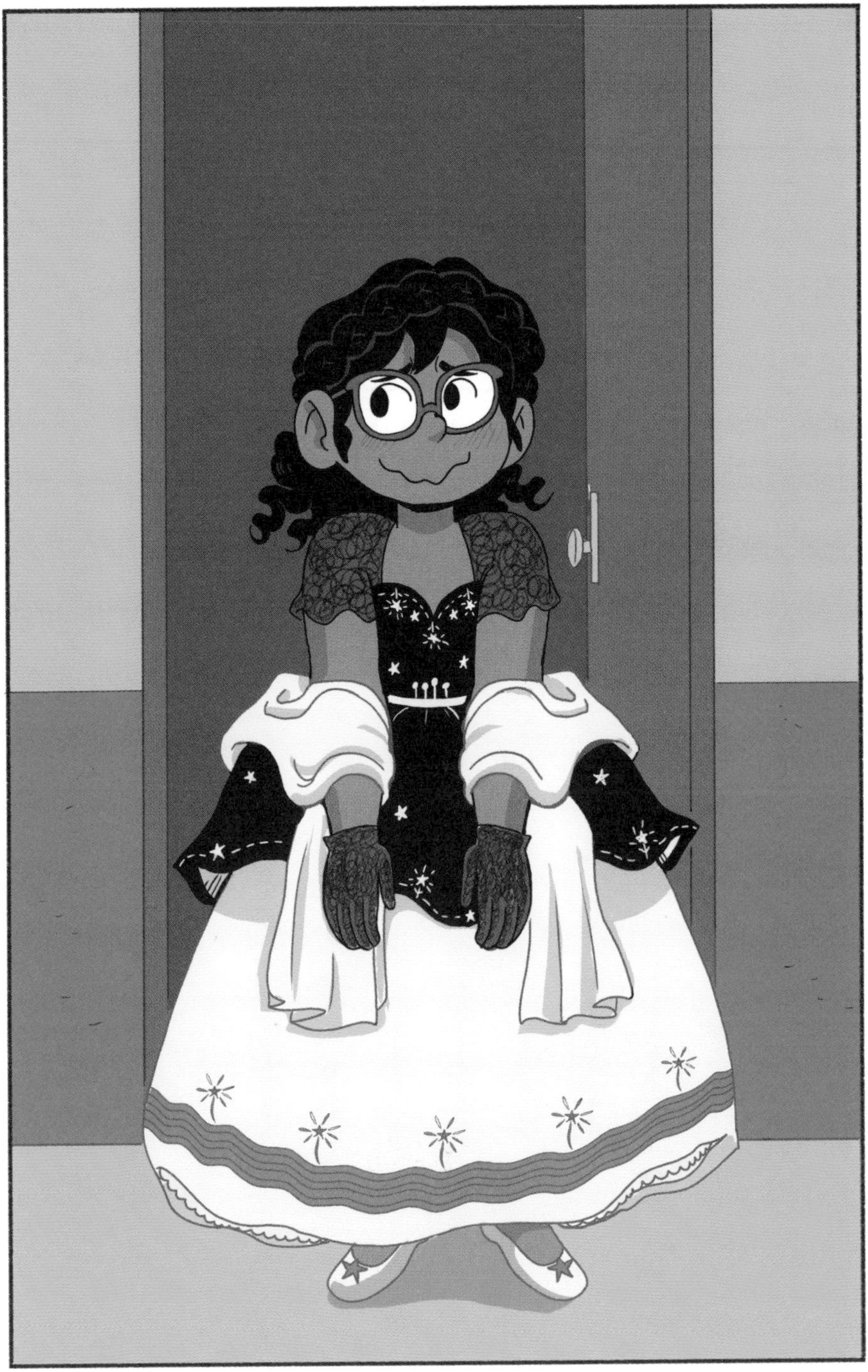

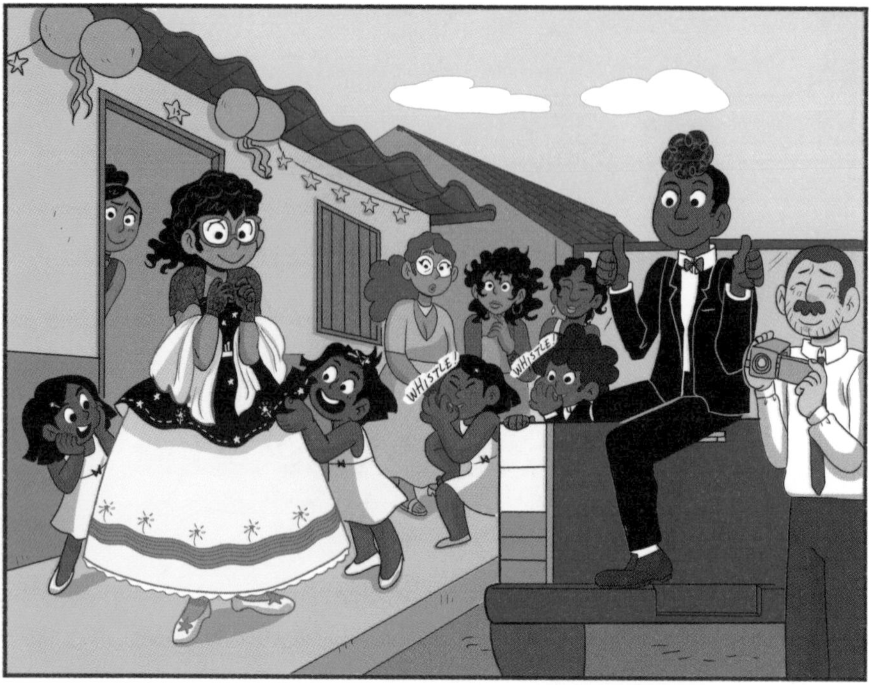
WHISTLE!
WHISTLE!

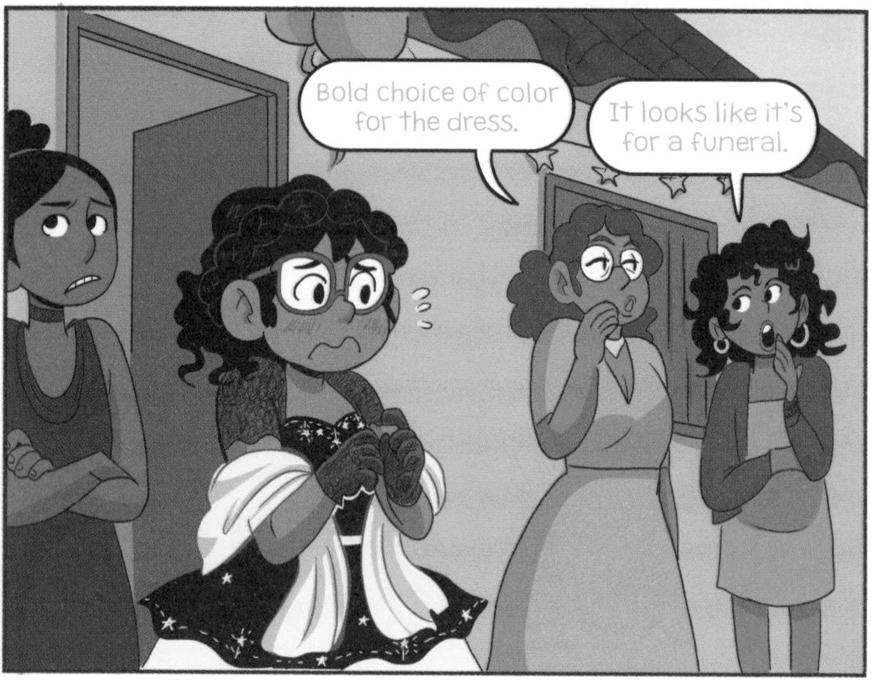
Bold choice of color for the dress.
It looks like it's for a funeral.

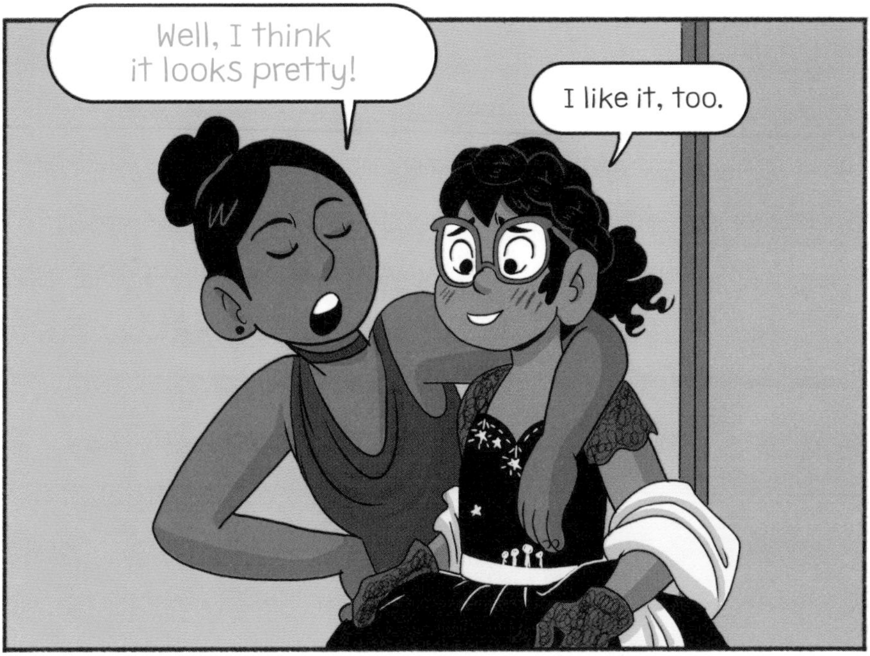
Well, I think it looks pretty!
I like it, too.

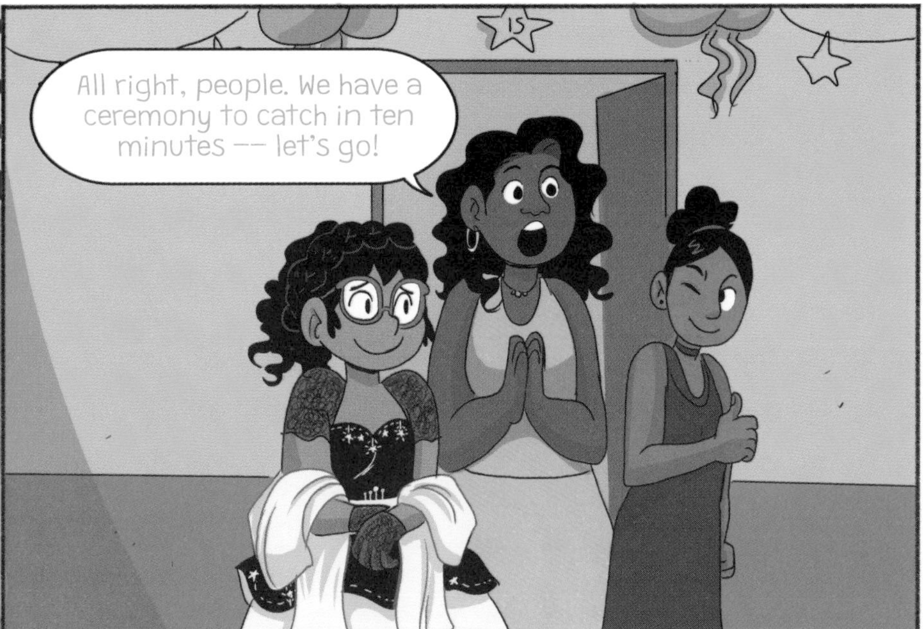
15
All right, people. We have a ceremony to catch in ten minutes -- let's go!

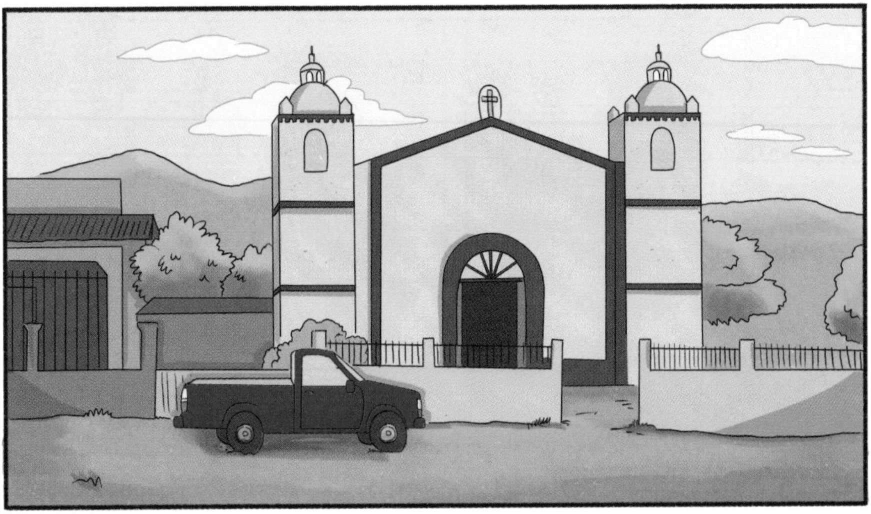

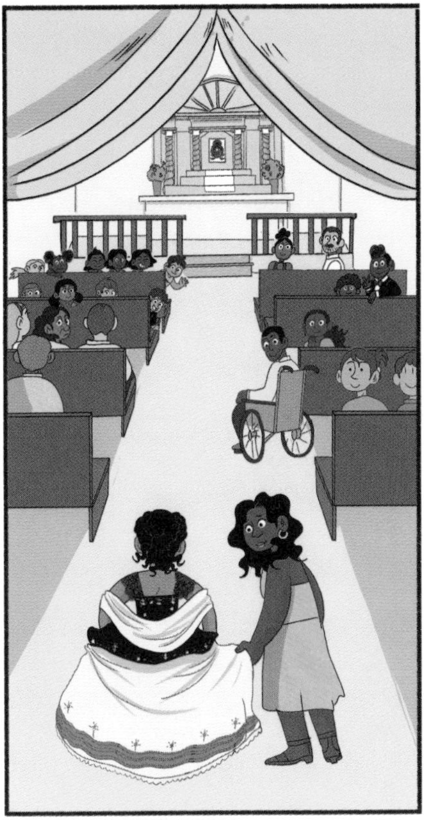

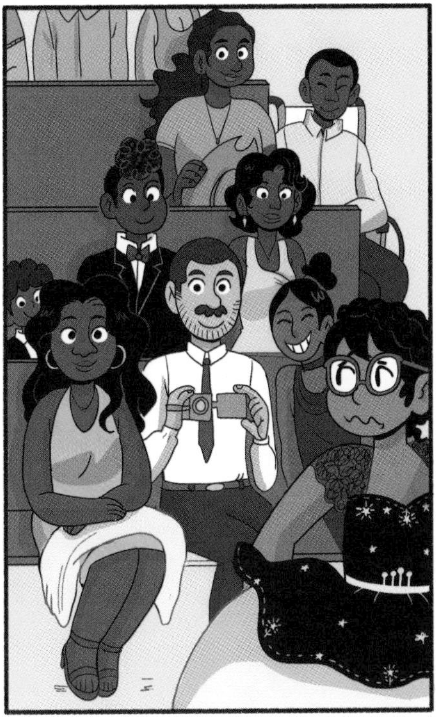

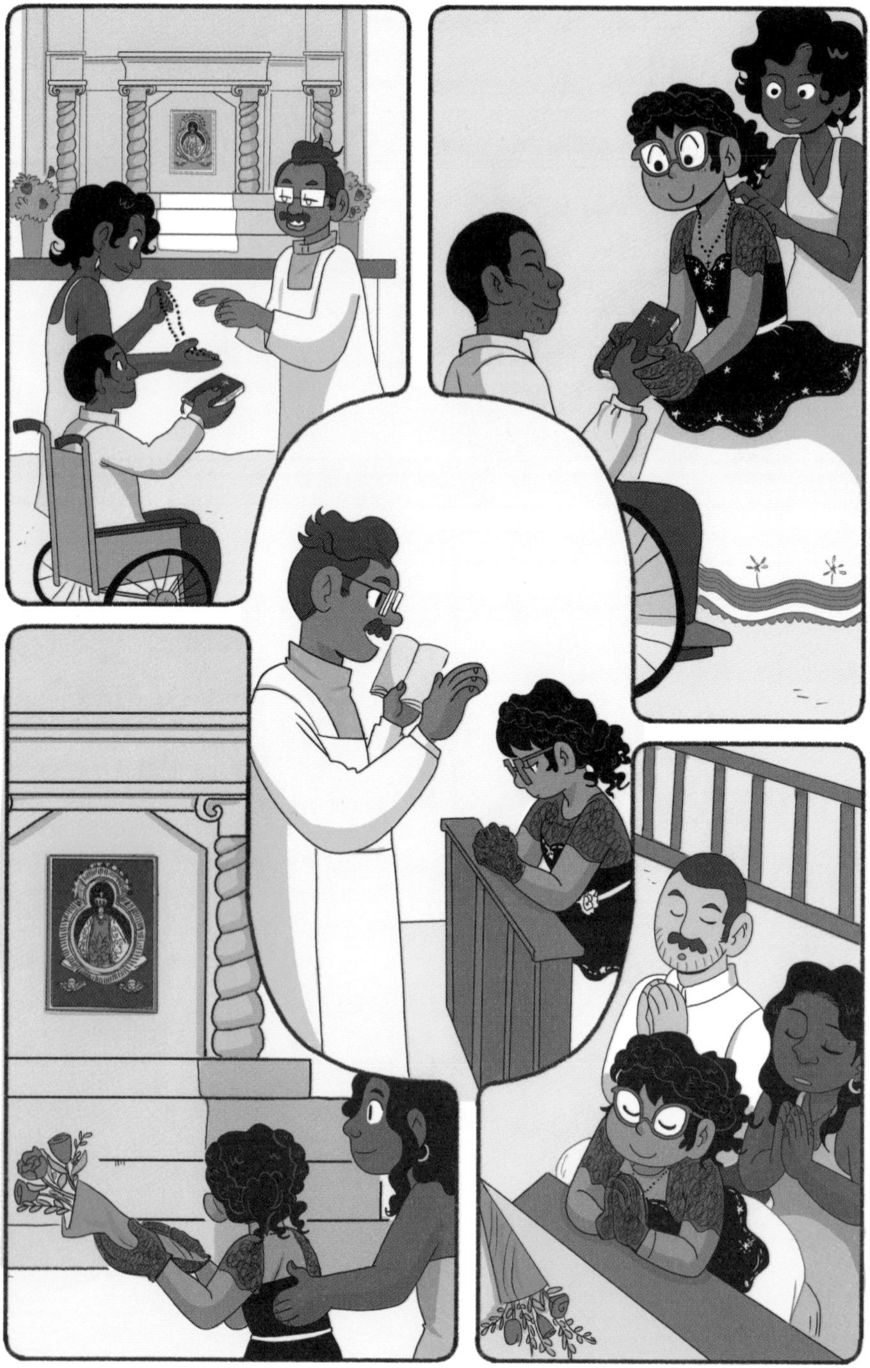

CHAPTER NINE

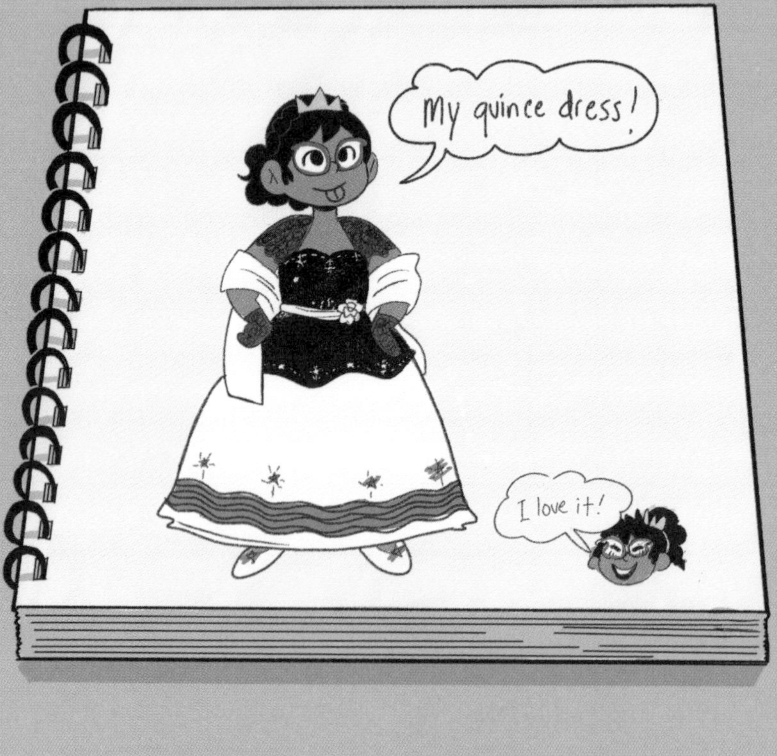
My quince dress!
I love it!

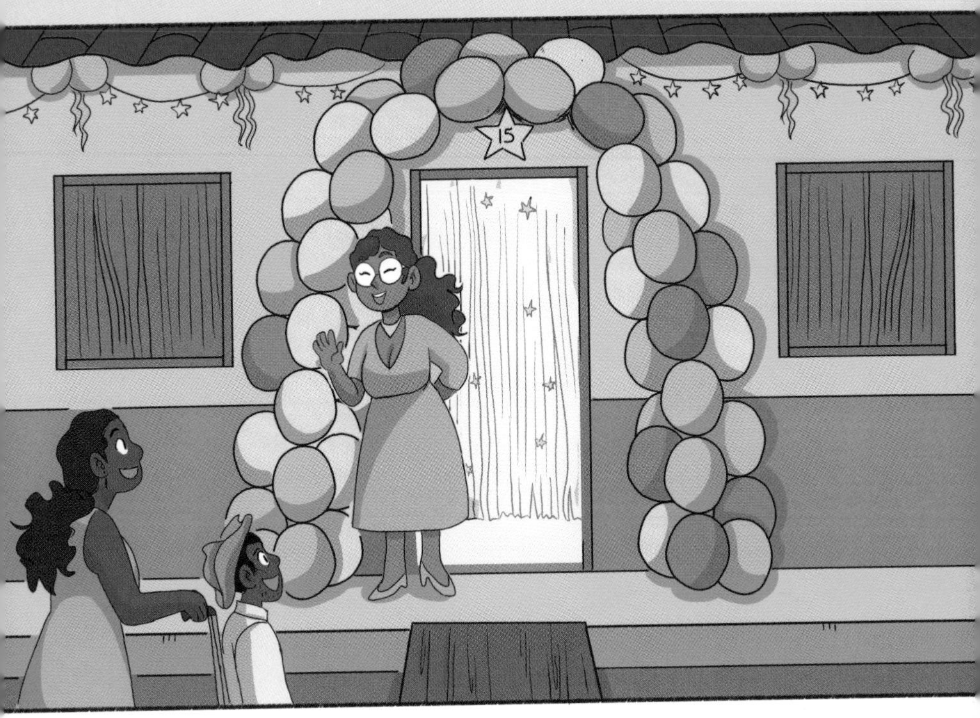
15

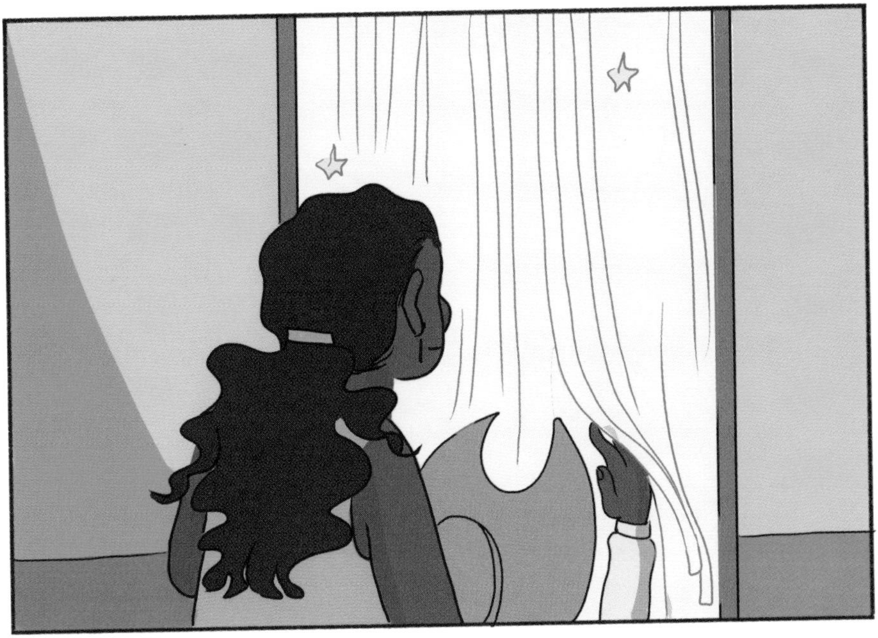

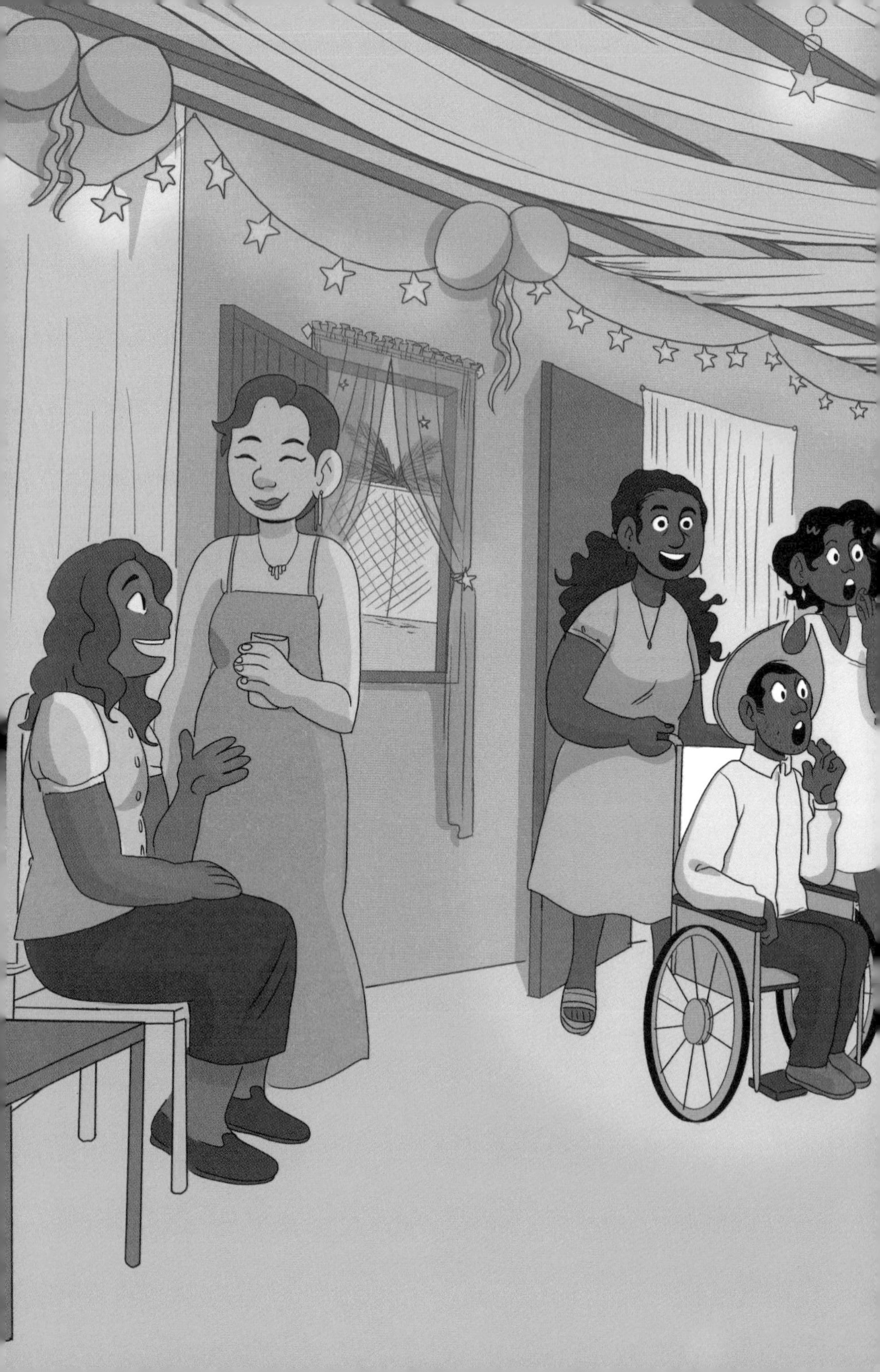

Thank you all for coming to this joyous event.

Tonight we are here with the lovely Gutiérrez family, who are presenting their princess for her quinces.

Places, everyone! Grab your partner!

And remember to SMILE!

You can do this, you can do it. Breeeathe.

You got this, cousin!

200

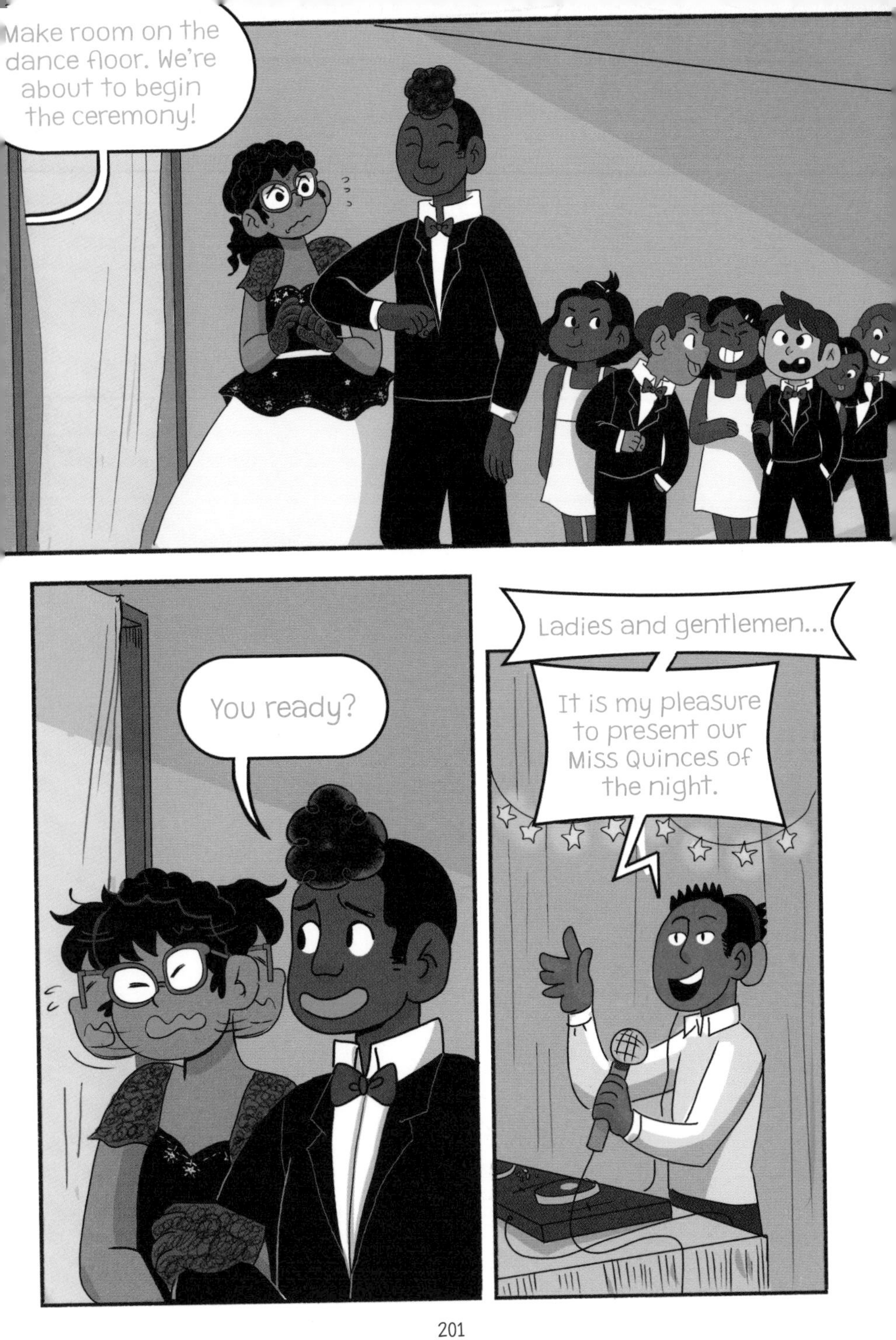
Make room on the dance floor. We're about to begin the ceremony!
You ready?
Ladies and gentlemen...
It is my pleasure to present our Miss Quinces of the night.

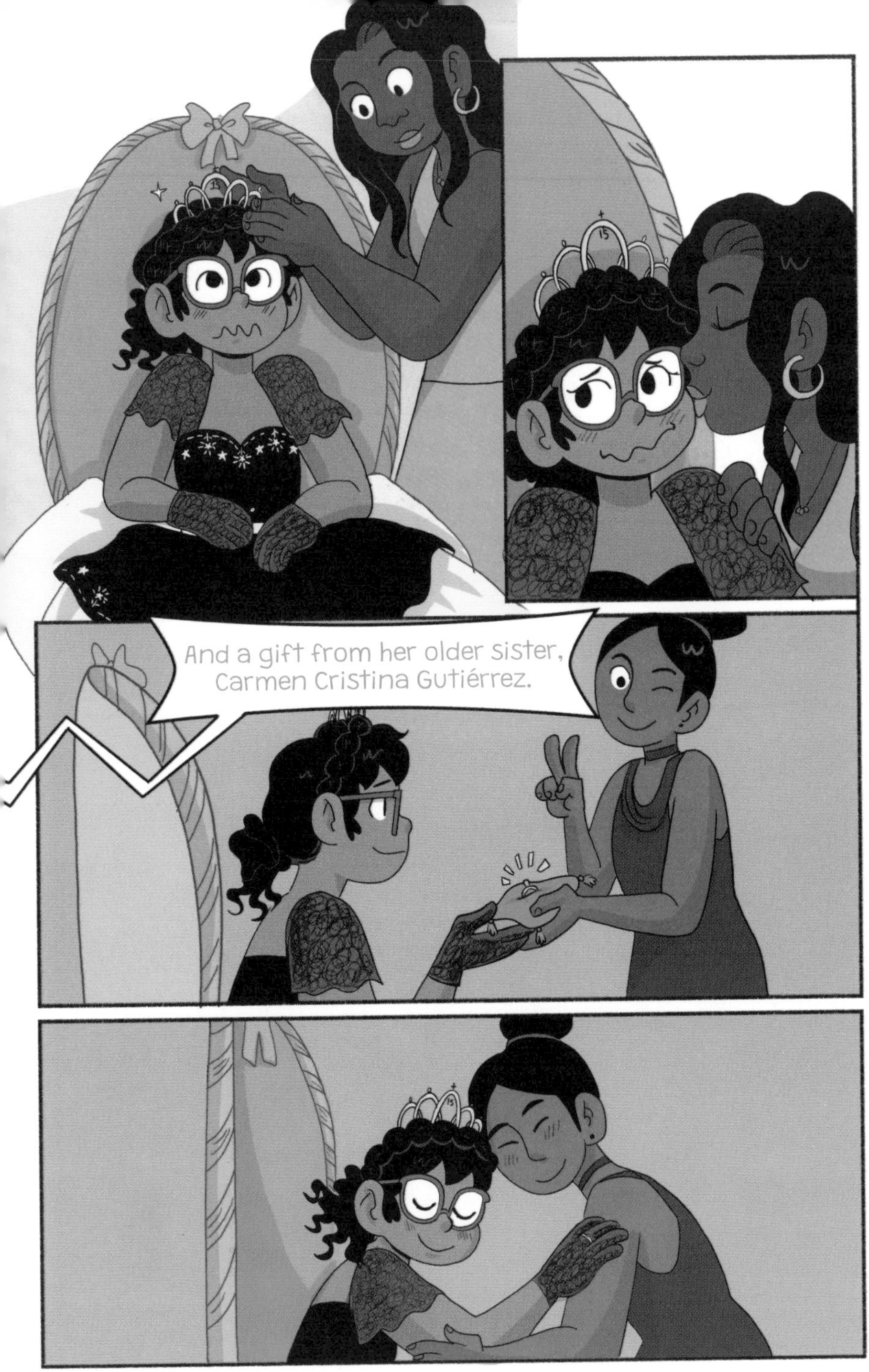
And a gift from her older sister, Carmen Cristina Gutiérrez.

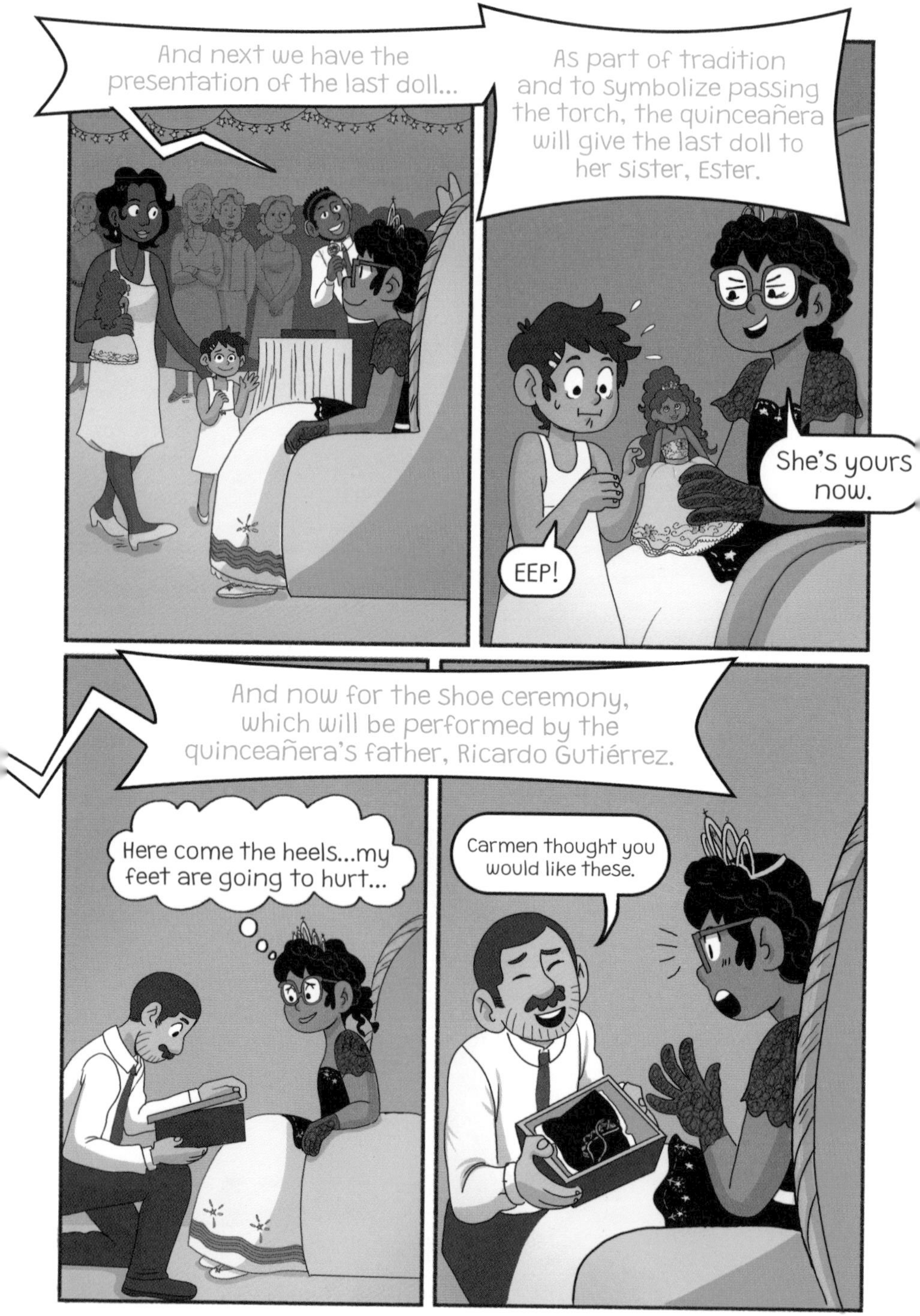
And next we have the presentation of the last doll...
As part of tradition and to symbolize passing the torch, the quinceañera will give the last doll to her sister, Ester.
EEP!
She's yours now.
And now for the shoe ceremony, which will be performed by the quinceañera's father, Ricardo Gutiérrez.
Here come the heels...my feet are going to hurt...
Carmen thought you would like these.

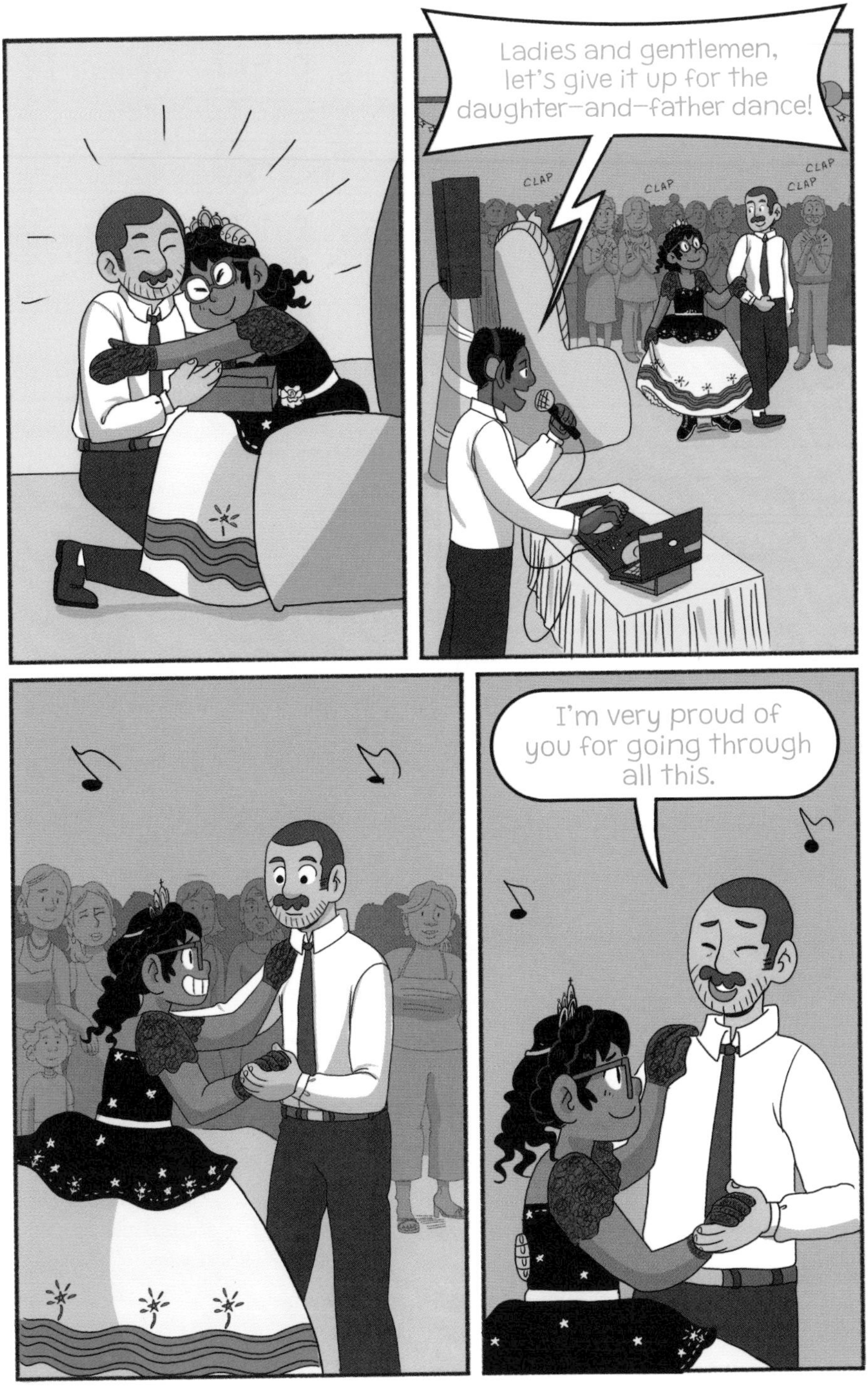
Ladies and gentlemen, let's give it up for the daughter-and-father dance!
CLAP
CLAP
CLAP
CLAP
I'm very proud of you for going through all this.

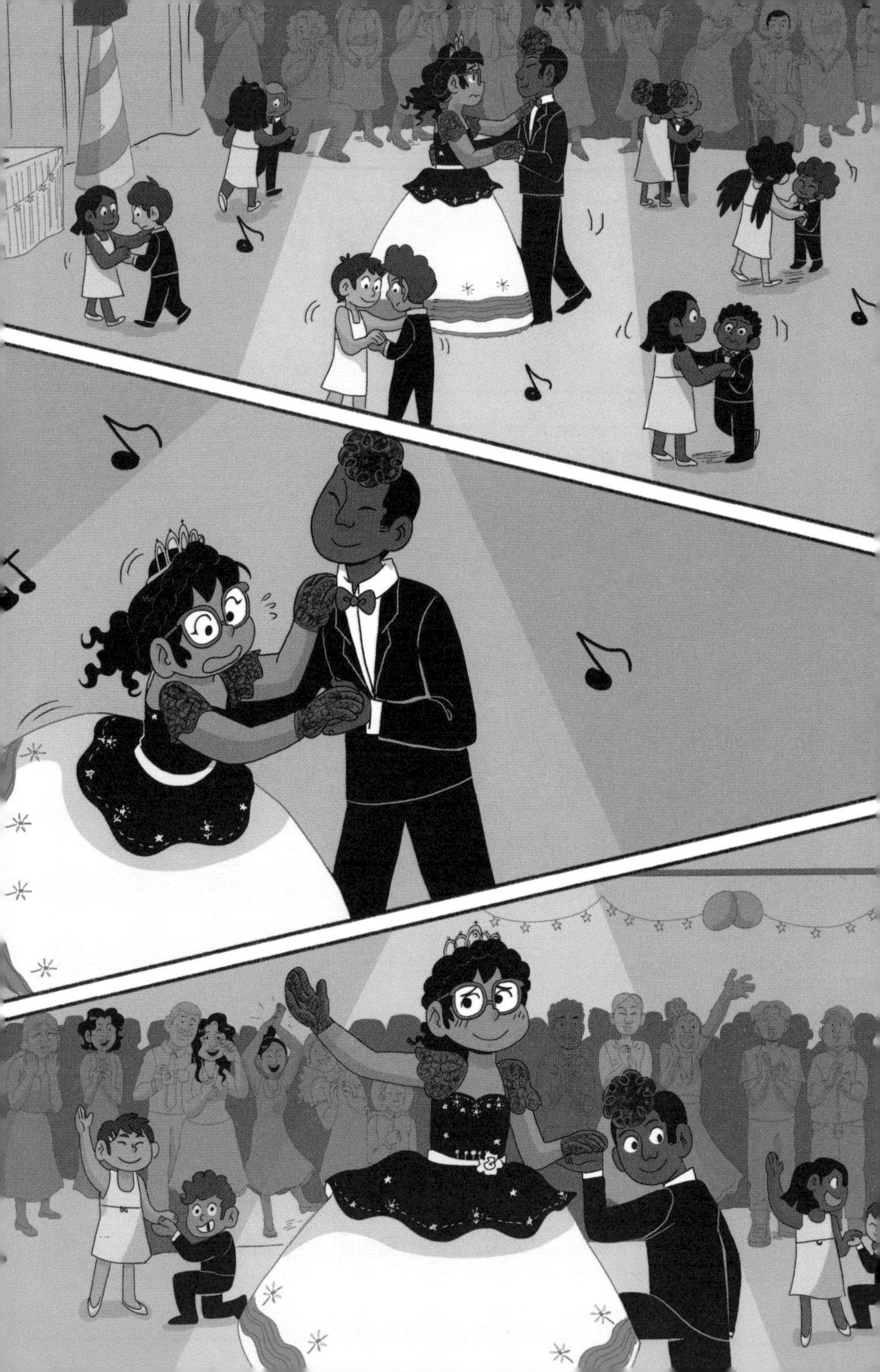

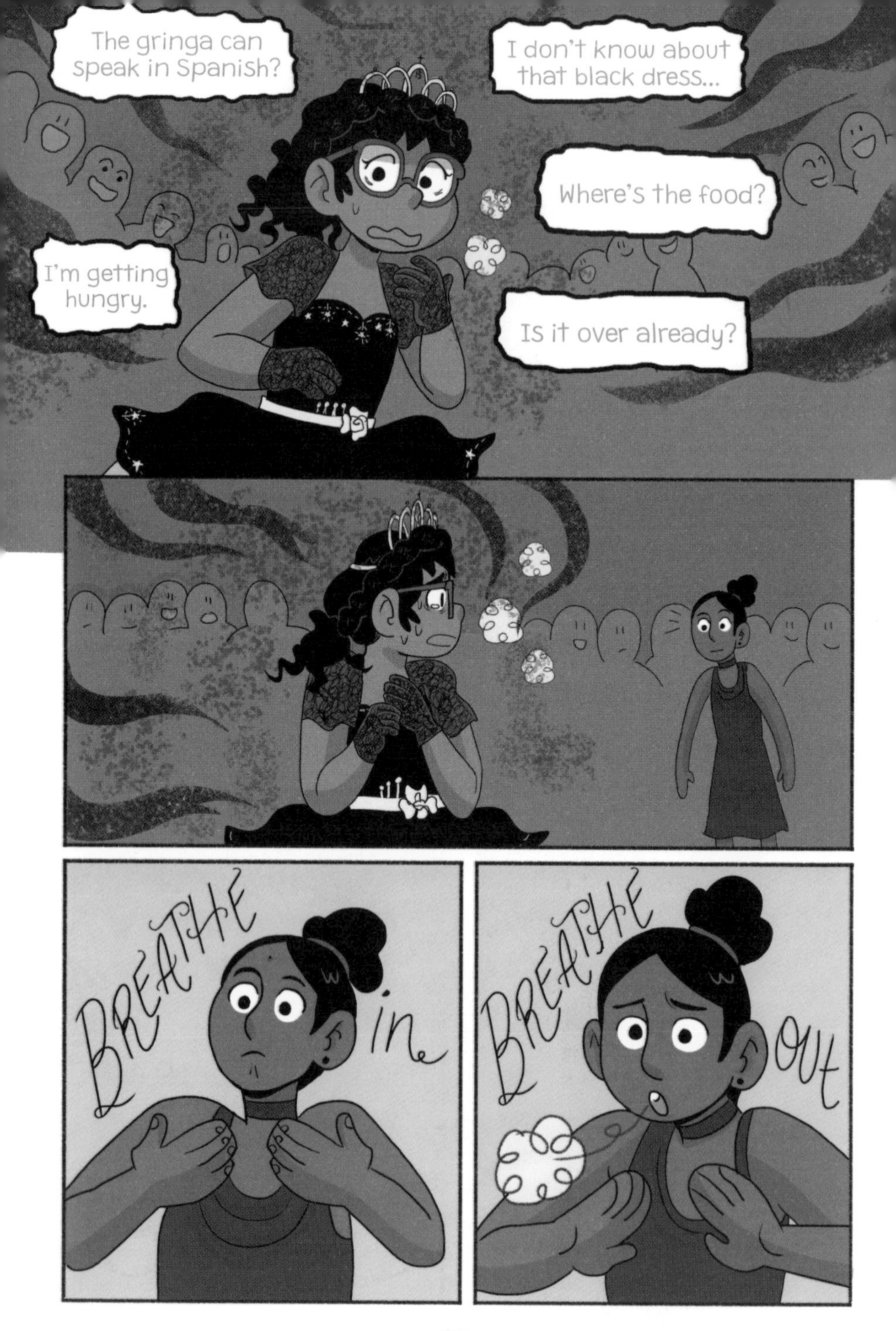
The gringa can speak in Spanish?
I don't know about that black dress...
Where's the food?
I'm getting hungry.
Is it over already?
BREATHE in
BREATHE OUT

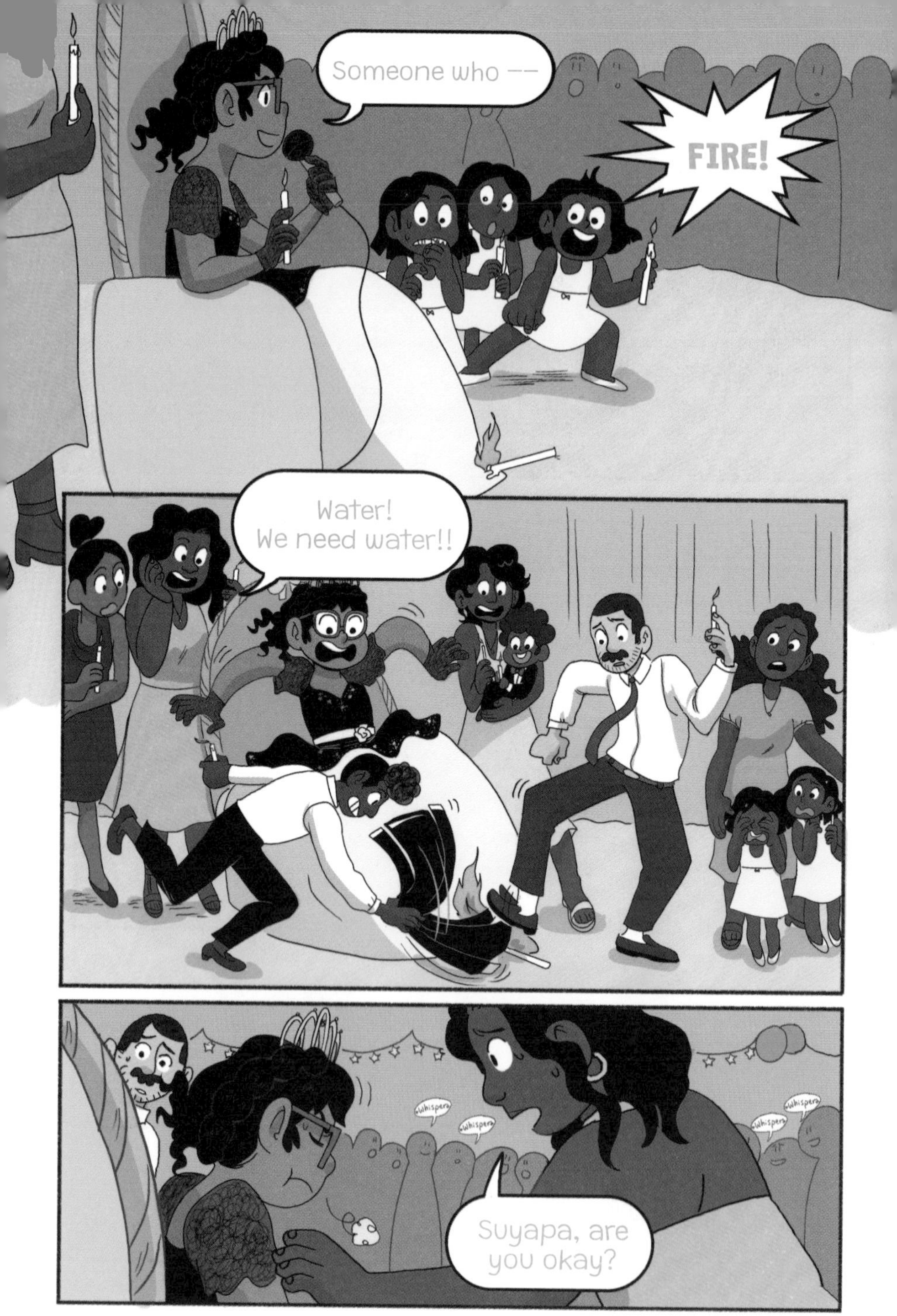
Someone who --
FIRE!
Water!
We need water!!
Suyapa, are
you okay?

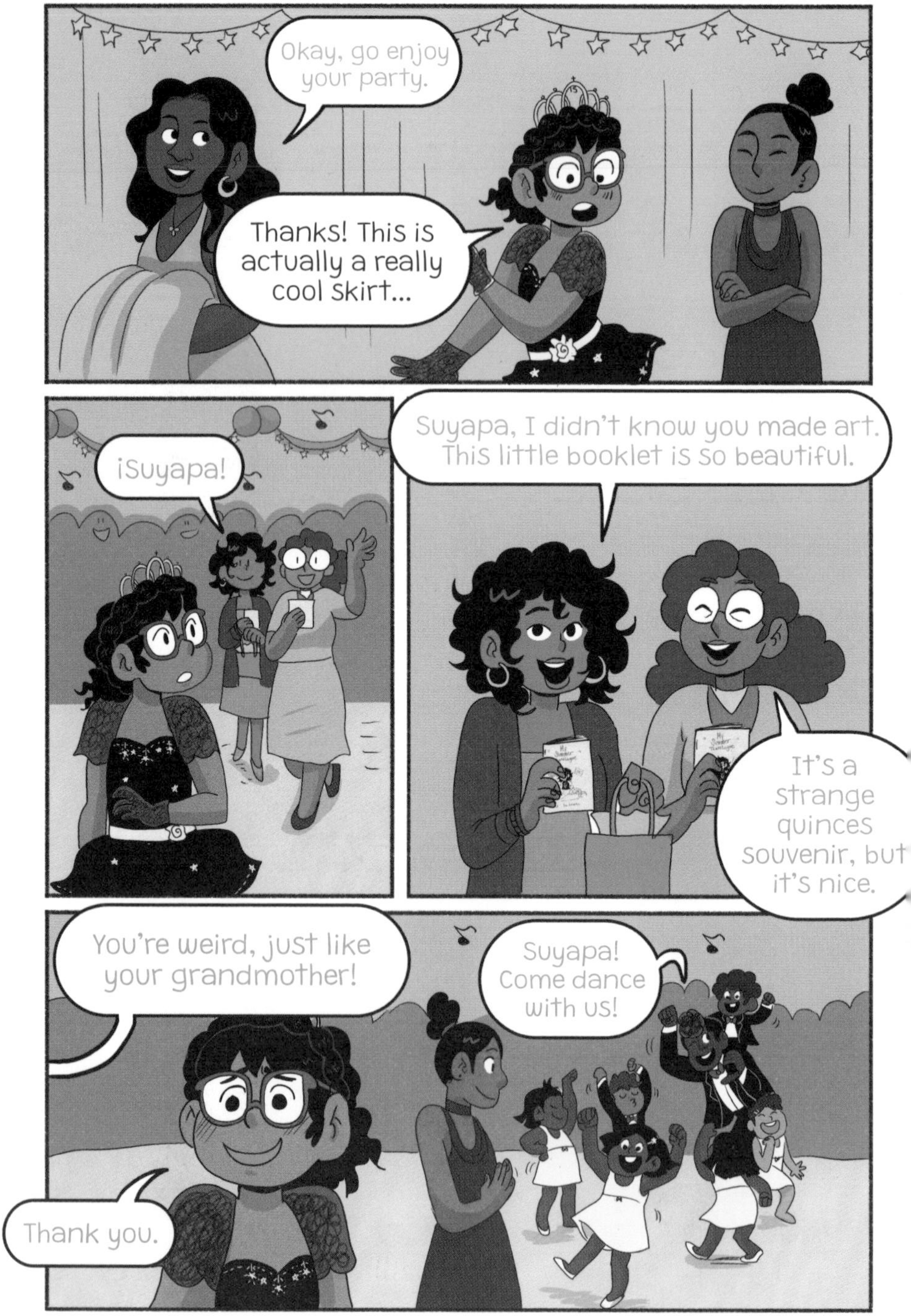
Okay, go enjoy your party.
Thanks! This is actually a really cool skirt...
¡Suyapa!
Suyapa, I didn't know you made art. This little booklet is so beautiful.
It's a strange quinces souvenir, but it's nice.
You're weird, just like your grandmother!
Suyapa! Come dance with us!
Thank you.

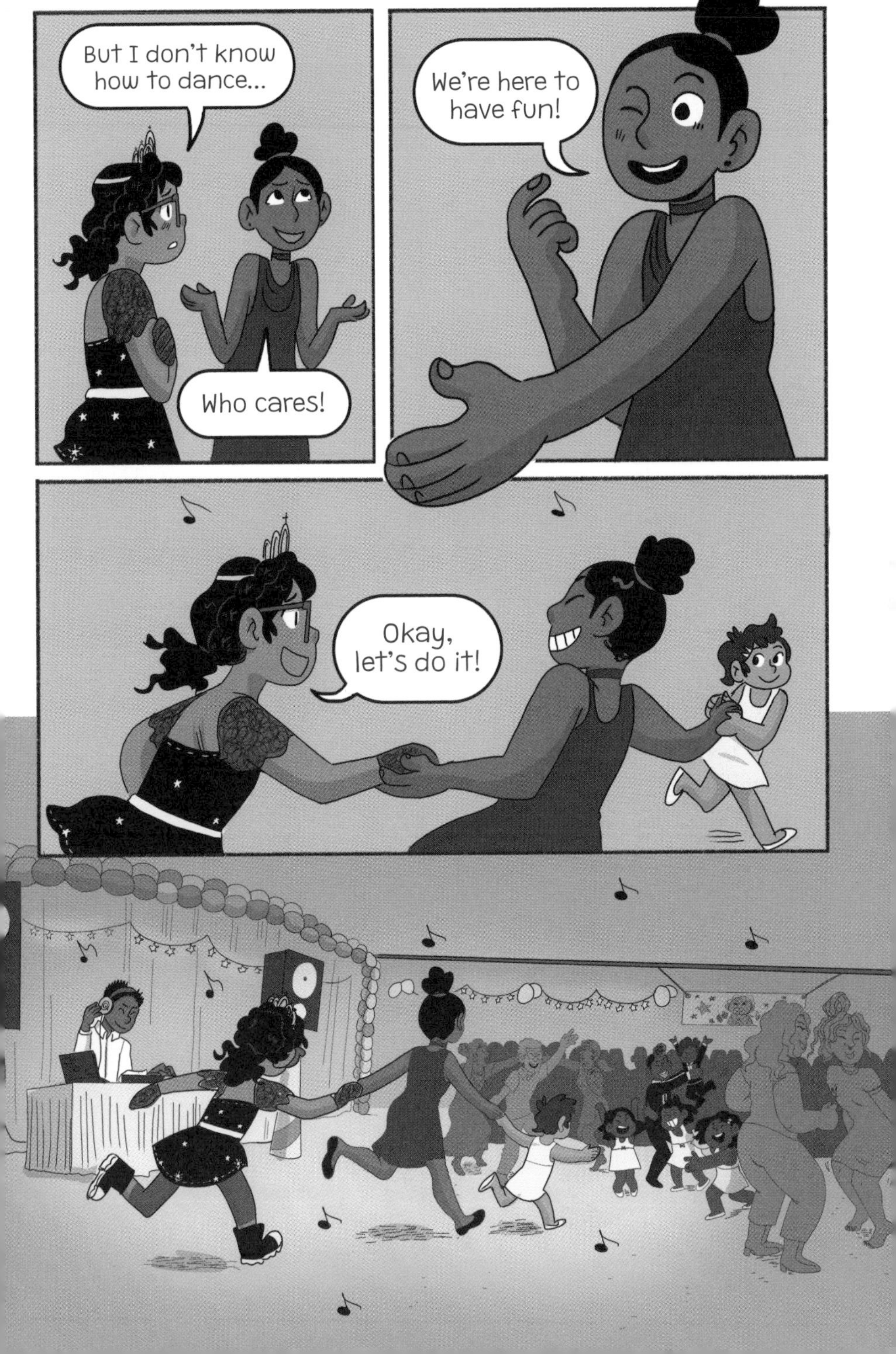
But I don't know how to dance...
Who cares!
We're here to have fun!
Okay, let's do it!

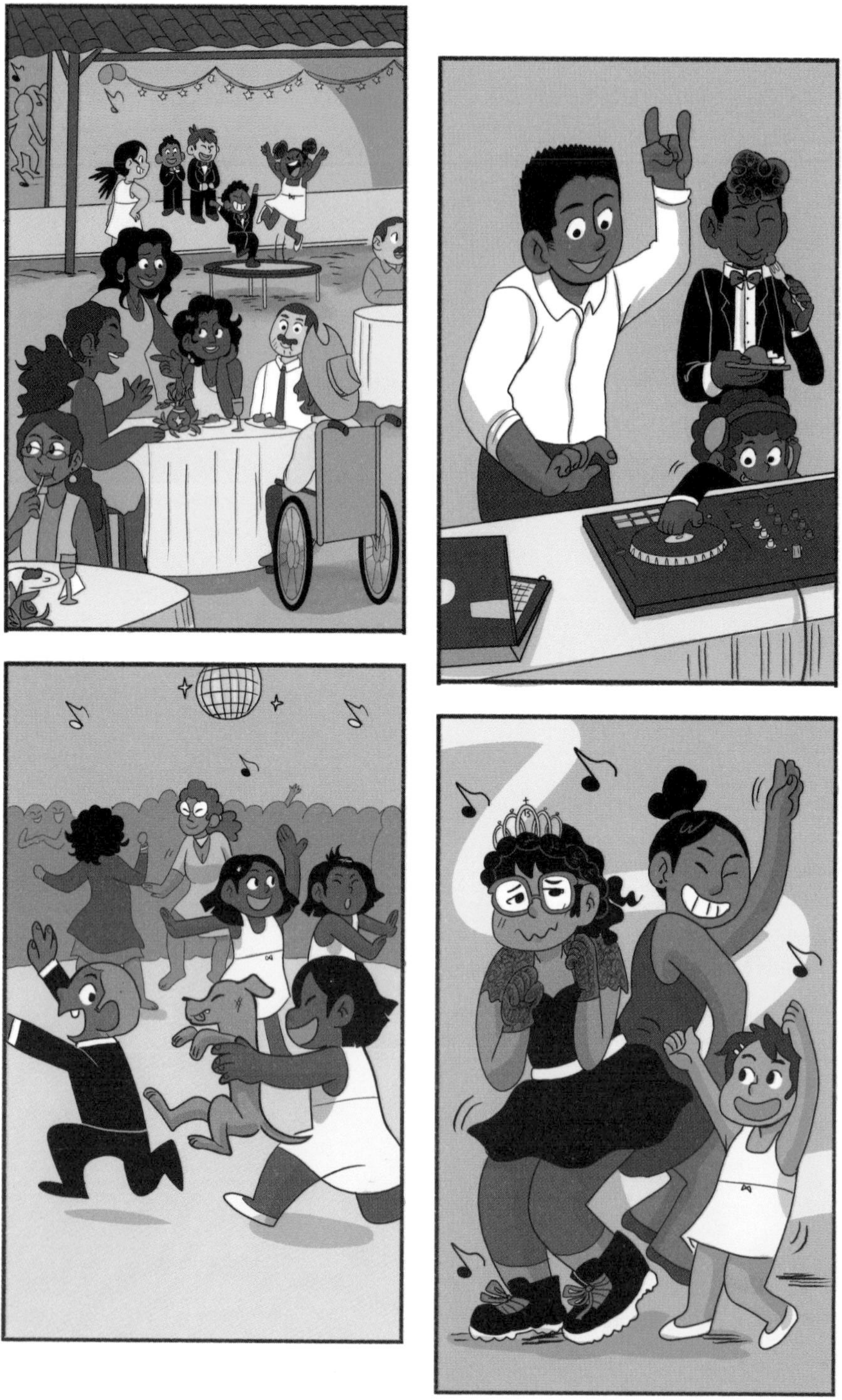

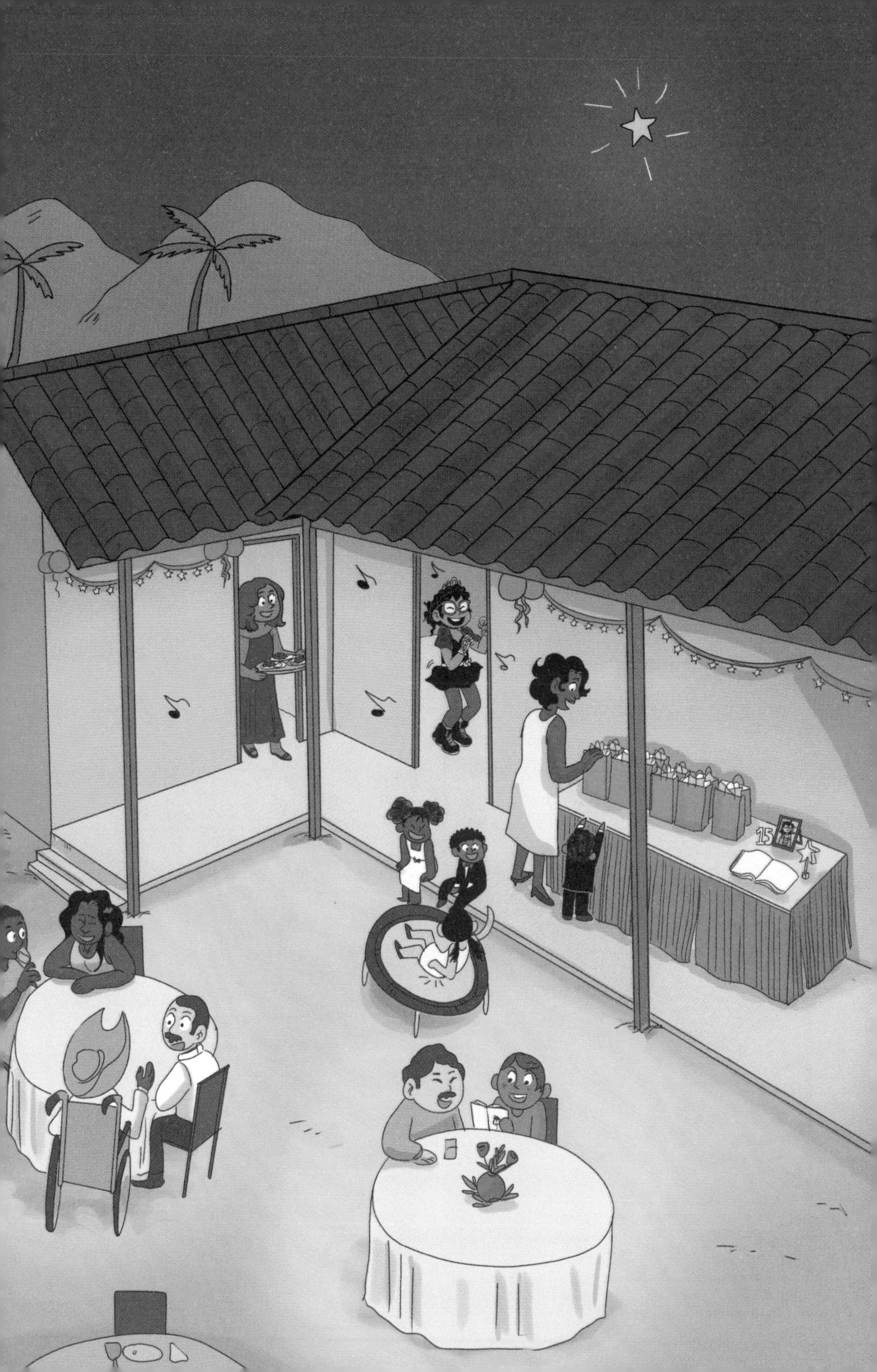
15

CHAPTER TEN

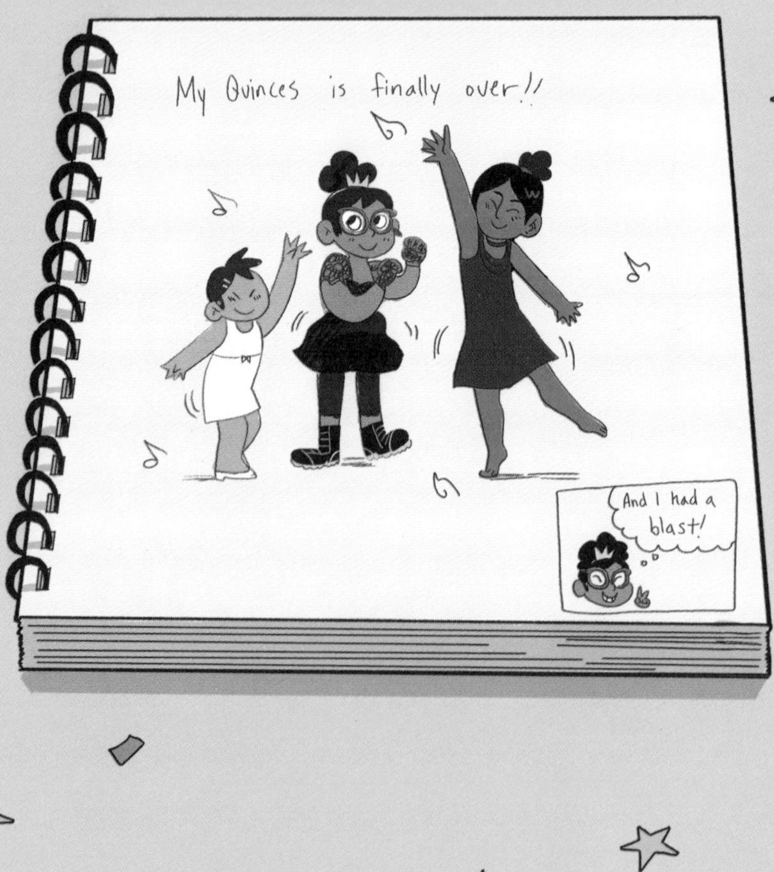
My Quinces is finally over!!
And I had a blast!

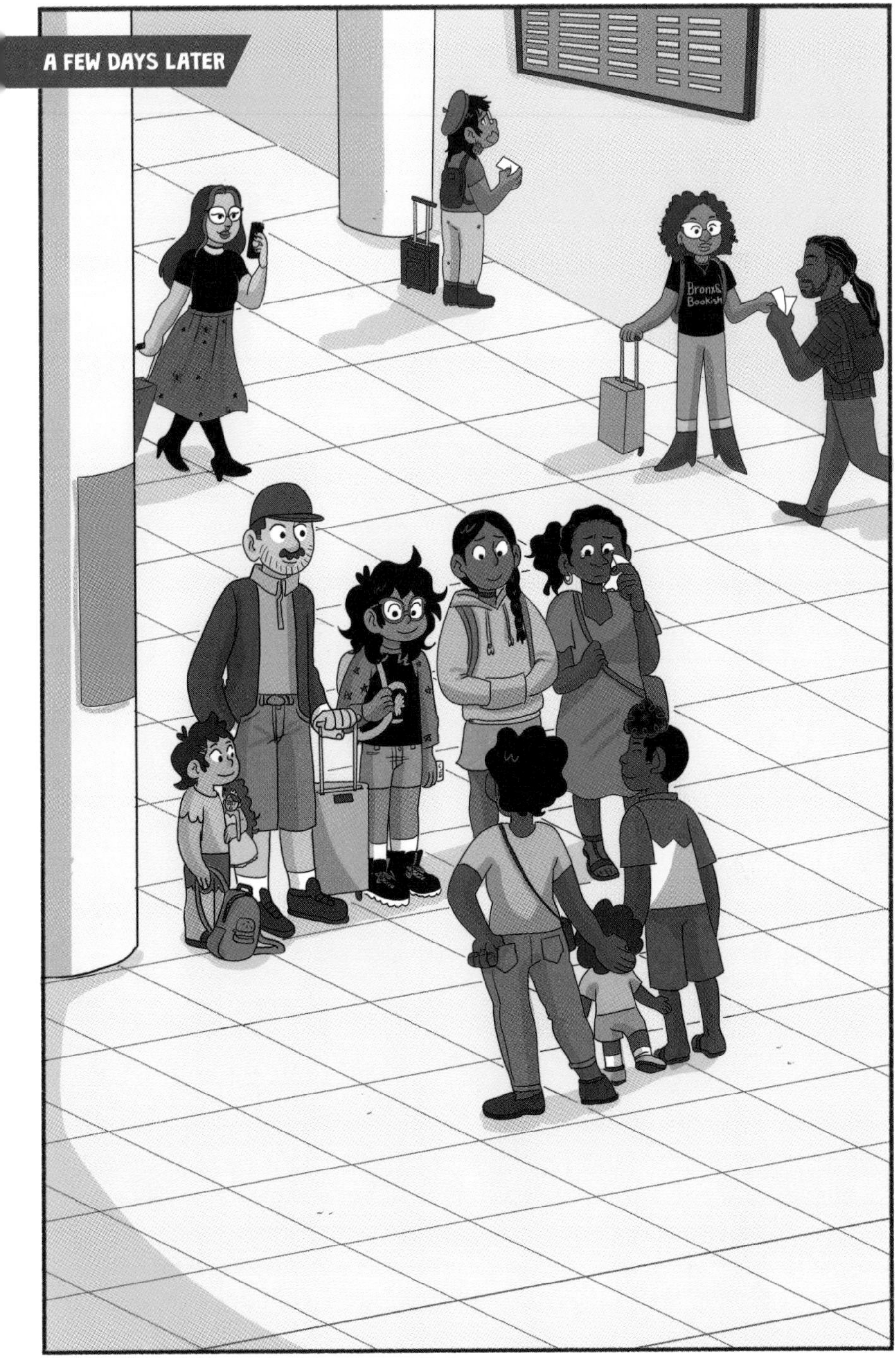
A FEW DAYS LATER
Bronx Bookish

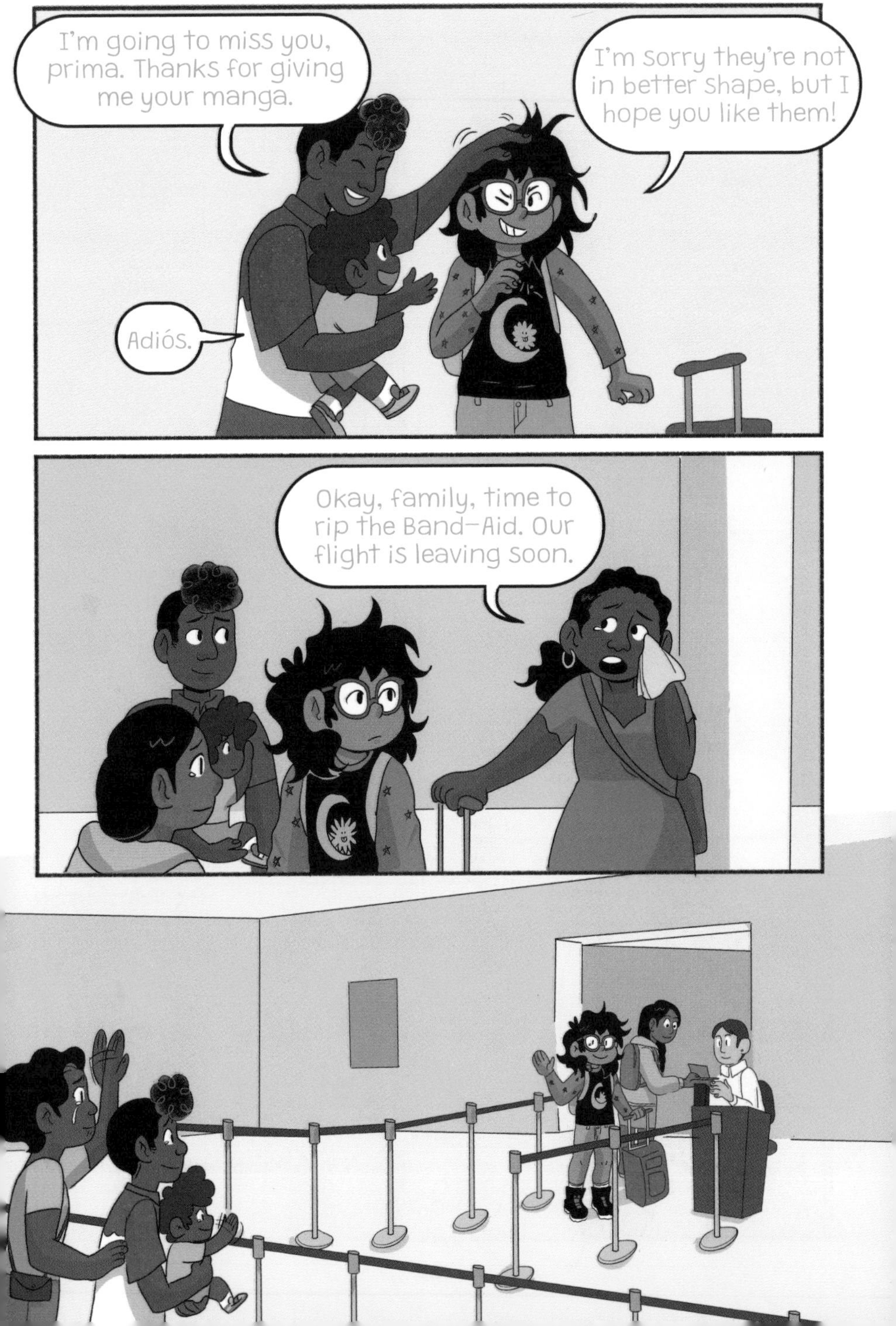
I'm going to miss you, prima. Thanks for giving me your manga.
I'm sorry they're not in better shape, but I hope you like them!
Adiós.
Okay, family, time to rip the Band-Aid. Our flight is leaving soon.

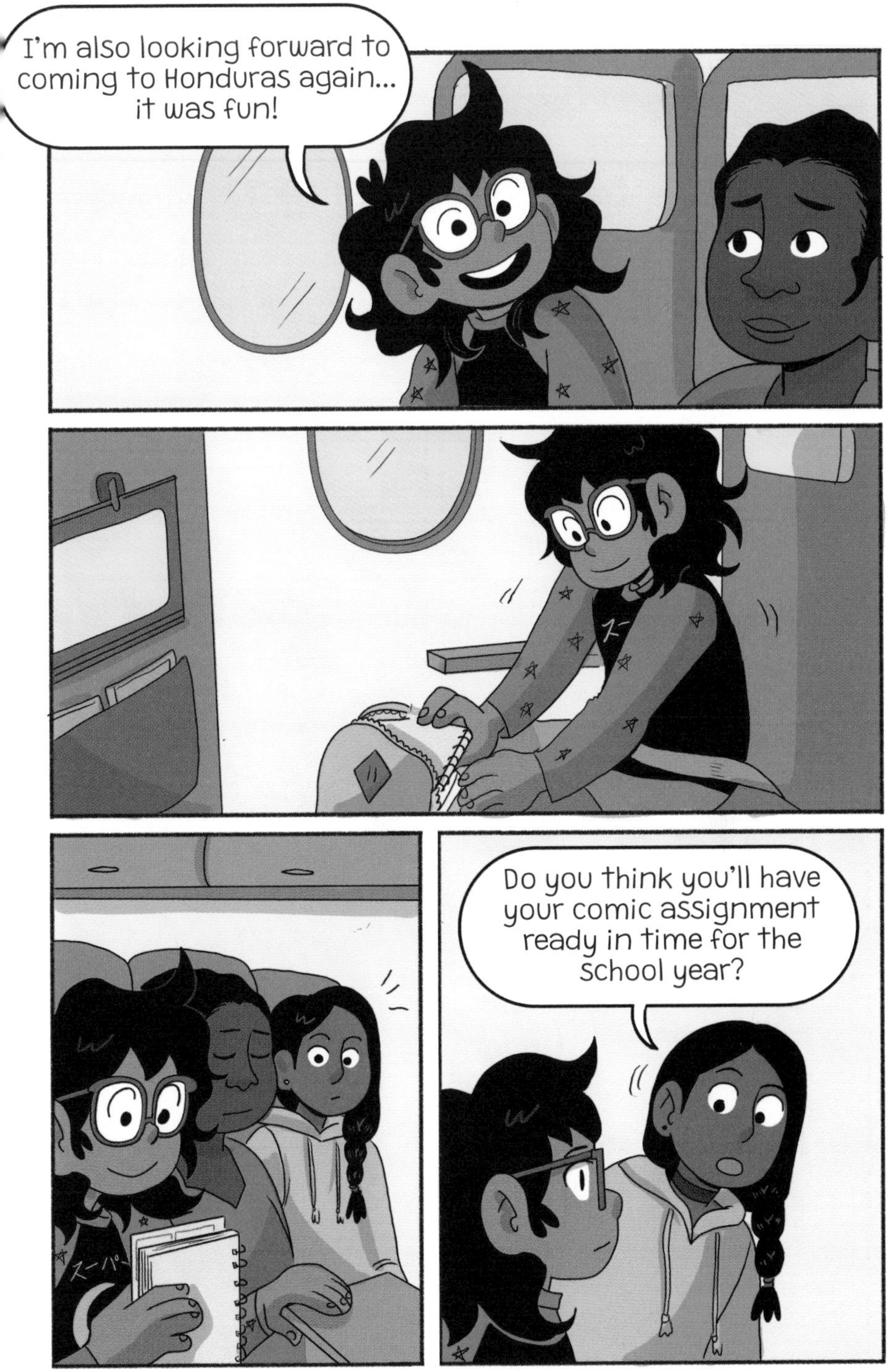

I'm also looking forward to coming to Honduras again... it was fun!
Do you think you'll have your comic assignment ready in time for the school year?

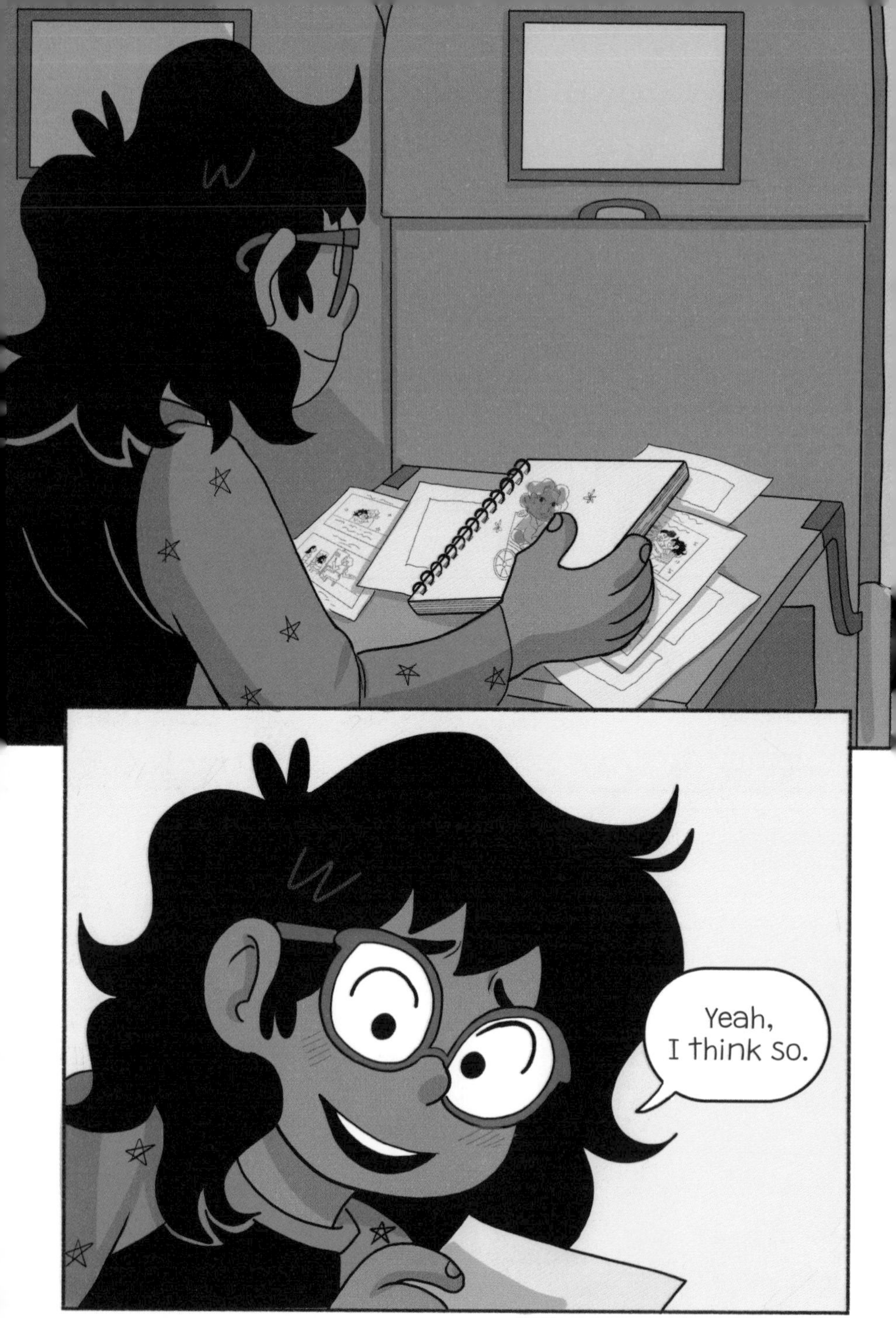
Yeah,
I think so.

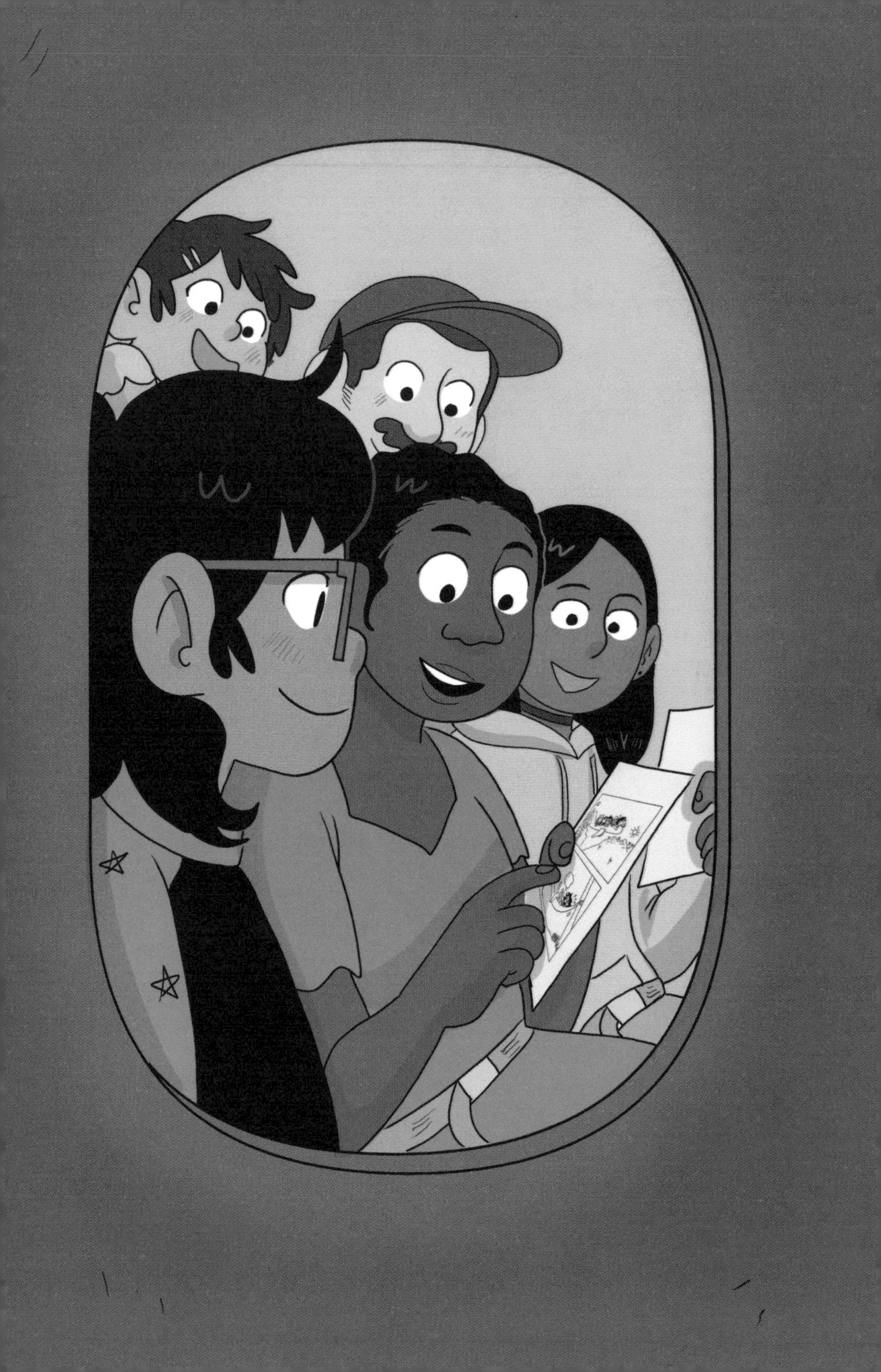

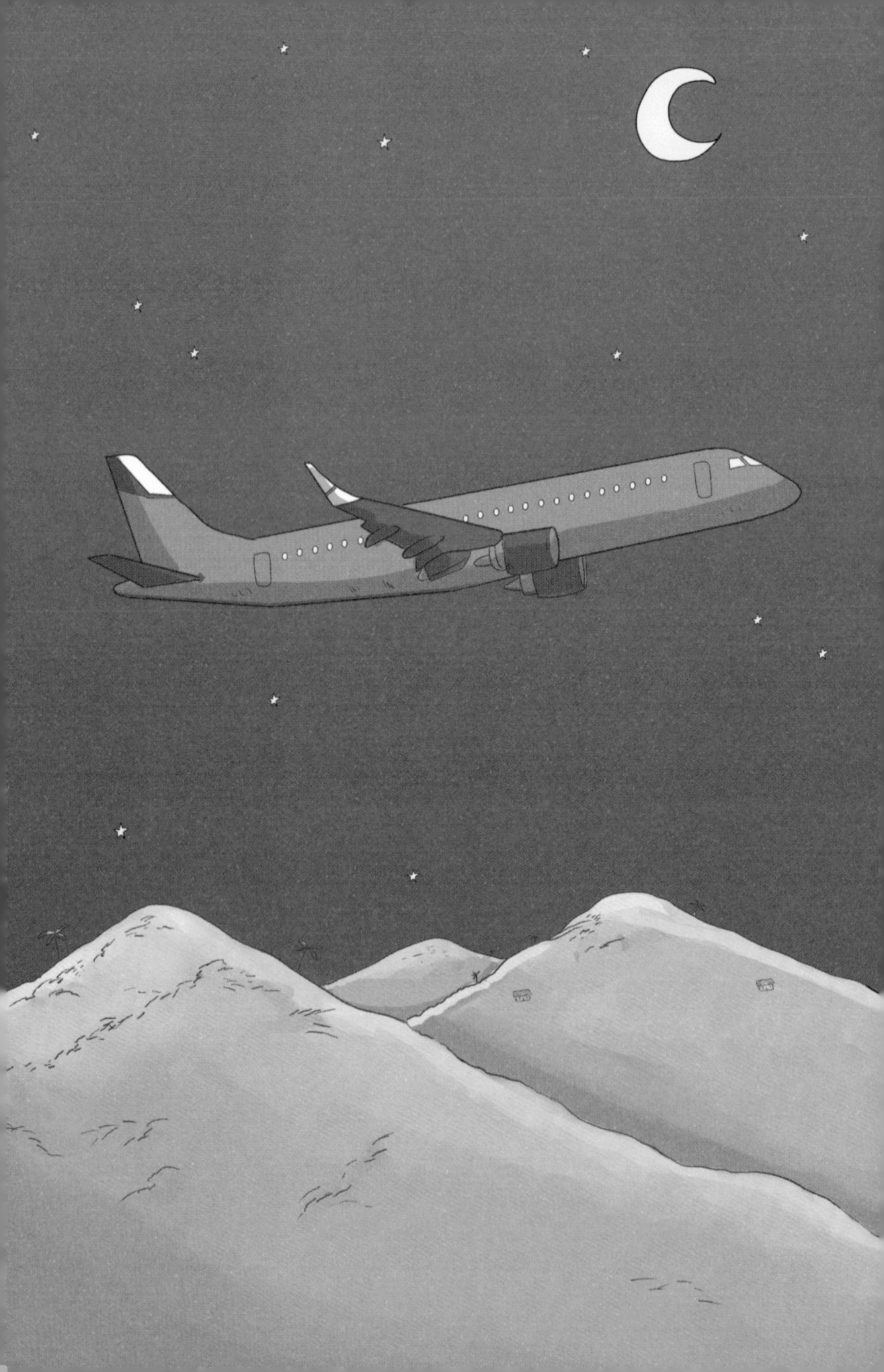

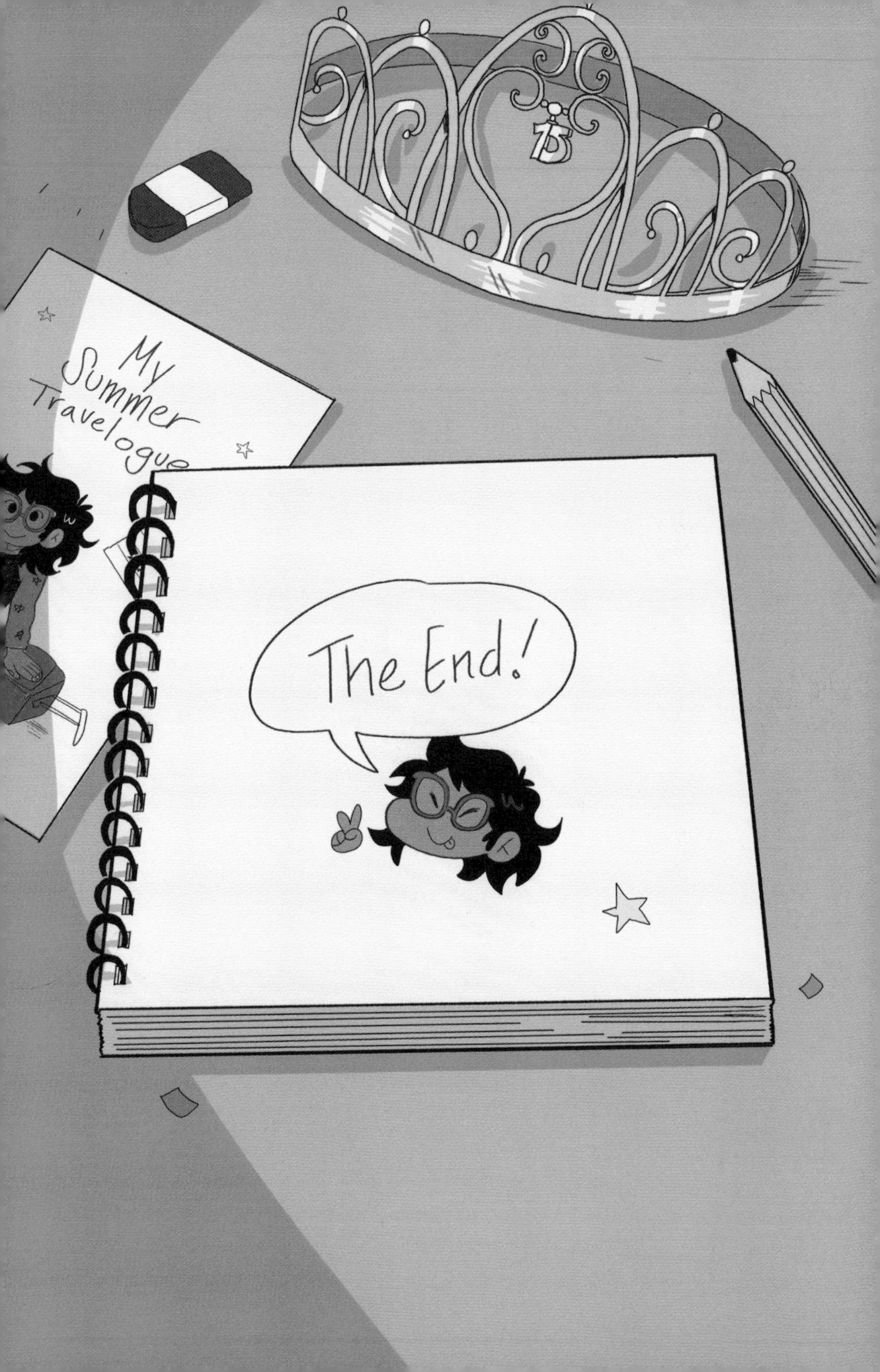

15
My Summer Travelogue
The End!

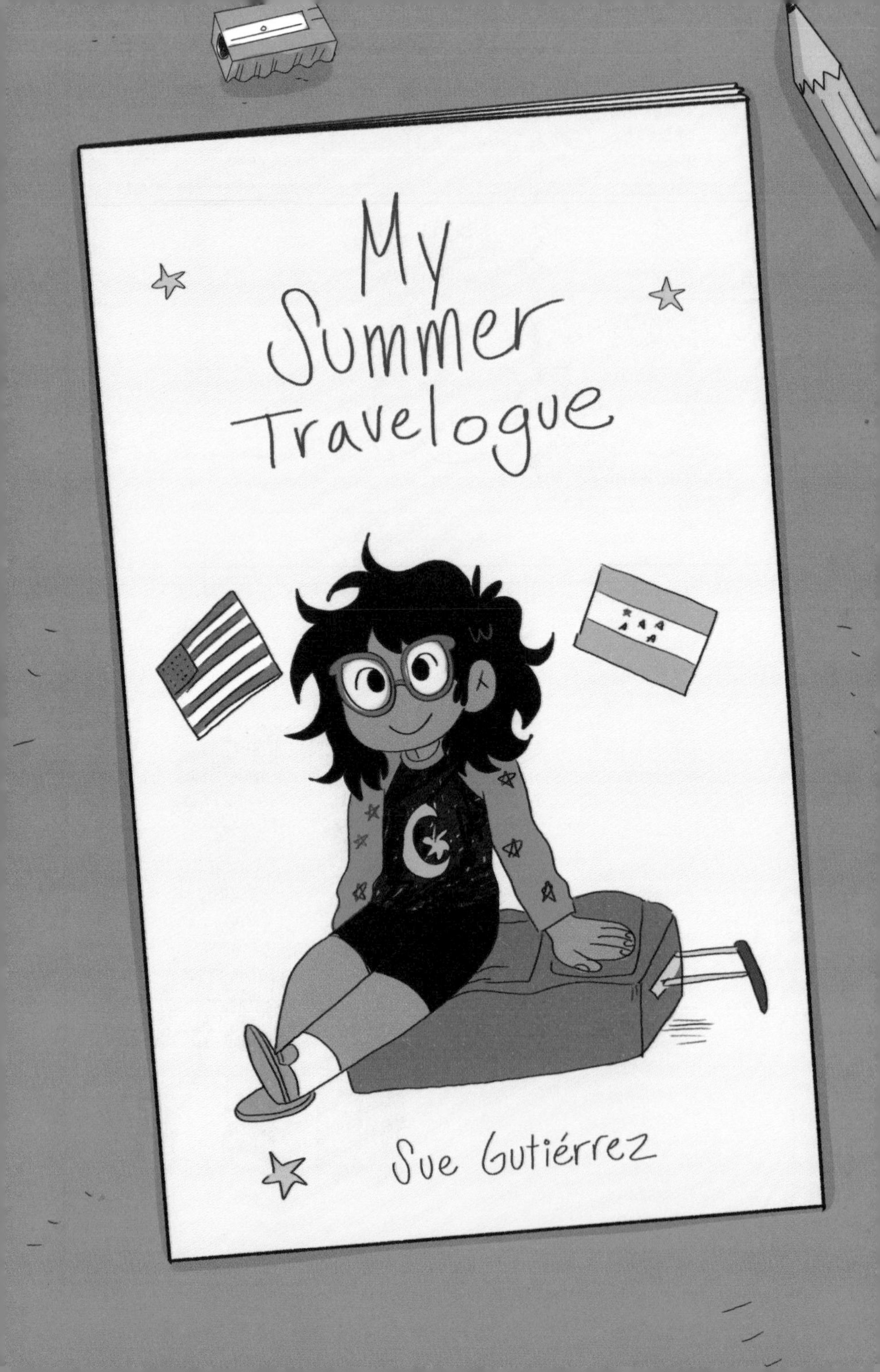
My Summer Travelogue
Sue Gutiérrez

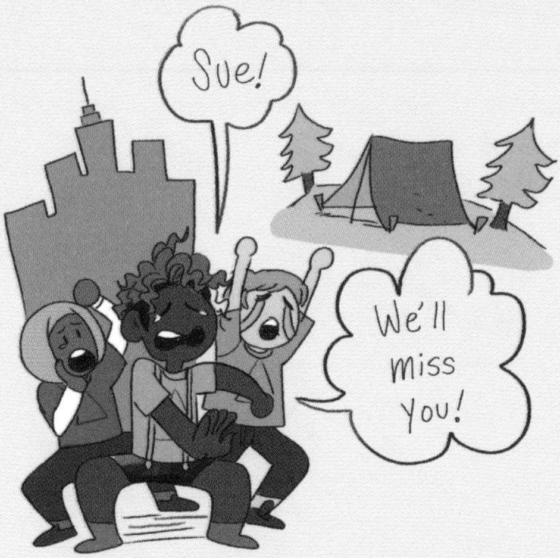
Sue!
We'll miss You!

This summer, the one thing I really wanted to do was go camping with my friends.

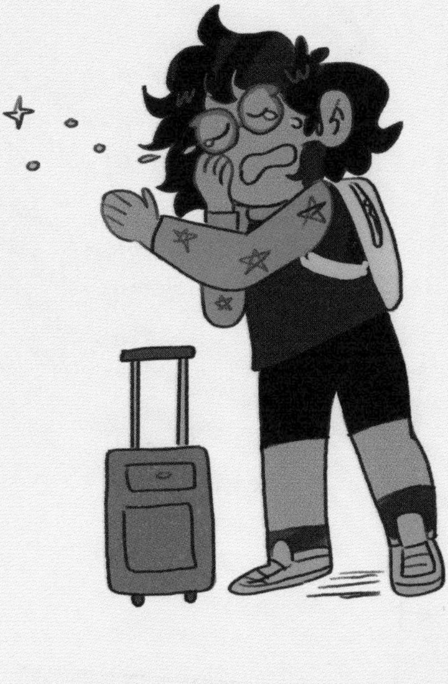

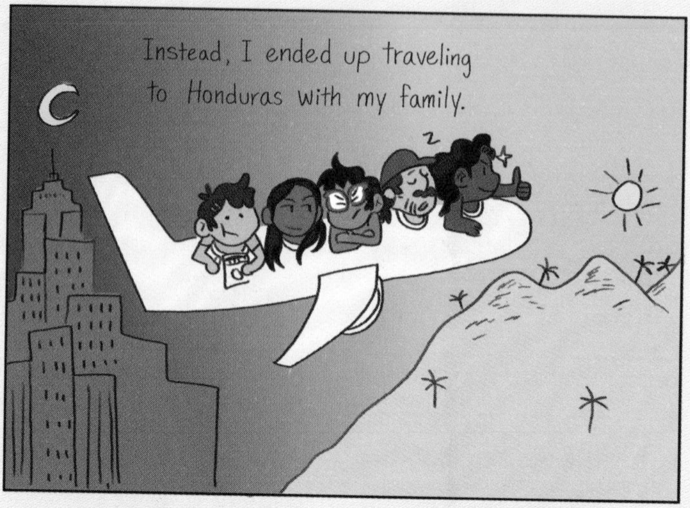
Instead, I ended up traveling to Honduras with my family.

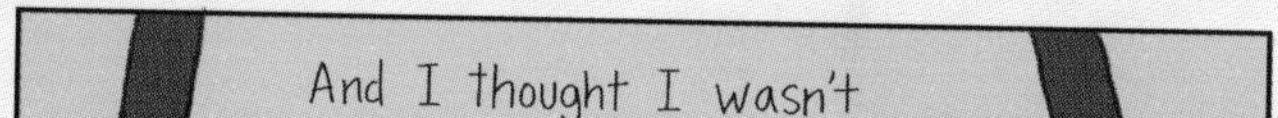
And I thought I wasn't going to do anything fun.
I'm so bored!

But to my surprise, my vacation was full of adventures like:

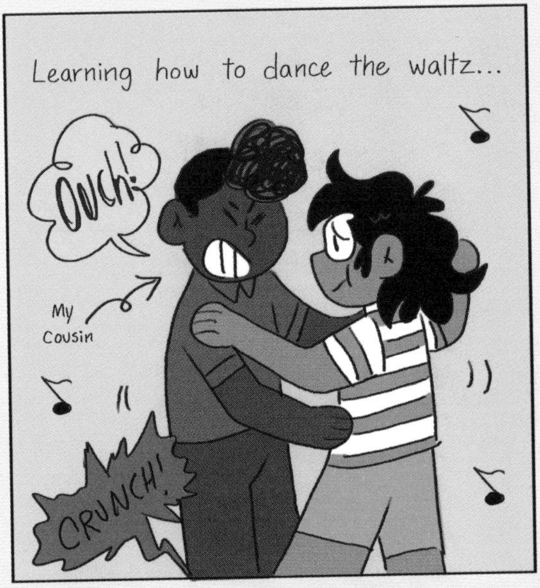
Learning how to dance the waltz...
OUCH!
My Cousin
CRUNCH!

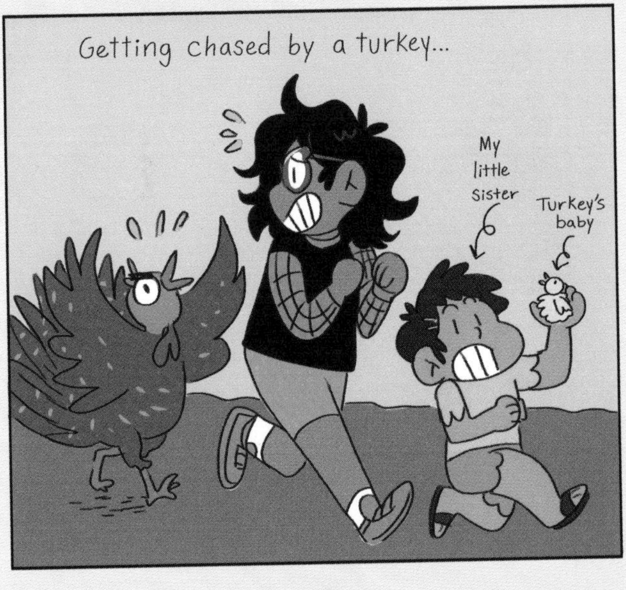
Getting chased by a turkey...
My little sister
Turkey's baby

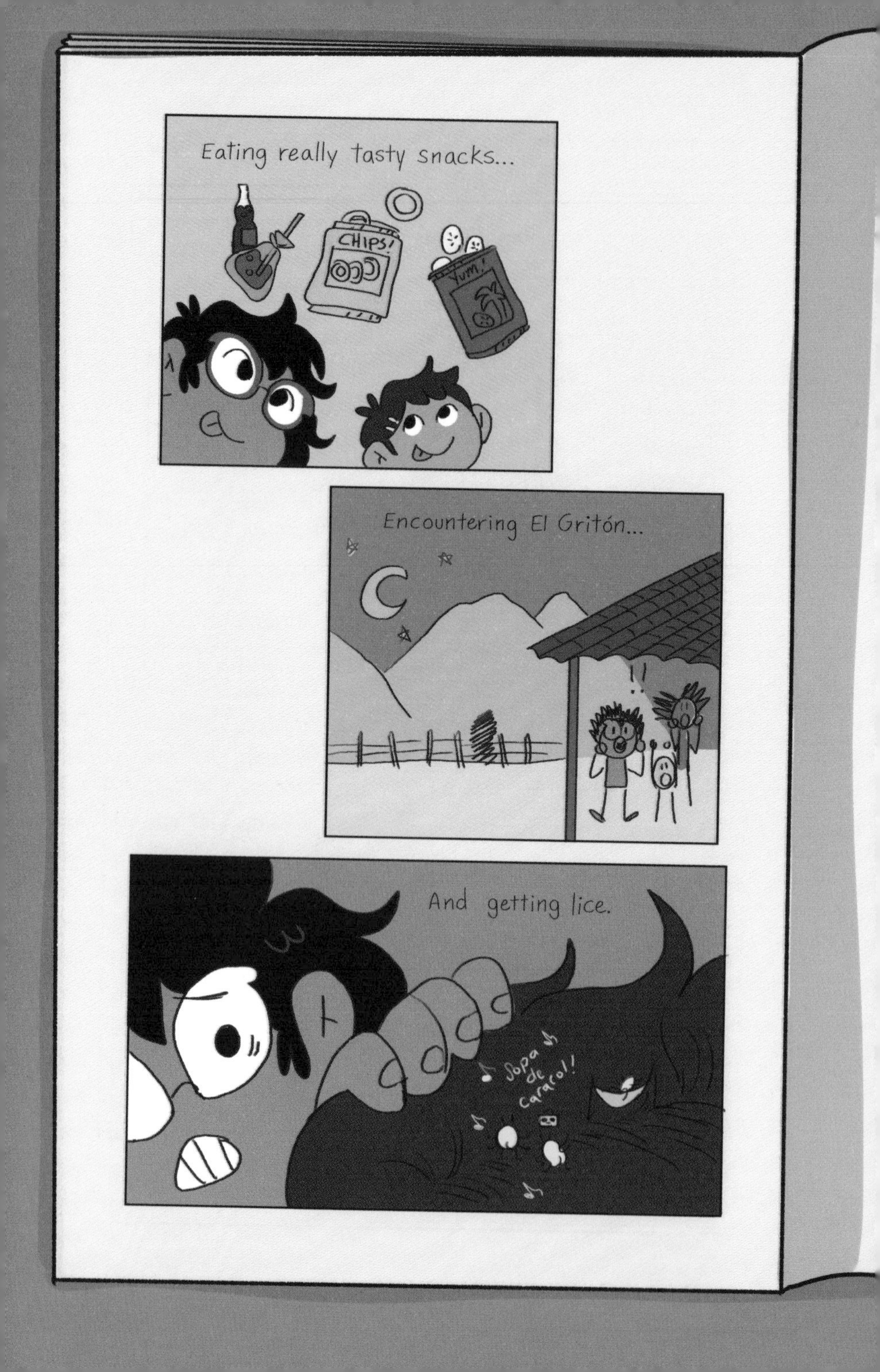
Eating really tasty snacks...
CHIPS!
YUM!
Encountering El Gritón...
And getting lice.
Sopa de caracol!

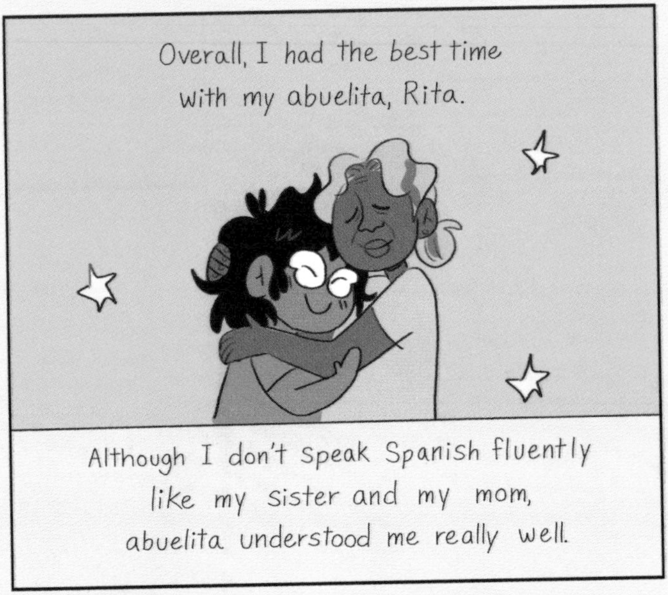
Overall, I had the best time with my abuelita, Rita.
Although I don't speak Spanish fluently like my sister and my mom, abuelita understood me really well.

She was weird like me and she didn't want to change that.

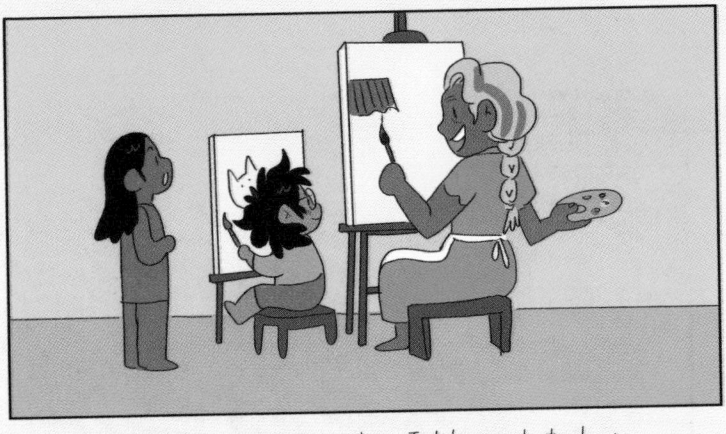

She's the reason why I like art today.

She taught me how to embrace my weirdness and let it shine bright in my own little way.

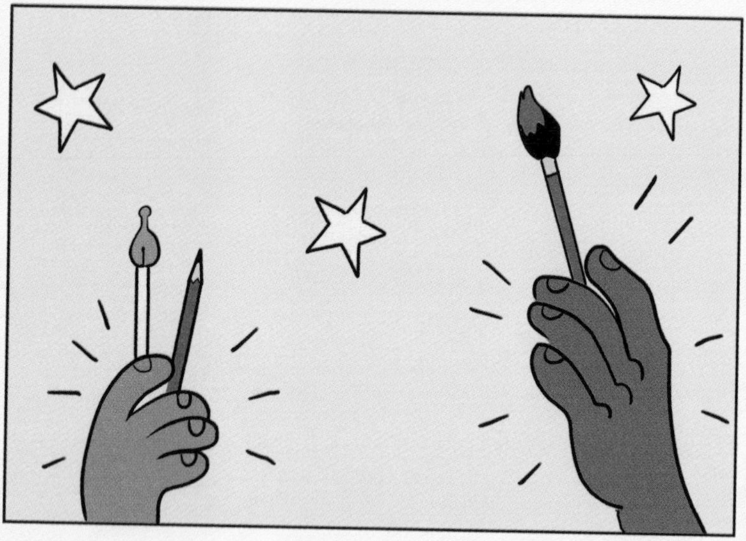

We will miss you, abuelita.
From one star to another...

You will always be loved.

Thank you for making
my last summer with you special.

-Suyapa Yisel Gutiérrez

Author's Note

Growing up in the United States, it was really hard to find any positive representation of Latine characters on TV or in movies. I didn't see much of the struggle that most Latine-Americans like myself faced during our adolescent years: the experience of "Ni de aquí ni de allá" (neither from here, nor from there). In other words, the lack of total belonging while being perceived as too American for our family, and too Latine for Americans.

As an awkward, nerdy teen trying to assimilate to my American social surroundings, I already felt like an outsider in my own immigrant household. Not being able to speak proper Spanish or share the same interests as my party-loving family, it's no surprise that we had a difficult time understanding each other! And just like my character Sue experiences, it was a struggle trying to forge my own identity within these two cultures. But, also like Sue, through the celebration of my quinceañera in my family's homeland, I was able to connect with my family and understand the cultural importance of this coming-of-age ceremony while embracing both aspects of my identity.

So, in a way, I created the story that I wished I could have read while growing up as the "weird kid." I want to show readers that it's okay to embrace your "otherness" and wear that identity with pride, like a shiny tiara. <3

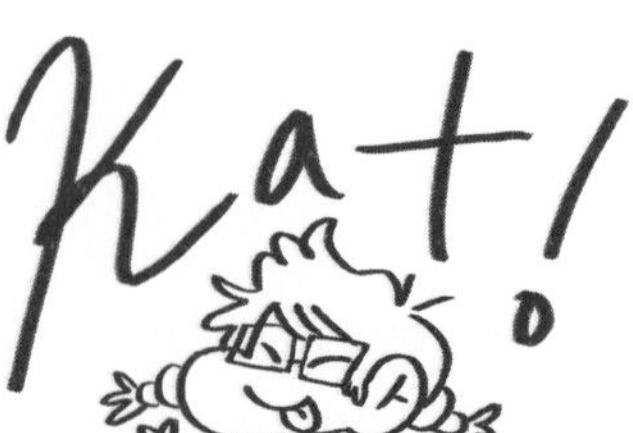
Kat!

A few notes about quinceañeras!

Whether it's an awkward stage in a young Latina's life or the day she's been dreaming about since she was a little girl, it's safe to say that a quinceañera is a very important celebration for many Latine families around the world. A tradition that dates back hundreds of years, quinces have come a long way since the Aztec and Maya versions of this coming-of-age ceremony. Eventually, with Spaniard influence, Catholic traditions were introduced, which most families include in their ceremonies today. And guess what? Marking the transition from childhood to adulthood isn't just for girls! Families sometimes hold quinceañeros for boys. Ultimately, everyone celebrates their quinces in their own fun way.

At the church

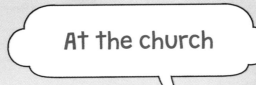

The quinceañera's day usually starts at the church, where the priest holds a religious ceremony surrounded by the young girl's family. Her godparents (or padrinos) accompany her, and serve as mentors by helping her stay on a path of spirituality and guiding her to become a reliable and responsible member of her community.

During the ceremony, the quinceañera is given traditional items that are blessed by the priest, such as the Bible and rosary that Sue receives. Then the quinceañera gives her bouquet of flowers, which symbolizes new life and beauty, to the Virgin Mary.

At the party

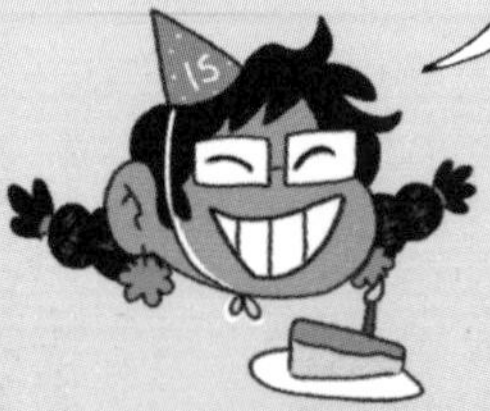

Unlike the church ceremony, the reception entrance is usually flashy and grand! The court of honor (Corte de Honor) consists of fourteen girls (damas) and boys (chambelanes) who have been chosen by the quinceañera. They escort her into the venue.

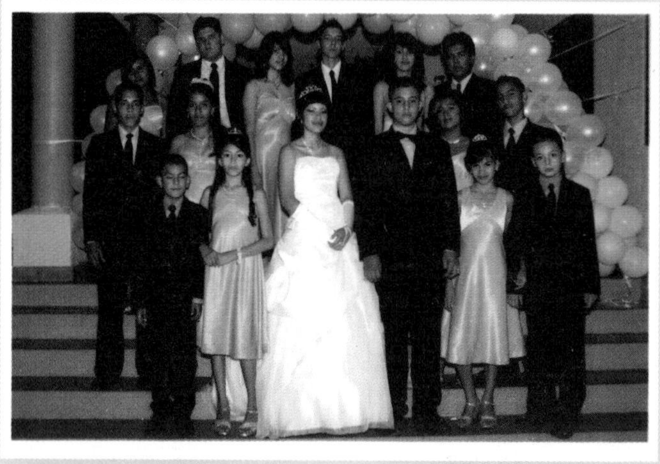

Parent-Daughter Dance: A heartfelt dance performed by the quinceañera and her parent or guardian as a symbol of guiding her from childhood to adulthood. It's one of the more emotional parts of the party, and someone will most likely cry. (I did!)

Examples of traditional quinces waltz songs:

"Tiempo de Vals" by Chayanne
"Quinceañera" by Thalia
"Vals de las Mariposas" by Tommy Valles
"De Niña a Mujer" by Julio Iglesias

Perfect for the parent-daughter dance!

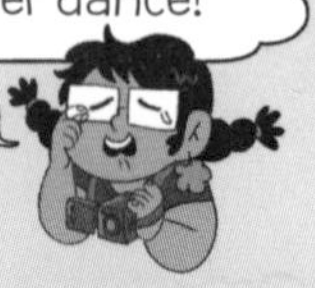

The Waltz: Considered to be one of the highlights of the quinces, the waltz must be performed well, so the quinceañera and her court practice for months in order to perfect it! And if she's lucky, after the waltz there might be a fun surprise dance (baile de sorpresa) that the court choreographed and prepared just for the party!

Last Doll Ceremony: Symbolizes the quinceañera's exchange of her childhood for responsibility and womanhood. Since she can no longer have childish toys, she passes on her "last doll" to her younger sister, if she has one.

Aside from the performances, another important part of the ceremony is the presentation of the quinceañera gifts, which each hold a significant and religious meaning. Here's a bit more info on the gifts that I included in Sue's story:

Tiara: A callback to the traditional tiara veil of the young girl's first communion, the quinceañera now wears a tiara as a symbol of being a princess of God. She may receive it at the church ceremony or at the party.

Ring: A reminder of the quinceañera's commitment to God and her parents.

Heels: The switching of flats into heels, usually by the quinceañera's father, represents the young girl's transformation into adulthood as she walks into a life filled with responsibility and maturity.

Whether the quinceañera ends up being a big party at a venue or a small intimate gathering at home, it's an event that requires a lot of planning! It's up to the family to work together and pull this event off. Thanks to my family and old quinceañera magazines, I look back fondly at the memories of my own quinces.

There's always that one aunt who is the life of the party!

Acknowledgments

Although I've been making comics and zines for a while, I still can't believe this book exists! As a kid growing up in the projects, I escaped into books for hours at the Scholastic store on Broadway. I never thought that I'd be given the chance to have my own books on shelves one day, so I'm honored that Scholastic gave me the opportunity to develop this story into something much more. Thank you so much!

I'd also like to thank . . .

My parents and sisters for letting me daydream for hours and indulge in creating comics at a young age. Thank you for pushing me to pursue my own dreams and teaching me how to get out of my comfort zone, starting with my own quinces when I was an awkward fifteen-year-old. ¡Los amo!

I'd like to thank and honor my bisabuela Mamita, who was a big inspiration for Rita. She passed away during the summer of my quinces, but I still have fond memories of her always being there for us. She was the most kind and strong-willed woman I've ever met. The universe is lucky to have an additional star in the sky. <3

My cheerleading team, Gloria and the Maldonado family, for sticking with me as I worked hard on this book. Thank you for always believing in me and encouraging me to follow my path no matter what. And to my cute pups, Mac and Roni, thanks for your cuteness and kisses.

My friends from the comics and zine community—thank you so much for being an inspiration of talent and compassion. I miss you all dearly! But especially my chosen family: Delta, Steph, Kelly, Moony, Sam, and Tim for always checking in on me and providing support in the most special ways possible. I love you!

My amazing agent, Linda Camacho, who is the most driven and intelligent Latina I know. Thanks for always having my back and believing in me from the start.

My editor, Cassandra Pelham Fulton, and my art director, Phil Falco, who believed in my vision and helped nurture this project from the start. Thanks, also, to David Saylor, Megan Peace, María Domínguez, Emily Nguyen, and everyone at Scholastic who worked on both the English and Spanish editions of this book. It wouldn't have been possible without all your hard work! Thanks!!

My awesome design team, Shivana Sookdeo, for her wonderful design work and title logo; Mariana Azzi for their superb coloring skills; and DUS'T and Pablo for assisting me with lettering. Thank you all for helping bring my vision to life!

Most of all, I want to thank my partner, Pablo A. Castro, the best cartoonist and person I know, for their expertise, incredible heart, and, above all things, their invaluable support during this whole process. Thank you for believing in me and my capabilities and for being my source of strength. I'm proud to be your partner!